THE
CHOICE

Alex Lake is a British novelist who was born in the North West of England. *After Anna*, the author's first novel written under this pseudonym, was a No.1 bestselling ebook sensation and a top-ten *Sunday Times* bestseller. The author now lives in the North East of the US.

🐦 @AlexLakeAuthor

Also by Alex Lake

After Anna
Killing Kate
Copycat
The Last Lie
Seven Days

THE
CHOICE
ALEX LAKE

HarperCollins*Publishers*

HarperCollins*Publishers* Ltd
1 London Bridge Street,
London SE1 9GF

www.harpercollins.co.uk

First published by HarperCollins*Publishers* 2020
20 21 22 LSC 10 9 8 7 6 5 4 3 2 1

A catalogue record for this book is available from the British Library

ISBN: 978-0-00-837354-2 (PB b-format)
ISBN: 978-0-00-837355-9 (TPB)
ISBN: 978-0-00-840364-5 (US only b-format)

Set in Sabon LT Std by Palimpsest Book Production Limited,
Falkirk, Stirlingshire

Printed and bound in the United States of America by LSC Communications

For more information visit: www.harpercollins.co.uk/green

To my three

PART ONE

Saturday, 7 March 2020

Look at him. I mean, just look. *Baggy, out-of-date jeans with brown leather brogues that have not seen shoe polish in years, shirt untucked over his spreading stomach. It's pathetic. No effort at all. Shabby. Second rate.*

I'm doing nothing wrong. He deserves everything he gets.

Out he climbs, his car – not washed, of course – parked on the road outside under a flickering streetlamp. He pauses, checking over his shoulder that everything is all right.

It's OK, he thinks, *everything's fine. He looks at the car. The kids are arguing in the back seat. One of them puts the interior light on, then off, then on again.*

He hesitates outside the local shop. He's about to go back and tell them, Stop it, you'll break the light, *but he pushes the door open and steps out of the early spring dark and into the shop.*

He can leave them there, for a few minutes. The car's unlocked – he doesn't want the alarm to go off – but no harm will come to them. He won't be in the shop long enough. His three-year-old daughter is buckled into a car seat, so she's going nowhere. His five-year-old middle son is erratic and wilful, but he won't get out of the car. He'll be too scared, and if he tries his big brother – all of seven years old – will stop him. He's sensible; a typical, rule-following first child.

So they'll stay in the car. Safe.

Brother, brother, sister.

Daughter, son, son.

The lights of his life, no doubt. Annoying, at times, and hard work, but he loves them. He and his wife are blessed. Their children are the most important things in the world to them.

Yet he leaves them in a car on the road, unattended.

It's not illegal. He probably knows that. He's probably checked. The law allows you to leave children in a car provided there is no undue risk.

Which is exactly the point.

He thinks the risk is acceptable, so small as to be easily dismissed. He won't be long, the kids won't get out of the car and they can't start it as he has the keys.

There are other sources of danger, of course – a runaway truck careering into the parked car and crushing it. An earthquake opening up a rift in the road underneath the car. A flash flood washing it and his children away.

All as near to impossible as makes no difference.

So he is right. The risk is small.

It is safe to leave them in the car for a few minutes while he goes into the shop. After all, what's the alternative? Get them all out, chase them around? And then there's the virus: it's hit Italy and Spain hard, and it could be the same here. People are nervous; they don't want their kids running around in a shop, picking things up and touching door handles and counter tops. He would have to corral them, which would turn a quick stop into an expedition.

At least that's the excuse he makes. The excuse a lot of parents make. In fact, it would not make it into an expedition. It would just make it take five minutes longer, which, when you think what might happen if you leave them alone and unprotected, is not all that much of a price to pay.

But never mind. It is very improbable anything will happen to them. The odds are vanishingly small.

It's one in a million that the kids are in danger.

And that's the thing. It might be a one in a million chance, but that doesn't mean it won't happen.

It means it'll happen one time out of a million.

One time in a million there will be a stranger out there with bad intentions.

But who? Who would it be?

He'll be asking that question for a long time.

Matt

1

Matt Westbrook stepped into the shop. It was one of the last of its kind – an independent local shop stocking a mixture of groceries, alcohol, newspapers, magazines and basic home cleaning and maintenance supplies – and he was the only customer.

He was only there because it was open and it was on his way home and Annabelle had texted to say they needed milk, coffee, bread, pasta, and beer or wine – and, if they had any, toilet paper and disinfecting wipes – and could he stop and get them on his way home with the kids?

Which was fine. She was recovering from a cold and didn't need to go out on a chilly night. He could pick up the stuff and do a big shop the next day at the supermarket. He wouldn't bother with the wine, though – they were trying for another baby, so she was off the booze and he didn't much feel like drinking alone.

They had three already, which was quite a handful, but

he had managed to persuade her to add one more. Norman, seven, was named after her late father, a physics teacher and one of the most creative and inspiring people Matt had ever met. Keith – named after the Rolling Stone, if anyone asked – had come next, followed by Molly. Each kid had brought with them worse morning sickness and harder labours: Norman was nine pounds, Keith ten, and Molly eleven. As far as Annabelle was concerned, that was nature's way of telling them to stop at three, but the years passed and the memories faded and, after a while, she had agreed to try for another.

His friends thought he was crazy, but he liked having kids. It was chaotic and busy, for sure, but he enjoyed it. More than that: he *loved* it. At work he daydreamed of sitting on the couch watching a movie with the three of them snuggled up to him and Annabelle, or of coming home and reading them a book.

And even though Norman was only seven he felt the time slipping away. He couldn't bear the thought there were only eleven years to go until he left for university or a career or whatever came his way, to be followed swiftly by Keith and Molly.

The first seven years had vanished in the blink of an eye, so eleven more was nothing. He wasn't ready for it, and the only way to stop it was to have more kids. Five, maybe, or six.

Annabelle might have something to say about that, but he'd cross that bridge when he came to it.

He looked out of the shop window at the car. The doors were still closed. The front doors were unlocked, but the rear doors were child-locked so, even if they tried, the kids wouldn't be able to get out. They'd have to climb into the front and go out that way, which was unlikely.

Still, he'd be as quick as he could. He didn't need a police officer walking past and seeing them and questioning where their mum or dad was. He was pretty sure it wasn't against the law to leave them there but he still didn't want to discuss whether it was good parenting or not to do so.

He grabbed a basket and moved around the shop. Milk, skimmed. A block of Irish cheddar cheese. A bag of pasta – fusilli, he noted, whatever that was. Coffee, not a brand he recognized and probably awful, but it would have to do. Bread, brown, unsliced – they had surprisingly good loaves here – and a warm baguette. He paused at the wine shelf. Maybe he would have a glass after all. Red, perhaps. It was cold, the nights drawing in. He picked up a bottle of Cabernet. That would do.

The checkout was at the far end of the shop. He carried his basket over and put it down.

'All right, mate.' The man behind the counter was in his fifties and had a Liverpool accent. 'Got everything you wanted?'

'Yes, thanks. Just grabbing a few bits.' He glanced around. 'Got any wipes?'

'We're out. Toilet paper's all gone too.' He shook his head. 'Load of fuss about nothing, if you ask me.'

'You never know,' Matt said. 'There's quarantine in parts of Italy.'

'Won't happen here, mate. But I'll sell people whatever they want to buy.'

The man punched in the prices, one by one. Easy to fiddle the take. Perhaps this place was a front for a gang, a place to quietly wash clean their ill-gotten gains.

'Twenty-seven fifty,' he said.

Matt hesitated and looked at the basket. Seven quid for the wine. A fiver for the coffee. He'd looked at the price of those. Which left fifteen-fifty for the bread, milk, baguette and pasta. How much was bread? Three pounds? Milk and pasta? The same probably. Which meant the baguette was outrageously expensive.

Or they all were.

The man looked at him, his expression questioning. For a moment Matt thought about asking for the prices of the bread, coffee, milk and pasta, but then the man interrupted.

'Everything OK, mate?'

He nodded, and handed over two twenties. If this was a front for a gang they didn't need to use it to launder any money. They were robbing people in plain sight.

'Thanks,' he said, and picked up his change and his shopping. It was definitely the supermarket next time.

2

As he left, Matt noticed the local newspaper had a story on the front page about a new signing for the rugby league team. It was the photo that caught his eye, a picture of a famous Australian playing for the Australian national team.

That would be quite the coup.

He was about to pick up a copy and go back to the counter – even this shop couldn't charge more than the cover price for a newspaper – when he glanced out of the window. A quick check on the kids, that was all; make sure they were still safely in the car.

He blinked, then looked left and right.

There must be some mistake.

The car was gone.

That was impossible. He had left it there only a minute ago.

But there was no car there. As if to make the point, a blue Mercedes pulled up and parked right where his car had been.

He must have parked it further up the street. It was strange; he would have sworn he'd left it almost exactly outside the shop. Maybe he had, and it was the angle from which he was looking out of the window that meant he couldn't see it.

Still. There was a church on the other side of the road, the main gate directly opposite the door.

And when he had got out of the car he had looked at that gate. He remembered it distinctly: his sister had got married there and a memory had come to him of her wedding day. It had been pouring with rain – a real deluge – and when Tessa and Andy came out all the guests had been holding umbrellas over the path to make a tunnel. They had walked through them to the main road and into the vintage silver Rolls-Royce that had taken them to the reception.

He had looked at the gate and remembered that day.

And when he had done so he had been standing more or less opposite it.

Which meant the car had moved.

His palms prickled with sweat. The kids must have taken off the handbrake, or somehow started the car and driven it off. He patted the pocket of his jeans. The keys were in there, so at least that was off the table.

He forgot the newspaper and jogged to the door. He needed to sort this out, right away. The man behind the counter coughed.

'Everything all right?'

'Yes. Just – I can't remember where I left my car.'

'Happens all the time, mate. People forget where they park.'

'It's not exactly that—' He stopped talking. There was no point explaining. He opened the door and looked up and down the street.

The car was nowhere to be seen.

He took a deep breath. His mind was starting to swim and he needed to concentrate. He couldn't afford to panic. He had to be methodical, but it was almost impossible to fight back the desire to scream and set off at a sprint in some – any – direction.

He looked left, to the village centre, and then right, to the swing bridge over the ship canal. In both directions the street was more or less straight, so he would have seen his car if it was there.

It wasn't.

'Where's the fucking car?' he murmured. It couldn't just be gone.

But it was. His car was gone, with his kids inside. He began to lose the battle against the fear and panic, because either they had moved it, or it had moved itself, or someone else had moved it. None of them were happy thoughts. As the thought sunk in, he clenched his fists, digging his fingernails into his palms. He had to *think*.

It couldn't have been driven away, because he had the keys – there was no way the kids had jump-started it – which meant it had rolled away – hard to imagine on a flat road, and even harder to imagine it had rolled out of sight – or it had been pushed away.

His kids couldn't have done that, so someone else would have had to do it.

And how far could you push a car in a few minutes? Maybe around a corner, but not much further than that.

A wave of relief broke over him. This was a prank. One of his friends, or more likely a few of them, after a beer or two – had seen the kids in the car and moved it to give him a scare. He pictured them, laughing as they released the handbrake and pushed the car down the street. There was a side street about thirty yards away, on the right. That's where they would have taken it.

That's where he would find them, standing by the car, laughing.

He would not be laughing with them. This was not funny at all.

He jogged towards the side street. Banner Road. He'd never noticed the name before; he'd remember it now. He slowed at the corner and turned.

There was a skip on the right and a white van parked on the left, but other than that the side street was empty.

The fear roared back and rose into a full-on panic. Where the *fuck* was his car? Where could it be?

He sprinted out onto the main road and looked up and down, once, twice, a third time.

Still nothing.

He ran back to the shop – to the last place the car had been – and stood outside the window, breathing heavily. His car was gone. His *children* were gone.

The shop door opened.

'You OK, mate?'

He turned around. The man from the shop – the owner, maybe – was standing on the threshold, arms folded, his eyes narrowed in suspicion.

'It's my car. It's gone.'

'What do you mean?'

'I left it here, but it's nowhere to be seen.'

'You sure it was here?'

'Yes.' He paused. Was it possible he had parked somewhere further away and walked to the shop? Had he misremembered looking at the church? No – he also remembered thinking he was only using the shop because it was more convenient than a detour to the supermarket, which would hardly have been the case if he had parked a walk away. Besides, he had checked on the kids when he got out.

'Yes. It was here.'

'What is it?'

'Discovery. Land Rover.'

The man stuck out his bottom lip. 'Nice vehicle. Maybe someone nicked it. Was it locked?'

'No, but—'

'Mate, you should lock your car.'

'I know, but—'

13

'I mean, it's easy to nick 'em if you can get in. Just plug a laptop into the data port and boom, job done. I heard it takes about fifteen seconds. You can't leave a car unlocked.'

'I only left it unlocked because—'

'There's no excuse, mate. You—'

'Listen to me!' Matt shouted. 'I left it unlocked because my kids were in there.'

There was a long silence.

'Fuck me,' the man said. 'You need to call the filth. Get the cops on this as soon as.'

'I know.' Matt took his phone from his pocket and unlocked the screen.

He was about to dial 999 when the phone buzzed. A message appeared.

Do not call the police.

He stared at it, his eyes wide. Dots scrolled under the message, and another appeared.

I repeat: tell no one and do not inform the authorities.
I will know if you do and you will never see your children again.

More dots scrolled, then another message appeared.

My instructions will follow. Await them.

3

Matt stared at his phone. The man from the shop walked over to his side.

'What is it?' he said.

Matt did not want to answer. 'It's OK. I'm fine.'

The man tilted his head and looked at him sideways. 'You don't seem fine.'

'I am. It's just – I'm fine.'

'Someone took your car with your kids in it, and you're fine?' He nodded at the phone. 'What was that?'

Matt had no intention of telling him, because if he told him the man might take it upon himself to call the police, which Matt was not yet ready to do – he might be, soon, but he needed to think this through.

Which meant being alone.

'Look,' he said. 'I appreciate the concern, but I promise. It's all OK. That was their mum. She has them.'

The man shrugged. It was clear from his expression that he didn't believe a word Matt was saying, but Matt didn't care.

'OK, mate,' he said. 'Whatever you say.'

He turned and walked back into the shop. Matt headed

for a bus shelter a few yards up the road and sat on the bench.

He read the messages again.

Do not call the police.

I repeat: tell no one and do not inform the authorities. I will know if you do and you will never see your children again.

My instructions will follow. Await them.

He tried to think through what all this meant. If the car wasn't nearby then it wasn't a prank – none of his friends would have gone this far, and besides, none of them knew how to steal a car. What had the man said? Fifteen seconds with a laptop plugged into a data port in the car? Sounded simple but so did loads of computer things, yet they were still way beyond the capabilities of him and his friends.

So someone had come to the car while he was in the shop, climbed in, started it somehow, and driven away.

With his children in the back seat. His stomach clenched and a cold sweat broke out on his head and neck.

It was crazy – the one time he had left his kids in the car and some random car thief had chosen that moment to steal it.

And then text him.

Which meant it wasn't a random car thief at all. If they had his number, they must have been targeting him – and his kids – specifically. But who the hell would do that?

He had no idea, but he did know one thing. This was *planned*. Someone had been watching, waiting for this opportunity.

The panic thickened, and his legs weakened. He let out a

low groan. If this was planned, that meant there was a reason. Someone wanted his kids.

But the kids weren't all they wanted, or the person behind it would not have sent him a message. They would just have disappeared.

So there was something else. But what? Was someone trying to punish him? He thought through all the areas of his life: family, friends, the law firm where he was a partner, any parents of the kids' friends or classmates that they had fallen out with. Was there someone he had slighted? Or who the kids had upset?

It was possible, but he couldn't think of anything, and surely anything sufficient to provoke this would have been obvious.

So what the fuck was going on?

In his hand, his phone buzzed.

I have his kids and his car. Easy to steal. Especially when you have the key. His spare, taken from the jar above the fridge in his kitchen, one day last summer when they were off on their family holiday. Too easy.

It's time to let him know what's happening.

Time to tear up everything he thought he knew and send him into a world of pain and confusion and fear.

I can't wait. He's had it coming for a long time.

I can't use the same phone, though. Hopefully he's not foolish enough to call the police, but there are no guarantees. The fucking idiot left his kids in an unlocked car, after all.

He assumed, like people do, that the world is safe. He assumed that what he sees around him every day – polite people, organized into nice little groups at work or at home, following the rules, saying please and thank you and worrying they might have upset someone – he assumed that this is how things are.

And he's right. Most people are like that.

But not all. Some of us see the truth. Some of us see that other people are mere tools to be used to get what you want. The idea you might deny yourself something because it could hurt someone's feelings is absurd. Why would you care about feelings? You either get what you want or you don't. To let other people's arbitrary emotional states obstruct you is fool-ishness. Worse, it is weakness.

And I am not weak. I was, once, and I learned my lesson. I suffered at the hands of someone who took what they wanted from me without a thought for what it did to me.

It made me who I am. Showed me the way I should live my life. I made sure to explain that to them before they died.

I also learned from them that you have to be careful. You cannot let people know you think of them as nothing but ways and means to get what you want. You have to learn to resemble them. Most of the time a smile and a question and an interested look is all it takes.

It's ironic: people love *me. They think I'm kind and helpful, because that's what I want them to think. They* trust *me.*

Which is very useful. Once you have earned somebody's trust it is the easiest thing in the world to abuse it.

Occasionally someone figures it out. My mother did, when she realized what I had done. Poor woman. It broke her heart.

I know what you are, she said, her eyes wide with shock. I've known it all along. I just didn't admit it to myself.

So I was putting her out of her misery, I suppose. It didn't have to be such a painful death, but there had to be something in it for me, didn't there?

Anyway, it's time to give Matt the next piece of the puzzle. It'll answer a few of his questions, inform him about the situation he's in, clear some things up.

But it won't help. Soon he will realize that for every question answered, more have been asked.

But first, the phone needs to be thrown away. The Bridgewater canal – oldest in the country, apparently – will be a fine place for it. No problem to pull over his dirty Land Rover Discovery and get out. The kids are unconscious. Hopefully the dose was correct. Not too strong. Not yet.

Pull the phone battery out, then two splashes as the phone and battery drop into the dark, oily water.

A new phone, booted up.

Type in his number – memorized, of course – and send the message.

Four words.

Four shocking words.

Watch sixty seconds tick by. One turn of the dial for the second hand. Analogue. No Apple Watch or Fitbit. Those things are a pain. Constantly buzzing and beeping. Measuring where you are and reporting it to some server. No, I don't want that.

Then the rest of the messages, followed by two more splashes.

Better safe than sorry.

Words Matt Westbrook should have paid more attention to.

Matt

Matt looked down at his phone and read the text message.
It was just four words.
Four *shocking* words.

This is a kidnapping.

He stared at the screen and read them again.

This is a kidnapping.

He slumped on the bench. His legs were shaking. Norman, Keith and Molly, the three people at the centre of his life, the three people he and Annabelle had built everything around, had been *kidnapped*.

He was sure, in that moment, that he'd never see them again. Something would go wrong and they would be gone forever.

He started to shake with sobs. They were his life now, for sure, but they were also his future. They were supposed to go to high school then university, to fall in love and get married, to have children. Or do something else. Become astronauts. Cure cancer. Form a rock band. Whatever. It didn't matter.

As long as they were there, in his and Annabelle's lives.

His phone buzzed again, and he turned to look at it. There was another message.

The ransom demand will follow.

Ransom? They were being held for ransom?

What did he have that anybody could possibly want? Money? He and Annabelle were comfortable but they were hardly in a position to pay millions, which was presumably what this person wanted. They wouldn't have gone to all this trouble unless they thought there was a large payoff at the end of it all.

If so, they were mistaken. He earned a reasonable salary from his law firm, and Annabelle made a steady income as a writer. She had published four novels, but none of them had earned anything like the kind of money that would make this worthwhile.

So he and Annabelle would not be able to pay. The kidnapper was going to ask for millions, in the mistaken belief their victims had it, and when he said he didn't have the money they would think he was lying, and hurt his children.

'Oh God,' he said, clutching his forehead. 'Oh God, please.'

'Are you OK?'

An elderly woman with a wheeled shopping bag, like the one his mum had had when he was a child, stood in the bus shelter.

'No,' he said. 'I mean, yes, I'm fine.'

'All right,' she said. 'Let me know if—'

Another buzz, another message:

Remember. Do not contact the police under any circumstances. I will know immediately if you do and you will never see your children again.

He let out a wail of terror. The elderly woman studied him.

'Are you sure you're OK?' she asked. 'Can I help? I could call someone?'

He stood up. His house was on the other side of the village, about half a mile away.

'I have to get home,' he said. 'I have to go.'

And then he started running.

Annabelle

1

Annabelle Westbrook sat on the couch, her legs tucked underneath her, and sipped her tea. It was lemon and ginger, and even though she knew it made no difference she felt like it helped with her cold. If it *was* a cold. There was some new virus going about and she had been lethargic and achy and running a fever, so there was every chance it was that. Either way, it had been a rough few days, but she was feeling better.

And she was starting to feel hungry. When Matt got back she would make something to eat. Maybe cheese on toast, with a splash of Worcestershire sauce on the top. When she and her brother, Mike, were kids that had been their dad's Sunday speciality; she associated it with memories of sitting around the kitchen table on Sunday evenings, their dad drinking a big mug of tea as they ate his cheese on toast. He was a creative and adventurous cook – after their mum had died he had had to learn, and he had turned out to be pretty good – and during the week he made tagines and curries and a *fantastic* lasagne and moussaka and whatever else he dreamed up when he came back from the school where he taught physics. It meant they ate late – at around 7 p.m. – but that was fine by her. She loved ending the day around the table with her dad and brother.

You have to eat together, her dad said. *Every day if you can.*

Sundays, though, were not for cooking. They were for spending together, as a family of three, small and tight and independent. They went for hikes and to football matches and on canoe trips and swimming in lakes and rivers and whatever else they felt like.

And then on Sunday evenings, all time for cooking consumed, it was cheese on toast, and it was her favourite meal of the week.

She felt ready for some this evening, thank God. It might perk her up enough to try for the baby Matt had persuaded her was a good idea.

She smiled at the thought. It was so sweet how much he loved being a father. It was clear he would have as many as she would allow, but four – if it happened – would be the limit.

Her phone started to ring. She had left it in the kitchen; it could wait. She cradled her tea and sank into the sofa.

A few seconds later it rang again. She closed her eyes and let it ring out.

It rang again. Whoever it was, was really trying. It could be her dad; there might be a problem. She put her mug on the carpet and walked into the kitchen.

She felt a jolt of concern when she looked at the screen. It was Matt.

'Hi,' she said. 'You need me?'

'Annabelle,' he said. 'Why didn't you answer?'

He sounded alarmed and her concern grew.

25

'I was in the living room. My phone was in the kitchen.'

'Good.' He was panting, his breath short. 'Is everything OK?'

'Yes,' she said. 'Why wouldn't it be?'

There was more heavy breathing. 'I'm on my way home.'

She noticed he had not answered the question. 'You sound like you're out of breath.'

'I'm running.'

She looked up at her reflection in the window. She was frowning.

'You're *running*? Why are you running?'

'I'll explain when I'm back.' He paused. His voice was tense and serious. 'I'll be there any minute. I need to know you're OK.'

'I'm fine. But it doesn't sound like you are. What's going—'

'I'll be right there,' he interrupted.

The phone went dead. Annabelle leaned on the table. Matt was running? Why wasn't he in the car? And why did he think she might not be OK?

What the hell was going on?

She held one hand to her stomach. Sweat prickled on her brow. The sick feeling was back.

Although this time it was not only the cold. It was worry.

2

She heard footsteps outside the front door a few minutes later and went to open it. He was standing on the step, a shopping bag in each hand, a packet of pasta poking out of a hole in one of them. His face was flushed and he was breathing heavily.

Her chest tightened in alarm. He had sounded terrible on the phone, but he looked worse.

And not only was he not in the car. He was *alone*.

'Matt,' she said. 'Where are the kids?'

He stepped into the house. His expression was rigid, but there was a wild look in his eyes. She realized with a start that it was fear.

'Sit down,' he said. 'You need to sit down.'

'I don't need to sit down,' she said. 'Where are the kids? Tell me where the kids are!'

He took her elbow and guided her into the living room and onto the sofa. Her tea was still on the carpet beside it.

Matt sat next to her. He was no longer breathing heavily; now he was taking short, shallow breaths. It could have been the running, but it looked more like he was trying not to panic.

'Matt,' she said. 'What's going on?'

He blinked, his expression almost puzzled. He opened his mouth to speak, but nothing came out.

'Matt! Where are the children? Tell me!'

'They're gone,' he said, his voice breaking. 'The children are gone.'

Matt

She didn't react for a few seconds, then, as the words registered, her mouth fell slightly open.

'Gone?' she said. 'What do you mean *gone?*'

He swallowed. His heart was racing and his mouth was dry and it was hard to speak. Annabelle was staring at him, her eyebrows knitted together in a deep frown.

'I . . .' he started, 'I went into the shop to get the stuff. I left the kids in the car—'

'Oh my God.' Her eyes widened. '*Matt*. What happened?'

'I wasn't gone long, maybe only a few minutes. I checked out of the window and they were OK, but—'

'Matt, what are you saying? Tell me what happened?'

'—after I paid and went outside the car was gone.'

'Gone?' He could see his words were not fully sinking in. 'How could the car be gone?'

'Somebody took it. But – Annabelle. The kids were in it. They took the kids too.'

His wife didn't answer. She folded her arms, then lifted one hand to her mouth, then put her hands in her lap.

'What?' she said, a barely controlled panic in her voice belying her attempts to compose herself. 'What did you say?'

'The car was gone. With the kids.'

'Maybe they took off the handbrake and it rolled away.'

'No. I checked.'

'Maybe you didn't check in the right place.' She stood up. 'We need to look for them. We can take my car. Maybe they drove it off somehow. Or the police moved it. If it was parked illegally the police may have moved it. Did you call them?'

'No,' he said. 'I didn't.'

'You didn't? Why not? We have to call them, now!'

'We can't.'

She was staring at him, her eyes wide, her nostrils flared. 'Why not? Of course we can call the police. Our children are missing!'

'We can't,' he said. 'There's more. And it's worse.'

Annabelle

She was reeling from his breathless arrival. She could hardly grasp what he was saying. His words were close to meaningless sounds, but she forced herself to focus.

He had told her he'd left the kids in the car, and the car had been taken.

The kids were gone.

He had not called the police.

She could make no sense of this. The kids were in their car and someone had taken it and he had not called the police.

But it was the last thing he had said that scared her the most. He had said there was more, and it was worse.

How could anything be *worse*?

For a moment she was not sure she wanted to find out. She had an overwhelming urge to close her eyes and pretend this was not happening. All she wanted was for this to stop, right now, and be over before it got going. Because whatever it was, it was not good.

But she had no choice.

'Matt,' she said. 'Just tell me.'

He looked at her, his face a mask of shock and fear. 'They've been kidnapped,' he said in a low voice. 'Someone is holding our kids for ransom.'

The word hung in the air between them.

'Kidnapped,' she said, the word odd in her mouth, almost as if she did not recognize – or could not believe – what it meant. 'Did you say kidnapped?'

'Yes.' His face was pale, the blood drained from it.

'OK,' she said. It sounded totally inadequate, but what was she supposed to say? This was a total catastrophe: normal language didn't work. But there was good news in this. Ransom meant you paid the kidnapper's price and they would release the hostages, which meant there was hope.

So this was good, in a way.

'What do they want?' she said.

'I don't know. They didn't say yet.' He held up his phone and showed her the screen. 'These messages came just after I left the shop.'

She took his phone and read the texts.

Do not call the police.
    I repeat: tell no one and do not inform the authorities.
I will know if you do and you will never see your children again.
    My instructions will follow. Await them.

He reached over and tapped the screen. 'Then these came from a different number.'

This is a kidnapping.

The ransom demand will follow.

Remember. Do not contact the police under any circumstances. I will know immediately if you do and you will never see your children again.'

So that was why he had not called the police. It made sense now, but she wanted them to know. They needed help with this.

'Shouldn't we tell the police?' she said. 'How would the kidnapper know? It could be a bluff to stop us involving them.'

'It could be,' Matt said. 'But it could be real. Maybe whoever it is knows someone. Or it's a cop. And if there is a way they could find out—'

'We won't see the kids,' she said. 'If it's true, we can't risk it. We have to wait. See what they want.' She looked at the phone. 'Were there any other messages?'

'No. That was the last one.'

'Did you call the number?'

'Not yet.'

'We should. I will.' She tapped the screen and lifted the phone to her ear.

'Are you calling?' he said.

'Yes.' She listened for the ringing to start, but it never came. It went straight to a recorded message.

The number you have called does not have a voice mailbox set up. Thank you.

Then the line went dead.

She put the phone down.

'What is it?' Matt said.

'An automated message saying no voicemail has been set up.'

'If they're using different numbers, they probably get rid of the phones afterwards.'

She pictured someone throwing a phone into a bin then taking a new one from a rucksack and typing in a number.

Matt's number.

'My God,' she said. 'They know your number. Which means this isn't random. It isn't someone who saw an opportunity and grabbed it.' She took a deep breath in an attempt to control the panic rising in her chest. It didn't work. 'This was planned,' she said. 'Someone was watching and waiting.' She felt a wave of nausea. 'They've been *watching* us, Matt.'

Matt stood and began to pace the room. 'I know.'

'But why? What do they think we have? What do they want?'

'I can't think of anything,' Matt said.

'But to go to all this effort . . .' Annabelle's voice tailed off. 'This is fucking unbelievable. Why would anyone do this? What do they want from us?'

'It must be money,' Matt said. 'What else is there?'

'But we don't have the kind of money that would make this worthwhile,' Annabelle said.

'Maybe they think we do.'

'But we *don't*,' she said. 'And if we say we don't they'll think we're holding out on them and' – she choked back a sob – 'and they'll hurt the kids. Matt, they're going to hurt my babies. We have to stop them. Please, we have to stop this!'

'How?' Matt said.

'I don't know,' she said. 'I don't have any ideas.'

And then, in her hand, her husband's phone buzzed.

This will be a shock for them. It will be the last thing they're expecting. They will be thinking the ransom will be for money, because they – in particular he, I don't blame her so much – are people of very feeble imagination.

Like the rest of the common herd, snouting around in the dirt for a few scraps, leaving the real prizes for those who can see the truth.

What else is there, they will think. What else could anyone want from them? The dirty Land Rover Discovery? No – that has already been taken. The three kiddoes? They too, have already been taken. Their house, as modest as his ambition? Impossible. How could they give me their house without me revealing who I am? It's hardly portable property.

So what else could I want?

His resignation? What would be the point? For him to humiliate himself? It's a pleasant thought, I admit, but please. *I am not that sort of petty-minded person. I am not that shallow.*

And he'll be humiliated enough, as it is.

Which leaves only one thing. That grubbiest of motives, money.

Which is, frankly, beneath me.

They don't know that, though, so they will conclude that I will be asking for cash. Lots of it. Which confuses them, because they aren't wealthy. Not poor, but nowhere near rich enough to make their kids the target of kidnappers looking for a ransom. I mean, think about what has gone into this. To pull this off required preparation and time. And a vastly superior nerve and intelligence. Let's not forget that. Even they will have worked out that the person who took his car and children must have been watching, waiting for an opportunity.

And they would only do that if there was a significant reward, which means a lot of money.

Which they don't have.

So they'll conclude it's a mistake. This is a mistake and someone thinks they're richer than they are, so they're going to have to say they can't come up with the one or two or three million they get asked for.

This will worry them. They will fear that the kidnapper will be angry if they say they can't pay. And eventually, if they keep saying it, the kidnapper will realize it's true and disappear, along with their children.

They are probably working out what they can offer. Sell the house, ask relatives. Maybe they can come up with half a million.

Tops.

But they don't need to worry. I won't be asking for money. I want something much more valuable.

And the time has come to let them know what that is.

I will tell them what I want, and they will give it to me. It will be a shock to him. A blow, a loss almost beyond imagining.

Not to her, though. Neither a shock, nor a blow. It will be welcome.

Time now, then, to introduce them to their new futures. Same method: take out a new phone. Type a new message.

Press send.

And wait.

Annabelle

The message was from another new number. Annabelle held it so that both she and Matt could read it.

> If you want to see your children again you will do exactly as I say. Understood?

She squeezed his upper arm. 'Jesus,' she whispered. 'This is actually happening.'

He glanced at her. 'I think they want a reply. For us to say we got the message.'

'OK,' she said. She typed a reply.

> Understood.

The reply was immediate.

> Good. And I see you have not informed the police. So we can move forward.

'They know,' Annabelle said. 'They know we haven't told the police.'

'It could be a bluff,' Matt said. 'Or a guess.'

'Maybe.' She pressed her head to his chest. This was unbelievable. They were having a text conversation with the kidnapper of their children. Her stomach heaved. She dropped the phone and staggered out of the living room. The door of the downstairs bathroom banged as she slammed it open and threw up in the toilet bowl. She stayed kneeling before it, her hands on the tiled floor.

Matt appeared in the doorway.

'I'm so sorry,' he said. 'If I hadn't left them—'

'Don't,' Annabelle said. She didn't want to go down this route, not now. She didn't know where it would end, because he was right, if he hadn't left them . . .

But that wasn't going to bring them back, and at the back of her mind she couldn't stop the idea that this was coming someday, whatever they did. This person was so determined, so twisted, that they were going to get to their kids one way or another, come what may.

'Ask for proof they're alive,' she said. 'I need to know my babies are OK.'

He typed a message and showed it to her.

Please send proof the children are well.

The reply was immediate.

Later. First, I tell you what I want.

'This is it,' Matt said. 'This is when whoever this is asks for something we don't have and we have to try and sort this mess out.'

'You still think it's money?'

'It's always money. What else could it be? We'll do whatever we have to, Annabelle. Sell the house. Ask my sister. Your brother. They can have everything we own.'

She closed her eyes. 'What if it's not enough? What if we're nowhere near having what they want?'

'We'll offer what we can,' Matt said.

'And if that's not enough?' Annabelle said. 'If they think it's too risky to be worth it to them and we never hear from them again?'

'We'll take the risk anyway. Beg them to return the kids. We'll promise not to pursue them if they do. We'll promise not to tell anyone. They can have everything and walk away.' He got to his feet. 'But we can cross that bridge later.' He held out her hand for the phone and typed a message.

What do you want?

They stared at the screen, waiting. The silence seemed to stretch forever, then the reply came.

The ransom is Annabelle. If you want to see your children again, you will exchange them for her.

The silence stretched on.

'No,' Annabelle said eventually. 'No, not this. That's crazy. It's impossible.'

'I'm going to call the number,' Matt said. 'Talk to them. This is madness.'

Before he could call, another message arrived.

You have my demand. It is simple and non-negotiable. Further instructions will come tomorrow morning. You will have one chance to agree. If you accept my terms, your children will be returned to you unharmed. If not, you will never see them alive again.

Matt pressed call. She watched as his face contorted in agony.

'Shit!' he said. 'Too late. Just a message saying there's no voicemail. The phone's dead. It's been switched off, or destroyed.'

Annabelle barely heard the words. She folded her arms tightly.

'Matt,' she said. 'It's me. *I'm* the ransom.'

'No. That's not going to happen. It's ludicrous.'

'Maybe,' Annabelle said. 'But it's happening. This is real, Matt.'

'There's a way out of this,' he said. 'There has to be.'

'Then what is it?' she said. 'What the hell are we going to do?'

PART TWO

Late July 2004

'You'll find someone else. You will. I know it. It doesn't matter what you say, you'll forget me and find some posh bitch.'

Matt didn't want to have this conversation. In the first place, there was no point, because they'd already had it about twenty-five times, and whatever he said to Lindsey – his girlfriend since Christmas – it wouldn't stop her from telling him that when he went to university he'd meet someone and leave her behind in boring old Stockton Heath, and in the second place, his heart wasn't in it. He thought it was entirely possible that he *would* meet someone else, and, the more she talked about it, the more attractive a possibility it seemed.

'I won't,' he said, aware there was a dangerous lack of conviction in his voice. 'We already talked about this. I'm going out with you.'

Lindsey propped herself up on her elbow. 'There'll be loads of girls there. And you'll end up falling for one of them.'

'I won't. I promise I won't.'

'You will. I know it.'

The first time they had gone through this pantomime – you will, I won't, you will – it had lasted for what seemed like hours, until Matt had realized that there was no way to convince her he had no intention of breaking up with her in favour of someone else. More to the point, he'd learned that she didn't want him to. What she wanted was a *promise* that he wouldn't, which he had discovered when he had asked her what he could say to make her believe him. Now, he went straight to it.

'What can I say to make you believe me?' he said.

'Promise me.'

'Promise you what?'

He knew what was coming. It was as though there was a script.

'That you'll never leave me. That you love me.'

He rolled onto his back. He didn't want to tell her he loved her. All he wanted was to go downstairs and smoke a cigarette in her parents' back garden, then see who wanted to go to the pub that evening.

'See?' she said, with a note of triumphant vindication in her voice. 'You won't say it. You *can't*.'

'I've already said it. Loads.' This was always how the conversation ended up: with him swearing undying love to her, and each time it felt a little bit less like the truth.

'You don't love me,' she said. 'You never have.'

Was she right? He didn't know. He'd thought he'd loved her, at one point, but how was he supposed to know if what he'd felt was love, instead of lust or just liking her a lot? They'd met at a friend's Christmas party and kissed, then talked on the phone for about two hours the following Sunday. In the weeks that followed they'd spent a lot of time together after school, and he had thought about her all the time, but now he wasn't sure what he had been feeling. He'd talked to Jamo about it, but that hadn't helped. He'd laughed and put on a stupid voice and said *It's the Matty Westbrook gameshow. Love, lust or like? What is Matty feeling?*

And this constant badgering didn't make it easier to figure out. It only put him off her.

'I do,' he said, eventually. 'I do love you.'

'Promise?'

'Promise.' She started to say something – probably a request for him to really, truly promise – but he swung his legs out of the bed and picked up his shorts. 'Let's go for a cig,' he said. 'And then make plans for tonight. I think Jamo and Danny are going into town.'

She did not reply. He realized he had said something wrong.

'Into town? Tonight?' She sat upright and pulled the duvet over her. There was a harsh tone in her voice, like she had had an unwelcome surprise. She shook her head. 'I thought we had plans tonight.'

'What plans?'

'You said you'd come over this afternoon.'

'I know. And here I am, right now. This afternoon.'

'Fine,' she said, spitting the word out. 'Go and have your cigarette, then go out with your fucking no-mark mates.'

He sat on the edge of the bed. 'What's wrong?'

'Wrong? Why would anything be wrong?'

'Come on, Linz. Tell me what's wrong.'

'I said nothing. Now, go and smoke your fag and then fuck off!' She shouted the end of the sentence, her face red and scrunched up in anger, then turned to face the wall.

'Lindsey,' Matt said, keeping his tone as neutral as possible. They had recently had a few arguments which had ended with Lindsey screaming at him, almost out of control, while he tried – without success – to placate her. 'If I did something wrong, I'm so—'

'If?' she hissed. 'If? You *promised* me we'd spend the night in together, and now you say you're going out in town? How is that *if* you did something wrong? How?'

'I didn't promise,' Matt said. 'I said I'd come over this afternoon and then—'

'It was a promise to me!' Lindsey shouted. 'You think you can come here and get a bit of action and then go off with your shithouse mates? You think you can have your fun and

45

then go into town to find some other girl to chat up? Fine. Do it. Go. Now. Leave.'

'Linz, come on. Please. I guess I misunderstood. If you want to stay in tonight, we can stay in. I'll get—'

She leaned forward, her eyes blazing. 'If *I* want to stay in? That's not good enough, Matt. I want you to *want* to stay in. I don't want to be the kind of girlfriend who *makes* her boyfriend do things. If you want to go out, go. I don't care.'

She didn't want to be the kind of girlfriend who made her boyfriend do things? He nearly pointed out the irony of this, given the last ten minutes of their lives, but he decided it probably wouldn't help matters.

'I want to stay in with you. But I thought—'

'Thought? I don't think you do much thinking, Matt. You just do whatever your mates tell you.'

'That's not true. We'll stay in together. OK? We can watch a film. You choose.'

She stared at him, slowly shaking her head. 'No. Go out.'

He closed his eyes. He felt his pulse throb in his temples. 'I'm not going out, Linz. I'm staying with you. OK? I'm staying with you.'

She shrugged. 'Fine. If you want to.'

'I do.' He pulled on his shorts and felt in the pockets for his cigarettes. He wanted one more than ever, now.

September 2004, Birmingham University

1

The woman behind the desk checked a list for his name. She put a tick next to it, then picked up an envelope and handed it to him.

'Right,' she said. 'That's you taken care of. You're in room 418 at Chamberlain Hall.' She pointed to a group of students standing by a table. 'Ask for Carla. She'll show you where to go.'

Matt took the envelope and thanked her. He turned to his parents. They were standing near the door to the university office. Lindsey was a few yards to their left. She had barely spoken on the drive down; he hadn't been expecting her to come, but she had showed up at the house as they were packing the last of his things into the car.

She had looked at the back seat, which, apart from a space for him, was full of bedding.

Where am I sitting?

I'm not sure. He glanced at his dad. *We could move a few things around.*

Lindsey, his dad said. *We'd love for you to come, but there's not a great deal of space.*

That's fine, she said. *I can squeeze in.*

There's really not enough room. It might not be safe.

It's OK, she said, and hunched her shoulders over. *I don't take up much space.*

His mum looked up from the boot, where she was stuffing boxes of quick-cook pasta into every available crevice.

Lindsey, she said slowly. *I think it's better for Matt to be able to focus on getting settled. And you had a chance to say goodbye last night.*

Lindsey looked at Matt. *What do you think?* she said.

He'd said the only thing he could. He didn't want a shouting match outside the house, after all.

I'd love you to come.

She smiled, and clambered into the car, making a space for herself in the middle seat, pillows and duvets spilling around her.

The drive had seemed to last an age. Lindsey stared ahead; his parents maintained a stony silence. He just sat there, wishing it was all over.

At least now they were there, and he was closer to the end of this. He walked over to his parents. 'There's someone called Carla over there. She's going to show me to the room. I'll be back in a sec.'

As he approached the students they all smiled at him. 'Hi,' he said, looking at them in turn and feeling like he was going to die of shame. 'Carla?'

A tall girl wearing grey sweatpants and a rugby shirt smiled at him. 'That's me.' She had a strong Liverpool accent. 'What's your name?'

'Matt.' He looked at the envelope. 'I'm in Chamberlain Hall. Room 418.'

'All right,' she said. 'Come with me.'

*　　*　　*

48

They walked by a small lake towards a large, grey building.

'That's Chamberlain,' Carla said. 'I lived in Shackleton my first year.'

She was on his left; Lindsey was on his right, holding his hand. His parents were behind them.

'What year are you now?'

'Third. I'm doing English. What about you?'

'Law.'

'Cool.' She turned to Lindsey. 'Are you a student?'

Lindsey waited a long time before answering. 'Not here.'

Carla's eyes flickered to his, her forehead creasing in a slight frown. 'Which uni are you at?'

Lindsey gave a little shake of the head and didn't reply.

'Linz is still at sixth form college,' Matt said. 'She's got another year to go.'

'Oh,' Carla said. 'I see. Anyway, we're nearly there. We can go in this door.'

They walked into an entrance hall. There were posters on the wall and a row of small letter boxes.

'For the post,' Carla said. She nodded towards a set of stairs. 'You're on the fourth floor.' She looked at Lindsey. 'I'll leave you to it. It's easy enough to find.'

There was an edge to her tone. Matt made eye contact with her. 'Thanks,' he said. 'For bringing us over here. I really appreciate it.'

She smiled. 'No problem. See you around.'

His mum and dad followed them into the hall. His dad raised an eyebrow. His smile was thin and forced.

'Right,' he said, when Carla was gone. 'Let's go and take a look at your new home!'

2

His room was small, with a single, wood-framed bed and a desk. There was a wire waste bin by a wardrobe. The walls were grey, although at one time they had been white; there were rectangular patches where posters had protected them from the accumulated grime.

Lindsey stood by the one window, staring out of it, arms folded, shoulders hunched. She looked almost in pain, as though the effort of containing all the emotion was hurting her.

He felt sorry for her.

'Hey,' he said, and put a hand on her shoulder. It was hard and tense. 'You OK?'

She shook his hand off.

'You just want me gone,' she said.

'I don't.'

'You do. Gone from here and gone from your life.'

She was right, but he wasn't stupid enough to say that.

'I don't want you to leave,' Matt said. 'Honestly. But I don't know what you want me to do. You can't stay here.'

'I know. But you could *want* me to. You could want to be with me.'

He no longer had anything to say. He still liked Lindsey – maybe loved her even, in some ways – but he'd had enough. She seemed intent on ruining their relationship. She needed to be constantly reassured that he loved her, that he was going to be faithful to her, that he wasn't interested in anyone else, and he could never say enough to convince her. It was exhausting. He genuinely liked her – she was smart and funny and kind and loyal, but it was all lost in the constant neediness.

'I do,' he said miserably. 'I really do.'

'No you don't.' She turned to look at him. Her face was red with fury. 'And I can't believe you did that to me earlier.'

He closed his eyes. What was this? What had he done now?

'Did what?'

'You know.'

'I don't,' he said. 'Honestly.'

'Yes, you do.'

He felt like screaming. He was supposed to be starting university, meeting new people, but instead he was arguing with his girlfriend, and he didn't even know why.

'What did I do?' he said. 'Tell me.'

'I shouldn't have to tell you,' she hissed. 'I'm not *going* to tell you. The fact you don't know goes to show you don't care about me.'

He rubbed his temples. All he had to do was get through this and she'd be gone. 'I'm sorry,' he said. 'Whatever I did, I'm sorry. I don't know what else to say.'

'So you don't want to know what you did?'

She stared at him. It was a challenge and he knew she would keep on until he asked her to tell him.

'Yes,' he muttered. 'What did I do?'

'You humiliated me.'

'I humiliated you? How?'

She put on a wheedling, sycophantic voice. 'Oh, Carla, she's not finished sixth form college yet. She still has a year to go.' She shook her head. 'You had to try and impress her, didn't you? Telling her how worthless I am.'

'But you *are* in sixth form college!' he said. 'What was I supposed to say?'

'Nothing,' she said. 'You should have said nothing.'

'How could I say nothing? She asked a question, and I gave an answer.'

'You should have said *nothing*,' Lindsey said. 'It's easy. You simply keep your mouth shut.'

'Right. Well, next time I will.'

'Don't dismiss me,' she said. 'Don't you *dare* dismiss me.'

'Look,' Matt said. 'I know this is a difficult day for you—'

'For me?' she said, in something like a triumphant cry. 'For me? What about you? Isn't this a difficult day for you, too?'

'Yes,' he said. 'Of course, but—'

'That says it all. That absolutely says it all.'

There was a knock on the door.

'Hey,' Matt said, glad of the interruption. He would have been glad of an earthquake, or plague of frogs. Anything to put a stop to this. 'Come in.'

The door opened. Two boys were standing outside his room. One was tall, with long, dark hair in a ponytail. The other was short and heavily built and had a shaved head.

'All right,' he said, in a cockney accent. 'I'm Sammy.'

'I'm Jason,' the other said. He sounded like he was from Newcastle. 'We're your neighbours. I'm next door and Sammy's down the hall.'

There was something thrilling about their accents: one from Newcastle, one from somewhere down south. It was exactly why he was here.

'Matt.' He beckoned them inside. 'And this is Lindsey.'

'Are you a student here?' Sammy said.

'She's my girlfriend. She came for the day.'

Lindsey glared at them. Jason glanced at Sammy. 'We'll come back later,' he said. 'Nice to meet you, mate.'

The door closed behind them. They were alone again. Lindsey walked over to the window and looked outside.

'I think we should go and find Mum and Dad,' Matt said.

3

DEAR MATT

WELL, NOT MUCH HAS HAPPENED SINCE I LAST WROTE, HA, HA. I'LL ACTUALLY BE SENDING THAT LETTER IN THE SAME ENVELOPE AS THIS ONE COS I WROTE IT LAST NIGHT AND I'M WRITING THIS ONE THIS MORNING.

THIS ONE WILL BE SHORT AS A LONG DAY OF COLLEGE BECKONS. IT'S NO FUN WITHOUT YOU. JANINE AND ALISON ARE ALWAYS WITH STEVE AND TOBY - DOING GIRLFRIEND AND BOYFRIEND STUFF WHICH ONLY MAKES ME FEEL TERRIBLE - SO I'M ALONE MOST OF THE DAY. I MISS YOU SO MUCH. THERE ARE NO WORDS FOR IT AND IT'LL NEVER GO AWAY. I DON'T WANT IT TO. ALL I WISH IS THAT IT DIDN'T HURT LIKE IT DOES.

I THINK ABOUT YOU ALL THE TIME AND I MEAN ALL THE TIME. I WAKE UP IN THE NIGHT, THREE OR FOUR TIMES, AND START WONDERING WHAT YOU'RE DOING, IF YOU'RE IN BED OR OUT IN A NIGHTCLUB (OR WITH ANOTHER GIRL, ALTHOUGH I KNOW YOU WOULDN'T DO THAT TO ME AND I'D KILL MYSELF IF

YOU DID. JUST KIDDING. I WOULDN'T ACTUALLY KILL MYSELF. I'D KILL YOU! JUST KIDDING, AGAIN). AND THEN I CAN'T SLEEP FOR AGES AND I'M TIRED AT COLLEGE SO I MESS UP DURING LESSONS, NOT THAT I COULD CONCENTRATE ANYWAY, BECAUSE I'M THINKING OF YOU!

HAVE TO GO NOW!! I KNOW YOU'RE BUSY WITH UNIVERSITY WORK (AND PARTIES AND PUBS, RIGHT?) BUT WRITE BACK, OK?

LOVE YOU, LOVE YOU, LOVE YOU.

L.

XOXOXOXOXOX

Matt lowered the letter. He felt in the envelope; there were yet more folded sheets of A4 paper. She wrote every day, always saying the same thing, and always begging him to write back. He had, at the beginning. The first letter he sent was long, explaining who everyone was (*you remember the lads who came in? Sammy and Jason? Well, they're my two best mates here now*) and what was going on (*there's a club everyone goes to on Wednesdays where it's a quid for two shots. I was in a right mess last night!*) but they had got shorter since then. And it had been a week since he sent one at all.

At least he wouldn't have to reply to this one. Lindsey was coming to stay tomorrow night – she was taking the train Saturday morning – so he could say he decided to wait to see her to tell her his news.

Which left tonight to have some fun with his friends.

He stuffed the letter back into the envelope and put it in his letter box. He could read it later. He had a lecture to go to, and then he, Sammy and Jason were meeting in the Student Union for an early pint.

4

He walked into the Student Union Bar. Sammy was standing with a tall, fair-haired man wearing cords and a jacket, and a woman with short, jet-black hair. The man was explaining something – he was probably a professor trying to hang out with the cool kids – and the woman – a student, he guessed – was leaning on the bar, a cigarette burning between her fingers.

'Matt!' Sammy said. 'Glad you could make it. This is Annabelle,' he said. 'And this is Guy. Guy's on my course. Fucking brainy. Knows everything. Shakespeare, Dickens, loads of poems. All that shit. He can quote it like it's going out of fashion.'

So, not a professor then.

'Hardly,' Guy said, although he looked pleased. He already had thinning hair and Matt tried to place his accent; it was neutral and hard to pick. 'Nice to meet you.'

The girl – Annabelle – raised her hand.

'Nice to meet you both, too,' Matt said. 'I'm Matt.'

'Hi,' Annabelle said. She took a drag on her cigarette. 'How's it going?'

'Good. You?'

She shrugged. 'Good enough. Do you do English with these two?'

'No. Law. I know Sammy from Chamberlain Hall.' She stood up, and he realized she was almost as tall as him. She had large, green eyes. 'Are you English too?'

'Maths,' she said.

'Bloody hell,' Sammy said. 'At least someone's doing a proper subject. Anyway, time for a pint. I'm buying.'

'That's good of you,' Guy said.

'Nah,' Sammy said. 'It's Happy Hour. Two for the price of one! Your round, next.'

5

Matt stubbed his cigarette out in the ashtray. It was over-flowing with ash and butts and he watched as the smoke curled up. He sipped his drink. It was a bottle of alcoholic tangerine-flavoured syrup. It was pretty foul but it was cheap, and strong.

The table was in a corner of the bar in the basement of the hall of residence. He sat on a couch that lined the wall and looked around. It was packed with students. Sammy and Jason were dancing on the tiny, sticky dance floor. They had contrasting dance styles; Jason shuffled from foot to foot, as though he thought he was the only person out there and everyone was watching him and he didn't want to embarrass himself. Sammy too gave the impression he thought he was the only person out there and everyone was watching him, but for the opposite reason: he threw himself around like a man possessed by a particularly vindictive demon.

Sammy banged into Annabelle and she laughed, then pointed to the table and said something. She started to walk over.

Matt felt his pulse quicken. It was strange; any of the other girls could have been coming over and he would have been fine, but not Annabelle. With her, it was different. He'd felt it as soon as they met. The second he'd seen her at the bar he'd been drawn to her. He had no idea what it was about her versus anyone else, but he didn't care.

It was real, and he'd felt it from her, too. But she had a boyfriend, so he was going to have to try and ignore those feelings.

'Done dancing?' he said, when she sat at the table.

'Safer over here,' she said. Her face was flushed. 'You not dancing?'

'I gave it a shot,' Matt said. 'And I agree with you. Sammy's a danger to himself and others.'

'Could I borrow a smoke?'

'If you give it back.'

She gave him a puzzled look. 'Sorry?'

'People always ask if they can borrow a cigarette, but they're not the kind of thing you borrow and return.'

'Oh. Never mind, then. I can do without.'

He had meant it to be funny, but it was not quite working out that way. He felt himself flush. 'It's fine. It's something we say at home. Me and my friends. It was a crap attempt at a joke.' He passed her his packet of Marlboro Lights. 'Here. Take one.'

'You sure? I don't have to give it back?'

He laughed. 'Of course. Have two.'

'Was that another joke?'

'Yes. Couldn't you tell?'

She shook her head. 'Afraid not.'

'I'll try harder next time. Or maybe not bother.'

'Don't give up. Practice makes perfect.' She lit the cigarette. 'So where are you from?'

'Warrington. You?'

'Richmond.'

'In London?'

'No,' she said. 'The Yorkshire one. You enjoying it? At uni?'

'Love it. How can you not?'

'I know, right?' She took a drag and blew the smoke out. 'What are you doing tomorrow night? There's a band night at the union.'

'I've got a' – he picked his word carefully – 'guest coming.'

'A guest? What kind of guest?'

'It's someone from home.'

'Someone from home? A friend? Your parents?'

'No. Someone else.' He paused. He didn't need to hide anything. It wasn't as if she was single, either. 'Girlfriend,' he said. 'She's called Lindsey.'

He was sure he saw a flicker of disappointment on her face – maybe a slight narrowing of the eyes or fading of her smile – but it was probably only wishful thinking.

She sipped her drink. 'That should be fun. She must be a serious girlfriend if she's coming to stay?'

'Since last Christmas. What about you and Guy?'

'Me and Guy!' She laughed. 'We're just friends. We've known each other for years. We were at school together in Richmond. He has a pretty serious girlfriend of his own. She's at Cambridge.'

She stood up and stubbed out her cigarette. 'God, it's hot in here. Do you want to go for a walk? Get some fresh air?'

'Sure. Now?'

'Why not?'

'Where to?' he said.

She shrugged. 'I don't know. The lake?'

'There's a lake?' he said.

'Yeah. You should have seen it on the way in.'

'That?' Matt said. 'It's more of a pond.'

'Maybe, but they call it a lake. I don't think pond has quite the same ring to it. Shall we?'

They headed for the exit. There was a terrace outside; people milled about, smoking and drinking. They walked along a path until they came to the lake.

It really was more of a pond.

'Another smoke?' he said.

'No. I don't actually smoke, if I'm honest. I just hold them and take a few puffs. Sort of like a French film star.'

'Is that what they do?'

'Don't you watch French films?'

'All the time. Well, when I'm not watching *Terminator* or *Predator*. Or Jean-Claude van Damme kicking ass and taking names.'

'Do you *really* watch those films?'

'Do you *really* watch French films?'

'No,' she said, and laughed. 'I don't.'

'Me neither.'

They fell silent. It wasn't awkward; it was comfortable. It was as though they'd known each other for a long time.

'So,' she said. 'Your girlfriend. Lindsey. What's she like?'

'She's nice.'

'Nice? God forbid any boyfriend of mine ever describes me as *nice*. It's the blandest, most meaningless adjective in the English language.'

'Worse than *OK*? Or *pretty good*?'

'Much worse. So, tell me. What's she like?'

'I dunno,' he said. 'To be honest, it's not been working out that well.'

'Oh? But she's coming to stay?'

'Exactly. It's – it's complicated.'

'Well,' she said. 'This is not like me, Matt, but I'm going to say it anyway. I think I like you. But you have a girlfriend. Who it's complicated with.'

'I know,' he said. 'I like you too.' He turned to face her. 'Isn't it weird? I feel like I really like you, already.'

'Yes,' she said. 'It's weird. But she's coming here tomorrow.' She leaned forward without warning and kissed him on the lips. Her mouth was warm and she smelled of perfume and then it was over.

'And I don't want to be in the middle of that,' she said. 'So let's go back inside.'

6

His first thought was *Why the fuck did I set an alarm?* and then, when, he looked at his alarm clock, *seven in the morning? Why do I need to get up at seven in the morning?*

Especially after last night. They had left the bar when it closed, and then gone wandering around the grounds. Jason had a bottle of Bell's whisky which he, Sammy and Matt passed between themselves. At some point Sammy had gone for a swim in the lake. He had left his shoes near the spot where Matt had stood with Annabelle.

The spot where she had kissed him.

The kiss. It was the reason he had been walking on a cushion of air all night. It was the reason he had worn a stupid, manic grin until collapsing into bed at four in the morning.

And it was the reason his alarm was set for seven.

He had to call Lindsey. Her train was leaving Warrington at ten o'clock, so he wanted to let her know before she left.

It was going to be a hard conversation, but it was only fair. He knew now that he didn't want to be with Lindsey. He hadn't for a while, but he had not known how to tell her.

But now Annabelle was on the scene he had no choice.

Plus, it was unfair to her to keep stringing her along. Regardless of Annabelle, the right thing to do was to tell her it was over.

But he was not looking forward to the phone call.

He got out of bed. He was still wearing the jeans and T-shirt from the night before. There was a sink in his room and he cupped his hands underneath the tap and splashed water on his face, then lowered his mouth to the stream and drank as much as he could stand.

Barefoot, he walked down the corridor to the phones. He took a fifty-pence piece from his pocket and fed it into the slot. That should be plenty.

He dialled Lindsey's number. It was her mum who answered.

'Hi, Sue,' he said, his voice hoarse. 'It's me. Is Linz there?'

'She's having her breakfast. Are you well? You sound like you've got a bit of a cold. She's very excited about coming to see you.'

His resolve wavered. She was not going to take this well. Maybe it would be easier to see her one more time. Get through the weekend and then let their relationship fizzle out.

He thought of Annabelle. Of the soft, warm kiss. Of how she had said she didn't want to be in the middle of this. He had to make sure there was no 'this' to be in the middle of.

So he had to do it. It was the right thing.

'I had a late night last night,' he said. 'No cold.'

'Right. I'll put her on.'

She called Lindsey. There was a pause, and then his girl-friend was on the line.

'Hi,' she said. Her voice was guarded and suspicious. 'I wasn't expecting a call.'

'No,' he said. 'How's it going?'

'Good. You sound awful. Are you ill? Is that why you're calling?'

'No. I wanted to talk to you.'

'Couldn't it wait until I get there?'

'I don't think so.'

He listened to her breathe. 'Go on,' she said.

'I – I've been thinking. And—'

'Are you breaking up with me?'

'No!' It was an instinctive answer. 'I mean, maybe.'

'Maybe, or yes?'

'Look, Annabelle, I—'

'What did you call me?'

He realized what he had done, and looked at the phone as though it was somehow to blame. 'Nothing.'

'You called me Annabelle. Who's Annabelle? Is she that slut that showed you to your room? No – that was Carla. It's a different one. Is that what's going on here? You're breaking up with me for some university slag.' She gave a harsh laugh. 'I knew this would happen. I *fucking* knew it. I told you. Well, let me save you the trouble. You're dumped, Matt. You'll never see me again.'

There was a click and the phone went dead. It had gone, weirdly, better than he had hoped. And, whatever else, it was over between them.

7

'I broke up with her.'

Sammy raised an eyebrow. He was still in bed, having woken up when Matt knocked on his door. 'That's a bit out of the blue. I thought you two were serious.'

Matt sipped his tea. 'We were, in a way. We started going out and it just sort of carried on. I liked her – I still do – but she was way more intense than I was. I was kind of glad to come to university, honestly. To get away a bit. And now I'm here – I guess I see it differently.'

Plus, he'd met someone else, and even in that fleeting kiss he'd felt something totally new. Maybe that was what Lindsey had felt about him; if so he could understand how she would do what she did. He couldn't get Annabelle out of his mind. Even in the moments after the phone call and with his head throbbing with a hangover he had remembered the kiss and thought of her and realized he was smiling.

Later this afternoon he was going to go and see her and tell her that he had broken up with Lindsey and then, he hoped beyond hope, they could repeat that kiss.

'How did she take it?' Sammy said.

'Not great. I got called a few names.'

'Well, at least it's done.'

'Yeah. She was supposed to be coming today but that's off.'

Sammy sat up. 'You didn't think it was better to tell her face to face?'

'No. It's a waste of a journey.' He hadn't been planning to say anything about Annabelle, but he found he couldn't keep it in. He wanted to tell the world. 'Plus there's someone else.'

Sammy smiled. 'Really? Someone at uni?'

'Yeah. I met someone last night. Well, I'd met them before, but last night I realized I liked them.'

'That's weird,' Sammy said. 'I did too.'

'You met someone?'

'Yep. We're going out tonight. Just for a drink.'

'Who?' Matt said.

'That friend of Guy. I thought they were an item, but they're not, so I asked her out. It was like, three in the morning. I thought I had no chance, but she said yes.'

He felt sick. 'Which friend of Guy? Annabelle?'

'Yeah. Her. She's fit as fuck.'

He wanted to scream *Don't talk about her like that*, but he just nodded.

Sammy stood up and grabbed a pair of jeans that were half under his bed. 'Who did you meet?'

'Oh,' Matt said, his mouth dry. 'It doesn't matter. No one you know.'

Saturday, 7 March 2020, 8.30 p.m.

Matt

1

Matt sat next to his wife, his arm around her. She was resting her head against his shoulder. After reading the ransom demand they had fallen silent. He didn't know what she was thinking; he didn't know what to think himself. It felt very lonely.

'Who can it be?' he said quietly. 'If we can figure that out then we have a chance of finding them.'

'I don't know anyone who would do this,' Annabelle said. 'I don't know anyone who *could*.'

'It can't be random,' Matt said. 'If it was just money it could be anybody, but it's you they want. There has to be a connection. Something personal.'

'Someone who hates me,' Annabelle said.

'Or the opposite,' Matt said. 'Someone who loves you.'

'But who?' Annabelle said. 'If that were the case it would have to be someone I know, someone I would recognize when I turn up to ransom the kids. What could they hope to gain by it?' She frowned. 'No, it's someone who hates me, Matt. They want to hurt me.' She looked up at him. 'Or it could be somebody who loves you and wants me out of the way.'

'No,' he said. 'It's not that. There's no one. I'd know.'

She started to cry. Matt held her tighter. It was all he could do; he felt totally helpless. And guilty. If he hadn't left them in the car, none of this would have happened.

'Then it's someone who wants to hurt me,' Annabelle said. 'That's the only explanation.'

'Who?' Matt said. He fought back his own tears. He couldn't believe they were having this conversation. It felt so unreal. 'Who would want to, and who could hide something like this?'

'It doesn't have to be someone we know,' Annabelle said.

'I think it does,' Matt said. 'They must know you, because they targeted you.'

'Right. But that doesn't mean *we* know *them*.' She paused. 'Perhaps they know me, but we don't know them.'

He didn't understand what she was driving at. 'Like who?'

'Like a fan. Someone who's read my books.'

He considered it for a moment. It made a kind of sense, but it also made things much, much worse. 'Then we have no way of working it out. It could be anybody.' Annabelle sat upright, her head in her hands. He got to his feet and began walking up and down the room. He felt like he was fizzing with energy, like his nerves were out of control. He wanted to do something. *Anything.*

But there was nothing to do.

'Has anything weird happened?' he said. 'Any fans got in touch, on Twitter or Facebook?'

'I can't think of anything,' she said. She picked up her phone. 'It might be very recent. I can take a look.'

She tapped on the screen. 'I don't see anything.'

'In the past?'

'Not that I can recall.'

On the arm of the sofa his phone buzzed. He walked over and snatched it up.

There was a new message.

This is what you asked for.

'What is it?' Annabelle said. He held up the phone and she read it. She frowned. 'What does that mean?'

The answer came quickly. The phone buzzed again and a photo appeared.

It was of the children. All three of them – Norman, Keith and Molly – asleep in the back seat of Matt's car.

Annabelle grabbed the phone. She stared at it. 'What's been done to them? They would never sleep like that. And Norman would know something was wrong. He'd be too worried to sleep. The kidnapper must have given them something.'

Matt's stomach tightened. What had they been given? What if the dose was too high? He leaned over and enlarged the picture. He examined their faces.

They were relaxed, their jaws slack. There was colour in their faces. They looked alive, at least.

The phone buzzed again.

They are fine. For now. They will not remain that way unless you do as I say. I will start sending pieces of them to you. First something small, like the tip of a finger. Then larger things. I will leave that to your imagination.

Annabelle grabbed the phone and typed a reply.

Who are you? Why are you doing this?

The reply that came ignored the question.

I will send my demands in the morning. If you do not meet them, or if you inform the police, this will be over and you will never see your sleeping beauties again. And I repeat: if you contact the authorities, I will know, and there will be no second chances.

Matt sat heavily on the couch. He studied his wife. 'This is for real,' he said. 'This is actually happening.'

2

Matt sat back on the couch. His head was spinning. It reminded him of a time early in his career when he had had to deliver a speech to a room full of lawyers and his mind had gone blank. Brain freeze, someone called it, and it was an accurate description. Everything stopped; all thought became impossible.

'This is insane,' he said. 'I don't understand it. The kids are gone, someone wants you as a ransom. And I have no idea what to do about it.'

He felt, for the first time in his life, completely powerless. There were no options. All they could do was whatever the crazy bastard behind this told them to do.

'I know,' Annabelle said, her voice close to breaking. 'It's just us, waiting to see what happens. And it's so unfair. What have we done to deserve this?'

'Nothing,' Matt said. 'No one deserves this.'

'What can we do, Matt? Is there anything?'

'No,' he said. 'I can't think of anything. But then I can hardly think at all.'

'Maybe we should get help.'

'From who? We can't risk telling the cops.'

'What about my brother?' Annabelle said. 'He might have an idea.'

'I suppose. But what if the kidnapper finds out? They said to tell no one.'

'How would they find out? And I'd like to see my brother.'

Matt nodded. He'd like to see Tessa, his sister, too. If nothing else it would make them feel less alone.

'OK,' he said. 'I'll call Mike.'

Mike answered on the second ring. He lived in Bebington, on the Wirral, where he had a building firm.

'Matt,' he said. 'How's it going?'

'Not great. Can you come over?'

'What's the problem?'

'I'll tell you when you get here.'

'You're calling at eight-thirty on a Saturday evening asking me to come over? What's going on, Matt? Is it the kids?'

'Can you come?'

There was a pause. 'It'll be an hour. OK?'

'See you then.'

He texted his sister.

Are you free?

She replied immediately.

Just finishing a shift at the hospital. Pooped, but you need me for something?
   Can you come over?
   Now?
   Maybe nine-thirty?
   Sure. Is everything OK?
   Will tell you when you arrive.

He put the phone down and looked out of the window. It was dark outside, and he imagined someone hiding in their garden, watching them. He got up suddenly and closed the curtain.

'What?' she said. 'Did you see something?'

'Only in my mind,' he said. 'I'm jumping at shadows.'

'Yes,' she said. 'But this time the shadows are real.'

Annabelle

1

Annabelle sat next to Matt on the couch, her legs tucked underneath her. Tessa had arrived a few minutes earlier and was opposite her in an armchair. She took deep breaths, fighting to control the panic.

It didn't help much. Every few seconds she was hit with an image of her children, locked in the car or in a strange room, crying out in terror or hunger for their parents, and she felt a physical pain that took the place of everything else in her world.

'So,' Tessa said. 'Are you guys going to tell me what's going on?'

'Let's wait for Mike,' Matt said. 'He'll be here any minute.'

'Do you' – Tessa nodded at Annabelle's stomach – 'have any news?'

Annabelle shook her head. She wished it was that.

The bell rang and Matt went to answer it. She heard the

front door open, and then her brother's voice. Mike walked into the living room.

'So,' he said. 'What's up?'

Annabelle looked from one to the other. She couldn't quite believe the words she was about to say. 'It's the kids. They – they've—' her voice broke and she started to sob.

Mike knelt next to her. 'Annie. What's happened?'

She couldn't reply; all her breath had left her and she was shaking with sobs. Mike wrapped his arms around her.

'They're gone,' Matt said. 'The kids are gone.'

'Gone?' Mike said. 'Gone where? What the hell is going on?'

She forced herself to inhale, slowly and deeply. 'They've been taken,' she said, eventually.

'Taken?' Tessa said. 'What do you mean?'

'The children have been kidnapped,' Matt said, his voice slow and heavy. 'We don't know who's responsible. But we know why. It's a ransom.'

'A *ransom*?' Tessa said. 'You're saying your kids are being held for ransom?'

'Right,' Matt said. 'For ransom.'

In the silence that followed Annabelle started to feel numb. It was a welcome break from the fear and panic. She supposed she might be in shock, her body trying to defend her from what was happening.

'OK,' Mike said, eventually. His voice was calm and measured. 'Someone has the children, and they want a ransom. How much is it?'

'It's not money,' Matt said.

'Then what is it?' Tessa asked.

Annabelle looked at each of them in turn.

'It's me,' she said.

2

Mike looked her in the eye.

'What does that mean?' he said, his voice even.

'It means that the kidnapper wants Annabelle in exchange for the kids,' Matt said.

'That's ridiculous,' Mike protested. 'There's no way that can happen. No way.'

'I know,' Annabelle said. 'But I'm starting to think it might be the only option.'

'No,' Mike said. 'There's another way.'

'What exactly did the messages say?' Tessa asked.

Matt picked up his phone and read out the text messages. Annabelle watched their eyes narrow and their frowns deepen. It had been shocking enough watching events unravel over a few hours, but they were getting the full impact in minutes.

The kidnap, the threats, the revelation of what the ransom was.

'They want you,' Tessa said. 'So it's someone who knows you. Any thoughts?'

'Have you been through everyone?' Mike said. 'Your colleagues at the law firm? Friends?'

'Everyone we can think of,' Matt said. 'And we still have no idea.'

Annabelle shifted on the couch. 'There's one possibility,' she said. 'Perhaps a fan. A crazy fan.'

'Jesus,' Mike said. 'So if that's it, it could be anyone.'

'Exactly,' Matt said.

Tessa folded her arms. 'What about the police?' she said.

'No,' Matt said. 'Too risky.'

'Are you sure?' she said. 'They have protocols for these situations. At least, I assume they do. When I work with them at the hospital – if there's been an incident where lives are in danger – they always have methods and systems to deal with it. They would keep it confidential.'

'What if they can't?' Matt said. 'That's what the messages say. The kidnapper will know.'

'I think you're right,' Mike said. 'At this point anyway. No police. They might not be happy to stay in the background. They might show up here or where the car was taken from. And then there'll be no hiding their involvement. We can't scare the kidnapper away. They're the only link to the kids.'

Annabelle listened in silence. The messages had been clear. Crystal clear. *I will start sending pieces of them to you.*

She closed her eyes. Somewhere out there her children – her babies – were in the care, if you could call it that, of a man – or woman – who had threatened to cut pieces off them and send them to their parents.

And who had also said no police.

I will know.

It could have been a lie, a way to make them fear the consequences of involving the authorities.

Or it could be true. Maybe the kidnapper had a contact in the police, or another way of knowing. Plus, like Tessa said, there was no guarantee that the police would do what she and Matt asked them to do.

78

And then she would never see her children again, which was unbearable.

'No,' she said. 'We're not telling them. I'm not putting the kids in danger.'

Tessa nodded slowly. 'Then what do we do?'

'I don't know,' Annabelle said. 'But not that.'

'Are you going to tell Dad?' Mike said.

'No,' Annabelle said. 'It'd only upset him.'

'I guess so,' Mike said. 'He's living with me now, and he's getting pretty frail.'

'You brought him back from the care home?' Tessa said.

'Yeah.' Mike shrugged. 'Could be unnecessary, but with this new virus, I thought it was best.' He came to the couch and hugged Annabelle tight. 'This is a mess,' he said. 'But we'll sort it out. Don't you worry. We'll sort it out.'

The words were comforting, and she wanted to believe them, but she didn't. She didn't believe them at all.

They will be at the fear and panic stage now. That idiot husband of hers will be thinking how powerless and useless he is. It is probably a familiar feeling for him.

He'll be wondering who would possibly go to all this trouble just to get Annabelle, thinking through all the possibilities, all the people he knows and all the people he's met. Anyone, anyone at all who might fit the bill.

He will never figure out who it is. Or why. He will think it is obsession, or revenge, or the product of a sick and twisted mind.

It is none of those. It is something far greater.

Even if, by an odd fluke, it crosses his mind, he will dismiss it.

And if he doesn't, I have my defences in place.

And in the meantime, I wait, and he waits.

But we are not the same.

He is waiting to find out what happens next. I am waiting to collect my prize.

Birmingham, October 2004

1

It had not worked out with Sammy and Annabelle, thank God. And Zeus. And Thor. And any other deity past, present or future. He had never been so relieved about anything in his life.

Not my type, Sammy said, after their first and only date. *We had a laugh but that was it. No spark. She wants to be a writer. Nice dream, but no chance.*

She wanted to be a writer. What Sammy saw as a naïve dream, Matt thought was thrilling. Why not try to be a writer? The worst that could happen would be you'd fail, which was no different from any other walk of life.

And now – both blissfully unattached – he and Annabelle were going out. That evening. He'd finally worked up the courage, two days earlier at the bar.

What are you doing Saturday?
Nothing.
Want to go somewhere?

Depends where.

I could surprise you.

She looked uncertain for a moment, then laughed. *You could try. But I'm not sure any of the usual haunts would be that much of a surprise.*

He nearly shouted in triumph, but he managed to keep it to a smile. *I've got an idea,* he said, hoping an idea would present itself in the next few days. *So Saturday it is.*

He'd said he would surprise her, and he was going to do exactly that. This wouldn't be one more lame evening in the corner of a smoky pub, or watching a shitty mass-movie. No – he was going to come up with something different. Edgy. Cool.

What would she like? What would impress her? She wanted to be a writer, so she liked cultural things. Theatre. Galleries. Music.

He looked for pop concerts. There were none on. He walked around the student union, looking at the flyers. There was a debate about whether Tony Blair was really a Labour politician. A student performance of a Russian play. A sit-in for peace.

No, thanks.

And then he saw it. A poster for the Birmingham Touring Opera. They were doing something called *The Two Widows* at 7 p.m. that evening.

He had no idea what it was, but it was perfect. They could meet at four, go for a drink and an early meal, then head to the opera. Surprise me, she'd said. Well, she'd be surprised all right.

I didn't know you were into opera, she'd say, impressed.

Oh, you know. I dabble.

Yes, this was perfect.

2

They met in the foyer of Chamberlain Hall.

'So,' Annabelle said. 'What are you thinking?'

He was thinking *My God you're the most beautiful person I've ever seen and I can't believe how I feel just looking at you, what the fuck is going on?* But he wasn't sure that was the right answer in the circumstances.

That was how he felt, though, and it made his head swim.

'Well,' he said. 'I heard that the opera was in town.'

The opera was in town? Was that what people said. It made it sound like the circus.

'The opera?'

'Yeah. The Birmingham Touring Company. They're doing *The Two Wives*.'

'By Smetana?'

Was it? 'Yeah. Smetana.'

She frowned. 'You mean *The Two Widows*?'

He felt his face and neck flush with heat. '*The Two Widows*. That's it.'

'And you want to go?'

'Of course.'

She smiled. 'I shouldn't judge by appearances, but I didn't take you for an opera fan.'

'Oh, you know. I dabble.'

'We're not really dressed for it.' She was wearing dark blue jeans and a red V-neck sweater. 'I might be OK, but' – she looked him up and down – 'I don't think Doc Martens, jeans and a T-shirt are going to cut it.'

He felt himself flush even deeper. He hadn't thought of his clothes.

'You think I should change clothes?'

'It is the opera. That you dabble in.' She smiled. 'So which operas are your favourites?'

He tried to think of one he knew. 'I like most of them.'

'Any in particular?'

There was only one vaguely opera-like thing he could think of.

'*Barcelona*,' he said. 'I like that.'

She frowned. 'Barcelona?'

'You know. By Freddie Mercury and' – he realized he did not know the name of the other singer – 'the opera woman.'

'Right,' she said. 'Any others? *Don Giovanni, The Magic Flute? Aida?*'

'Love them.'

She folded her arms and looked at him with a wry, amused expression. Was she making these names up? It was possible.

And he really had no idea.

'OK,' he said. 'I know nothing about opera. But you said to surprise you.'

'This is certainly a surprise.'

'Then it worked,' he said.

She laughed, long and hard. Even though she was laughing at him it was the best sound he'd ever heard.

'Well,' she said. 'That was kind of weird. But cute. In a desperate way. Maybe we should just go to the pub instead.'

'What?' he said. 'I've bought the tickets. And I want to find out why these wives—'

'—widows—'

'—widows are so merry. Let's go and change into our opera clothes. I'll meet you here in twenty minutes. And I'll be in my shirt and tie, OK?'

3

He had no idea what was going on, why the widows were merry, or how they made the noises that came out of their mouths, but he could tell that the opera was spectacular.

And he felt – in a way he never had before – grown up. He was wearing a shirt and tie. They had sherry at the bar. And Annabelle looked unbelievable. She was in a knee-length black dress and in his mind they were Brad and Jen or Frank and Ava or some other famous couple.

At the interval they sat at a small marble-topped table in the corner of the bar and had another glass of sherry.

'You like it?' he said.

'I *love* it.' She smiled at him and he thought *Oh God, a smile for me. For me. We're together. We're actually together.* 'What do you think?'

'I don't really know what's going on,' he said. 'But it's still totally captivating. It's weird – if you put an opera CD on for an hour I'd be totally bored, but watching it – it felt like it was ten minutes.'

'I know. Captivating's the right word.' She sipped her sherry. 'And so stylized. They have to act, but while singing. It's amazing.'

The bell rang to signal it was time to return to their seats. As they headed for the double door that led to the concourse, he put his arm around her waist. He felt the heat of her body through her dress, and then, in a moment he would never forget, she put her arm around him.

And it was obvious they *fitted*.

It was, to that point, the best thing that had ever happened to him.

4

When he woke, the first thing he thought was *When can I see her?*

After the opera they had gone to the lake where she had kissed him. There was a bench; it was damp and he had brushed it down, then put his jacket on the wooden surface.

Don't be soft, she said. *You'll ruin it.*

You'll ruin your dress.

It cost me ten pounds in the River Island sale, she said. *Your jacket is much more valuable. It's quite cool, actually.*

It's my dad's. He had it in his wardrobe. It's pretty old.

They call that vintage. Your dad had good taste.

They sat and talked for a while. Her mum had died when she was eleven and she and her brother had been raised by their dad, a physics teacher. He was an opera fan – along with hiking, model-making, jazz and woodwork – and had taught her a bunch about opera, along with how to make furniture, how to navigate in the thick fog of the Howgill Fells and how to bivouac overnight if you got lost, but, most importantly, he'd taught her to trust in her own abilities and skills and follow her dreams.

He told her about his parents, not that there was much to tell. He felt colourless and drab next to her.

Around two in the morning she shivered.

I'm going to bed now, she said. *You can walk me back to my room.*

They parted at the door to her building.

See you soon? he said.

I can't wait.

Those were the last words she had said before turning and walking through the door, and he thought of them now.

He had heard them and said them countless times, but never understood they could be literally true. The thought of waiting to see her was unbearable.

When he got down to the foyer of Chamberlain Hall there was a note stuck to the outside of his letter box. He grinned. It must be from Annabelle, telling him where they should meet.

It wasn't. It was from the university office.

Please phone Lindsey Daley.

Just those four words. Lindsey must have called the university and left a message for him.

His euphoria was swept away by a feeling of dread. He did not want to call and speak to her – he was pretty sure she would want to give it another try, reconcile, get back together. But that was not on the cards.

He wasn't sure why she thought it would be.

He might as well get it over with. He went to the phone boxes and put a couple of coins in. She answered on the second ring.

'It's me,' he said. 'I got a message from you.'

'Oh,' she said. 'Right. How much money did you put in?'

'Twenty pence. That's all the change I have.'

'I'll call you back. What's the number?'

'What's going on, Lindsey?'

'I'll call you back.'

He gave her the number.

'So,' she said. 'I have news.'

'Right.' He paused. 'What is it?'

She gave a little cough.

'You're not going to like this.'

'Like what?' The sensation of dread deepened.

'Promise me you won't be angry.'

'Why would I be?'

'Promise you won't.'

'How can I, if I don't know—' He stopped himself. This was pointless. 'I promise.'

'That's not a real promise. You're only saying it.'

'Lindsey, tell me what it is. Please!'

There was a pause. 'I'm pregnant.'

It took a few seconds for the meaning to sink in.

'Pregnant? With a baby?'

'Yes. With a baby. Your baby, before you ask.'

'How?' he said. 'We used protection. Condoms. Every time.'

'They're not one hundred per cent.'

He tried to think of a time something had gone wrong. There were none. 'I don't get it.'

'It happens. Nothing is foolproof.'

He couldn't think of what to say. He couldn't think of what to think. All he knew was that this was not good. 'So what do we do?'

'I know this is weird, but you need to call your sister.'

'Tessa?'

'Unless you have another sister, yes.'

90

'What's Tessa got to do with this?'

'I can't tell you. I don't want you to shout at me. And I think you'll listen more to her. So please, call Tessa.'

The phone went dead.

Call his sister? She wasn't friends with Lindsey. They were in the same year at school, but they only knew each other through him.

He dialled home. His sister picked up immediately.

'Hi,' she said. She sounded uncomfortable. He could picture her expression; when she was about to say something that might be controversial, she got a look on her face that was part tentativeness, part determination.

'I'm in a phone box. Call me back.'

The phone rang a few seconds later.

'So,' he said, when he picked up. 'I just talked to Lindsey. She told me – something – and said I need to call you.'

'I know. She said she'd ask you to call me.'

He shook his head. 'I don't get it. Are you guys friends now?'

'Good friends. We go out every weekend.'

He closed his eyes. For fuck's sake. He simply couldn't shake her.

'You do? And she told you what happened?'

'Of course she did. She told me earlier this week at college.'

'And you didn't call me?'

'She asked me not to. She wanted time to think before she talked to you.'

'Right,' he said. He looked over his shoulder. A girl with dark red hair was waiting to use the phone booth. He gestured to his watch and gave an apologetic shrug. 'What did she want to think about?'

'About her options.'

There were *options*? Other than an abortion. His mouth was dry, and it wasn't a hangover.

'And why did she want me to call you?'

'Because she wanted me to tell you what she's going to do. She didn't want to tell you herself. She said you'd be angry.'

What he wanted to do was shout *that's a bloody excuse. She's playing games*, but that would make him sound angry. Which would be kind of proving her point. He took a deep breath. 'What's she going to do?'

'She's made up her mind, Matt. She's thought about it a lot.'

'And?'

He had a horrible, sinking feeling that he knew exactly what Tessa was going to say.

'She's going to have the baby.'

'No,' he said. 'No way. She's not thinking about it clearly. She's too young. We're both too young!'

'She wants to have the baby.'

Matt took the receiver from his ear and rested it against his chest. Lindsey was pregnant, and she was going keep it. She was going to be a mum.

He was going to be a dad.

He lifted the receiver to his ear. Tessa was in the middle of saying something.

'—and she's a nice person. Honestly. She's lovely.'

'I don't doubt it,' he said. 'But I don't want a baby with her.'

'I know,' Tessa said. 'It's such a huge thing. I've kind of been in shock these past few days. It's been *so* hard to say nothing. I tried to tell her it might not be a great idea, but she's made up her mind. It's her right to do that, Matt.'

'I know. But she needs to unmake it.'

'I don't think she will.'

'You're her friend now. Tell her this is a big mistake.'

Tessa sighed. 'I told you: I tried. This isn't good, Matt, but she's going to do it, and you have to face up to that.'

'Jesus,' Matt said. 'This is a fucking nightmare.'

'There's one other thing,' Tessa said. 'Lindsey wanted me to mention this, too. She thinks you might listen to me.'

'What now?' he said. 'Is it twins?'

'That's not funny. And no, it isn't.' She paused. 'As I said earlier, I've got to know her and I like her a lot. She's a great person, Matt. She knows she got it wrong with you, but she's learned from it. She loves you, and she knows that you love her too, deep down.'

'I don't, Tessa.'

'Maybe. But you should give her a chance. You should consider it.'

'Consider what?'

'Getting back together with her.'

There was no possibility of that. None. All he could think of was trying to persuade her not to go through with it.

'I don't think that's on the cards, Tess,' he said. 'It wasn't working out.'

'I know,' Tessa said. 'But I promised Linz I'd talk to you about it. At least ask you to think about it.

'There's nothing to think about. We weren't right for each other.'

'She's changed.'

'I don't think so,' he said. 'And anyway, there's someone else.'

His sister did not reply for a few seconds. 'Annabelle?'

'Yes. How do you know?'

'That's the name you called her.'

'I see. Well, we're kind of together now.'

'Yeah,' his sister said. 'But is that only because you and Linz parted on bad terms? If it wasn't for that, you might never have fallen for her.'

'The thing is, Tessa, I like her. We've only been on one date but we clicked. I didn't feel that way about Lindsey.'

'You've been on *one* date, Matt. That's nothing.'

'I know. But . . . we clicked, that's all I can say. Look,' he said. 'I can see why she wanted you to talk to me, but it makes no difference. We're not getting back together. And Lindsey needs to talk to me herself. You have no idea how serious this is.'

'I do,' Tessa said. 'Which is why I agreed to help. I don't want to be caught up in this. It's been killing me, Matt. I've been so worried. I can't sleep.'

'Shit, Tessa. You don't need to put up with this. I'll deal with it, OK? I love you, but this is between me and Lindsey.'

'I love you too,' Tessa said. 'Good luck, big brother.'

He had a shower and a cigarette and a coffee, then he called Lindsey. His sister had evidently got there first.

'You didn't wait long, did you?' she said.

'For what?'

'To replace me. Tessie told me about Annabelle. She's been around a while, huh? That was the name you called me. You'd hardly left home, and already I was nothing to you.'

Tessie? No one called his sister Tessie.

'I don't want to argue about this,' Matt said. 'There's no point. I met someone else. I'm not trying to hide it.'

'You're pathetic. I can't believe you're going to be the father of my child. I'm going to have to put up with you for years.'

'Then don't do it,' Matt said. 'You don't have to have the baby.'

'How *dare* you!' she shouted. 'It's my body and my baby, and you don't get to tell me what to do!'

'I wasn't telling you what to do. I was just saying—'

'I hate you, Matt. I can't believe I ever thought you were the one for me. I *hate* you.'

94

'I'm sorry,' he said. 'I am. I don't want to upset you, but I don't know what to do or say, Lindsey. We can talk about it more, if you like.'

'There's nothing to talk about. I'm having the baby and you can do whatever you want. See it, be there for it, or ignore it. I don't care.'

'I'll be there for it, of course,' he said. 'I'll—'

The phone went dead. He hung up and slumped against the wall of the phone booth. This was a disaster.

There was only one thing he could do, and it was the last thing in the world he wanted to do.

He was going to have to go home and sort this out.

'I thought it was all over?' Annabelle took a drag on her cigarette. 'You guys broke up?'

'We did.'

'Then why do you have to go home to see her?'

There was another note in his letter box when he got back from the phone call – how he wished it was the only note he'd got that day – saying *Meet me at our bench at noon. A xx*

Our bench. They had a *bench*.

'She called and left me a message to get in touch. She had news.'

'Oh?' Annabelle looked wary. She folded her arms. 'What kind of news?'

He was not going to lie. What he had with Annabelle was already too precious. He didn't want to start off with lies, apart from ones about liking opera. 'She's pregnant.'

She blinked, eyes wide. 'That's some news. You're the father?'

He nodded. 'Apparently.'

'Didn't you guys – you know. Use protection?'

'Condoms. I guess they're not foolproof.'

95

'Did one break or something?'

'No. I don't think so. I don't remember that happening.'

'Then they're pretty reliable.'

He shrugged. 'Not reliable enough.' He took her free hand in his. 'I wanted to tell you,' he said. 'I don't want anything hidden between us. I'm going to tell you the truth, always. So, in that vein – I really like you, Annabelle. I want you to know that, as well.'

'I like you too. A *lot*.'

He felt a wave of relief. 'That's fantastic.'

'But—'

But. That one word was like a knife slipped between his ribs.

'But what?' he said.

'But I think you need to sort this out,' Annabelle said. 'It's a big deal, for you and for Lindsey. You need to make sure you get this right, and I don't want to distract you from that.'

'You won't,' Matt said. 'We can just take it slow. I'm not going to get back together with her, whatever happens. It doesn't need to change things for us.'

'You're going to be a dad,' Annabelle said. She had tears in her eyes.

'Not necessarily,' he said. 'That might not happen.'

'But while it might that changes *everything* for us.' She took his hands in hers. They were warm and soft. 'So go home and do what you need to do. And when the dust settles we'll see where we are.' She leaned forward and kissed him, then stood up, and walked away from their bench.

5

'Hi, Matt.' Lindsey's mum, Sue, opened the door. 'You're back! How's university?'

He had gone home first and Tessa had told him that Lindsey had not informed her parents about the pregnancy; she was worried they would force her to have an abortion, so she was planning to keep it a secret as long as she could.

'It's great.'

'Lindsey said you're enjoying it. She was hoping to visit more often but she mentioned you have a lot going on.'

'Yeah,' he said. It was clear that Lindsey had not told her parents they had broken up, either. 'It's pretty busy.'

'Well, I'm glad you made it home. She's been missing you. She's upstairs.'

Lindsey was sitting on her bed, reading a magazine. When he came into the room she looked up at him with a sweet smile. There was no trace of the hatred she had expressed so forcefully that morning.

'Hi, stranger,' she said. 'Long time, no see.'

'Right.'

She patted the bed. 'Take a seat.'

He stayed standing. He looked at her stomach. There were no signs of her pregnancy.

'So,' he said. 'You're pregnant.'

'We're pregnant.'

He ignored her clarification. 'Do you want to talk about it?'

'Sit down,' she said. 'You're making me feel uncomfortable.'

He looked around for a chair. There had been one at her desk, but it was gone. He wondered whether she had removed it so he had nowhere to sit, but caught himself. It was probably just downstairs.

He sat next to her on the bed.

'So. We're going to be parents.'

'If you have the baby. There's still time to change your mind. We haven't talked about it yet.'

She laughed. 'You can't understand,' she said. 'But I have no choice. I *have* to have this baby. It's my child. I can't do anything to hurt it.'

'I understand. But for the record, do I get any say?'

She shook her head. 'But I know you're a good man, Matt. I know you'll want to do the right thing for our baby, whatever you think just now.'

'I will. I'll do the best I can. But—'

'I knew you would.' She smiled. 'I knew I could count on you. I knew you'd be ready to give it a try.'

He frowned. 'Give what a try?'

'Us. The baby.'

He got to his feet. 'Lindsey. I don't want to sound mean, but it's over. There's no us.'

'There is, and there always will be. We've created this child together. That'll never go away, and all I want is what's best for the child. Don't you want the same?'

'Of course, but—'

'What "but" can there be?' she said. 'We have to put the

baby first. If it doesn't work out, that's fine. But we owe it to our child to give it a try. And I think we can do it, Matt. And a second ago you said you'll do the best you can.'

That was not what he meant. 'Look,' he said. 'I'm not ready for this.'

'Matt. This is your child. You have to face up to your responsibilities.'

'I'm at university.'

'That's fine. You can come back on the weekends. The baby's due in late May, so you'll be nearly done with the year by then. And we can move there together for your second year.'

She was smiling at him, her hands folded over her stomach. He wanted to run from the room and never come back.

'I don't think that's going to work,' he said.

'We can give it a try! It's only a bit of weekend travel!'

'Not that,' he said. 'Me and you. We broke up. It was over.'

'It *was* over. But that's only because you left for university. If you'd stayed here we'd still be together. And this is a sign you should have. This is a gift from the universe.' She sat upright. 'You have to stay with me, Matt. You can't *abandon* me. What will people think? What will your parents think? Your sister?'

'When are you going to tell your mum and dad?'

'When the time is right.'

'And what would we say in the meantime? About me coming back at weekends?'

She shrugged. 'That we got back together.'

'I need – I need to think,' he said.

'OK,' she replied. 'But you know what you have to do, Matt.'

Saturday, 7 March 2020, 10.00 p.m.

Matt

Tessa put her hand on his elbow. 'You have tea?' she said.

'In the kitchen,' Matt replied. Mike was sitting by Annabelle; she looked pale and ill. He didn't feel much better himself, but he had to keep moving, keep thinking this through, keep trying to find the answer.

Although up to now there were no answers.

'Where in the kitchen?' Tessa asked.

'The cupboard above the kettle. You know where the tea is.'

'Come with me,' she said, and caught his eye. She walked out of the living room and he followed her into the kitchen.

'What is it?' he said.

'There is another possibility,' she said. 'You didn't mention it, so I wanted to add it to the list.'

'What do you mean, "another possibility"?'

'For who this could be.'

Matt studied his sister. He knew the expression on her face. It was the one she got when she was about to say something that might be unpopular. 'We needed to be alone for you to tell me?'

'It might be better.'

'What are you getting at, Tess?'

'It's possible there's someone else,' she said.

'Someone else?' There was no time for this cryptic bullshit. 'I don't get it. Just say it.'

'Another man,' Tessa said. 'Someone who's in love with Annabelle.'

'We went through that. There's no one we know. It could be a fan, but other than that there's no one.'

'No one *you* know. Annabelle might know them.'

It took a moment for him to understand what she was suggesting. No wonder she had looked uncomfortable.

'You think she's having an affair?'

'No, I don't. I'm only saying that it's a possible explanation, and you shouldn't rule it out. Maybe it was a fling, and the guy became obsessed. Or she flirted with someone and they took it to mean something it didn't. It happens, Matt.'

'No,' he said. 'She wouldn't do that.'

'I agree. But it's worth considering.'

'In any case, she'd have said. Our kids' lives are at risk!'

'She might be hoping there's another way to solve it. One that doesn't involve you finding out.'

He felt a twinge of doubt. Was this possible? It would explain it, that was for sure. But it would mean Annabelle had had an affair – or something of that nature – and then lied to him when the man she'd had an affair with had kidnapped their kids.

It was almost impossible to believe.

But then the entire thing was almost impossible to believe.

'What do you suggest?' he said.

'Ask her.'

'She won't like it. Do you want to?'

'Not with our history,' said Tessa. 'We're friends now, but you know.'

He did know. They had not got off to a great start. It wasn't their fault, but still.

'OK,' he said. 'I'll mention it.'

Annabelle

Matt and Tessa came back into the room. Matt looked shaken and frightened. Tess had a serious look on her face. She did not meet Annabelle's gaze.

Matt sat next to her on the couch. He nodded at Tessa and Mike. 'I need to speak to Annabelle alone,' he said. 'Only for a moment.'

'What is it?' she said, when they were alone.

Matt seemed almost nervous. He folded his arms. 'You had any more ideas?'

'About what?'

'About who it might be?'

'No.' She caught his eye. 'Have you?'

'I did have a thought,' he said. 'A possible explanation.'

'And?'

'Tessa – we were talking and she had an idea. About who might be responsible.'

'Tessa?' she said. 'What did she say?'

'What if it's someone who's in love with you?'

'We went through this already. There's no one.'

'Maybe someone you don't want to tell me about.' He looked away, unable to hold her gaze.

'Like who?'

'Annabelle,' he said. 'This is a possibility, that's all. No one is saying it's true. But we owe it to our kids to examine every avenue, right?'

'Right.' She paused. She didn't like where this was going, and, if the expression on his face was anything to go by, neither did he. 'What avenue is this, Matt? Who might be in love with me who I don't want you to know about?'

'Someone who – if you had' – he inhaled deeply – 'if you had had an affair, or a fling, or even simply gave someone reason to think—'

'If I had had an *affair*?' Annabelle said. She could barely believe what he was saying. 'Are you suggesting I have a secret boyfriend?'

'No,' Matt said. 'But if there *was* someone.' He paused and lifted up his hands, palms facing her. 'I'm not accusing you of anything—'

'It sounds like you are.'

'—but think about it. One explanation could be a jilted lover. A one-night stand—'

'This is insane, Matt. Stop talking. Please.'

He looked away. 'I'm not saying you did anything, Annabelle. But theoretically this is an explanation and we have to explore every possible avenue. That's all.'

'Was this your sister's idea?'

They looked at each other in silence.

'Yes,' he said. 'She mentioned it.'

'Of course she did.'

'It was only an idea. She was being helpful.'

'Well thank God she's not trying to be disruptive.' She took a series of deep breaths. This was no time for them to argue, and besides, she didn't really blame him. It was no surprise he had come up with this after talking to Tessa. In recent years they had become closer, but it seemed Tessa was still ready to believe the worst of her.

'Listen,' she said. 'I'm going to accept that you and your sister are simply trying to explore every avenue. But let's put this to bed once and for all. I'm not having, nor have I ever had, an affair. Or a one-night stand. Or an ill-advised kiss at a Christmas party. I love you, and I would never do that to you. I've never even wanted to.'

The tension – some of it, anyway – drained from his face. 'I never thought different,' he said. 'It was . . . I had to ask.'

'After Tessa mentioned it.'

'Yes. But she wasn't trying to accuse anyone—'

'Forget it,' Annabelle said. 'And let's get back to finding our children.'

Birmingham, November 2004

1

Matt ran down the stairs of Chamberlain Hall. The bus to the station left in two minutes and it was a three-minute walk. If he missed it, he'd miss his train, which would put him into peak commuting hours on a Friday evening and a more expensive ticket.

Which he could do without. It was bad enough he was going home for the weekend – again – and he didn't need to pay over the odds for the privilege.

He and Lindsey were giving it a try. She was loving it all: him, them, the pregnancy.

He was loathing every second.

On Tuesday she'd left a message for him to call. He'd wondered for a moment whether something had happened to the baby – he hated himself for the small burst of hope the thought gave him – but the pleasure in her voice when she picked up the phone made it clear there was no bad news.

I'm twelve weeks today, she said.

That's wonderful.

It is. After twelve weeks the likelihood of something going wrong is much lower. We're going to be parents, Matt!

He had ended the call terrified. Terrified about becoming a father, terrified by how much Lindsey was thrilled by it and terrified about what the hell was going to happen to his life.

A voice interrupted him.

'You in a hurry?' It was Guy. He was through the door, his arm around a girl Matt had met in the first week and not seen since. She was called Trixie, and was one of the most beautiful people he had ever met. It was amazing to him that she would ever deign to be seen with anyone other than a film star, but evidently Guy was in that category.

'Got to get a bus. If I miss it, I'll miss my train. And then—' he held his hands up. 'I have to go.'

'Oh,' he said. 'I can give you a lift.'

'You have a car?'

'Yeah. Want a ride?'

'That would be amazing,' Matt said. 'You sure?'

'Absolutely. You need to go straight away, right?'

'Right.'

Guy smiled at Trixie. 'You want to come?'

She shook her head. 'I'll wait in your room.' She held up a sheaf of papers. 'I can read through the script.'

Matt watched her walk up the stairs. He glanced at Guy. 'Script?'

'We're in a play I wrote. That's the script. You should be in it. I've got the perfect part for you.'

'Thanks, mate,' Matt said. 'But I've got a lot going on. I have to be back home at weekends.'

'Is that why I haven't seen you around?'

'Probably. I've been back a lot.'

'Family trouble?'

'You could say that.' There was a long pause. 'My girl-friend's pregnant.'

'You have a girlfriend? You and Annabelle had a thing, right?'

Annabelle. The sound of her name was like a punch in the stomach. And the fact that she had been talking about him to Guy made things even worse. There was an entirely different life he could have had, and it was in touching distance.

'Yeah,' Matt said. 'We went out a few times.'

'She seemed a little sad about you breaking up,' Guy said. 'But I guess if you're going to be a dad it must be a serious relationship.'

'It is. Kind of.' Matt paused. 'Do you see Annabelle much?'

'Not all that often. But from time to time.'

He was about to ask if she had another boyfriend, but he stopped himself.

'Say hello from me, would you?'

'I will,' Guy said.

'And tell her I liked her too.'

Guy gave him an odd, pitying look. 'Everything OK?' he said.

'Yes. It's . . . it's complicated.'

'It always is,' Guy replied. 'Going to New Street?'

2

His dad met him at the station.

'Back again,' he said. 'How's it going?'

'Good.'

'You must be missing Lindsey?'

'Yeah.'

They walked down the platform. The car was parked outside.

His dad started the engine, then turned to face him.

'Is everything OK, Matt?' he said.

'Yes. Fine.'

'Is there anything you want to talk about?'

'No.' There was plenty; the pregnancy for starters, but Lindsey had made it clear she didn't want anyone to know in case her parents found out. She was terrified they would make her have an abortion.

'Only your mother and I think it's odd that you come back every weekend.'

'It's just to see Lindsey.'

'You don't seem that happy when you're home.' He paused. 'You seem . . . weighed down.'

'I don't know, Dad. I'm fine.'

'Well, if you ever want to talk, I'm here to listen. You can tell me anything, you know that, right? I'm your dad, and most of the time I'll be able to help. So, anytime you want to talk, I'm ready to listen. No judgement, OK?'

'Thanks, Dad.'

'And if there are any problems, we can find a solution.'

Not for this we can't, he thought. *There's no solution to this.*

3

Lindsey took his hand and placed it on her stomach. The skin was smooth and warm.

'The baby's three inches long,' she said. She smiled at him. 'It's a little person. *Our* little person.'

He felt as though he should be sensing something underneath his palm, as though the presence of another human being should register in some way.

He felt nothing. Her stomach was exactly as it had always been.

'When do you start showing?' he said.

'In a few weeks. It's different for everybody.'

'You'll have to tell your parents.'

She shrugged. 'It's winter. I can wear baggy clothes. I don't want them to know.'

He took his hand from her stomach. 'You don't think we should tell them? It's a big deal.'

'No!' She shook her head. 'Don't you *dare* say anything. They'll try to stop us having it.' She scowled, her eyes hard. 'They're my parents, Matt. It's not your choice to tell them.'

'OK,' he said. 'I was only asking.'

4

His sister was talking to him, but he wasn't really listening. He was thinking about what Lindsey had said.

They're my parents, Matt. It's not your choice to tell them.

'Matt,' Tessa said. 'I asked you a question.'

'Sorry,' he said. 'I was miles away. What were you saying?'

'I asked if you love her.'

'I don't know, Tess. There's a lot going on. It's hard to tell what I feel.'

Tess rolled her eyes. 'She's a great person,' she said. 'We've been spending a lot of time together and she's so lovely. I know you had a few arguments – she told me she shouted at you sometimes – but she said she's more relaxed now.' Tess shrugged. 'Maybe it's the baby. She feels more secure now she knows you two will be together.'

He felt a sense of rising panic. He was trapped and he was going to stay trapped. This baby was forever. He was too young to do this, too young to know how to deal with it. He needed help.

He needed his parents, and, unwittingly, Lindsey had given him the key.

They're my parents, Matt. It's not your choice to tell them.

Which was true, but his parents were *his* parents, and it was *his* choice what he told them. And, like his dad had said, no judgement.

'Tess,' he said. 'I have to talk to Mum and Dad.'

5

His dad looked at his mum. She was cradling a glass of white wine.

'We thought something was going on,' he said. 'And we're glad you told us. This is not something you have to deal with on your own.' He leaned over the kitchen table and squeezed Matt's elbow. 'We'll help you with this, son. I promise.'

Matt felt 100 per cent better. Even though nothing had changed, it seemed like everything had changed. 'Thanks,' he said.

'What do Lindsey's parents think?' his mum said.

'They don't know,' Matt said.

She blinked. 'They don't know?'

'She doesn't want to tell them. I thought she should, but she said it's not my decision.'

'Did she?' his mum said. 'I see.' She sipped her wine. 'This is something her parents need to know about,' she said. 'She's seventeen, and they are going to be massively affected by this. They have a right to know.'

'I said I wouldn't tell them,' Matt said. 'I promised.'

'Maybe you did,' his mum said. 'But I didn't.' She looked

at her watch. 'Nine fifteen. It's not too late to call, is it, Colin?'

'No,' his dad said. 'I think it's OK.' He took a deep breath. 'I won't lie, Matt. This is a serious situation. But it'll be fine. One way or another, it'll work out.'

'I don't see how,' Matt said. 'I'm going to have a baby.'

'For starters, you'll be finishing university,' his dad said. 'If you want to. We'll take care of the baby if needs be. Your life will go on, son.' He pursed his lips. 'But there's a long way to go yet.' He glanced at Wendy. 'Time to make that call. You want me to do it?'

His dad handed him a bottle of beer. 'Well,' he said. 'I told them.'

'How did they take it?'

'I talked to Craig.' He sipped his beer. 'I think he was in shock. He didn't say much, to be honest. I explained that it had happened during the summer and Lindsey didn't want to tell anyone. I didn't give any reasons why. She can explain that.'

'They're probably talking to her right now.'

'Yep. You can expect a phone call from her sometime soon, I'd imagine.'

Shit. He wasn't looking forward to that call at all. She'd be irate; it had been a while since she'd really lost her temper at him – the last time was before she'd found out she was pregnant – but he was pretty sure she still had it in her to go off on one.

'I also said that we'd support whatever decision Lindsey took, and would stand by the child, but that we wouldn't expect you to let it get in the way of your studies. If you want to – and I hope you do – you can complete university. Your mum and I will help with the baby. And if you decide that Lindsey's not the right person for you, then we'd support

115

you breaking up with her. Obviously you – and we – would have to make sure you fulfilled your obligations to your child, but that doesn't necessarily mean settling down and getting married at nineteen years old.'

'OK,' Matt said. He didn't know how to say what a relief it was to hear his father say this; it was like a door in a dark room opening to show a path leading out into the light. 'Thanks. I mean it. Thank you.'

'I want to say something else, Matt. Maybe you and Lindsey will go on and be happily married for seventy years. I hope you do. But if you and her aren't going to be happy, there's no point – and you need to know that's an option. Marrying your mum was the best decision I ever made; she's been the source of my happiness – along with you and Tessa – for the last twenty-five years. And she will be for the next twenty-five. I want the same for you.'

'Thanks, Dad. I love you. You too, Mum.'

'I love you too, son.' He finished his beer. 'Now I suggest you put on the TV and wait for that phone call.'

The phone call came late, after Matt was asleep. He was woken during the night by the phone ringing. He looked at the alarm clock: 2.45 a.m.

He was about to get out of bed when he heard his dad's voice.

'Hello?'

There was a pause.

'That's fine, Craig. I'd rather you called if it's important.' Another pause.

'What?' His voice was shocked, but also something else. Angry, maybe. 'Why would—'

This time the pause was long. A couple of minutes at least. Then his dad sighed. 'I'll talk to him. I don't know what he'll do, Craig, but I'll talk to him. Thanks for calling.'

116

Then came a click as he put the receiver down.

Matt listened as his dad climbed the stairs. His tread stopped outside Matt's door.

'Dad?' he called out. 'Is that you?'

His door opened. 'Hi,' his dad whispered. 'You awake?'

'The phone woke me.'

'Oh. That was Craig. I was going to let you sleep.'

'I heard your conversation. What's happened?'

His dad sat on his bed. 'He talked to Lindsey. He and Sue didn't think it was a good idea to keep the baby, so they tried to discuss that with her, but she refused to countenance it.'

He took a deep breath.

'He said they told her they thought part of the reason she wanted the baby was to keep you and her together, so they explained what I'd said, about you not being under any obligation to do that, unless you wanted to.'

He squeezed Matt's shoulder. 'He said that she got very worked up and had a kind of fit. She was having trouble breathing, so they decided to take her to hospital. She didn't want to go, but they insisted.'

He shook his head. 'In the car she calmed down and said she didn't need to go to the hospital, but Sue wanted to take her anyway. She was worried she would have another fit, and she was worried about the baby. So Lindsey owned up.'

'What do you mean, "owned up"?'

'There's no baby.'

'She lost it?' Matt said.

'No. There was never any baby. She made it up. She told them you'd broken up with her after you went to Birmingham and she was worried she'd lost you, so she made it up. She knew a doctor would figure it out, so she told them the truth.'

'There's no baby?' He felt two stone lighter, like he was

117

floating above his bed. This was over. Tomorrow he could go back to Birmingham and get on with his life.

'Craig and Sue are very upset. They want to talk to you tomorrow morning.'

Matt felt bad for them. For Lindsey, too. But he was also angry. There was no guarantee he could pick up where he had left off with Annabelle.

'I don't know. I don't want to talk to Lindsey.'

'I understand that. They'll come here. And then I'll drive you to Birmingham and we can forget this whole sorry mess ever happened.'

6

He was woken by a knock on the door.

'Lindsey's mum and dad will be here in half an hour,' his mum said. 'And then we'll drive you back.'

He got out of bed and packed his bag, then went downstairs. He was finishing his breakfast when the doorbell rang.

His dad answered the door and brought Craig and Sue into the kitchen. They were unsmiling, their faces lined and tired.

'Hi,' Matt said.

'Hi, Matt,' Sue said. She looked close to tears. 'We just wanted to say sorry. From us. Lindsey can do her own apologizing.' The words were rushed, as though they had been rehearsed.

'You didn't deserve this,' Craig said. 'We're truly sorry.'

'That's OK,' Matt said. 'It's fine now.'

'For you,' Craig said. 'But I've a feeling for Lindsey this is only the beginning.'

Sue glanced at him and gave a little shake of her head. She took a lilac envelope from her handbag. 'She wanted us to give you this,' she said. 'You don't have to take it, but I said I'd try.'

'I'll take it,' Matt said. 'Thank you.'

Sue handed it to him. Up close he saw she had tears in her eyes. 'You're a good lad, Matt,' she said. 'We'll miss you.'

7

He read the letter in the car.

DEAR MATT

 WELL I GUESS IT'S ALL FUCKED ANYWAY NOW SO I MIGHT AS WELL TELL YOU THE TRUTH. I LOVE YOU, MATT, I LOVE YOU AS MUCH AS ANYONE EVER LOVED ANYONE ELSE. MORE, PROBABLY. AND I KNOW WE'RE MEANT TO BE TOGETHER. I MADE UP THE BABY TO SHOW YOU THAT. I WAS GOING TO TELL YOU THE TRUTH AS SOON AS YOU'D REALIZED THAT YOU AND ME IS WRITTEN IN THE STARS.

 IT'S FATE, MATT, AND YOU CAN'T ESCAPE FATE.

 SO GO AND HAVE YOUR FUN BUT I WONT GIVE UP ON YOU. I'LL BE HERE FOR YOU, ALWAYS. AND I KNOW YOU'LL COME BACK EVENTUALLY BECAUSE YOU'LL SEE WE'RE MEANT TO BE TOGETHER. THAT'S THE TRUTH, MATT. IT HAS TO BE. THERE'S NO WAY I CAN FEEL LIKE THIS IF IT'S NOT REAL. THE UNIVERSE ISN'T THAT CRUEL. I DID A BAD THING BUT I DON'T DESERVE TO LOSE YOU FOREVER.

121

SO BYE, FOR NOW. BUT REMEMBER I LOVE YOU.
AND I'LL NEVER GIVE UP ON YOU. NEVER.
   L

He folded the letter up and put it in the side pocket of his rucksack. He felt bad for her, and, in a strange way, he understood what she was saying. He felt the same way about Annabelle. It felt so right, it couldn't be wrong.

They pulled up outside Chamberlain Hall.

'Righto,' his dad said. 'Here we are.'

'Thanks, Dad.'

'You want me to stay? We could go for a pint?'

He hesitated, then his dad laughed.

'I'm only kidding. I've got to mow the lawn. You go and find that girlfriend of yours. Love you, Matt.'

'Love you too, Dad.'

He picked up his rucksack and got out of the car. He'd been planning to drop it off in his room, but he changed his mind. He was going straight to find Annabelle.

Sunday, 8 March 2020, 4 a.m.

Matt

Somehow he had fallen asleep. Not for long – twenty minutes, maximum – but one minute he was sitting on Norman's bed, in the place he had read countless stories to his elder son, and the next he was opening his eyes.

And remembering why he was in his son's empty bedroom at four in the morning.

They were waiting for instructions from the person who had kidnapped his children, and who was demanding his wife as a ransom.

His wife, Annabelle.

Not money. Not a huge news story so they could make a political point.

Annabelle.

They wanted her to exchange herself for her children. And then what? What did they want to do with her? Kill her? Keep her in captivity? Was this someone who hated her and wanted revenge? Or a crazed fan who was obsessed with her?

Whoever it was, they must be insane. There was no way he and Annabelle would go along with this. It was ridiculous.

At least, that was his initial thought. But the more he

thought about it, the harder it was to see any viable alternative. They could involve the police, but Annabelle had ruled that out. They could refuse, but then what would happen to the kids? Or they could do as the kidnapper asked – which was unthinkable.

Three alternatives, none of them acceptable.

And so, for now at least, there was nothing to do but wait. He stood and walked out of Norman's room into his and Annabelle's bedroom. He lay next to her and stared at the ceiling. It was going to be a long few hours.

Sunday, 8 March 2020, 6.03 a.m.

Annabelle

1

She was lying in bed next to Matt, neither of them able to sleep, when the next message came.

Again, a new phone number. Again a photo.

Annabelle stared at it, studying every detail.

In it, the children were lying under a blanket. Norman was holding an iPad and he and Keith were looking at the screen, their faces lit by the glow from the screen. Molly was asleep next to them. It was hard to see where they were; the wall behind them was not well lit, but it looked like it was metallic.

A van, then. Or a warehouse. Or something else. A shipping container.

Matt put his hand on her shoulder. 'They're alive,' he said. 'At least they're alive.'

It was cold comfort. Before she could reply, the next message followed. She held the phone up so they could both read it.

As you can see from the photograph, your children are safe and unharmed. For now. If you wish to keep them that way, this is what you will do.

They waited, dots scrolling along the bottom of the screen.

At 5.30pm today, you and Annabelle will come to the location for the exchange. Details will be sent at 5pm, along with further instructions. I will be monitoring the surrounding area and if there are signs of anyone else, the exchange will be cancelled and your children will be gone for ever. There will be no second opportunity.

The dots scrolled again.

Once the exchange is done, Matt will leave with the children. Please indicate your acceptance of these terms immediately. The offer will expire in one hour.

Matt put his arms around her and pulled her towards him. She could not bring herself to respond. She felt hollow and broken.

'Let's go downstairs,' Matt said. 'Talk to Mike and Tessa. I think I heard someone moving around.'

2

Mike was sitting on the couch, a mug of coffee in his hands. Annabelle sat next to him. Matt stood by the window, looking out into the dark morning.

The door to the living room opened and Tessa walked in. 'I couldn't sleep,' she said. 'I heard you all down here.'

'We got another message,' Annabelle said.

'What is it?' Mike said. 'What does it say?'

'Take a look,' Annabelle said. She was suddenly overwhelmed by a sensation of utter hopelessness. This was getting worse and worse. 'Take a fucking look.' She passed him the phone and folded her arms around herself. 'Sixty minutes to decide what to do,' she said, as much to herself as to others in the room. 'Five of them gone already. What do I do? It's impossible.'

She turned to Matt. She barely recognized him; his eyes were wide, his pupils dilated, his forehead creased. He looked as though he was suffering intense physical pain.

'Matt,' she said, 'I don't understand what's happening. I have no idea what I should do. Tell me what to do.'

'I don't know,' Matt said. 'I'm sorry.'

'There's only one option, isn't there?' she said. 'There's

only one thing I can do. It's what *any* mother would do.'

'No,' Matt said. 'No.'

'But what choice is there?' Annabelle said. 'Our children are in danger. And if this is the only way to make them safe, I have to do it.'

'There's another way,' Matt said. 'There has to be.'

'What?' Annabelle said. 'What way?'

Matt stared at her. He didn't know what way, but he didn't want to admit it. Saying it would make it real.

Tessa cleared her throat.

'There could be a possibility,' she said. 'I don't know if it will work, but we could consider it.'

'What is it?' Annabelle said.

'It might be a long shot,' Tessa replied. 'But there's someone I know who might be able to help.'

Birmingham, December 2006

1

She lay next to him, her hips tight against his in the narrow single bed.

'I have to go and pack,' she said. 'I can't believe term is over.'

He rolled on his elbow and kissed her. 'Don't,' he said. 'Stay here. We can live in my room over Christmas, eating beans on toast.'

'You have a toaster?'

'Beans on bread, then.'

'It's an attractive offer,' she said. 'But I don't think it's going to work. Plus I'd miss my skiing trip.'

'Of course,' he said. 'The skiing trip.'

He was glad she was going skiing; he loved her and he wanted her to be happy.

But he was also sad. Because he was not going to see Annabelle for twelve days.

Twelve whole days.

She was going home today. And then tomorrow she was going skiing for a week in Chamonix. Then she would be at home in Richmond for Christmas, and then at her cousins' house in Scarborough for Boxing Day and then, finally, they would be reunited on 27 December, when he was catching a train and going to stay with her.

He couldn't bear the thought of it. Over the last two years – other than for a few days here or there – they had been inseparable. One night, as they lay together, arms and legs entwined, she had said to him, *I didn't know it was possible to feel like this.*

Me too, he said. *I want to be with you all the time.*

I know. I knew I liked you when we met, but I had no idea it would turn into this.

It was the same for me, he said. *As soon as I met you I was drawn to you. What is that? That feeling you get right from the start?*

I don't know, she said. *All I know is it's real and I love you.*

I love you. The words were like a magic charm. He took them everywhere with him. To lectures, the library, the pub: I love you. She. Loves. Me.

And now she was going skiing. She had invited him – all he had to pay was flights and lift tickets and ski rental – but it turned out those things weren't cheap, and were not something his dad was prepared to invest in.

Dad, he'd said, on the phone a few weeks earlier, *please. It can be my Christmas present, and birthday present. For the next decade.*

Matt, his dad said. *It's pretty expensive. I would if I could, but I don't think we can make it work.*

'OK,' she said. 'Time to go. I've not even started packing.' She swung her legs out of the bed and stood. She picked up a T-shirt and pulled it over her head.

'Stay,' he said. 'It's nice and warm in here.'

'I don't have time.'

He sat up and put his hands around her waist. He kissed her stomach.

'Do you have time for this?' he murmured.

It turned out she did.

When he had packed, he went to Annabelle's room. It was empty, her belongings in bags by the door. She hugged him tight when he walked in.

'I'm going to miss you,' she said. 'I don't know how I'm going to get through the next two weeks.'

'Twelve days,' Matt said. 'Only twelve days.'

'That doesn't help.'

'I know.' For a moment he thought about saying *Don't go. Let's never be apart. You can come to my house*, but he bit his tongue. It sounded too much like Lindsey. She was going skiing, and that was that.

There was a knock on the door. She kissed him and opened it. Guy came in, car keys in his hands.

'Hi,' he said. 'Ready?' He held up the keys. 'Car's downstairs. Can I help with a bag?'

'Thanks,' Annabelle said. 'Do you want to leave soon?'

'I was thinking of it. My uncle wants me to help him with something later today.' He smiled at Matt. 'Sorry to tear you two apart.'

'You guys going back to Richmond together?' Matt said.

'Yes,' Annabelle said. 'My dad's busy, so I asked Guy.'

So this was it. Goodbye for twelve days. He picked up the heaviest bag. 'I'll give you a hand.'

2

'So, how was the term?' His dad glanced at him from behind the wheel. 'Enjoy it?'

'It was good.' Matt looked out of the window. He didn't want to talk. It was worse than he had anticipated. He felt wretched; he knew it was pathetic, but he couldn't help it. He felt bereft without her. The world seemed pointless.

'Is that it?'

'It was good, Dad, all right?'

'One more year and you're done. Hard to believe you'll have a degree and be heading into the world of work. I'm very proud of you, Matt.'

He didn't reply.

'I said I'm proud of you.'

'Thanks.'

'Is everything OK?'

'Yeah. Pretty much. You know.'

His dad tapped his fingers on the steering wheel. 'Annabelle's going skiing?'

'Right. It's twelve days.'

'That's not terribly long,' his dad said. 'And you know what they say. *Tempus fugit.*'

'Tempus what?'

'*Tempus fugit*. Time flies.'

He turned away. His dad was quoting Latin to make him feel better. This was worse than he had thought.

'Yeah,' he said. 'Tempes Flugit.'

Back at home, his mum handed him a mug of tea.

'Well,' she said. 'Your dad and I got you an early Christmas present.'

She went into the hall. When she came back she was carrying a black carrier bag. She handed it to him.

'Try it on.'

Matt frowned. 'What is it?'

'Take a look.'

He opened the bag and took out a winter coat. It was brown with light blue patches under the arms.

'See if it fits.'

He stood up and pulled it on.

'It looks good,' his mum said. 'Do you like it?'

'Yes,' he replied. 'But what's it for? I don't need a coat.'

'It's warm,' she said. 'It was on sale. It's a second. There's a slight stain on the shoulder.'

'Thanks,' he said. 'It's great.'

'Glad you like it.'

'It would be good,' his dad said slowly, 'for skiing.'

This was fucking unbelievable. They knew how he felt about Annabelle going skiing without him and now they had bought him a ski jacket, just to rub it in.

'I'm not going skiing, though,' he said. 'So maybe you should return it. I don't want you to waste money.'

'I can't return it,' his mum said. 'It's a second. And it was a bargain. You can have it for Christmas.'

He bit his lip. It was a lovely, thoughtful present and he didn't want to be ungrateful, but part of him wanted to scream, *I don't want it! I don't need a new coat to remind me where my girlfriend is!*

'Gosh,' his mum said. 'Look at him. Look at that face.' She laughed and hugged him. 'You're thinking we're a bit cruel and insensitive, aren't you? Do you honestly think I'd waste money on a coat like that for no reason? Tell him, Colin.'

'Tell me what?' Matt said.

'You're going skiing,' his dad said. 'Two days from now. I found a cheap flight, and a friend has skis and boots you can borrow. He said they won't be perfect for you, but they'll be good enough.'

He realized after a second that his mouth was open.

'For real?' he said.

'For real,' his mum said, with a wide smile. 'Like we said, it's an early Christmas present.'

'And birthday,' his dad said. 'For ten years. That was what you agreed to, right?'

'Twenty years,' Matt said. 'This is amazing. Thank you! Does Annabelle know?'

'Not yet. Her dad does. We arranged it with him a few days ago, but we agreed we'd keep quiet. Make it a surprise. You can tell her.'

3

He stood on a moving runway which took him, and the gaggle of four- and five-year-olds he was with, gently up a shallow incline.

If he was totally honest, he did not enjoy skiing at all. He felt guilty about it, after his parents had paid for the plane tickets and bought him the ski jacket, but he just didn't really like it.

It didn't help that he had two choices: spend the days pottering about on the baby slopes, or try to join in with Annabelle and Mike and some French friend of theirs called Jacques and spend the days terrified of dying.

The day before, he had joined them for a run. By the time he had finally emerged at the bottom, they were waiting by a log hut, sipping coffees. Annabelle had said, *Why don't you get a bit of practice in before coming with us again?*

I'll be OK, he replied.

It's not you I'm worried about, she said. *There are kids up there.*

Great. She was worried he was going to flatten a child. Either way, he was stuck down here while she and her ski buddies zipped from peak to peak. Not only did he feel guilty; it was embarrassing, and it would only get worse when they sat in a bar drinking beer and talking about what they had done during the day.

Oh my God, the powder was amazing today!

I'm thinking of telemarking tomorrow. Anyone interested in going off-piste?

What could he add? *I managed to overtake a toddler this afternoon? I'm making real progress!* So he'd sit there, not really understanding what they were all talking about.

At least there would be beer.

Speaking of which, it was nearly 3 p.m. Maybe he'd get started early.

4

'There you are!'

Annabelle walked through the crowd to the table he was sitting at. Her cheeks were flushed and tanned from the fresh air and sun, although there were white circles around her eyes where her goggles had been.

'Hi,' Matt said. 'Have a good day?'

'Fantastic. It was amazing. You?'

'Oh, you know. I was one of the fastest in my group.'

She laughed. 'Are you feeling sorry for yourself?'

'A bit.'

'You'll get better,' she said. 'Everyone starts somewhere.'

'I suppose. I feel a bit left out. And a touch inadequate.'

She sat next to him, her boots clumping against the table. 'You know one of the things – one of the many things – I love about you?'

'Go on,' Matt said. 'Tell me. Maybe a few of them.'

'It's your honesty. Lots of guys would sit there feeling their masculinity had been challenged, then they'd get drunk and try to prove how tough they were by punching someone.'

Matt held up his beer. 'This is my third. And I think that guy at the bar is looking at me funny.'

She giggled. 'You tell me you feel left out and inadequate – which we all do sometimes – but you don't take it as an affront to your manhood. It's so refreshing.'

'Well,' he said. 'I'd rather be able to ski, but at least that's something.'

'It's everything,' Annabelle said. 'You're mature and smart and funny and I love you. And – in case you were wondering – I want to spend the rest of my life with you, even if your skiing leaves something to be desired. Does that make you feel better?'

Better? Had she just said she wanted to spend the rest of her life with him? Better didn't cover it.

'A bit,' he said. 'And I feel the same way. Do you think we will spend our lives together?'

'Do you want to?'

'Yes.'

'Then we will,' she said. 'Nothing could keep us apart, Matt. Nothing.'

Sunday, 8 March 2020, 6.15 a.m.

Matt

'So what's the idea?' Matt said.

Tessa pursed her lips. 'I don't know if it'll work, but it could be worth a try.'

'Let's hear it,' he said. 'Who do you know?'

'A guy called Rob,' Tessa said. 'He's a friend of Andy's. A retired cop. He fitted our burglar alarm system before we got divorced. Andy said he does other private detective type work. We could call him. Get a bit of advice, at least.'

Matt looked at Annabelle. He could see she was not convinced.

'What are you thinking?' he said.

'I'm thinking he may tell the police.' She shook her head. 'That can't happen.'

'I don't think he will,' Tessa said. 'He has no reason to, and we can ask him to keep quiet before we tell him anything. He might have an idea, Annabelle. We should try. And I don't see any other options.'

'I think she's right,' Matt said. 'We could at least talk to him. But it's up to you, Annabelle.'

'OK,' she said. 'We can talk to him.'

* * *

Tessa laid her phone on the arm of the sofa and put it on speakerphone. A man's voice answered.

'Hi, Rob,' she said. 'Sorry for the early call. This is Tessa Westbrook, Andy's wife. Ex-wife, actually. You fitted our alarm system.'

'No problem.' His voice was clear on the speaker. 'I'm an early riser. Is there something wrong with it?'

'It's not the alarm. It's something else. Something a bit unusual. Before we go any further, I have to ask you if you can promise not to tell anyone what we're about to discuss. Especially the police.'

'Look,' he said. 'If you've done something wrong and you tell me, I can't promise—'

'No one's done anything wrong. It's not that. It's' – she looked at Annabelle, who nodded her agreement – 'it's a friend. We need advice on what to do if someone's been kidnapped.'

'Kidnapped?' he said, his voice suddenly urgent and alert. 'Has someone been kidnapped?'

'Yes,' Tessa said. 'And we need to know what to do.'

'Jesus,' he said. 'Who is it?'

'I'll put the parents on. You're on speaker.'

Matt leaned towards the phone. 'Hi, Rob. My name's Matt Westbrook. I'm Tessa's brother. My wife, Annabelle, is here, as well as my brother-in-law, Mike.'

'Nice to meet you all. Why don't you tell me what happened?'

'It's my kids. I have three – Norman, Keith and Molly. I left them in the car while I went into a shop – Holt's in Stockton Heath – and when I came out' – he paused, and swallowed – 'they were gone. The car as well.'

'Holy shit,' Rob said. 'You sure it wasn't just someone stealing the car?'

'No. I got a text message a few minutes later. It said "Do not call the police".'

'What?' Rob said. 'So whoever took them had your number?'

'Yes,' Matt said.

'Which means this was planned.'

'It seems that way,' Matt said.

'Look,' Rob said. 'This is serious. You need to involve the police. They can deal with this.'

'We can't,' Annabelle said. 'The kidnapper made it clear they would know if we do and we would never see the kids again.'

'How would they know?' Rob said.

'I don't know,' Annabelle replied. 'But if there's any possibility they could, then it's too risky. That's why we called you. Can you help?'

'I can try,' Rob said. 'Have you asked for proof of life?'

'We got a photo of the kids. They look fine. Alive at least.'

'OK. That's good.' He paused. 'I'm still struggling to get my head around this, but you want to establish as much contact as you can. Negotiate. Ask for another photo, this time with a clock or something in the background that shows the time. A TV show that's on right now. A football game.'

'We can't,' she said. 'We've tried calling the numbers, but the kidnapper uses a different phone every time, so the previous numbers just go to voicemail.'

'Right,' Rob said. 'They're trying to maintain control of the situation. What about the ransom?'

They had agreed not to tell him what the kidnapper was asking for. They wanted advice; they did not want Rob thinking he needed to involve the authorities.

'It's money,' Annabelle said. 'A lot.'

'It always is,' Rob said. 'I think you should pay. All you want is your kids back – which is actually a reason not to involve the police. The police are going to want to get your kids back, but they're also going to want to apprehend

141

whoever did it, so they might take a different approach to you. So pay. Try to negotiate so it doesn't look like it's easy for you to come up with the ransom, or the amount will increase, but in the end you have to pay. You have to give this type of person what they want. It's the only way.'

'We have to give them what they want,' Annabelle said, her voice flat. She was staring into the distance. 'That's what you're saying.'

'I know it's hard to swallow, but it's the best option. It's the only one.'

'How do we know they'll return the kids?' Matt said. 'We can't trust someone who would do this.'

'No, you can't. But if you hand over the money, there's no incentive to keep your kids, because then you *would* call the cops, and no kidnapper wants that. Too much hassle, plus there's always the chance the cops will find them. The alternative's much simpler: return the kids and walk away with the cash. Keeping hold of three kids is way too risky. So I'd say you should pay.'

'And if we say no?' Annabelle muttered.

'There may be one more opportunity to pay,' Rob said. 'Or not. And your kids will be at huge risk. With no cash on the horizon there's no incentive to hang around, or keep the kids alive.'

'Thank you,' Annabelle said. 'This has been very helpful.'

'I'm sorry,' Rob said. 'But if you do this right you can get your kids back. Call me if you need more advice. Maybe when you get the instructions. There might be something I can help with. And good luck. This is a tough situation.'

'We will,' Matt said. 'And thanks.'

He cut the call.

'Well,' Annabelle said. Her lips were quivering and her voice was on the edge of breaking. 'That was quite clear. We have to pay the price.'

Matt put his arm around her and held her tight. 'No,' he said. 'There's no way we can do that.'

'Matt,' she said. 'If we don't and I never see the kids again, I'll never forgive myself. If it's a choice between me and them suffering, I'd take me every time.'

He closed his eyes. She was right, he knew she was. But that didn't make this any easier.

'If we do,' he said. 'I'll never see you again.'

'You'll have the kids. And they'll be safe.'

'But I love you, Annabelle.'

'I know. And I love you too. But they're our children, Matt.'

'No,' he said. 'I'm not ready to accept this. Not yet. We'll come up with something.'

'OK,' she said. 'But if we don't, we're going to pay the ransom. It's the only option.'

Annabelle

Annabelle walked out of the back door and into the garden. It was dark and cold but she needed fresh air, and some space to think. Now she had made up her mind she felt oddly calm. The panic and the fear were still there, but at least she had clarity. There were no more decisions to agonize over; she had resigned herself to what was going to happen. Someone wanted *her* – who, she could not imagine – and they were going to get her. There was nothing she could do to stop it. Matt was hoping to come up with something to stop this, but that was unlikely. It was obvious whoever it was had planned this for a long time, and they were going to make sure it worked.

Well, let them.

She had a plan, too.

Nothing specific – how could there be, when she didn't know who this was or what they were expecting? – but a plan nonetheless.

She would give them what they wanted. She would hand herself over to save her kids.

And then they would find out that maybe she wasn't what

they wanted after all. With nothing left to lose, she would do whatever it took to get back to her family, and she would make them pay for this.

One way or another, she would make them pay.

In her pocket, her phone buzzed. It was a text message, from Guy.

I was in Brighton yesterday at a literary thing and bumped into the woman who runs the Standwich Literary Festival. She wants to know if you want to do it. It's in early May. You'd be perfect. Interested? No hurry, but let me know when you have a chance to think about it. I'm going hiking today but we can talk later.

Guy – as well as being one of her oldest friends – was her agent. After they had left university he had joined a small agency, and – with a little help from Matt – had sold her first book. It had been odd working with him at first, but she was used to it now.

She typed a reply:

Don't know if I can. Will fill you in later.

Are you busy?

Kind of. Something came up.

Everything OK?

She paused before replying, but then decided she wanted him to know.

Not really.

The phone rang seconds later.

'Hi,' Guy said. 'What's going on?'

'It's pretty fucked up, Guy.'

'Is it Matt? Are you guys OK? Is someone ill?'

'No. It's the kids.'

'What about them?'

Now she was about to say it, it sounded absurd.

'They've been kidnapped, and they're being held for ransom.'

He did not speak for a few seconds.

'Is this a joke?'

'No. Someone took them. Last night.'

'Someone *took* them? How?'

'They were with Matt. He went into a shop to get some bits and bobs, and left them in the car – he didn't want them running around touching stuff, with that new virus – and when he came out, they were gone.'

'Are you sure it wasn't a car thief?'

'Yes. We got a ransom demand.'

He inhaled sharply. 'How much? Pay it. I'll pay. I can mortgage the agency. I can get whatever you need. We'll sort this out, Annabelle.'

'Thanks,' she said. 'But it's not money. It's me.'

'What on earth do you mean?'

'They want me, in exchange for the kids.'

'That's ridiculous!' He made an exasperated snorting noise. 'You can't swap people like that. This isn't the Mayor of fucking Casterbridge!'

'That's what they want.'

'They won't get it!' he said. 'How's Matt?'

'Thinking of options.'

'Good. I'm on my way. I can help with this.'

'No,' she said. 'There's no need. I'm just glad of someone to talk to. See if I'm insane for doing this.'

146

'Doing what?'

'There's only one choice.'

'No!' Guy said. 'You can't.'

'If I don't, the kids are dead and then I'll have to kill myself. This way they'll be alive. It might be a terrible choice, but that's the way choices work, right? You take the least worst one, however bad.'

'Look,' Guy said, 'there has to be another way!'

'I don't think there is. I need the kids to be safe, and this is the only way I can get that. I'll deal with whatever comes afterwards.'

'I'm coming to your house,' he said. 'And that's final.'

'No. I want to spend this time with Matt.'

There was a long silence. 'Fine,' he said. 'But call if you need anything. OK?'

'I will.' She put the phone down and went inside. Matt was standing by the fridge, pouring milk into a cup of tea.

'Who was that?' he said.

'Guy. I've been invited to a literary festival in May. I was telling him it isn't an option.'

'So you've made up your mind, then?' Matt said. 'You're going to do it?'

'I don't see another way.'

'Me neither,' Matt said. 'But I don't think it has to end there. I've got an idea.'

The clock is ticking. That fool of a husband will be desperate, searching for some way to keep his wife safe.

There is no way. Because the choice is hers and there is no doubt what she will choose. She will come to me. I have given her everything she needs.

She will be able to say – truthfully – that this is what any mother would have done in the circumstances.

Well, maybe not any. Not mine. Mine would have done nothing. That's what she did when I asked her for help.

She could have chosen self-sacrifice. She chose to leave me to my fate.

But the overwhelming majority of mothers would choose their children.

Not Annabelle Westbrook, though, she is like my mother. Her children are a burden; pretending to love them is a chore. Only I know that, which is why I am doing this for her.

Anyway, in the eyes of the world, she does the honourable thing. Such an act of self-sacrifice! A martyr to motherhood! An inspiration to us all.

When the story comes out, she will be a hero.

And she will have what she has wanted all along.

How could she have had it otherwise? She could not leave her family. She would never truly get away from them. She was trapped.

But now I have created the one situation in which she can leave them and remain free of any guilt or blame.

A situation in which she has no choice. In which she has to pay the ultimate price for her children's freedom.

And she knows this.

And I cannot wait to see her gratitude.

Grappenhall Library, 2009

1

The boy – maybe ten years old, copper-coloured hair, dark, almost black eyes – put his hands on the desk.

'Hi,' he said. 'Do you have all the Harry Potter books?'

'Are you looking for one in particular?' Annabelle asked.

'*The Order of the Phoenix*,' he said. 'That's where I'm up to.'

'We do have it,' Annabelle said. 'We have quite a few copies, and they're very popular, but I think one just came back in. If it did, it'll be on the returns cart.'

'Oh,' the boy said. 'Can I take it out?'

'Yes. That's what we're here for.'

'Do you know where the returns cart is?'

Annabelle smiled. 'I do. Would you like me to show you?'

The boy nodded, and she walked to the end of the counter. There was a cart with all the returns on it, ready to be put back on the shelves. She ran her finger over the spines.

'Here it is,' she said. 'Let's check it out. Do you have your library card?'

The boy handed it to her. She scanned the barcode and called up his account. The list of books he had taken out covered the screen. Oscar – she read his name on the card – was an avid reader.

'There you go,' she said, and handed him the book and his library card. 'Enjoy your reading, Oscar.'

2

It was her dream to see her book on the shelves of a library. Her dream, and the dream of thousands – tens of thousands – of other people who were writing novels and poems and plays.

It was a dream she did not think would ever come true. The first novel she had written, during her last year at Birmingham, was in a drawer in a desk in the house she and Matt were renting while he finished his legal training. It had been the most inspiring and the most dispiriting thing she had ever done. The feeling of holding a completed manuscript in her hand had been amazing. She had written a novel, one hundred thousand words that all, more or less, fitted together to make a coherent whole. Semi-coherent, at least. It had taken over a year and she had poured everything into it.

It was thrilling to hold it in her hands.

It was also incredibly depressing, because no one was ever going to read it. Never mind getting it published; not even her friends and family – not even Matt – were going to read it.

Because it wasn't any good. Worse, it was boring. She'd read it a few times, and each time it got worse. The main character – a woman in her early twenties – came across as whiny, the plot was thin, the ending weak. But the problem went deeper than that. It was forced; it didn't sound like her.

She hated it. She loved that she'd done it, but she hated the novel itself.

And so she started again, and this time it worked. The first line came to her unbidden and then the rest followed.

I told them I was trouble.

She loved it at every stage. Sketch, rough draft, final draft. The main character, Janet, mid-twenties, was mysterious and intriguing. She was engaged to Marcus – they had got engaged soon after they met, to the shock of her friends, because, on the face of it, their relationship was not a healthy one.

Marcus was cold and distant and rude to her and to her friends; they all assumed she would see she had made a mistake and break up with him.

But she claimed to everyone she was happy and had no intention of ever leaving him. They joked she must be trapped.

It wasn't a joke.

She had a secret, and Marcus had discovered it when they met. If she ever left him, he would tell the world.

And she could not let that happen.

But she could not marry him. Which meant – although he did not yet know it – Marcus was not as safe and secure as he thought he was. Janet had a plan to escape, and she knew the perfect person to help her with it.

She *loved* it. So did Matt. And she sent it out to the three agents she had selected – after hours of research – as the most suitable to represent her book.

Only one replied, with a cursory: *Thank you for sending your novel. We receive a lot of submissions and unfortunately yours is not something we think we can take on at this point.*

So she tried some more. Months went by, and then they too politely declined. It wasn't what was selling at the moment, or they had another book too similar to it, or it was promising but not for them.

Eventually she had sent it to every agent and every publisher she could find. None of them were interested.

The only one she hadn't tried was Guy. He had taken a job as an editorial assistant at a small agency in Oxford.

Why not ask him? Matt said.

It's not fair. He'll feel obliged. And it's no good. No one wants it.

I love it, Matt said. *I'm not just saying that. I really do.*

Which was great to hear, but meant the same as your mum or dad saying they liked it.

That was, nothing.

3

She watched the copper-haired child leave and glanced at the clock. Another thirty minutes, then she was meeting Matt – and Kathryn and Andy and Rick and Jim – in the pub.

Her phone buzzed. She had a text. It was from Guy.

Can you call? Or are you at work?

She replied.

Working. But it's quiet.

A few seconds later the phone rang.

'Hi,' Guy said. 'I wanted to catch you before the office closes for the weekend. There's someone here who wants to talk to you.'

'Someone where?'

'At the agency.'

'Really? Who?'

'She's called Becky. She's an agent. Kind of my boss.'

'Why does she want to talk to me?'

'I'll put her on.'

There was a scratching noise and then a woman's voice came on the line.

'Hello,' she said. 'Is this Annabelle?'

'Yes.'

'So you're the author of *Still Waters*?'

Annabelle froze. How did she know about her book? She'd deliberately not sent it to the agency where Guy worked.

'Yes. That's me.'

'Well, I wanted to say congratulations. I loved it.'

'I—' Annabelle said. 'I don't understand. How did you read it?'

'Guy gave it to me. He said it was by a friend so he didn't feel he was able to be an impartial judge, but he thought it was good. So he asked me to read it. And I loved it.'

'How did Guy get it?'

'You didn't send it to him?'

'Erm . . .' she hesitated. This could all wait. 'Not exactly. But never mind. You liked it?'

'I *loved* it. Now, tell me. Have you sent it to any other agents?'

'One or two.'

'And have any of them offered representation?'

'No.'

'Good. I'd like to offer to represent you. My agency, anyway. It would be Guy who would be your agent.'

'Oh my God,' Annabelle said. 'This is incredible.'

'I hope you'll consider us. We're a small agency, but a good one, I think. And Guy will be an excellent advocate for your book. He's already shown that by giving it to me. So, think about the offer and let us know. Take all the time you want.'

All the time she wanted? That was about three seconds. 'Can I accept now?' Annabelle said.

'Would you like to think about it?' Becky asked.

156

She should. She really should.

'No,' she said. 'I think I want to accept.'

Becky laughed. 'Excellent. Then we'll draw up the paperwork. It'll be in the post next week. Congratulations, Annabelle. We look forward to working with you. Enjoy the weekend. I'll hand you back to Guy.'

'Well,' Guy said. 'You can see why I was so eager to reach you.'

'Guy,' she said. 'What exactly happened? How did you get my book?'

'I think you'd better ask Matt,' he said. 'He's got a bit of explaining to do.'

'Did he send it?'

'I'm afraid so.'

'I told him not to!'

'He mentioned that. He made me promise not to say anything if I didn't like it. But, as it turned out, I *loved* it. So maybe don't be too angry with him.'

Angry? There was no room for angry.

Other than the day she had met Matt, this was the best day of her life.

Sunday, 8 March 2020, 6.45 a.m.

Annabelle

Matt was looking at her with an earnest expression. It was, to tell the truth, a little desperate.

'So what is it?' Annabelle said.

'We track you. And when the kids are safe, we get you back.'

She nodded slowly. 'How? They're going to search me. I can't imagine they'll let me have my phone so you can look on the "where's my phone" app?'

'I don't know yet.' He sipped his tea. 'Maybe a tracking device, something like that.'

She shook her head. A tracking device would easily be discovered, unless it was some James Bond type thing she ate or hid inside her body, and where would they get something like that?

'How would I hide it?' she said.

'I don't know. But there must be a way to keep track of you. And it doesn't need to be for long. As soon as I have the kids, I can call the police.'

She pictured herself in a car with a faceless kidnapper,

looking out of the window as her family receded from view. She knew it probably wouldn't be like that, but that was the image that came to mind.'

'I just wish there was a way you could follow me,' she said. 'I wish you could fly, so high that you were invisible, like an eagle, then swoop down and rescue me.'

He stared at her, his mouth slowly falling open.

'Annie,' he said. 'There is a way I can do exactly that.'

'How?'

'A drone.'

She was about to dismiss the idea, but she paused. There was a problem, though. 'Won't it be obvious, buzzing up there?'

'I don't know,' Matt said. 'But maybe we can find one that flies high and quietly. And is fast.' He held up his hands. 'I don't have all the details yet. But it could work, Annie. Someone could operate it from a distance and follow it as it follows you.'

'What if they do see it?' she said. 'And think it's the police? They might hurt the kids.'

'We'll make sure it can't be seen.'

'If it can, we're not using it.'

'But if it can't? What do you think?'

She thought it *might* work. She doubted it, but it might. If it did, great. And if there was no risk of being spotted then they had nothing to lose. Either way, whoever was behind this was going to find out she was not a passive piece of meat to be traded. She was not going to let them take her family from her without doing everything in her power to stop them.

But that was for later.

'Where would you get a drone?' she said.

'I was thinking of asking that guy, Rob. He might know where we could start. You OK with that?'

'Let's do it,' she said.

Matt

1

Matt held the phone up so they could all hear.

'This is Rob.'

Matt cleared his throat. 'We spoke earlier. About the kidnapping.'

'I remember,' Rob said. 'Something come up?'

'Well,' Matt said. He glanced at Annabelle. 'There was something we didn't mention.'

'Oh yeah?' The welcoming note in his voice was gone, replaced by a guarded tone. 'What was that?'

'It's the ransom. It's not money they want.'

'You said it was. Lots of money.'

'I know. We didn't want to tell you the truth.'

'Why not?'

Annabelle leaned towards the phone. 'You'll understand when we tell you.'

'Go on,' Rob said. 'What do they want?'

'It's me,' Annabelle said. 'They want me.'

'Come again, love. I don't think I caught that.'

'It's my wife, Annabelle,' Matt said. 'She's the ransom. They want her in exchange for the kids.'

'What the fuck?' Rob said. 'So what do you need from me?'

'You said – when we spoke earlier – that we have to give them what they want,' Annabelle said. 'And you're right. I can't leave my children in danger.'

'Yeah,' Rob said. 'But this is different.'

'Not really,' Annabelle said. 'It's just that the price isn't money. Nothing else changes. We still can't involve the police, we still can't refuse the demands.'

'It's your call,' Rob said. 'But this is a very fucked-up situation.'

'I know,' Matt said. 'So we need to have a plan. And we do.'

'What is it?' Rob said.

'It might sound crazy,' Matt said. 'But we're thinking of a drone.'

'That doesn't sound crazy at all,' Rob said. 'Not easy, but not crazy.'

'You think it'll work?' Matt said.

'I don't know. I'll have to think more about it.'

'How soon can you get here?' Annabelle said. 'We have to reply to the kidnapper in the next twenty minutes.'

'Where do you live?'

Annabelle gave their address.

'I'll be there in ten,' Rob said. 'Hang tight.'

2

Ten minutes later the doorbell rang. Matt went to open it. There was a tall, heavily built man in his mid-forties standing outside. He had close-cropped hair and hard grey eyes. He held out his hand.

'Rob Carter,' he said. 'I assume you're Matt?'

'Come in.' Matt ushered him through to the living room. 'Take a seat. This is Annabelle. My sister, Tessa. My brother-in-law, Mike.'

'Nice to meet you.' Rob sat in an armchair. 'So, you have quite the situation.'

It wasn't a question.

'Yes,' Annabelle said. 'We do.'

'And you're definitely going to pay the— do what they're asking?' Rob said.

'We are,' Annabelle said.

'And you want to track Annabelle after the handover?' Rob said. 'On the way here I considered a tracking device, but I think a drone makes sense. The kidnapper could find the tracking device easily, and I suspect they'll look. They'll be expecting it. So yes, a drone.'

'Do you think it's possible to follow me with a drone?' Annabelle said.

'It certainly is,' Rob said. 'There's some pretty sophisticated kit out there. A lot of criminals use drones for exactly this purpose.'

'In kidnappings?' Matt said.

'No. To follow cars they want to steal. Expensive ones. They follow them from the drone and watch the owner walk away, then they move in.' He took off his jacket. 'The drones are impressive. They can do around forty miles per hour, with a control range of three to five miles, depending on the terrain. Either way, you can control them from a distance, so no one would know you were there. And they can live-stream what they see.'

'So you think we could make this work?' Matt said.

'Yes, with one caveat,' Rob said. 'They don't fly for that long. Maybe thirty minutes. Forty max. So you have to hope that's all you need.'

'It will be,' Matt said. 'We'll call the cops as soon as we have the kids. They can pick up Annabelle.'

'It could work,' Rob said. 'But there are no guarantees.'

'It's all we have,' Matt said.

'How do we get one,' Tessa said. 'Can you buy them?'

'Not these ones,' Rob replied. 'These are commercial drones. They're also regulated; you have to register them with the Civil Aviation Authority. And you can't just fly them anywhere. They're geofenced – which means they won't go into certain areas, such as near airports or prisons or other sensitive sites. You might need it to, if you're following someone.'

'So what do we do?' Mike said.

'Get hold of one,' Rob said. 'As well as someone who can operate it. They're not the kind of things you can start using without any experience.'

'Any ideas where?' Tessa said.

'I might know someone,' Rob said, 'who has unregistered drones which have been modified so they can go wherever their operator wants.' He folded his arms. 'She might let you rent a drone, and provide an operator. It won't be cheap though.'

'Who is she?' Matt said. 'Is she a—'

'Don't ask,' Rob said. 'Because I won't say. It's someone I know from when I was in the police. Tell me if you're interested and I'll see what I can do.'

'How much?' Matt said.

'Let's start with ten thousand. Can you pay that? And it needs to be cash.'

'Yes,' Matt said. He looked at Tessa, Mike and Annabelle.

Tessa nodded. 'I can go to the bank and get some of it.'

'Banks are closed,' Mike said. 'It's Sunday. I've got the cash in my account. I'll give you a cheque.'

'No,' Rob said. 'No cheques.'

'Then what do we do?' Annabelle said.

'I'm not sure,' Rob replied. 'But she'll need cash.'

'We'll figure it out,' Tessa said. She looked at her watch. 'Five minutes to go.'

Matt glanced at his wife. 'Annabelle?'

'Tell him we accept,' she said.

Matt typed the message. He stared at it for a long time, then pressed send.

Chester, 2011

1

She walked, hand in hand with Matt, through the shopping mall.

It was her first book reading, at an independent bookshop in Chester. The owner had sent a message to Guy saying she'd read *Still Waters*, loved it, and would Annabelle like to do a reading? Would she like to? She'd have killed for it.

A book reading.

Her book.

Still Waters by Annabelle Anderson. They were engaged and she had considered writing as Annabelle Westbrook, but it felt premature. If there were further books she would write under her maiden name; she liked the anonymity, as well as the alliteration of the name.

Plus, Matt had said it was best to have a surname starting with 'A' as most people browsed from the start of the shelves, and that was where the A's got put.

She had chosen three key passages to read, one from the start, and two from the middle. She knew what she was going to say, and had tried to anticipate the questions she might get. She pictured the scene: her, sitting by a table with a stack of copies of *Still Waters* on it, her book in her hand. Rows of people sitting in chairs brought from a storeroom at the back. Would there be enough? How many chairs did a bookshop typically have? If people had to stand, that was fine. She'd make a joke about it. Modest and self-deprecating, of course.

They turned a corner, and there it was. The site of her first reading.

There was a sign in the window:

AUTHOR EVENT
BOOK SIGNING
Annabelle Anderson, reading from her debut novel
Still Waters
6 p.m., 30 October 2011

Matt made an excited face. That was the great thing about him; she knew he truly wanted the best for her. His excitement was genuine; with friends there was sometimes the sense that they secretly wanted you to fail, that they saw themselves as competitors. But not Matt. They were a partnership.

And in a year they'd be married.

'OK,' Matt said. 'Here we go. Are you nervous?'

'A bit,' she said. 'Excited, mainly.'

They walked into the shop. To the right was the counter; to the left there was a table in an area that someone had cleared. There were four rows of chairs; Annabelle counted them quickly. Eight in each row, so thirty-two in total. That would almost certainly not be enough.

A woman walked over. She had short blond hair and a muscular build. 'Hi,' she said. 'I'm Nicole. You must be Annabelle?'

'Yes. Thanks for having me.'

'My pleasure. Thanks for coming.' Nicole gestured at the chairs. 'Still fifteen minutes to go, yet. People tend to arrive at the last second. Would you like a drink? We have water. That's it, I'm afraid.'

'Thanks. I'm OK for now.'

Annabelle's pulse sped up. Nicole had sounded like she was apologizing for the lack of people, like she was trying to make Annabelle feel better.

Should she feel bad? Was this a poor turnout?

No. People would come. People arrived at gigs and football games at the last second, so why would a book reading be any different? She could start a few minutes late to give them an opportunity to get here.

She walked over to the fiction section. Ever since the book was published two weeks back she had been unable to pass a bookshop without going in to see whether her book was on the shelves. And there it was, two copies, side by side. She fought the urge to take it and put it cover outwards – she had succumbed more than once in other shops, but it would be a bit embarrassing here.

'Here for the reading?'

She turned to the door. Nicole was smiling at two women in their fifties. They were standing in the doorway. One of them shook her head.

'We were looking for the latest *Diary of a Wimpy Kid*. For my grandson.'

'We have that. Come in.'

The two women walked inside. They looked at the empty chairs.

'Who's doing the reading?' the woman who had asked for the *Diary of a Wimpy Kid* said.

'Annabelle Anderson,' Nicole replied. She pointed at Annabelle. 'She's a local author.'

A local author? Was that why she was doing this reading? Because she was a *local* author? Annabelle had been thinking it was because she was a good author.

'Hi,' Annabelle said. 'Welcome.'

'Thank you,' the woman said. 'What time does it start?'

'At six,' Annabelle replied. 'Just a few minutes.'

'Will it last long?' the woman said.

'Not too long,' Annabelle said. 'I'll try to keep it brief.'

'Well,' the woman said. 'I suppose we can stay.'

2

With a minute to go, there were five in the audience; the two women looking for *Wimpy Kid*, Matt, a man in his sixties who was staring at his phone, and a woman in her mid-fifties who sat, clutching a copy of *Still Waters* against her midriff.

Annabelle stood by the history section. There were maybe thirty books piled on the table in front of the chairs, so presumably Nicole had been expecting around that many guests, and that many book sales.

As it was she would get four, maximum, although since one woman already had it and the other two were here for *Diary of a Wimpy Kid*, it was more likely she would sell one, and that assumed the man was a potential customer, and not just someone looking for a way to pass half an hour in a warm room in the company of others.

She wanted to apologize, buy the thirty books herself, and run out of the bookshop.

Nicole walked over, a bottle of water in her hand. It was unlikely she'd make enough money to cover the cost of it.

'Well,' she said. 'Should we get started?'

'Yes,' Annabelle said, trying to put as much of a note of

optimism in her voice as she could. 'Let's get this over with.' She felt suddenly guilty at the way the words had come out. They had sounded negative and ungrateful and she did not want Nicole to think she was blaming her.

'OK,' Nicole said. 'I'll do an introduction and then hand it over to you.'

She walked to the table and clapped her hands together.

'Welcome,' she said. 'And thank you for coming. I am delighted to have as our guest—'

There was a loud crashing noise from the door. Annabelle looked up. A man was standing at the entrance, a large pile of books at his feet.

'Sorry,' he mumbled. 'I knocked into the table.' He began to pick them up, but Nicole waved a hand.

'Take a seat,' she said. 'We're just getting started. I'll deal with those later. It's no problem.'

The man shuffled over and sat down. He was tall, mid-thirties, and balding. He walked with a stoop, as though trying to make himself as inconspicuous as possible.

'OK,' Nicole said. 'Like I was saying, I am delighted to have Annabelle Anderson as our guest. Annabelle is the author of *Still Waters*, which had been described as a "twisty tale of a relationship gone desperately wrong". It is her debut novel, and no doubt the first of many. I read it and enjoyed it immensely. Ladies and gentlemen, Annabelle Anderson.'

There was a smattering of applause as Annabelle took the few steps to the table.

'Thank you, Nicole, for such a lovely introduction.' She sat in the chair next to the table and picked up the copy of the book she had made her notes in. 'And thank you for being here.' She opened the book. 'I thought I would do three readings from the book, and then open it up for questions.'

She cleared her throat, and began.

170

3

The *Wimpy Kid* seekers left as the last of the brief and almost apologetic applause finished. Annabelle's talk evidently hadn't inspired them to buy a copy of the book.

The man in his sixties picked up his phone, looked at the screen, then got to his feet. He lifted it his ear.

'Hello?' he said. 'Hang on one second.'

He caught Annabelle's eye and gave an apologetic half-shrug, then headed for the door.

An imaginary phone call, Annabelle thought. *Not even original.*

'Well,' she said, looking from the woman in her fifties to the man who had knocked over the books. 'Thanks for coming.'

Nicole stood up. 'There are books for sale on the table,' she said. 'Annabelle will sign them, if you wish.'

Form a queue, Annabelle thought. *Both of you.*

The man in his thirties walked up to the table. He picked up a copy of the book and riffled through the pages. He didn't pause to read any of the words before fixing her with an intense stare. His eyes were a dark blue, under wild, uncombed hair.

'I'm a writer, too,' he said suddenly.

'Oh,' Annabelle replied. 'Congratulations. What do you write?'

'Poems.' He took a thin book from the pocket of his battered canvas coat. It looked home-made, the pages printed and stapled together. 'This is my book.' He held it out to Annabelle. 'Here. Take it.'

'That's very generous,' she said, glancing at Matt, who moved a step closer to her. 'But I couldn't. It's yours.'

'I want you to have it. That's why I came!' He gave a short, harsh laugh. 'We're both writers! We have to stick together.' He thrust it at her again. 'Here. It's yours.'

The book, printed on light green paper, hovered between them. Annabelle reached out a hand and took it. 'Very kind of you,' she said. 'I look forward to reading your poems.'

He nodded. 'I'm Carl,' he said. 'My name's on the front.'

She looked at the cover. There was a clumsy line drawing of a cat, below the words, all in capitals, POEMS AND SONGS by CARL JAMESON.

She opened it. There was an inscription, in block capitals:

TO ANNABELLE
FROM ONE WRITER TO ANOTHER; WE SHARE
A SPECIAL BOND
YOURS MOST FAITHFULLY
CARL JAMESON

'Thank you, Carl,' she said.

He nodded again and held up the copy of her book he had taken. 'Can I have this?' he said. 'A swap?'

It seemed impossible to say no. She'd have to pay Nicole for it later. 'Certainly,' she said. 'Would you like me to sign it?'

'Yes. Put "To Carl, from your fellow writer, Annabelle". Like I did. OK?'

172

'OK.' She wrote the message, exactly as he'd said it. Something told her he would check. She handed the book to him. 'Good luck with your poetry, Carl.'

'Do you want to talk about it? Writing?' he said.

'I'd love to,' Annabelle said. 'But maybe another time.' The lady in her fifties was still in her chair, holding the copy she'd brought in with her. 'But I think I need to sign someone else's book.'

His face flickered with disappointment. 'Oh. All right. Another time, then.'

'Yes. Another time.' She looked past him at the woman. 'Would you like me to sign that?'

The woman stood up and handed her the book.

'I *loved* it,' she said, in a soft voice. 'I felt the pain. I thought to myself, here is someone who really understands *pain*. It helped me, at a difficult time in my life.' She looked left and right, then lowered her voice. 'I went through the same thing. I hope it's over for you.'

'Yes,' Annabelle said, unsure what else to say. 'It's only a novel, obviously. A story.'

'Nothing's only a story,' the woman whispered. 'Especially not this.'

'That's so wonderful to hear,' Annabelle said. 'Thank you for saying that.'

'It's my pleasure.' The woman smiled. 'Would you sign it for me?'

'I'd be delighted.' Annabelle opened the book. It looked like it had been read more than once. 'Who should I make it out to?'

'Rachel,' the woman said. 'Make it out to Rachel.'

When Rachel had left, Annabelle looked at the table.

One fewer book on it than at the start. Nicole was putting away the chairs.

'I'm sorry,' Annabelle said. 'That was a bit of a waste of your time.'

'Don't worry,' Nicole said. 'At least you had five show up. We've had worse.'

'Really? I wouldn't have thought it could be much worse.'

'We had zero, once. No one came at all. And only one, another time. So five is pretty respectable.'

'That makes me feel a little better, I suppose.' Annabelle gestured at chairs. 'Can Matt and I help tidy up?'

'No, that's fine. It won't take me long. Thanks for offering, though. You two go off and enjoy the evening. Have a drink somewhere.'

'By the way, I owe you for a book. That guy took one. He swapped it for his volume of poetry.'

Nicole laughed. 'Was that what he was saying?'

'Yes. One writer to another. He was very particular about the message I wrote in his book.'

'You get all sorts,' Nicole said. 'Come to the till and I'll ring it up.'

'Drink?' Matt said as they left.

'I need one. That was embarrassing.'

He put his arm around her shoulders. 'No it wasn't,' he said. 'And who cares, anyway?'

'It bloody was,' Annabelle said. 'There was an audience of five. One was you, two were there by accident, one swapped his hand-made pamphlet of poems for a book which I had to pay for, and the other already had one.'

'When you put it like that,' Matt said. 'You do have a point. Although, look on the bright side. By buying a book for that guy you generated sales of minus one. That's got to be some kind of a record.'

'Thanks,' Annabelle said. 'That's not exactly what I wanted to hear.'

'How about a drink? Drown your sorrows?'

'Now you're talking,' Annabelle said. '*That* was what I wanted to hear.'

Sunday, 8 March 2020, 2 p.m.

Matt

The doorbell rang just after 2 p.m. Rob was standing outside. He had left a few hours ago and now he was back, accompanied by a slender, tall woman. She had a thin face, her hair pulled back in a ponytail.

'This is Brenda,' he said.

'All right,' Brenda said, in a strong Birmingham accent. She did not smile.

'Come in,' Matt said. 'Follow me.'

He showed them into the living room. Annabelle was upstairs, resting in bed. Tessa and Mike were standing by the window.

Brenda nodded at Tessa and Mike, then looked at Matt.

'Payment?' she said. 'Has to be upfront.'

'We . . .' He paused. 'The banks are closed. This came up last night. But we'll give you the money. I promise.'

She shook her head. 'I can't take promises to the bank. Sorry.'

'Then what do you want?' Matt said. 'Jewellery? My watch? The car? You can have anything.'

'No,' she said. 'Cash. That's what the boss wants and what the boss wants, she gets.'

Tessa stepped away from the window. 'I can get cash tomorrow morning, as soon as the bank opens. I'm a doctor. I have money.'

'I believe you, love,' Brenda said, 'I really do. But I don't have any wiggle room.'

There was a cough from the door. Annabelle was standing there, her eyes sunken.

'I'm Annabelle,' she said. 'My children are gone, and I'm the price of their safety. Did Rob explain that?'

'He did, love.'

'Are you a mother?'

'I am,' Brenda said.

'Then you'll know how desperate I am. And that we'll find a way to pay you. You have to trust us.'

'There's the rub,' Brenda said. 'My boss doesn't trust anyone she doesn't know. It's nothing personal, but that's how it is.'

'She knows me,' Rob said. He folded his arms. '*You* know me. I'll guarantee it. If they don't pay, I will.'

'Let me make a phone call,' Brenda said. She left the room. A few minutes later, she was back.

'You guarantee it?' she said. 'You know what that means?'

'I do, and I do,' Rob replied.

'Then we have a deal. So. Tell me everything you know.'

Annabelle

Brenda listened as they explained everything that had happened. When they had finished, she puffed out her cheeks.

'Any idea who this is, love?' she said.

'None,' Annabelle said. 'That's what makes it so hard.'

'And you find out the location around five p.m., right? Handover five-thirty p.m.?'

'Right,' Annabelle said.

'Good,' Brenda said. 'There'll be enough light. This is what I think's going to happen. The location is going to be quiet and hidden away, but with more than one way of getting in and out. When the kidnapper has Annabelle, the children will be returned. There'll be a delay in handing the kids over so they can get away from the location without you following them.'

'What do you mean, delay?' Matt said.

'They'll make it take a while – have the kids walk to you, something like that.'

'But we'll be watching,' Matt said.

'We'll be watching,' Brenda said. 'I'll be close enough – maybe half a mile – so that Rob and I can come and pick you up. Someone else needs to get the children. Then we track Annabelle.'

'I can get the kids,' Mike said.

'I'll go with him,' Tessa added.

'What if the drone is visible?'

'It won't be,' Brenda said. 'It'll be too high. And even if it is, once the kids are with us it doesn't matter. All that matters is we don't lose Annabelle.'

'And if the drone can't keep up?' Tessa said.

'It will, unless they go on the motorway,' Rob said. 'Which I doubt will happen.'

'Why not?' Annabelle said.

'Because they'll stick to back roads. Motorways aren't safe. Not enough ways off. It's easy to apprehend someone on a motorway.'

'Then, once we have the children, we call the cops,' Tessa said.

'Right,' Rob said. 'Once the cops are informed, Brenda's involvement is over.'

'You know,' Brenda said, looking at Annabelle. 'You might want to think about being ready to do something. Once the kids are safe.'

'Like what?' Annabelle said.

'Take something with you. Something sharp. A blade, or another weapon. The kidnapper's probably going to restrain you – handcuffs, something like that – but there'll be an opportunity to attack them. And if you have a weapon, your chances will be much higher.'

'It's a good idea,' Rob said. 'You could conceal something in a shoe, or a sleeve. A large nail, or a screwdriver. Anything.'

'And the sooner you use it,' Brenda said. 'The better.'

Annabelle looked at Matt. He was nodding, but she didn't think this would work. She didn't think that whoever was doing this was foolish enough to make it that easy, but she didn't want to say that. She didn't want to break Matt's heart.

Plus, it was something to think about.

'Good idea,' she said. 'Let's do it.'

They settled on the head of a hammer sewn into the cuff of her coat. It was a large puffer coat, so the hammer-head didn't stick out. It did make it hang a bit strangely, but if she put her hand in her jeans pocket it was reasonably well disguised.

'You use that,' Brenda said. 'The first chance you get, and as hard as you can.'

'I don't know if I can,' Annabelle said.

'You can,' Brenda replied. 'There's no doubt. Just remember what they've put you through. Someone has chosen to do this to you, and they deserve to be hit with that hammer as hard as you can swing it. Harder.'

'I will,' Annabelle said.

'There's something odd about this,' Brenda said. 'Something personal. But whoever is doing this is deluded. Deranged, almost.'

Annabelle stared at her. *Deluded. Deranged.* A memory came to her of the last time she'd heard those words together. It was a long time ago, but the memory was as clear as if it had been the day before.

'Matt,' she said. 'Do you remember before we got married there were those messages?'

He nodded slowly.

'Do you think – do you think they have anything to do with this?'

'Maybe,' he said. 'But how would that help? We never found out who that was.'

'I know. But it's something.'

'What happened?' Tessa said.

'I haven't thought of it since,' Annabelle replied. 'But it was pretty weird.'

Summer 2012

1

The message came from an anonymous account. It was a Hotmail account; the name was just a string of letters and numbers.

You don't have to do this.

That was all it said. Annabelle would never have opened the message – she would have assumed it was spam – were it not for the subject.

Your Wedding

Since she was getting married in three weeks, that had caught her eye and she had opened it.
And there it was.

You don't have to do this.

It was unsigned. She read it again. Someone had sent it, someone who knew she and Matt were getting married. That was quite a lot of people.

She felt a flush of anger. Who would send something like this? It wasn't as though she was demanding everyone treat her like a princess on her special day – she was trying to be reasonable – but she didn't need this. It was either someone who didn't want her to get married – who, she had no idea, since the only other serious boyfriend she'd had was now living in Paris with his French wife – or someone who thought she needed rescuing. Either way, it was selfish.

She deleted it. Whoever it was, she wanted nothing to do with it.

2

The next morning, when she had made her coffee, she opened her laptop. There was another email.

It was a follow-up to the previous message.

I'm serious. You don't have to do this. It's not too late.

She was about to delete it, but paused. It was better to put a stop to this, once and for all. She typed a reply.

I don't know who this is, but please stop sending me messages.

The reply came immediately.

I know what he does to you. I know you are unhappy. You don't have to go through with this. There's still time.

What – and who – the fuck was this? She sent a reply.

I have no idea what you are talking about. I don't want to hear any more from you.

183

She watched her inbox with bated breath. For a minute or two there was nothing, and then the reply came:

You don't have to lie to me, Annabelle. Just say the word, and I can get you out of this. I know you're scared, but trust me.

Trust them? An anonymous emailer warning her not to get married? Not likely.

Who is this? she wrote

A friend.

Which friend?

There was another few minutes delay.

I can't say. Not until you agree to call it off. I can come for you later today. Don't be frightened, Annabelle. He won't be able to hurt you. You'll be safe, finally.

She heard footsteps upstairs, and then the sound of Matt coming down the stairs. She moved the cursor to the delete button. Her hand was shaking.

She deleted the message, and then blocked the sender.

The door opened, and Matt came in. He leaned down and kissed her.

'Is there more coffee?' he said.

'I made a pot. There's plenty left.'

He looked at her half-empty mug. 'Want a refill?'

3

'Did you mention it to Matt?' Miriam, her oldest friend and maid-of-honour – a title which sounded vaguely ridiculous to Annabelle, given the number of boyfriends Miriam had been through – sipped her prosecco. They had been at the wedding dress shop, getting the final alterations done, and were having a celebratory drink in a wine bar in Liverpool.

'Not yet.'

'Why not?'

'I don't know. I don't want to piss him off.'

'You haven't done anything,' Miriam said.

'I'm not worried he'll be angry at me. I just – I don't know. I didn't say anything this morning and then I came out to meet you. I'll probably tell him tonight. Not that there's much to tell.'

'Who do you think it was?'

Annabelle shrugged. 'I have no idea. Truly.'

'Maybe one of your many fans,' Miriam said. 'A stalker. Now you're a literary celebrity.'

'I think I have about five fans,' Annabelle said. 'At least, that's what the sales of my books would indicate.'

'The new one's doing OK,' Miriam said.

'Kind of,' Annabelle said. 'But it's not exactly flying off the shelves. It's not *on* most shelves.' Every time she passed a bookshop she went in to see if *Deep Cover* was there. It was not. Guy had told her not to worry; writing careers took time to build. He quoted a statistic about how many thousands of books were published each year, and how many titles bookshops bought.

The upshot was that there were a lot more published than appeared on the shelves.

So the fact you're not in every bookshop in the country is not a problem, OK?

It was a valiant effort, but it didn't make her feel much better.

'So, not a fan,' Miriam said. 'But then who?'

'I can't think of anyone. And all this "I'll rescue you" stuff – it's weird.'

'I can think of two possibilities,' Miriam said. 'It's a joke, in which case you have to figure out who has such a crappy sense of humour, or it's a test. Someone wants to see if you are truly committed to the marriage.'

'No one has a sense of humour that crappy. And as for a test – who would think I need rescuing? I love Matt, and anyone who knows the first thing about us knows that.' She sipped her drink. 'If it is a joke, I'll bloody murder whoever did it.'

Miriam puffed out her cheeks. 'Matt might want to test you.'

'Maybe. But he wouldn't do this. It's not like him.'

'No,' Miriam said. 'But this is a big moment, and people do strange things. He may want to be one hundred per cent sure. I know it's unlikely, but of the two' – she shrugged – 'that's where I'd put my money.'

'OK,' Annabelle said. 'I'll talk to him.'

4

'No,' Matt said. 'Of course I didn't! Why would I do that?'

'Miriam thought it may be a test,' Annabelle said. 'To see if I'm committed.'

'It'd be a pretty shit test,' Matt said. 'A random person emails you and you say yeah, sure, I'll run off with you. If I was going to try and test your commitment, I'd come up with something better than that.'

'Then what is it?'

'I don't know. Can I see the emails?'

'I deleted them.'

'That's OK,' Matt said. 'They'll be in your deleted emails for a while.'

She opened her laptop and logged into her email account.

'Here they are.'

He read the emails.

'This is so weird,' he said. 'I mean, I could see someone declaring their undying love for you so that at least you knew they felt that way before you got married, in case you reciprocated. But this? This is just weird. They want to *rescue* you?'

'Could it be a joke?' Annabelle said.

'It could. But by who, I have no idea.' He laughed. 'Whoever sent this is deluded. Deranged, even. There's a crazy fucker out there monitoring your life.'

'Matt!' Annabelle punched him on his arm. 'Don't say that!'

'It's a joke!'

'Well, it's not funny. I'm scared! A bit, anyway.'

'Why? You're worried they may kidnap you before the wedding? I doubt it. It's some idiot messing around. Probably someone who saw we were getting married, got your email address and wanted to mess with you. I doubt we even know them. Forget about it. If any more come, tell them to get lost.' He kissed her. 'It'll be fine. Don't worry.'

'Sure,' she said. 'But make sure we lock the doors tonight, OK?'

Sunday, 8 March 2020, 4.55 p.m.

Annabelle

1

Annabelle closed her laptop. She and Matt were in the office looking for the emails to see if there was any clue to who had sent them, but they were all gone.

'We should have paid more attention at the time,' Matt said.

'We were focused on the wedding,' Annabelle said. 'And they just stopped.'

'Do you think they're linked to this?' Matt said.

'I don't know. They could be.'

Matt put his arm around her. 'If they are,' he said. 'Then this goes back years.'

Annabelle closed her eyes. The idea that this had been bubbling away in the background for a decade or more was terrifying.

'I don't even want to think about that,' she said. 'It's—'

Matt's phone buzzed and he snatched it up.

'It's the kidnapper,' he said. He tapped the screen. It glowed, reflected in his eyes.

When he looked up, his face was pale.

'What is it?' Annabelle said.

'No,' he said. 'No, this can't be true. It can't.'

'What is it?' Annabelle said. 'What does it say?'

Matt's hand shook. He looked older, his eyes dull, his expression fixed. His smile was one of the first things she noticed when she met him. It was a full-face smile, his mouth wide, his cheeks high and his eyes bright. He almost looked startled, as though he was about to gasp in amazement or burst into fits of giggles. It was infectious and she had found herself smiling in return. It was part of what drew her to him; being with him was always fun.

Now, though, the smile was gone. He barely looked like himself. And this was only the start of this nightmare. Who knew what toll it would take by the end?

'What does it say?' she said.

'Read it,' he said, and passed her the phone.

The handover will take place at 5.30pm. You need to arrive – only the two of you, or the deal is off, without any negotiation – at the GPS coordinates I will send after you reply confirming you will be there.

You will find a gate. Stop there. Matt – get out of the car and open the gate, Annabelle – drive through the gate until told to stop. It will be obvious when that is.

Matt, wait until Annabelle and I have left. Then you can retrieve your children.

There is one other thing. Annabelle will be naked other than a bathrobe. She will have no belongings with her whatsoever. If this requirement is not met, or if there is any attempt to conceal a weapon or tracking device of any kind, the swap will be aborted.

190

'That's the end of the hammer,' Annabelle said. 'I'm going to be totally defenceless.'

They went into the living room. Rob and Brenda were standing by the window. Matt called into the kitchen for Mike and Tessa.

'Another message,' Annabelle said.

'What is it?' Rob said.

She gestured at the coat with the hammer-head sewn into the sleeve.

'This is useless,' she said. 'I can't take anything. No weapons. No phone. Nothing.'

'That's why it's concealed,' Brenda said. 'So they won't know you have it.'

'They've thought of that. They want me to be naked. It's in thirty minutes.'

Brenda gestured at the phone. 'Can I see?' she said.

Annabelle handed her the phone.

'Well,' Brenda said. 'We still have the drone, and if it's in thirty minutes it can't be that far away. We need to be ready to go.'

'You need to tell him you want to see the kids,' Rob said. 'Check they're OK. This is very one-sided. It doesn't feel great.'

'What should I say?' Annabelle said.

'That you'll be there, but you want to see the kids before you go through the gate.'

'OK,' she said, and began to type.

We will be there but need to see the kids before the swap. They need to be visible and safe.

She pressed send. Seconds later the reply came.

Not possible. I do not want your children. If you do as I say, they will be returned unharmed. If you do not, you will never see them again.

Annabelle closed her eyes. Her stomach contracted and she retched. In her hand the phone buzzed.

This is the only option. You have one minute to confirm these arrangements or it is off.

Rob read the message. 'You have to go with it,' he said. 'This guy means business.' He paused. 'I'm sorry to be so blunt, but that's how it seems to me.'

'You sure?' Brenda said. 'If the children are hurt – or killed – there's no deal. The only way the kidnapper gets what they want – Annabelle – is by keeping the kids safe.' She put her hand on Annabelle's arm. 'We – you – could call their bluff.'

'No,' Annabelle said. 'I'm not calling anyone's bluff. Not when the price of getting it wrong is the lives of my children.'

'Annabelle,' Matt said. 'We can't do this. I can't let you.'

'You have no choice.'

He stared at her. 'I can't lose you,' he said. 'I can't.'

'I know.' She reached for his hands. 'But there's no alternative.'

She typed a message.

Confirmed.

When the reply came, there were no words, just a set of GPS coordinates. She read them to Matt and he typed them into his phone.

The door opened and Mike walked in. He was followed by Tessa.

Matt held up the screen to show the map.

'That's it,' he said. 'That's where it is.'

2

So, finally, the plan was this:

They would go to the rendezvous and follow the instructions they had been given. She would be defenceless and near-naked and alone. They would hope that their children were returned to Matt.

And then Brenda and the drones would follow her. She had three drones – enough for two hours – so they should be able to follow Annabelle until the police were informed and could go and get her.

She sat in the passenger seat. Matt drove, following the directions on the screen of his phone. They were in her blue, ten-year-old Golf. She was wearing a black dressing gown. Underneath she was naked. She had an image of the police stopping them and asking why she was dressed like that; it would be quite hard to explain.

Despite Matt sitting next to her, and all the activity at the house, she felt totally alone. In less than half an hour she'd be – what? A prisoner? Dead? She had no idea, and that terrified her.

Matt's phone rang. The name of the caller came up on the screen.

'It's Sammy,' she said.

'I've not spoken to him in a while,' Matt said.

'You want to answer?'

He paused and she looked at him. He and Sammy had been very close in the years after they left university, but since the wedding – the stag party, actually – things had not been the same.

'No,' Matt said. 'Let it go to voicemail. I'll call him when this is all over.'

She put a hand on his knee and squeezed it.

'Matt,' she said. 'I love you.'

He made a soft, strangled sound and she saw his lips quiver.

'I love you too,' he said.

'You know, people talk about love at first sight and whether it's possible, and I never say much, but I know it is. From the very first time we met I knew you were going to be special in my life. I didn't know how special, but I knew you were different. Now, looking back, I know what that was. It was love.'

'Annabelle,' he said, his voice breaking. 'You're my life. I can't imagine how I could carry on without you. I keep thinking about all the time we've been together. I can't do it without you.'

She felt a sudden, shocking horror at the situation. She wanted to shrink to nothing, disappear. She wanted never to have existed.

'I feel the same,' she whispered. 'You'll be OK, I think. Make sure you tell the kids their mum loves them. Every day.'

'I can't think that way,' he said. 'We won't lose you. We have the drones.'

'I know,' she said. 'I know. But just in case. I want you to know that I love you and I trust you to bring up our children the right way.'

195

They approached a roundabout and a woman's voice came from the phone.

Turn left at the next junction.

'It's down here,' Matt said. 'Another mile or so.'

She looked at the clock: 5.54.

Six minutes left with her husband.

Six minutes until her kids were safe.

They followed the road. It was lined with industrial units. After a few hundred yards it turned into a rutted track. It was unlit, and the car jolted as they hit potholes and rocks.

Somewhere above them, a drone tracked their progress. Half a mile or so behind them, Brenda and Rob watched the images it relayed to them. Mike and Tessa were parked beside them, waiting for the signal to come and get the kids.

Eventually the track turned left into a wooded area.

And there was the gate.

The woman's voice came from the satnav. 'You have reached your destination.'

They slowed to a stop. The clock on the dashboard showed 6 p.m.

Annabelle turned to Matt.

'Bye,' she said. 'Goodbye, darling.'

Summer 2012

Sammy climbed on a chair in the middle of the room. He was holding a bottle of vodka in his right hand, and a cigarette in his left. His face was flushed, and he wobbled on the chair.

'Oi!' he shouted. 'Everyone listen up!'

Matt and about twenty-five of his friends – some from university, some from home – were in a barn in North Wales, having spent the day at an adventure centre. During the morning they had run around a forest with paintball guns shooting each other; after a few beers at lunch they had spent the afternoon racing go-karts. The results were predictable. After a three-car pile-up two of the participants in Matt's stag do had gone to hospital, one, a friend from work called Barry, with a broken wrist, and the other, Matt's cousin, Simon, with a fractured elbow. Sammy, who was driving the third car, claimed to be fine, but had been walking with a limp ever since.

The guests gathered around Sammy.

'Right,' he said. 'Now for the main event! Get over here, Matt.'

Matt glanced at Jason. 'What is this?' he said. 'What's he got planned?'

'Don't know,' Jason said. 'But I'm guessing it involves that vodka.' He shrugged. 'Sorry, mate. You put him in charge of your stag do.'

Matt walked over. Guy was standing on the edge of the group. He raised an eyebrow as Sammy jumped off the chair and pointed to it.

'Take a seat,' Sammy said, and handed him the vodka. 'And have a swig of this. You'll need it. Dutch courage.'

Matt laughed. 'What are you planning?' he said.

'Sit down,' Sammy replied. 'You'll see.'

Matt sat on the chair. As soon as he was seated, he saw Scott and Tony, two other Birmingham friends, step forward. He was surprised to see they were holding ropes – he wondered, for a moment, why they had them, before realizing it was obvious why – but before he could do anything, they had wrapped one around his chest and the other around his knees.

They pulled them tight.

'OK,' Sammy said. 'Get ready, Matt! It's your last week as a free man, and we're going to give you a night to remember!'

The door to the barn opened and two women came in. They were dressed in very short silver dresses and high heels, and they were greeted by loud cheers.

'Say hello to Lexi and Candy,' Sammy said. 'Come on in, girls.'

Matt caught Sammy's eye. 'I don't think this is a great idea,' he said. 'I thought we agreed, no strippers?'

'A stag do's not a stag do without strippers,' Sammy said. 'Relax, mate.'

Lexi and Candy stood in front of him and started to sway backwards and forwards.

'I'm Candy,' the one on the left said.

'And I'm Lexi.'

Lexi looked about his age; Candy was quite a bit older. She pulled down the straps of her dress and straddled him. She started to grind her pelvis against his, and pushed her breasts into his face.

198

He felt her nipples against his cheeks, and turned away.

'Look,' he said. 'I really don't want—'

Candy lifted her hips up and leaned against him. He felt hands move up his thighs to his belt.

'Take them off!' Sammy said. 'Give him his treat!'

Matt squirmed in the chair but the ropes were too tight; besides, Candy was pinning him down.

'Stop!' he said. 'I don't want to do this!'

He felt the waistband of his jeans loosen, and then they were being pulled down. He felt a hand on the outside of his boxer shorts, rubbing his penis.

'Jesus,' he said. 'Please. Leave me alone!'

He looked up at Sammy, about to tell him one more time to put a stop to this, and froze.

Sammy had a video camera in his hand.

He was *recording* this? Was he insane? The last thing you did was document something like this. If Annabelle ever saw it – and Matt would spend his marriage terrified that she would, somehow – she'd have nothing to do with him. He didn't want this in the first place, and now it was going to be on video.

'Sammy!' he said. 'What are you doing?'

He looked at Guy, who was watching, arms folded, his face expressionless. Next to him Jason was frowning.

'Guy!' Matt said. He shook his head. 'No!'

Guy shook his head. He stepped forward, and put his hand on Lexi's shoulder.

'OK,' he said. 'That'll do.'

She stood up. 'I thought he wanted the full works?'

'No. That's enough.'

The guests laughed; some booed good-naturedly.

Candy shrugged. 'No refunds.'

'That's fine,' Guy said. 'Thanks for coming.'

*   *   *

Tony and Scott untied the ropes and Matt stood up. He turned to Sammy. He was staring at them, the video camera by his side.

'What's the problem?' he said.

'What's the problem?' Matt said. 'What the fuck were you thinking? I mean, strippers, maybe. But getting them to do whatever you had planned – and what was that, by the way? Were they going to give me a blowjob? Or fuck me? With you filming it? Are you *totally* crazy?'

Sammy snorted. 'I thought it'd be funny. And you'd like a memento.'

'Well, it wasn't. And I don't.' He held his hand out. 'Give me the camera. I want to delete that.'

'Scared the wife will see it?' Sammy said. 'Whatever you want, mate. Seems marriage does change a man, after all.'

'Yeah,' Matt said. 'Seems it does.'

Late Summer 2012: Wedding Day

Annabelle entered the church, her left arm in the crook of her dad's elbow, her right in her brother's. When she had first told them she and Matt were getting married, she had suggested that both of them walk her down the aisle. Her brother had coughed and looked a little nervous.

It's normally the father who gives the bride away, he said.

That's another thing, Annabelle said. *I don't want to be given away. I just want to be accompanied on my wedding day by the two most important people in my life. I don't belong to anyone now and I won't after the wedding. So if this means I'm not being given away, then all the more reason to do it this way.*

Well, her dad said. *It's tradition, petal, but if you'd prefer to do something else, that's fine by us. It's your wedding day, not ours.*

She looked down the aisle. Matt had turned to watch her, a smile on his face. She smiled back and began to walk down the aisle.

The church, St Wilfrid's in Grappenhall, was over nine hundred years old. She thought of how much had happened in those centuries, how many weddings and christenings and funerals had taken place in these stone walls. Hundreds of thousands – maybe millions – of people had sat in the aisles and witnessed the most important events in the lives of the people they loved.

For a moment she felt dizzy, and she leaned on her dad. He paused and held her by the elbow.

'OK?' he muttered.

She nodded and took a deep breath, and they continued down the aisle.

'So,' the vicar said. 'Before we move to the vows, there is a question I must put to those here today. I expect the answer to be no, but I have to ask.' She looked up at the congregation. 'Should any person here know of any lawful impediment why Annabelle and Matt may not be joined in holy matrimony, let them speak now, or forever hold their peace.'

She paused, and Annabelle had a sudden conviction that someone was going to stand up and say, *Don't do it, I told you, you don't have to. Come with me and I'll rescue you.* Then she would see who it was who had sent the emails, because part of her was sure they had not gone away. Yes, there had been no more emails, and after a while she'd stopped thinking about who had sent them, and whether they would try anything else to sabotage her wedding, but she hadn't forgotten.

Because it felt like sabotage – not a joke, or a test, but an attempt at sabotage.

And why would they stop?

She glanced over her shoulder and scanned the faces. No one was moving. She looked at the door, expecting it to burst open, and then the vicar spoke.

'Excellent,' she said. 'Annabelle and Matt, you will now make solemn vows of your love for each other in front of your friends and family. We'll start with you, Matt.'

He repeated her words; they were so familiar – to have and to hold, in sickness and in health, for better or for worse – and yet, now they applied to her and Matt, so strange. She had heard them so many times they had lost their meaning,

202

but as she heard him say them, the meaning became clear.

And then it was her turn. It went in a blur, and suddenly she was saying *I do* and realized she was smiling and Matt was smiling back at her, and then the vicar asked Guy, their best man, if he had the rings, and he stood up and handed them to her, and the vicar told her to hold out her hand, and Matt was saying *With this ring I thee wed*, and then she did the same.

'I now declare you,' the vicar said, 'husband and wife.' She leaned forward and placed a hand on each of their forearms. 'Congratulations. You may kiss.'

They did, a sort of awkward halfway house between a peck on the lips and a full-on, passionate, open-mouthed kiss, then looked up to see everyone clapping and cheering.

Annabelle glanced at the doors. Still closed. Still no one there to sabotage her wedding.

And now it was too late.

Sunday, 8 March 2020, 5.31 p.m.

Matt

Matt looked at his wife, the dressing gown pulled tight around her. 'No,' he said. 'No.'

It was more a statement of disbelief than a rejection of what they had planned. Now they were here he could not believe this was actually happening. He had thought – somehow – it would be resolved before it came to this.

But now they were here, and it was *real*.

'We have to,' Annabelle said. 'The kids.'

He squeezed his eyes shut, tears filling them, then reached out to her for one last time. They hugged, and he felt the warmth of her body beneath the dressing gown.

'No,' he said. 'No.'

She pulled away. 'I love you,' she said.

'I love you too.' He opened the car door, stepped out and unlatched the gate. The rusty hinges creaked as it opened.

She put the car in gear and drove slowly past him. He pressed his hands to the glass, feeling the car slip away from him.

He watched as she drove along a track. When she was about a hundred yards away the brake lights went on and the car stopped.

A figure had stepped into the road. It was tall and wore dark jeans and a dark hoodie.

It raised a finger to its lips, then held out its left hand. It was holding something.

Matt squinted to see what it was.

It was holding handcuffs.

Annabelle

She drove slowly along the road. Once she glanced in the rear-view mirror to see Matt staring, his face blank, his hands slightly raised.

It was too painful, and she did not look again.

She was just starting to wonder if they had done something wrong – come to the wrong location, or at the wrong time, perhaps – when a figure stepped out of the trees on the left.

There he was.

If it was a he. The figure was tall for a woman, but it was also slender and thin-hipped.

The kidnapper wore dark jeans and a hoodie, which hid their face. Slowly, they raised their right index finger to their lips, then held out their left.

A set of handcuffs dangled from their hand.

The kidnapper gestured for her to get out of the car, then mimed taking off her dressing gown.

She opened the door and swung her bare feet onto the ground. It was cold and stony.

'You want me to take this off?' she said.

A nod. She was about to unbelt it and shrug it off, but she paused. She didn't want to be naked. If her kids were

206

watching, that was not what she wanted them to have as their last sight of her.

'Are my children here?' she said.

Another nod.

'Where?'

A shake of the head this time, and a repeat of the mime of removing the dressing gown.

'OK,' she said, and took it off.

The kidnapper examined her, then picked up the dressing gown and tossed it to her. She put it back on; she was glad of the warmth. The kidnapper held out the handcuffs and she put her hands out. The handcuffs snapped as they went around her wrists. The metal was cold, and bit into her skin. She had never worn handcuffs before.

The kidnapper straightened up then and took a piece of black cloth from a pocket. It took her a few seconds to realize what it was.

A hood.

'No,' she said. 'Please. Let me see my children first.'

A pause, then a nod. The kidnapper pointed to the trees on the other side of the road. There was a narrow, rutted track, and a few yards along it she saw Matt's Land Rover.

'They're safe?' she whispered. 'I'm here!' she shouted. 'I love you!'

The kidnapper held an index finger up to their lips to shush her.

She ignored the signal.

'Norman! Keith! Molly!' she shouted. 'I love you!'

The kidnapper ran around the car and grabbed her by the throat. The hand squeezed hard and the words died in her mouth.

With the other free hand they reached into their pocket and pulled out a metal ball with leather straps either side. It was pressed to her lips, but she kept them closed.

The pressure grew. Her lips were pushed against her teeth; she worried they might split, but she did not want the ball gag in her mouth.

The grip around her throat tightened. She felt like she was going to pass out, her vision blackening from lack of oxygen.

She nodded, and the pressure on her throat lessened.

'OK,' she said. 'OK.'

She opened her mouth, and the ball gag was pushed in, then the hood was jammed over her eyes.

She heard her car door opening, and then there was a shove in her back and she fell into the rear seat. The door slammed shut.

2013 Christening

Having a baby – a son, he was a father to a son – was everything he had thought it would be and nothing like he had expected. The love, the wonder, the overwhelming desire to keep Norman from harm were all things he had expected.

What he had not expected was how intense they were. He had no idea before he picked up his son for the first time and lay on the hospital bed with Norman on his chest, just how immediate and complete the feeling of absolute devotion would be.

He'd known this person only minutes, and yet he was already the most important thing in his life.

He and Annabelle. Matt had looked at her, lying next to him in that hospital bed, and he had seen a different person. She had metamorphosed. He had thought he had loved her as much as he could but in the instant he met his son a new world had opened up to him. She was his wife and lover, his life partner, his best friend, and now she was the mother of his child. She had borne this child, given him this most precious thing. Without her there would be no Norman.

Without her, there would be nothing.

Without them both, his life would be meaningless.

Which he wished he could say. They were in the church – St Wilfrid's, the same one they had been married in – getting Norman christened, and he wanted to turn to his friends and family and tell them what the baby he was holding at the front of the church and the woman by his side meant to him.

He wouldn't, though.

He would think it, and hope Annabelle guessed it somehow, but he wouldn't say it. He wondered why not. Was it because he thought it was a sign of weakness? That it made him look vulnerable? He *was* vulnerable, and showing that would not be a sign of weakness, but of strength, strength he did not yet have.

Maybe next time.

'OK,' the vicar said. 'Could you hand Norman to me?'

She held out her hands and Matt placed Norman in them. He was asleep, and he twitched at the moment of transfer, then settled again.

'A beautiful child,' the vicar said. 'Congratulations. And sleeping too. Although that may not last.'

She held him close to the font and scooped up water from a pewter bowl. She poured it over his head.

'I baptize you in the name of the Father . . .'

Norman woke, and screwed up his face. She poured more water on him.

'. . . and of the Son . . .'

He started to cry, a plaintive noise that grew quickly into a wail. The vicar scooped up more water, and tipped it over his forehead. The crying got louder. Matt stepped forward, but Guy – Norman's godfather – put his hand on his forearm.

'It's OK,' Guy muttered. 'Nearly done.'

'. . . and of the Holy Spirit. Amen.' She smiled. 'There,' she said. 'He's awake. I'll pass him back to you.'

Matt took his son, and held him close to his chest. He kissed his head.

'It's OK,' he said. 'It's OK.'

Norman's cries stopped. Annabelle put her arm around him and kissed him on the cheek.

'You're the best dad ever,' she said. 'And one day Norman's going to get you a mug with it on to prove it.'

Sunday, 8 March 2020, 5.35 p.m.

Matt

He heard Annabelle shouting. He couldn't make out the words but there was no doubt it was her voice.

She was naked, and handcuffed. He stared at her naked back; he knew that body so well. He watched as she put her gown back on and the hooded figure handcuffed her. He started to run towards the car, but he stopped himself.

The kidnapper had made it very clear what would happen if he didn't stay put, and, as far as he could see there was no sign of the kids.

But Jesus Christ, it was hard to ignore her.

And what if it was all a lie? What if the kids weren't there? What if this was all a ploy to get Annabelle *and* the kids?

That fear had been at the back of his mind all along, and it suddenly lurched front and centre, bringing with it a racing heart and a sickening dread.

He groaned and sank to his knees. The ground was soft and cold. How had they been so stupid? It was obvious now that this had been the plan all along: take the kids, and use the promise of returning them to get hold of Annabelle as well.

There was still no sign of the kids. Annabelle shouted

again, and the kidnapper jumped forward. He put his hands around her throat, and the shouting stopped.

That was enough. He was going to go and get his family back. He stood up and looked around for a weapon. A stick, a rock. Anything. Nothing, if necessary. He had nothing to lose.

And then the kidnapper opened the rear door of the blue Golf and shoved Annabelle into the car. Seconds later, the car was driving away.

Matt sprinted after them. It was pointless; the car was gone, but he kept running anyway. When he reached the point where the car had been, he stood and looked wildly around.

To the right he saw his Land Rover. He ran towards it; the keys were on the back bumper. He snatched them up and unlocked the door, then yanked it open.

They were there. All three of them.

Molly in the middle. Keith on the far side. Norman right in front of him.

'Daddy,' Norman said. 'You came.'

'Of course I did. Of course I did.' He leaned into the car, grabbed Norman in a hug, then reached over the seat to Molly and Keith. 'My God. You're safe.'

'Where's Mum?' Norman said. 'We heard her shouting. Where is she?'

'She's—' Matt said. 'I'll tell you everything later. But for now we have to go.'

'I want Mum!' Keith said. 'Where did she go? She was here a second ago.'

'Can you get her?' Norman said. 'We want to see her.'

'I will. I promise. It's complicated—'

His phone rang. It was Rob.

'We're tracking them,' Rob said. 'Perfect visual. They're heading for the A49. We can cut through where you are and pick you up. Do you have the kids?'

'Yes.'

'They OK?'

'Seem so.'

'Good. Is your car there?' Rob said.

'Yes.'

'Leave it, there'll be forensics in it. We'll be there in minutes. Hang tight.'

The phone went dead.

'Dad?'

He turned. Norman was standing by the rear door.

'Where is she?' he said.

'I don't know. But we'll find her. I promise.' He held out his arms and hugged Norman. It felt wonderful to be with him again. 'I promise we'll find her.'

He hoped it was not a promise he was going to end up breaking, for his sake as much as the kids'.

2013: Christening Party

1

After the ceremony they went to the London Bridge Pub. Most of the guests from the christening were there, happy to have a Sunday afternoon drink with family and friends. These were the only times people saw each other these days – between kids and jobs and moves to new places there was not much room for nights in the pub.

Matt sipped a glass of red wine. Norman was asleep again, strapped to his chest in a baby carrier. He loved wearing his son; on week nights he strapped him on when he got back from work and walked around the house, and on weekends he took him for long hikes while Annabelle napped or went out with her friends. He walked along the canals and through little-used paths and snickets that led to remote churchyards and dense copses and abandoned barns. There was a Neolithic stone circle not too far from their house, which he had read about online and taken Norman to see. As they walked, he explained to his son what they were passing and why it mattered. At six months old it wasn't likely he would understand, but Matt was sure some of it was going in, one way or another.

Annabelle's brother, Mike, walked over. 'Let's have a photo

of the parents and godparents,' he said. 'Now a good time?'

He had offered to take photos; he had an interest in photography and an expensive camera, and had been snapping away throughout the ceremony.

'Sure,' Matt said.

'I'll round them up. You go and stand by the fireplace.'

Matt walked over. By the time he reached the fireplace, the others were on their way.

'Matt and Annie in the middle,' Mike said. 'Guy, you stand next to Annie and Miriam, and Tessa, you stand by Matt.'

Matt unclipped the baby carrier and took Norman out. He held him facing the camera. Mike took a few shots, then rotated the bezel of the lens and moved a few steps back. He took some more, then moved to the side.

'How about one with Annabelle holding Norman? And then Miriam, Tessa and Guy?'

Matt passed Norman to Annabelle and Mike took more photos. Then Miriam and Tessa had their turn.

'Only Guy left,' Mike said. Guy held out his hands and Tessa handed Norman to him. He held him away from his body, his hands under Norman's armpits.

'Here,' Matt said. 'Put him in the crook of your elbow.'

Guy held Norman a little closer. He was stiff and awkward. 'Not my strong suit,' he said. 'I like babies, but I don't have much experience. It's weird. You don't know how to hold them.'

'It comes easily,' Matt said. 'I had no idea before he was born, but you soon pick it up.'

'You're a natural,' Guy said. 'That's obvious. You were made to be a dad. I could see that from the start.' He paused, and looked over Matt's shoulder. He gave him a warning glance. 'Someone wants to say hi,' he said, his forehead creased in a frown.

Matt turned to see what had caught his attention. At first

he didn't recognize her. She was very thin and her hair was short, but after a few seconds he realized who it was.

'Lindsey,' he said. 'Hi.'

'I wanted to come and say congratulations,' she said. Her voice was slurred and her eyes were unfocused. It was obvious she was extremely drunk. Matt glanced at his watch. It was half past three in the afternoon.

'Thank you,' he said.

'I'm so pleased for you,' she said. The words were hard to make out. 'I always knew you'd have a good life.'

'Again, thanks,' Matt said.

'You got everything you wanted.' She swayed as she looked at him. 'Better off without me, weren't you? You were right to get rid of me. I'm a fucking hot mess.' Her voice rose at the end and more than a few heads turned to look.

Annabelle was standing with Miriam. She came over to Matt and put her hand on his back.

'Hi,' she said. 'I'm Annabelle.'

'I know who you are,' Lindsey said. 'And I want to say congratulations to you too.'

'Thank you,' Annabelle said. 'Remind me of your name again?'

'It's Lindsey.' She leaned forward, her eyes wide. 'Lindsey.'

Matt watched as Annabelle put it together. 'Oh,' she said. 'I see.'

'Yeah, you see. You remember me? I'm the sorry bitch you stole Matt from.' She paused. Matt could see the conflict play out on her face, see the desire to stay cool and in control fight with the anger.

The anger won.

'You slut,' Lindsey said. 'You *fucking* slut.'

'I'm sorry,' Guy said. 'But that's enough.' He put his hand on Annabelle's elbow. 'You and Matt go elsewhere. I'll deal with this.'

'Who the fuck are you?' Lindsey said, swivelling to Guy, her face livid. She was holding a bottle of Budweiser and Matt thought she might hit Guy with it.

'I'm a friend of Matt and Annabelle. This is an important day for them and it doesn't need to be ruined by you, or anyone else. So, if you wouldn't mind, please leave.'

'*If you wouldn't mind, please leave,*' Lindsey said, in a mocking tone. 'Who invited Prince fucking Charles? Fuck you, you posh cunt.'

She looked at Matt, then Annabelle, then Guy, and then back to Matt.

'Your turn will come,' she said. 'Mark my words. Your turn will come.'

A man appeared behind her. He was tall and wiry, curly brown hair poking out from under a baseball cap.

He put his hand on her shoulder; she started, then whipped around. As soon as she saw him, she started to sob.

'Hey,' he said. 'It's OK. Let's leave.' He pulled her close to him. 'Come on, petal,' he said. 'Time to go.'

He led her away from Matt. As they walked past Tessa, the man said something to her. Tessa touched him on the shoulder and gave a little shake of her head, then followed them to the door of the pub.

As they left, the man turned and stared at Matt, with an expression in his eyes that was something like hatred.

2

'Jesus,' Guy said. 'That was like a medieval fairy tale. Wicked witch turning up at the feast. Who was that?'

'An ex,' Matt said. 'From a long time ago.'

'Why was she here?' Annabelle said. 'Who told her?'

The door of the pub opened. Tessa came in and glanced at Matt. He caught her eye and then she looked away.

'Tessa?' he said. 'Did you tell her?'

'No,' Tessa said. 'Not exactly.'

'Or not at all?'

'Not exactly.'

'What does not exactly mean?' Annabelle said. There was an edge in her voice. She knew Tessa had remained friends with Lindsey after Matt had broken up with her. He had told her – perhaps it was a mistake – that Tessa had tried to persuade him to reconcile with Lindsey. It had led to the first real argument he and Annabelle ever had.

She's my sister, he'd said. *She's loyal to her friends. I know it's annoying. But that's all it is. Loyalty.*

She's trying to break us up. And she will, if you don't tell her to stop all this bullshit.

There was no way he was risking their relationship because

of Tessa's friendship with Lindsey, and he had told Tessa exactly that. She called Annabelle a bitch who didn't deserve her brother. He left her to cool off and things eventually settled down. Annabelle seemed to have forgiven her and moved on.

Still, there was an edge in their relationship that was never far from the surface. And right now it was in the open, given that Lindsey had just showed up in the pub after their first son's christening, apparently because of something Tessa had done.

'So?' Annabelle said. 'What does "not exactly" mean?'

She held up her hands. 'I saw her last week in town and she asked after Matt. I mentioned that you guys had a son, and then said, "The christening is next week actually, at St Wilfrid's." And she said, "I suppose you'll be at the pub afterwards for a drink?" and I said, "Yeah, that's the normal drill" or something like that.' She puffed out her cheeks. 'I had no idea she'd come. I didn't invite her.'

'For God's sake, Tessa,' Matt said. 'What were you thinking?'

'I'm sorry! I didn't *want* to ruin your christening. I mean, Jesus. It's not my fault she showed up, is it?'

Annabelle gave her a sweet smile. 'No, it isn't. Don't you worry about it. It's fine. I hope she's OK. She seemed to be struggling a bit. I mean, Matt and her broke up a long time ago. I'm surprised she's still thinking about it.'

Matt stuck out his bottom lip. 'I'm a very sought-after man,' he said. 'Losing me could scar a person for life. Once you've had sight of the mountaintop, life in the valleys is unbearable.'

Annabelle rolled her eyes. 'I think you know what I mean.'

'You're right,' Tessa said. 'She's had a really hard time. I don't know exactly what happened, but at one point she disappeared. She was living with her parents and just vanished. They found her a week later, in a homeless shelter in Birmingham.'

'Who was the guy?' Matt said.

'Her boyfriend. He's called Anton. They've been together a while. He's been good for her.'

'Are you still friends?' Annabelle said.

'Not as such,' Tessa said. 'But I stay in touch. And it's a small town. I've seen them out together. She was doing better, but from today's evidence she's had a relapse. Anton was upset about it.'

'I hope it works out for her,' Matt said. 'But I don't need her to be part of my life again.'

'No,' Annabelle said. 'That would not be good.'

Matt looked at his sister. 'So maybe don't share details of our private affairs in the future, OK?'

Sunday, 8 March 2020, 5.41 p.m.

She is mine, now.

It is done. Finally. She is in the back of the car.

Mine.

I can barely contain my excitement. I want to take off this hood and turn and smile at her and say, Look, it's me!

I want to see her reaction, I want to glory in the moment.

But I will have to wait for that. I want this to be as special as possible, and now is not the right time. I have set up the perfect tableau *at our destination.*

And I have waited this long. I can wait a little longer.

Matt

A few minutes later, two cars came through the gate and up the track. Mike and Tessa got out of the first one and sprinted over.

Mike grabbed Norman in a hug, then picked up Keith in one arm and Molly in the other.

'Oh my God,' he said. He wiped tears from his eyes. 'I'm so glad you're OK.'

Rob got out of the second car and beckoned to Matt. 'Let's go.'

Matt hesitated. He looked at his kids. Now he had them back, he did not want to let them out of his sight ever again. He took a deep breath. He had to. He had to get Annabelle back. Everything else – even the kids – had to wait.

'Come on,' Rob said. 'I'm sorry. But we have to go.'

Matt hugged all three of his children. 'Uncle Mike and Aunty Tessa will take you home. I'll be there soon. Take care of them until I'm back, OK?'

'No,' Keith said. 'I want you to stay here.'

He felt his heart breaking.

'I know. But I have to go, and I won't be long.'

'Can we come?' Norman said.

'Not this time.'

'We could help,' Norman said.

'Matt,' Rob interrupted. 'We have to go.'

'I'm going to get Mum,' Matt said.

'You're going to get Mum?' Keith said.

'Yes.'

'OK,' Keith said. 'Then you can go.'

Annabelle

She was wedged in a tight gap. When he had shoved her into the car he had pushed her down between the front and back seats; she had heard a click and the front seats had pushed back, trapping her in the footwell.

She supposed he didn't want anyone seeing a hooded person through the car window. It was simple, but effective.

And very painful. There was something pressing hard into her chest. It hurt, but worse was her arm. It was twisted in an unnatural position, and the pain was steadily increasing as the seconds ticked by.

The engine started and the car began to move. For a few minutes the road was bumpy, but then it got smoother. They must be on a main road. She wondered in which direction they were heading, and whether, somewhere above them, a drone was tracking their movements.

She hoped so. She hoped they arrived at their destination soon, and then Rob and Mike and Matt and the police and whoever else they could muster would come and rescue her and she'd see her kids again, her amazing, wonderful kids.

That is, if they were still alive. All she had seen was the

car. She had been hoping for a shout in answer to hers, but there had been nothing.

There was no proof her kids were OK. And that made the pain in her arm feel like nothing.

And it made her dangerous. Because once she felt there was nothing to lose, there was no telling what she would do.

She felt the car slowing to a halt and heard another vehicle pass. Traffic lights, maybe. Then the car started moving again and she was pushed to the right as they made a turn.

She had been trying to map their location in her mind, but already it was pointless. She had no idea where they were.

She lay back, her head resting on something hard. Less than two feet from her was the person who had kidnapped her. She still had no idea who it was, or why they wanted her. It was possible it was a fan, but how would they have been able to plan this? How would they have had Matt's phone number?

The car slowed to a halt again. Another traffic light? She rubbed her head on the seat. The hood lifted, and she managed to shake it off. She tried to twist her body free.

She was pinned in position. Her shoulder ached. This was pointless.

It was also an opportunity to do something, and it could be her last one. If she could get herself free before they started moving, she might be able to disable the kidnapper somehow, or kick out a window and shout for help.

Anything. She didn't care how much it hurt or how badly injured she might get. Anything was better than this.

She pushed her feet against the side of the car and arched her back.

Her arm moved into a more comfortable position and she felt a bit of space open up around her.

She tensed every muscle in her body and pushed again.

And she felt herself move.

2014

The Knot – her third book – had been published a month before. It was the story of Maxine, happily married to Nigel, both of them hoping for a child. Then, out of the blue, she falls ill. Very ill. She has a year – maybe two – to live. Maxine is forced to assess her true priorities and realizes – to her surprise – that her husband is not one of them. She does not want to spend her final year with a man she does not love.

Her husband, however, does not agree. He is glad, though, to know what she truly feels about him.

Because it turns out he is not what he seems, and neither is her diagnosis. Someone is weaving a knot about her and it will not be easy to disentangle herself.

It had been well reviewed and she had been asked to come to a large bookshop in Manchester to do a reading. She was reluctant; the readings she had done in the past had been sparsely attended, but the shop owner said she expected quite a few to be there, so she had decided to accept.

And it had been worth it. There were about fifty people there and most of them had bought a book for her to sign. She worked through the queue of people until there was just one person left. She looked at him, and realized his face was familiar.

It took her a moment to place him, and then he spoke.

'I was waiting till the end. So we could talk.' He took out

a small, hand-bound book from the pocket of his trench coat. 'I've got another book out too.'

'I remember you,' she said. 'You're a poet, right? You came to a reading when my first book was out.'

A wide grin spread across his face. 'I gave you my first book. We swapped. Did you read my poems?'

She hadn't – when she got home she had taken the book he had given her out of her bag and put it down on a shelf and hadn't seen it since, but she wasn't about to say that, so she told him, 'I really enjoyed it.'

'Which was your favourite? Of my poems?'

'Gosh,' she said. 'I don't know. I did enjoy them, though.'

He flinched, his left eye twitching. 'You don't have a favourite?'

'It was a long time ago,' Annabelle said. 'I don't remember all that well. I barely remember what I read last week! But I do remember enjoying them.' He didn't look convinced and she decided to change the subject. 'Which is your favourite?'

'Of my poems?'

'Yes. Do you have one you like the most?'

'"The Nightingale",' he said. 'It's about a beautiful bird trapped in a cage which is eventually set free.' He leaned over the desk. 'It's a bit like your new book.'

'I suppose so,' Annabelle said. 'Have you read it?'

He shook his head. 'I read the reviews. I haven't got my copy yet.' He put the hand-bound book on the table. 'Can we swap again?'

'Absolutely,' Annabelle said. She took a book from the pile and opened it. 'Remind me of your name again?'

His eye twitched again. 'Carl Jameson. Can you write "To Carl, with thanks from one writer to another." That's what I put in yours. Except not to Carl. To Annabelle.'

She wrote the words he had requested then closed the book and handed it to him.

'I can't wait to read your new poems,' she said. 'Congratulations.'

He clutched the book to his chest.

'Same to you,' he said.

Sunday, 8 March 2020, 5.44 p.m.

Matt

Matt sat in the back seat. Brenda was in the front alongside Rob. She had a tablet on her lap. The screen showed a car – Annabelle's blue Golf – driving along the road. She had another tablet open showing a map with a dot moving across it.

This was *working*.

Matt watched as the Golf paused at a traffic light.

'How far is that from us?' Matt said.

'About half a mile, as the crow flies,' Rob said. 'But we have to get onto the A49 first, which means heading to a junction a bit south of here, then travelling north to them. Maybe a mile in total.'

Matt glanced at the speedometer. They were going sixty miles per hour, so they would cover that mile in about a minute, but presumably the traffic light would change, maybe in half that time.

Which would leave them half a mile away.

Closer.

'Let's go,' Matt said. 'Maybe we can get there before they move on.'

Rob accelerated. He felt his hope rise. This was the chance they had been waiting for.

This was it.
His phone buzzed.
It was a text from Guy.

How's it going? Just finished up the literary festival and wanted to check in.

Matt replied.

We have the kids.

Thank God. Annabelle?

With the kidnapper. But we have a plan.

What is it? You don't have to tell me, if you're in the middle of it. I'm just worried about her.

I got someone with a professional drone and she's tracking the car. But I have to go. Going to call the police.

Good luck. Keep me posted.

He put his phone down and turned back to the screen. The traffic light turned green.
The car didn't move. Maybe Annabelle had found a way to stop it.
'Speed up,' he said. 'Faster.'

Annabelle

She relaxed, resting her muscles. She could feel the reduced pressure in her arm and the relief was blessed. She wanted to wallow in it, but there was no time.

She drew her strength into her legs and pushed as hard as she could, then harder again.

And then she started to slide up the back seat.

She stopped and moved her arms, testing that she was free.

What was she going to do? She looked at the door, her eyes drawn to the handle. She should wait a moment, recover her strength, then dash out of the door and get away from here. She didn't know where she was but it didn't matter. Once she was out of this car she would be free and she could deal with whatever came next.

It would be child-locked. The kidnapper would have seen to that.

Her only option was a direct attack. She gave a weak groan, like someone in distress, and manoeuvred herself slowly and silently into a crouching position.

Then she launched herself at the back of the black hood, smashing her elbow against the driver's head.

It banged hard against the steering wheel and she fell forward, her hips and legs getting caught on the passenger seat. She lifted her arm, remembering what Brenda had told her. *Hard as you can. Don't hold back. You'll only get one chance.*

She swung, and the kidnapper slipped away from her, twisting in the seat. One hand shot up and grabbed her around the neck. The other slammed into her sternum and pushed her slowly backwards.

The hand around her neck started to squeeze.

She looked out of the window. Maybe someone would be seeing this.

There was no one. She watched the traffic light turn green.

'Sorry,' a low, rasping voice said, and then the world went black.

PART THREE

Sunday, 8 March 2020, 5.50 p.m.

Why did she do that? Why?

It is so irritating. I did not want to hurt her, not at all, but she gave me no choice. Was I supposed to let her hit me? What if someone saw? This would all be over. She would have ruined it.

Stupid Annabelle. Stupid, stupid *Annabelle.*

She could have made this easy, but now she will have to suffer. I cannot risk that again. Maybe she is a bit confused. I will explain it to her and she will forgive me. She will understand.

But I am not sure I do.

I am left with a question: why did she do that? Why did she try to ruin this?

It is not what I expected.

And that makes me nervous.

Annabelle

It was the pain in her shoulder that brought her round. At first she just had the sensation that something was hurting, that maybe she was sleeping awkwardly, lying on her arm in an uncomfortable position. Then she started to think no, it was worse than that, it really hurt, and then she was not sleeping at all.

Because the pain in her shoulder wasn't bad any more. It was *excruciating*.

It all came back to her: the attempt to attack the driver, the hands around her neck, the certainty that she was being choked to death, and then the fade to black.

She opened her eyes. She was still in the car, wedged in behind the seats. Her hands were still cuffed, although her right arm was twisted, her elbow caught between the corner of the front seat and the frame of the car.

Which was the cause of the pain in her shoulder; her elbow was pulling it away from her body.

She lifted her arm an inch, intending to bring it closer to her ribs and relieve the agony, but a sharp, searing, *unbelievable* pain ripped through her shoulder.

It felt like the tissues and muscles and ligaments in her shoulder were being torn apart, and it *fucking* hurt.

She let out a groan, the gag still in her mouth, then used her left arm to try and lever herself up a few inches. She had to do something to lessen the pressure in her shoulder.

It worked, a little, but now she was leaning on her good arm, which she would not be able to do for long. She turned so that her weight was on her hips, and screamed – with the gag it came out as a kind of grunt – as her right arm did not follow.

Bones in her shoulder moved. She felt the top of her arm press against her ribs.

Which should not be happening. Her shoulder was not in the place it was supposed to be.

She twisted her head and looked up. The back of the kidnapper's hooded head was visible.

'My arm,' she tried to say. 'It's broken.'

All that came out was unintelligible garbage.

The head tilted and turned. The face was hidden under the hood.

'Help,' she said. 'Help me.'

There was no response.

Beneath her the chassis of the car hummed. It felt like they were moving quickly. She glanced at the window. Overhead lights passed by at short, regular intervals.

They were on the motorway.

Which meant the drone could not keep up with them. Their plan had assumed they would stay on back roads, but the kidnapper had gone on the motorway after all.

Which meant she was on her own.

Although maybe not. If Matt knew the drone would lose them, he would call the police, and the police would know which motorway they were on, and could find her. Block the exits. Anything.

That was what Rob had said. He had said *motorways aren't safe. Not enough ways off. It's easy to apprehend someone on a motorway.*

So even though the drone would have lost them, it was good they were on a motorway.

But she was still shoved in the back of her car, her shoulder in pieces. A thudding panic joined the pain and the edges of her vision darkened.

The world began to swim. She felt herself slipping away. She let herself; it was blessed relief.

Matt

On the screen he watched the car pull onto the M56.

'Shit,' Matt said. 'They're going on the motorway.'

'What?' Rob replied. 'We're going to lose them.'

'You said they wouldn't do that,' Matt said, fighting the urge to shout at him. 'You said they would avoid motorways.'

'Looks like I was wrong,' Rob said. 'Call the police. Now. Tell them what's going on, and where they are.'

'M56, direction Manchester, just joined at junction ten,' Brenda said. 'Tell them that.'

Matt picked up his phone and dialled 999.

'Emergency, which service do you require? Fire, police or ambulance?' the dispatcher said, her voice brisk and calm.

'Police. It's urgent.'

Another voice came on the line. This time it was a man. 'Hello. What is the nature of your emergency?'

'It's a kidnapping,' Matt said. 'It's complicated.'

There was pause. When the man spoke again his tone was more urgent. 'OK. What is the location of the emergency?'

'It's not fixed. I'm in a car. We're following the kidnapper. They have my wife.'

'Sir,' the man said. 'This is not a hoax, I hope?'

'No!' Matt said. 'And it'll take a long time to explain. Time we don't have. My kids were kidnapped and the ransom was my wife. We were following the car she's in, but we lost it.'

'Where exactly are you, sir?' the man said.

'On the A49, heading towards the M56,' Matt said. 'That's where the car went. It's on the motorway, heading towards Manchester.'

'Can you repeat that?'

'The car we are following – the car with my wife in it – just went onto the M56 at junction ten, and is heading towards Manchester. But we can't see it any more. Our drone can't keep up.'

'Your drone?'

'Never mind. It's a blue Golf.' He gave the registration. 'You need to find it. Soon.'

'What's your name, sir?'

'Matt Westbrook.'

'And your address?'

'Twenty-four Pepper Avenue, Stockton Heath.'

'I hope this is not a hoax, Mr Westbrook.'

Matt took a deep breath. 'Look,' he said. 'It's urgent. And it isn't a hoax.'

'OK,' he said. 'We have your number. I'll put out an alert. We'll do everything we can.'

Matt put the phone down.

Rob glanced at him. 'There's a fair possibility it ends here,' he said. 'Going on the motorway is a big mistake. There are cops on that motorway right now and there are cameras on every exit. There's nowhere they can hide.'

'I hope you're right,' Matt said. 'Because if not, I'm getting the feeling I'll never see her alive again.'

Annabelle

When she came round this time, she realized the car was no longer moving. The searing pain in her shoulder, however, was ever present.

She opened her eyes. It was dark out, although there was the glow of lights somewhere outside.

The lock clicked and the car door opened, then the front seat moved forward and the pressure in her shoulder eased. The hooded figure appeared above her.

Two hands reached down and grabbed her under the armpits. Her shoulder screamed in agony and she grunted, the ball gag muffling the sound.

'Sorry you're hurt.' The voice was gruff and forced, like someone trying to disguise how they sounded. There was something in it she recognized, but it eluded her.

The kidnapper dragged her out of the car. They were in a car park, outdoors and next to a white van. The side panel was open; she was shoved inside.

She lay on the metal floor as the door slammed shut. The floor was cold; she curled into a ball to keep herself as warm as she could.

The door slammed shut.

Her right shoulder throbbed, but at least in this position there was nothing pressing against it. The pain began to subside to a bearable level.

After about a minute, the door opened. The kidnapper was silhouetted in the frame.

For a moment, she thought she recognized the silhouette. Again she had the feeling that there was something familiar about it; again she couldn't quite grasp the knowledge. It slithered just under the surface, elusive.

The kidnapper stepped inside and clicked on a torch. Three dirty yellow straps were hanging from a hook on the wall.

The kidnapper sniffed, then gestured for her to get into a sitting position, before dragging her alongside the strap and pulling it across her arms and chest. Once the strap was cinched tight, it was secured with a buckle.

She breathed out, the air forced from her lungs; when she tried to inhale she could only take a shallow breath.

The next strap also went into a hook, then over her thighs, securing them flat to the floor. The third strap went around her ankles.

The kidnapper opened the side panel, stepped out into the car park, and was gone.

Matt

They sped along the motorway, well above the speed limit, flashing past car after car.

None of them was Annabelle's blue Golf.

Up ahead was the blue motorway sign for junction nine. Matt shook his head.

'Shit,' he said. 'They could have gone off there.'

Rob nodded. 'It's possible. They're moving too fast, so without the visuals from the drone we've got no way of knowing where they are. But my bet is they'll have stayed on.'

'In about ten miles this motorway runs out and we'll be in Manchester,' Brenda said. 'And then they could be anywhere. I think we should pull off and wait. Let the police do the searching. Plus I need to land my drone. You need to stop soon, or you'll be buying my boss some new kit.'

'I don't give a fuck about the drone!' Matt said. 'I want to find my wife!'

'She's right. There's nothing we can do now, mate,' Rob said. 'Time to let the professionals have a go.'

Matt stared out of the window. He knew Rob had a point, but the thought of stopping made him feel sick. At least if he was still looking for her he was doing something. Stopping meant accepting she was gone.

Which she was.

They had tried, but they had failed.

Already he was wondering if they could have done something different, something better.

Probably. And he knew he would never stop wondering what.

But it wouldn't change anything.

Annabelle was gone.

Now the only hope she had was the police.

Annabelle

She wasn't sure how long she lay in the van. More than a few minutes, for sure, and less than an hour, but other than that she couldn't tell. It was dark and silent and freezing and smelled of oil and grease.

And her shoulder was causing serious pain. Now she was still she could feel the bone at the top of her arm – she had no idea what it was called – pressing against the side of her chest. She tried to brace it against the yellow strap and push it back, but as soon as she did the pain flared up, white-hot.

The only relief was that it still moved, so it wasn't dislocated.

Once she heard a car, and she tried to bang against the floor and sides of the van, but the straps held her motionless, which was presumably what they were for. The kidnapper really had thought of everything.

What was not obvious was why.

And when she thought of the options the pain in her shoulder seemed irrelevant, because they were all horrifying.

Torture. Rape. Murder. She tensed her whole body to try

and contain the panic, but she could feel her mind fraying. Every one of those possibilities was beyond horrific.

The front of the van opened. It shook as someone got in. The engine started, and they began to move.

There was a sliding sound and a panel between her and the front opened. The kidnapper looked back at her, then a hand snaked out and removed the ball gag. It fell to the floor.

'Who are you?' she said, her voice hoarse. 'Why are you doing this?' And why had the ball gag been removed? It was almost as though, now no one could hear her, her captor wanted to minimize her discomfort.

There was no answer. The panel slammed shut and they began to move. She slumped against the wall.

So they had switched vehicles to a van. That was the plan. They had pulled off the motorway and parked next to this van to put anyone following them off the scent.

But there was a flaw in the plan. It would be easy enough for the police – she hoped Matt had called them – to track her car as it exited the motorway – there were cameras everywhere – and so they would know where it went.

Say, into a car park.

And if they're smart, Annabelle thought. *They'll see this van leave the same car park and wonder who was in it.*

It was a slim hope, but it was hope nonetheless, and, for a moment she felt better.

She rested her head against the side of the van. Her shoulder pulsed with pain.

Suddenly, the hope vanished. Her chest tightened and she was overwhelmed by panic. Adrenaline flooded her muscles and she felt a surge of strength. For a moment she was sure she could break free of the straps, then she could open the hatch and reach through and throttle the kidnapper, or open the door and leap out when the van was stationary.

She clenched her fists and strained against the straps.

They did not move. Of course they didn't. The idea she would have a sudden access of strength that would snap them was foolish. This wasn't a movie.

This was real. This was actually happening.

The panic gripped harder. She had no control, no options, and her children were gone. And she still had no answer to the question: why do all this? Why not just grab her off the street? And why her?

There had to be a reason, and that was what frightened her the most. There was something huge behind all this.

A scream rose in her throat, and, once it started, she could not stop it.

Wynne

Detective Inspector Jane Wynne took the call in her kitchen. She had just put two glasses next to a bottle of Italian red wine – she had no idea what it was but it had cost £15 so she hoped it was good, since her guest had mentioned she was a wine drinker – and was peeling an onion to start making her signature spaghetti bolognese, when her phone rang.

She knew the number. It was Detective Sergeant Michael Dudek, newly promoted and her partner for the last six months.

She glanced at the time. It was nearly 6 p.m.

She didn't want to answer it. She knew what it meant. It meant the red wine would go undrunk and the spaghetti uneaten.

But she had to. That was the job. Not for the first time she wondered whether it was worth it.

She answered the call.

'Dudek,' she said. 'How wonderful to hear from you.'

'Right,' Dudek said. 'Sorry to bother you, boss. But I thought you'd want to hear this.'

'What is it?'

'It's pretty unusual,' Dudek said. 'I've never come across anything quite like it.'

That was not something cops often said. Wynne felt a rising curiosity.

'OK,' she said. 'Sounds intriguing. Tell me more.'

'It's a kidnap,' Dudek said. 'A really weird kidnap.'

'Weird? How?'

'It's a mother of three kids, Annabelle Westbrook. I don't have all the details, but she was the ransom—'

'What do you mean, she was the ransom?'

'Like I said, I don't have all the details, but it seems she was the price of her own kids being returned. She went with her husband to the swap.'

'She did *what*?' Wynne said.

'She went to the place the kidnapper told her to. She and her husband and took an ex-cop and tried to track the kidnapper's vehicle with a drone. But they lost them.'

'Are they insane?' Wynne said. 'Why didn't they call us?'

'I don't know. But they didn't. Anyway, the kidnapper took the wife and the husband tracked them as far as the M56, heading towards Manchester.'

'How long ago was this?'

'About thirty minutes since it was called in. We put cars on the exits to try and pick them up.'

'And?'

'They'd already left the M56. Junction nine.'

'How do you know?'

'They're on camera. Clear as day.'

'Where did they go?'

'Into the truck stop. There's a big car park there.'

'Let me get this right,' Wynne said. 'Someone kidnapped three kids and held them ransom. The price was their mother, who accepted this and made a plan for her husband to follow her with a drone?'

249

'Right.'

'But he lost her, because they went onto the motorway. And now they're in a truck stop.'

'You got it.'

'Presumably they went there to switch cars?' Wynne said.

'That was what I thought,' Dudek replied.

'So we just stop every car that comes out. And look on camera for any that already left. Focus on vans, that kind of thing.'

'That was the plan,' Dudek said.

'Was?'

'Was,' he confirmed. 'Because a few minutes after Annabelle Westbrook's blue Golf went into the truck stop, it came out again.'

'And? Where did it go?'

'Towards High Legh. We lost them along the way, though. It's a country road and there are no cameras.'

'Shit.'

'But there's good news.'

'Which is?'

'There's nowhere to turn off that road before you *do* get to a camera, at an all-night garage. And they haven't passed there yet.'

'So they're somewhere on that stretch of road?'

'It looks like it. They've been there for about half an hour.'

'Are there houses? Places to hide?'

'A few. And there's a pub. We're heading there first.'

Wynne looked at the bottle of wine. She put the cork back in. She could call Sheila and postpone.

'What's the name of the pub?' she said. 'I'll meet you there.'

Matt

Rob pulled up outside the house and parked next to Mike's Volvo. The Land Rover was still where the kidnapper had left it. Matt supposed the police would want it for forensic stuff; he didn't want to ever see it again.

'Sorry,' Rob said. 'But it'll work out.'

Matt opened the door. 'Thanks.'

'Be in touch if you need anything.'

'I will.'

He got out of the car and walked towards the front door. It opened before he reached it.

Norman stood there, his hand on the Yale lock, silhouetted in the door frame.

'Daddy,' he said. 'Where were you? Did you find her?'

Matt held his arms out and grabbed him in a tight hug. 'I was out,' he muttered into his eldest son's hair. 'Not yet. But I will. I promise.' He blinked away his tears. He didn't want to alarm his son. 'How about you? Are you OK?'

'Yes,' Norman said. 'I'm fine.'

Matt took a deep breath. 'Were you hurt?'

Norman shook his head. 'No.'

'What happened?'

'We were in a van. There was a tablet. We just stayed in there. We got food and stuff.'

'OK. You might have to tell someone about it.'

'The police?'

'Yes.'

'To help them find Mum?'

Matt was surprised Norman had figured out what was going on so easily, but then he was often struck by how much his eldest son understood about the world. He assumed it was always that way with the firstborn; they grew up so much faster than you anticipated, so you were always surprised by what they were capable of.

Which was good, because what was coming was going to test all of them.

'That's right,' he said. 'To help them find Mum.'

'OK. I'll talk to them.'

'Where are Keith and Molly?'

'Watching TV.'

'How are they?'

Norman shrugged. 'They're good. When we were – when we were gone, I told them everything was OK. Molly really missed you and Mum, so I made up stories. About animals and things. They were pretty good!'

'How was Keith?' His middle son was quiet, and very sensitive. With Norman you knew what he was feeling, because he told you. Keith, though, bottled it all up.

'OK,' Norman said. 'I know you and Mum worry about him, so I made sure he was all right.'

Matt's throat tightened. 'You're fantastic,' he said. 'Thank you for taking care of them. They must have been scared.'

Norman looked at him. He hesitated, and his lips started to quiver. 'I was scared, too.'

He pulled his son closer. 'I'm here now. And everything's going to be fine.'

'But what about Mum?' Norman said. 'We need her.'

'We do,' Matt said. 'And we'll find her. The police are looking.'

'How do you know we'll find her?' Norman said.

He blinked. 'Because we have to,' he said.

His phone rang. It was not a number he knew; it could be the kidnapper. His shoulders tensed.

'Go and watch TV,' he said. He didn't want Norman to hear him talking to the kidnapper. 'I'll be there in a minute.'

Norman gave him a searching look, then walked towards the living room. Matt answered the call and lifted the phone to his ear.

'Hello,' he said. 'Matt Westbrook.'

He was expecting a man's voice, perhaps with a new ransom demand, but it was a woman who spoke.

'Mr Westbrook? This is Detective Inspector Jane Wynne. I'm in charge of your wife's case. I wanted to give you an update.'

'There's an update?' he said. 'Did you find her?'

'Yes, after a fashion. Your wife's car left the M56 and went into the truck stop at Lymm. We have it entering on CCTV.'

'Is that where she is? Did you find her?'

'Not exactly. Her car left a few minutes later. We tracked it to a relatively small area.'

'Where?'

'On the road leading to High Legh. We're pretty sure they set off in that direction and stopped en route. There's a camera at a garage along that road and they haven't gone past it. So the car is somewhere on a short stretch of that road.'

Matt tried to quell the swelling hope. 'Are you going to look?'

'I'm on my way there now.' DI Wynne paused. 'I want to

be clear. We don't know what we'll find. It's just a lead, at this point. But I want you to know we're doing all we can.'

'Thank you,' Matt said. 'Do you want me to come there?'

'Not yet. I'll call you as soon as we know anything. And I'm going to need to get your version of events, Mr Westbrook, and to talk to your children. I'll be in touch soon.'

'OK,' Matt said. 'Good luck.'

Sunday, 8 March 2020, 6.40 p.m.

Wynne

1

Wynne's phone said the pub was a mile further up the road. She was behind a white van; they passed a forty-mile per hour sign and it sped up to exactly forty. A white van driver with a strict respect for speed limits. Rare, in her experience. She chided herself for the prejudice.

Not because she cared about prejudice in itself, but because prejudice led to bad assumptions, and they led to bad detective work.

Half a minute later she turned into the pub car park. It was quite full; there were a lot of people visible through the pub windows.

At the rear of the car park she saw a squad car. DS Dudek's red Vauxhall Astra was parked next to it. She slowed to a stop and got out.

Dudek was standing by a blue Golf with two uniformed officers. He turned to her and gave her a thumbs down.

'This is the car,' he said. 'But she's not here. It's empty.'

'They could be in the pub?' one of the officers, a man in his late twenties, said.

'Possible,' Dudek said. 'But my guess is they aren't having a leisurely drink while the kidnapper works out the next stage in his dastardly plan.'

'Worth checking, though,' Wynne said. 'Do you have a photo of Mrs Westbrook?'

The officer nodded.

'Show it around. See if anyone saw her. Also ask if anyone saw the car arrive.' She looked around. The Golf was parked in the corner, maybe fifty yards from the pub. 'No doubt they parked here for a reason,' she said. 'But someone may have seen them. You can both go. It looks busy in there.'

The two officers set off for the pub. Wynne looked at Dudek.

'So why do you think the kidnapper would have driven it here, having first pulled into the car park of the truck stop?' she said.

'Because he realized there was CCTV at the truck stop.'

'You're assuming it's a he,' Wynne said. 'But let's go with that for now. If he knew there was CCTV at the truck stop, then he must have realized the CCTV would show him leaving,' Wynne said. 'So he's back where he started.'

'So he comes to the pub,' Dudek said. 'To switch vehicles.'

'No,' she said. 'Not here. He'd have to drag a woman – either unconscious, or, if she was awake, struggling and screaming – from one vehicle to another. It's too public.'

'So why come here?' Dudek said.

Beyond the car park was a field. Wynne gestured across it. 'Maybe he took her that way. On foot.' She paused. 'But that raises the same objection. If she's unconscious, he'd have to carry her. And if she's conscious and on foot, why wouldn't she resist? Try to draw attention? Or just run into the pub. There's something we're missing.'

She looked around the car park. She pictured the blue Golf pulling in and driving to the far corner of the car park. The driver's side door opening and a figure in a hoodie getting out, then opening the rear door and reaching in to pull out a slumped, unconscious body.

That was impossible. Far too risky.

She pictured the kidnapper opening the car door and ushering Annabelle Westbrook out, then leading her over the wall and into the field.

Impossible, too. Even if she was drugged it would draw attention.

So if both were impossible, what did that leave?

It hit her, and she closed her eyes.

'Shit,' she said. 'I can't believe we missed this.'

'What did we miss?'

'Think about it. There's no way he could have brought her here. What would he do with her? It's too public. Which leaves only one option: he didn't bring her here.'

'But the car's here.'

'Yes. But she wasn't. The whole thing was a diversion. Annabelle was never here.'

'But the kidnapper was,' Dudek said. 'Unless someone else drove the car.'

'No one else drove the car,' Wynne said. 'He was here. Just not with her.'

'Then where was she?'

'The truck stop,' Wynne said. 'There'll be a corner that isn't covered by the cameras. He had a car – or a van, something like that – waiting there, and transferred her. Then drove her Golf here, and walked back. It's what? Two miles? So at a brisk walk that's twenty-five, thirty minutes?'

She looked at her watch.

'What time did the Golf leave the truck stop?'

'About fifty minutes ago.'

'So he arrived here forty-five minutes ago, then walked back. We need footage of every vehicle leaving the truck stop in the last twenty minutes. And any people entering the truck stop on foot, although I'm guessing he found a way in that the cameras can't see.'

'What I don't understand,' Dudek said, 'is why? Why do all this?'

'Because the kidnapper knows we know the first car he took her in, and we'd have every traffic cop in the country looking for it as soon as Annabelle Westbrook's husband called us. He needed to switch.'

'But now we'll track every car – or van – that left the truck stop. It'll be harder, but we can do it.'

'I know,' Wynne said. 'So maybe this bastard's not as clever as he thinks he is. But that's good news for us, and bad news for him. Let's go. We need to review that footage.'

2

'Pause it there,' Wynne said. 'Now go back a few seconds. Play.'

They watched a white van, old-ish, nondescript and unmarked, pull out of the truck stop. It headed in the direction of the pub – the Bear's Paw – they had just left. It moved steadily, observing all posted speed limits.

'That's it,' Wynne said. She clenched her fist. The time stamp was 6.40 p.m. Right as she was arriving at the pub. 'That's them. I saw that van. I was behind it.'

'We can't be sure,' Dudek said. 'There are other vans.'

'True,' Wynne said. 'But I'll bet you'll see all the others leaving the truck stop ten or twenty minutes after they arrive. Thirty at most. We need to check them all, obviously. But this one you'll spot arriving a day or two ago.'

'We'll check,' Dudek said. He rewound the footage until the van was back on screen. 'And in the meantime we'll issue an alert for that van.' He wrote down the licence plate. 'And we'll pull up the names of everyone who's ever owned it.'

Annabelle

The road grew bumpy. The jolting sent bolts of pain through her shoulder, but the yellow straps made it impossible to move to a more comfortable position.

She had hope, though. The police would have found her car and figured out what had happened, and then they would see the van leaving on CCTV. They'd find her. She believed they would. She *had* to believe they would.

And in the meantime, there was the agony.

From the bumps, she assumed they were on a quiet country track. It made sense; why not hide away? Eventually, though, they'd have to go out on the open roads, and then – surely – someone would spot them.

The van slowed to a stop. She heard the front door open and close, and then the panel door slid along its rails and the night air flooded in.

The kidnapper stood, face hidden under the hood, and lifted a hand, thumb up, then down.

It was an enquiry as to whether she was OK.

She shook her head.

'Doctor,' she said. 'I need a doctor.'

The kidnapper bent down and undid the yellow strap that

was around her chest then undid the handcuffs and gently moved her right shoulder.

She opened her eyes wide in agony.

'No,' she said. 'Please. Leave it.'

She saw a syringe in the kidnapper's hand; it was unsheathed and she felt it prick her skin.

Whatever was in the syringe did not take long to work; within minutes she started to feel woozy. The kidnapper unstrapped her and guided her to the panel door of the van.

She looked out. They were on a scruffy piece of wasteland. There was a pond to their right, the surface oily in the moonlight, and an agricultural structure to the left.

Next to the van was an Audi estate.

Had she seen that car before? She thought she had, but her mind was going foggy and she couldn't place it. It was hard to think. Hard to know.

But what she did know, through the fog of the drug, was that all hope was gone. The police would be looking for the van, which was why they were switching to the Audi.

The boot clicked open and a hand gently pushed her into a sitting position, then tipped her in. She did as she was told, her mind crying out for sleep.

The kidnapper reached behind her and brought out a pillow then tucked it under her head. It was an oddly tender gesture.

Which was her last thought, before she slipped into unconsciousness.

This is not what I wanted, and I am annoyed.

Yes, it has gone well, in the sense that it worked, but everything I do works. I need more than that.

I want it to be perfect.

A work of art. A testament to my genius.

So yes, it went as planned. I took the Golf to the pub, then walked back to the van. They'll see that leaving on CCTV, but they'll never find it, and if they do, so what? We're in the Audi.

And now we are on the way to our final destination.

But there was one imperfection spoiling it all.

I hurt her.

Yes, she attacked me, so it's really her fault, but still: I did not want to hurt her.

I wanted her to be comfortable until we reached the final destination, when I could reveal myself to her. It would have been the perfect ending.

And beginning.

Yes, I could have avoided all this by telling her everything as soon as she was in the car, but I wanted more than that.

I wanted it to be extra-special. That – if anything – is my failing. I wanted it to be too good.

I am too good.

But that is not what happened. I will make it up to her, though. And this time it will *be perfect.*

Monday, 9 March 2020, 8 a.m.

Wynne

Detective Inspector Wynne studied Matt Westbrook closely. He was haggard and drawn. He looked like he hadn't slept, which was more than likely.

He sat on the couch in his living room and rubbed his eyes.

'So,' she said. 'You and your wife had no ideas who this might be?'

'None,' he said. 'When we found out it was a ransom, we assumed someone wanted money – and that they'd made a mistake targeting us, since we don't have enough to make this worthwhile. But when we found out the ransom was Annabelle . . .' His voice tailed off and he shrugged. 'We had no idea who it could be.'

'And you have thought through all areas of your lives? Family, friends, work? Nothing unusual springs to mind?'

Matt Westbrook started to shake his head, then hesitated.

'There's nothing, really,' he said. 'But there were some weird emails, right before we got married.'

'Emails?' Dudek asked. 'From who?'

'They were anonymous. Saying things like "you don't have to go through with this". That kind of thing.'

Wynne looked at Dudek. 'And you have no idea who sent them?'

'None. They stopped, and we didn't think too much about them. We thought maybe it was a stupid joke.'

'They stopped?' Wynne said. 'Do you still have them?'

'We looked. They're gone.'

'Good to know,' Dudek said. 'But it doesn't help much.'

'No,' Wynne said. 'But it is interesting. If the emails are linked, then this dates back to the time of Mr and Mrs Westbrook's wedding.'

'If,' Dudek said. 'We don't know they're linked.'

'True,' Wynne said. 'There's something else I'd like to explore. Mrs Westbrook is an author?'

'Yes,' Matt said.

'I assume you considered that it might be a fan?'

'We talked about it, but it didn't help. It could be anyone. And whoever's behind this knew so much about us. My phone number, where we live. The kids' names. It seemed more likely it was someone who knows us.'

'That information is relatively simple to get hold of.'

'You think it was a fan?' Matt Westbrook said.

'If it was someone you know, that would be easy to find out. Whoever it was would have to have been missing from their day-to-day lives for the last forty-eight hours, and that would stand out. So I think it is very possible it is a fan. Or someone outside your circle of friends. But I know that doesn't help.'

Matt flinched. 'It could be anyone,' he said.

'Yes, but we have the details of the van,' she said. 'That's the main thing at the moment. Do you happen to know of any fans she has interacted with? Does she have Twitter, Facebook? A website?'

'All of them, I think.'

'Do you have her password?' Dudek said.

'They should be on her phone,' Matt said. 'I'll unlock it. You can take it, if it helps.'

'Thanks,' Dudek said.

'Did she ever mention a fan who tried to get too close?' Wynne said.

Matt looked up as he thought. 'Not really. Not recently, anyway.'

'Not recently?' Dudek said. 'There was someone in the past?'

'Kind of. I mean, it was hardly anything, but there was a guy who came to a couple of her readings. He said he was a poet and gave her his books in exchange for hers. I think he had no money. He was a bit – I don't know what the word is these days – but a bit *off.*'

'Off in what way?' Wynne said.

'Very intense. He wanted her to write specific messages in the books. He came to at least two readings.'

'Do you know his name?' Wynne said.

'No,' Matt replied. 'But I can find out. I think she kept the books of poems he gave to her.'

Matt

Matt opened the door to Annabelle's office. It was, in theory, a shared office, but he rarely used it for anything other than a quiet moment reading the news.

The chair, an old leather office chair on wheels, was pushed back from the desk. She must have left it there. When was that? Was she working at the desk a couple of days ago, in the moments before all this happened?

He sat down and pulled the chair up to the desk. Her laptop was open, the screen dark, on the surface; there was an empty mug next to it. The tab of a green teabag hung over the side. On the left of the desk there was a manuscript, covered in edits and notes. Behind that was a photo of the five of them around a sunny pub table. He remembered it well; they had been walking in the Lake District and stopped for lunch.

He was overwhelmed by a sense of her presence. This room was hers; she had occupied it and shaped it. She was part of it. It was unthinkable that it could exist without her.

But it did. She was not here, and this was what she had left behind. His throat was constricted, his stomach hollow. This must be what it was like when someone died, he thought.

The world they had lived in was still there; only they were missing.

He pushed the thought away. She was not gone yet. He could not think like that.

It would drive him mad.

He scanned the shelves above the desk, going over the books one by one. He wasn't sure what he was looking for, but he knew it was slim. It could easily be hidden between two books.

And then he saw it. Next to her first novel there was a small gap. He slid his finger into it and pulled it out. A slender, home-made book of poetry. He took it out and opened it. There was an inscription, in block capitals.

TO ANNABELLE
FROM ONE WRITER TO ANOTHER; WE SHARE
A SPECIAL BOND
YOURS MOST FAITHFULLY
CARL JAMESON

This was it. This was the guy. It had to be. He headed out of the office to show it to DI Wynne.

Wynne

Wynne opened the door of Dudek's Astra and sat in the passenger seat. In her hand she held the volume of poetry Matt Westbrook had given her. Outside, Dudek was on the phone.

He finished his call and got in the car.

'Put in a request for his address and any details we have on him,' he said.

'Good. We'll go and talk to him.' She turned to Matt Westbrook's house. There was something about this case that had been bothering her, and now she knew what it was.

'You look thoughtful, boss,' Dudek said. 'What is it?'

'There's something confusing here,' Wynne said. 'I've been thinking it over.'

'What is it?'

'The motive. I can't put my finger on it.'

'They want Annabelle.'

'Right. But if that's all it is, why do it this way?'

'He's obsessed. Or she. You know how it works. The motives are always the same: money, revenge, love. A crazy fan. Ex-boyfriend. A friend she pissed off. We can't rule anything out yet.'

'I get that,' Wynne said. 'But if what they want is Annabelle, why do it like *this*?'

'What do you mean, exactly?'

'If all they want is Annabelle, why kidnap the kids? Why not simply take her? And if they want revenge, why not just kill her? Why bother with the kids at all?'

'Yeah,' Dudek said. 'I see what you're saying. He could have kidnapped her. It would have been a lot easier. Pick her up somewhere and then disappear. All this – the messages, exchange, switching to a van – could have been avoided.'

'Which suggests there's a reason for it,' Wynne said. 'There's something more going on. The kidnapper wants something. Maybe to send a message of some kind.'

'Like writer to writer,' Dudek said. 'It is sort of poetic.'

'Yes,' Wynne said. 'Exactly, like writer to writer. I think it's time to pay Carl Jameson a visit.'

Annabelle

The first thing she thought when she woke up was that she had slept on her shoulder in an uncomfortable way. It ached with a dull throb.

The second was that she had a terrible hangover. Her mouth was dry, and she had a piercing headache. Oddly, her mouth hurt, as though it had been bruised.

What did I do last night? she thought. *Did we go out?*

She stretched out her left hand to reach for Matt. She needed a hug, and, if she could persuade him, a glass of water and an aspirin.

He was not there. There was *nothing* there. Her hand flopped into space, which was weird, because she always slept on the right side of the bed.

And then she remembered.

The car. The kids. The reason her shoulder hurt. The reason her mouth hurt.

She opened her eyes.

The room was totally dark. She lay there, waiting for her eyes to adjust, but there was nothing to adjust to. She twisted on the bed, feeling behind her with her good arm. There was a wall. She ran her hand over it, hoping for a switch. There was nothing.

Then she froze.

Was she alone in here? Was there someone with her, sitting beside the bed, watching? She pictured the figure in the hoodie, here, now, arms folded, watching . . .

She listened. For a second she thought she heard someone breathing, thought she could detect the sound of a heart beating.

She realized it was hers.

'Hello?' she said. 'Is anyone here?'

There was no answer.

She moved her legs to the right, feeling for the end of the mattress. It was a double bed, at least. She shuffled across it, and sat on the right-hand edge, her left hand in front of her. She inched forward until she felt a wall, then gradually raised her hand until she was standing and her arm was above her head. She reached as far as she could, but did not get to the ceiling.

A high ceiling, then. Probably not a basement.

She swept her hand down in an arc, keeping it on the wall. When it was almost at ninety degrees to her body, her fingertips brushed something. It felt like a raised piece of wood; a window frame, she assumed.

She felt around the edge, then into the middle. Her fingers did not touch glass or the fabric of a curtain. Rather, there was a hard, plastic cover. A shutter, maybe.

She inched along the window, her left hand – the right was uselessly strapped to her body by the sling – running along the bottom of the window frame.

And then the window frame ran out, and, at the far side of the window, her fingers met a rod, dangling against the wall.

She pulled it, but it did not lengthen. She turned it to the left, then to the right and it began to rotate.

Gradually, dull spots of light appeared in the window. They merged into lines and the blind started to rise. After a few seconds it was up, and she was looking out of a window.

It was a view that was somehow familiar. A lawn sloped about fifty feet to a small stony beach, on the shore of a placid, grey lake. It looked like a large body of water, the far side about three hundred yards away.

And she realized that she knew this place.

She had the same feeling she'd had when she saw the kidnapper, face obscured by the hoodie. There was something about that slender, thin-hipped build and the measured, precise way they moved that she recognized.

It was the same now. She had seen this place before. She hadn't been here, but it was familiar. It wasn't the Lake District – there were no mountains – and she racked her brains for other bodies of water that she knew. Budworth Mere. Carsington Water. They were this kind of size, but it wasn't them. She knew them. Maybe it was somewhere famous, maybe it had featured in a film or TV show.

God, it was frustrating. It was right there in her memory, but agonizingly out of view. She was sure that if she could just figure it out, it would hold the key to what was going on.

But it slipped away.

She turned to look at the room. To her left was a double bed. On the far side of the bed was a table with a lamp. To her right was a door. It was closed and, she had no doubt, would be locked. On the far wall was a desk, above which were shelves filled with books.

On the desk was a bottle of champagne, with two plastic flutes next to it. It looked set up for a romantic celebration.

She felt a shudder of apprehension.

The books were mainly fiction, a mixture of classics, Booker winners, modern authors. There was little that wasn't considered literary.

On the top shelf was a set of encyclopedias. There were six volumes, so hardly the Britannica, but something.

And next to them were copies of her books.

All four of them.

The most recent, *This Is Not the End,* on the desktop itself.

Plus the translations.

All four into French, German and Spanish. The first two into Italian and Greek. The second one into Polish. The first into Korean, too.

There was a copy of everything.

What the *fuck* was this?

She ran to the door and tried the handle. It didn't move. She hammered on it.

'Hey!' she shouted. 'Open this door! Come here and tell me what's going on?'

The words faded into the silence.

And then there was the sound of footsteps outside, and the scrape of a key in a lock.

Wynne

1

DI Wynne sipped a mug of coffee. DS Dudek sat opposite her, a piece of A4 paper in his hand.

'Here's what we know about Carl Jameson,' he said. 'Thirty-nine years old, unmarried. No kids. Lives in a terraced house in Padgate with his mum. About ten years back he got arrested for shoplifting. Got off with a warning. That's about it.'

'Plus he's a poet and a fan of Annabelle Westbrook,' Wynne said.

'That too.' DS Dudek folded his arms. 'If he has her, where would he keep her?'

'Good question. An abandoned building? Or in the house. Maybe his mother knows what he's done. Maybe she helped him. Stranger things have happened.' Wynne finished the coffee. 'Let's go and see him.'

DI Wynne knocked on the door. There was no doorbell; the door looked like it needed painting. Two houses down, a man in his forties came out. He was wearing overalls and carrying a flask.

He studied them. 'Everything OK?'

'Yes, thank you,' DI Wynne said.

The man didn't move. 'You looking for Edith?'

'Her son,' DS Dudek said.

'Carl?'

'Yes. Does he still live here?'

'Aye,' the man said. 'He does.' He sniffed. 'Are you police? Is Carl in trouble?'

'We are the police,' Wynne said, then gave her standard response to these kind of questions. 'We're making routine enquiries.'

'Involving Carl? I don't see what you'd need from him.'

'What's your name, sir?' Wynne said. The man flinched. No one liked giving their name to the police, however innocent they were.

'Jim Franks,' he said.

'Are you related to Carl Jameson?' she asked.

'No. Just a neighbour. Known him since he was a baby. He's a good kid.'

'I'm sure he is,' Wynne said. She was about to knock again, when there was the sound of a lock being drawn and the front door opened.

A woman, in her seventies at least, looked at them.

'Hello,' she said. She looked worried, her eyes moving from DI Wynne to DS Dudek. 'Is everything OK?'

'I'm Detective Inspector Jane Wynne,' Wynne said. 'And this is DS Dudek. I take it you are Edith Jameson? We have some questions for your son, Carl. Is he here?'

'Yes,' she said. 'I'm Edith Jameson. And Carl is in the front room. Do you have any identification? Sorry to ask, but – you know.'

Wynne and Dudek held up their warrant cards. 'Take your

time,' Wynne said. Edith Jameson's neighbour was still watching them. 'If you have any concerns, we're happy to have your neighbour join us.'

'That's OK,' Edith said. 'Come in.'

Inside the hall, Edith gestured at a closed door. 'He's in there,' she said. 'He's up, but let me check he's ready.'

She knocked gently on the door, then eased it open and looked inside.

'Carl,' Wynne heard her say. 'There's people here to see you.'

There was a muffled response.

'OK. I'll let them know.'

She turned back to look at them.

'He says can he have a few minutes?'

Wynne nodded. 'Of course.'

'Would you like a drink while you wait?' She smiled. 'Tea?'

'No, thank you,' Wynne said. 'I just had one.'

'Do you have coffee?' DS Dudek said. 'I'm not much of a tea drinker.'

'Oh,' she said. 'I don't. Neither of us drink coffee. Although, come to think of it, I did have instant, a while back. Let me check the cupboards.'

'That's fine,' Dudek said. 'No need to go to any trouble.'

'Water, then?'

'Really, Mrs Jameson,' Wynne said. 'We don't need anything. But thank you for offering. It's much appreciated.'

'Not at all,' Edith said. She gave a quiet cough. 'If I could ask – what is this about, exactly?'

'Do you recognize the name Annabelle Westbrook?' Wynne said.

It was clear from the puzzled expression on her face that she did not, or at least, wanted them to think she did not. Wynne was getting the impression that deceit of that kind was not in her repertoire, however.

'Who is she?' Edith said.

'Someone we're making enquiries about,' Wynne said.

'Do you think Carl knows her?' She frowned. 'He's never mentioned her. He doesn't have all that many friends, Mrs—'

'Wynne. Detective Inspector Wynne. We think he may know her. He's certainly met her on at least two occasions. She's a writer. He attended her readings.'

The frown fell away. 'Do you mean Annabelle Anderson?'

Wynne glanced at Dudek.

'Maiden name?' he said.

'Or pen name,' Wynne said.

'I'll check.' Dudek took out his phone and tapped on the screen. After a moment, he nodded. 'That's it. She publishes as Annabelle Anderson.'

'Well, he loves her books,' Edith said. 'He's a big fan. He was saying not so long ago that she had a new book out.'

'Really?' Dudek said. 'When was that?'

'I'm not sure. Maybe sometime around Christmas?' Edith shrugged. 'But he hardly knows her. He's just a fan.'

There was a noise from the room, and a voice called, 'Come in.'

Wynne smiled. 'Well, it seems we can ask him for ourselves.'

2

Dudek walked in ahead of her. The minute he was inside, he turned to look at her with an expression she couldn't read.

She immediately saw why.

Carl Jameson was not simply in this room; he *lived* in this room. There was a bed against the back wall, a large TV facing it, and bookshelves lining the rest of the room.

Carl was sitting by the side of his bed.

He was in a wheelchair, his head tilted to the side and resting against the headrest. His legs and arms were wasted, and there was a tube that extended from the frame of the wheelchair to his lips.

Wynne was familiar with what it was for. It was a sip-puff tube, through which he could control the chair.

'Carl Jameson?' she said.

'Yes.' His speech was slurred and difficult to understand.

'We had a few questions we wanted to ask you, about Annabelle West—' she caught herself, 'Anderson.'

'Is she OK?' His eyes narrowed; the concern seemed genuine.

'She's missing,' Wynne said. 'We're trying to establish her whereabouts.'

'I don't know where she is,' Carl said. 'But I hope she's

OK.' His eyes flickered to a bookshelf. 'She signed her books for me. She read my poems. She liked them.'

'Her husband mentioned that,' Wynne said. She paused, then added. 'He said she was a big fan.'

'Really?' Carl said.

'Yes.'

Dudek looked at her, puzzled. She'd explain later.

'When was the last time you left the house?' he said.

'Yesterday. Mum and I go out every day.'

'And two nights ago? You were here?' he said.

'Yes,' Carl replied. 'What happened to Annabelle?'

Wynne looked at Dudek. There was no point going any further. Whoever had met Matt Westbrook at the exchange was tall and thin and not in a wheelchair. She smiled.

'Thank you, Mr Jameson,' she said. 'You've been a great help. We'll let you get on with your day.'

'What happened to Annabelle?' he said, his voice rising, despite the effort. 'What happened to her!'

In the hallway, Edith Jameson opened the door for them.

'You didn't know his condition, did you?'

'No,' Wynne said. 'We didn't.'

'Well, now you do,' she said. 'And he had nothing to do with whatever has happened to Annabelle Anderson. I'd appreciate it if you didn't come back. I don't want to upset him again.'

'I understand,' Wynne said.

'He's had a hard life,' Edith said, tears forming in her eyes. 'When he was born there were complications. I don't know if it was that, but he was never like the other kids. And in the last few years he got this disease – motor neurone disease. I don't know if it's linked, or just a cruel twist of fate. But he hasn't long left, and I don't want you to disturb him again.'

279

'We won't,' Wynne said. 'And I apologize for upsetting him today. But we have to follow the enquiry where it takes us. We won't bother you again though.'

'If she's OK, would you let me know?' Edith said. 'He would like to know that.'

'Of course.' Wynne backed out of the door. 'Goodbye, Mrs Jameson.'

'It's not him,' Dudek said as they walked to the car. 'So what next?'

'We find that van,' Wynne replied. 'Or we've got nothing.'

Matt

1

Matt put the phone down and sank into the sofa. Wynne had told him about the meeting with Carl Jameson, who it turned out was both in a wheelchair and dying.

Which left them with nothing.

He looked at his kids. Norman and Keith were playing Minecraft; he normally hated watching them getting so absorbed in a computer game, but it was a relief they had something to take their mind off their mum. Molly was on his lap, her face tilted up towards him. It was the way she had always lain on him since she was a baby.

And on Annabelle.

That morning, Norman had woken first and got into bed with him.

Is Mum still gone? he said.

Yes.

When's she coming back?

I don't know. Soon.

How soon?

As soon as we can find her. The police are looking.

Are you looking?

I am. Do you remember anything about the kidnapper, Norman?

He tensed. *Not really.*

The police will want you to tell them everything you can. Is that OK?

He paused. *It's OK. If it helps find Mum.*

Keith was different. He lay curled up next to Matt, not speaking. Matt kissed the top of his head.

How are you?

He answered quickly. His voice was quiet and strained, as though even this one word was an effort. *Good.*

Are you worried? About Mum?

A bit. A pause. *Yes.*

It's normal to be worried. But we'll find her, OK?

OK.

He hated the feeling of lying.

His phone buzzed. He looked down. It was Guy.

'Guy,' he said. 'Hey.'

'Matt. Is now a good time?'

'As good as any.'

'Is there any news?'

Matt brushed his lips against Molly's forehead. 'None good.'

'What's happened?'

'They thought they had a suspect,' he said. 'A fan who had come to her readings. But it turned out to be nothing. We're still at square one.'

'Damn,' Guy said. 'How are the kids?'

'Good, considering. They're worried. We all are. I think the police are going to talk to them today.'

'Do you think they'll need any help? Counselling?'

'Maybe. But hopefully Annabelle will be back this afternoon and all this will be over. I don't want to dwell too long on the alternative.' He knew that soon he would have no choice; the alternative would become reality.

'I hope so too. I'm heading into the office for a few hours, but let me know if there's anything you need? I'll have my phone on.'

'I will,' Matt said. 'Thanks.'

The problem was there was nothing Guy could do. There was nothing anyone could do.

2

What did it do to you to lose your mum when you were seven? Or five? Or three?

He supposed a lot of children went through it. Parents died. Not all the time, but it happened. There were counsellors trained in dealing with bereavement, methods to help children understand and process their grief, then move on and live normal lives.

Not easy, but possible.

But what if your mum traded herself to save you after you were kidnapped? There were no methods for dealing with that, no well-trodden paths that led to understanding and acceptance. There would be guilt and pain and bewilderment and who knew what else.

And then there was him. Every time he closed his eyes he saw her getting into the front seat of her car and driving away. Heard the shout as she saw her children.

And every time he felt a stab of anguish that he had not stopped it, that he had agreed to let her trade herself for the children, that he had not called the police or raised a private army or done something.

But they couldn't have risked telling the police and there

was no way Annabelle was going to leave the kids with whoever had taken them. And they had tried everything to track him.

Their children had been in the hands of a kidnapper. He could still remember vividly how that had felt. He had been desperate and panic-stricken, like the world was going to end at any moment and there was no price too high to pay to bring them back.

He would gladly have sacrificed himself, but that was not what was being asked.

The price was Annabelle and she was always going to pay it.

But how would they explain that to the children?

He glanced at his watch. DI Wynne was due in five minutes to talk to the kids.

Molly was still lying on his chest, her eyes closed. Norman and Keith were playing Minecraft, building their virtual world.

It was a moment of peace and he forced himself to enjoy it.

He did not think there would be many more.

Annabelle

Annabelle pictured herself springing on the kidnapper as soon as the door opened, wrestling him to the floor, then sprinting away.

That was hardly going to happen. She was in reasonable shape but she had never been in a fight in her life. Moreover, she had one working arm and the kidnapper was likely to be wary. Her chances of overpowering another adult with one arm and without a weapon or the element of surprise were limited.

She tensed and straightened.

She called the kidnapper to mind. Taller than the average woman, yes – maybe five ten, five eleven – but that slender, thin-hipped build . . .

The handle turned, and the door began to open.

Matt

The doorbell rang just before midday. Matt got to his feet. Tessa was coming to look after the kids. Matt wanted to be there when DI Wynne talked to them, so Tess was going to entertain the two who were not being interviewed.

He was a single parent, for the moment.

He opened the door. It wasn't Tessa; it was Mike.

'Hi,' Matt said. 'I wasn't expecting you.'

'Tessa called me. She had to go to the hospital.'

'Oh,' Matt said. 'I see.'

'She said to tell you she was sorry, but there was a pile-up on the M6 so it's all hands on deck. She had no choice.' Mike shrugged. 'Life as an A and E doctor, I suppose.'

It was, in a strange way, a reminder that life went on. For Matt, everything was suspended, but out there people were getting into car accidents and having babies and living and dying as they always did.

He was about to shut the door when another car – an old Mazda – pulled up.

DI Wynne got out of the passenger side. She was with another woman, who looked to be in her late twenties or early thirties. She was not in uniform and was not dressed in a long, floral dress. She wore glasses and had her hair pulled up in a ponytail.

She did not look like a cop, Matt thought.

'This is Rory Hall,' Wynne said. 'She'll be the one questioning the children. She's trained in this kind of thing. I'll be present and may suggest things to her that she can ask. And you'll need to be there too.'

'Come in,' Matt said. 'The kids are in the living room. Would you like me to get them?'

Rory Hall smiled. She had a lively, warm gaze, and emanated a sense of energy and intelligence.

'Not yet,' she said. She had an Australian accent. 'I'd like to talk to you before I meet the children. It's useful for me to get a sense of who they are, and how best to treat them. I'd also like to know what they've told you, if that's OK?'

'Of course,' Matt said. 'We can go into the kitchen. This is my brother-in-law, Mike. He's going to look after the children.'

'So,' Rory said. 'Why don't you walk me through it?'

Matt started at the beginning: he told her how he'd parked outside the shop and the car had been gone when he returned. At first he'd suspected the kids had done something, and then wondered if it was a prank.

But then the messages came. And the photos and the demands and then the handover.

'Could I see the photos?' Rory asked.

He handed over his phone.

Rory studied them. 'Thank you,' she said, eventually. 'What have the children told you, Mr Westbrook?'

'Not too much. Norman said they were fine. No one hurt them. He said Molly missed me and Keith was quiet, so he tried to reassure him.'

'You must be proud of him,' Rory said.

'I am.'

288

'Is there any sign of trauma?'

'No. They're worried, obviously. About their mum. I'm trying to keep things as light as possible, though.'

'That's a good idea. I think I'm ready to talk to them now.'

'I love them,' he said. 'Please remember that.'

Rory put her hand on his. 'I will,' she said. 'I know this is a terribly difficult time, Mr Westbrook, but they're lucky to have you.'

Matt listened as she questioned the children.

She had a clear method. She started each interview by introducing herself, and telling the child she was interviewing who she was and where she was from, then asked if they had heard of Australia.

Norman had. He asked why she was here.

'Because I fell in love,' Rory said, with a warm and genuine smile. He could see why she was good at this job.

'Who with?' Norman said.

'A guy called Frank.'

'Is he from Australia?'

'No. He's from here.'

'Is he nice?'

'He is. Now, I heard you had quite an experience. Would you be able to tell me what happened?'

'Yes,' said Norman. 'After Dad went to the shop, we were sitting in the car. A man got in. He told us, "Don't worry, your dad sent me."'

'What did he sound like?' Rory said.

'I don't know.'

'Was his voice high, like this' – she spoke in a high-pitched voice – 'or lower, like your dad?'

'High. I think.'

Rory glanced at Wynne. 'Was it a woman's voice? Or a man's?'

'A man,' Norman said. 'I think.'

'Good.' Rory said. 'Did the man have an accent?'

'Not really,' Norman said. 'Just sounded normal.'

'OK. So after he got in the car, then what?'

'He drove us somewhere, then gave us Coke. Mum and Dad don't normally let us have that. And then we fell asleep.'

'And when you woke up?'

'We were in a metal room. I think it was maybe a van.'

Wynne handed Rory a piece of paper. Rory showed it to Norman. It was the photo of him and Keith watching something on an iPad, while Molly slept beside them.

'Do you remember this?'

'Yes. He gave us more Coke and we fell asleep in there. The next time we woke up, we were on the way to the forest. Then Dad came.'

'Did you see the man's face?'

'No,' Norman said. 'He always wore a hood.'

'Thank you,' Rory said. 'I think those are all my questions. For now.'

'Did I help?' Norman said.

'Heaps,' Rory said. 'You helped *heaps*.'

It was the same with Keith and Molly. Afterwards, DI Wynne, Rory and Matt sat in the living room.

'What did you think?' Matt said.

'The kids seem to be fine, for the moment,' Rory said. 'Although I'm going to recommend that they see a doctor for a physical – and a tox screen as well – and then that they see a paediatric psychiatrist, as well as a counsellor. They're going to need strategies to cope with this.'

'I agree,' Matt said. 'And did you learn anything?'

'Well,' Rory said. 'I thought it was interesting that the voice was high pitched. I don't think we can rule out this being a woman.'

Wynne nodded slowly. 'I agree,' she said.

'Anything else?' Matt said.

'I'm afraid not,' Wynne said. 'I'm afraid that at the moment there is very little to go on. But we have other lines of enquiry.' She got to her feet and glanced at her watch. 'DS Dudek should be here shortly. We're going to want to talk to your brother-in-law, if that's OK?'

Wynne

1

Mike Anderson sat in the armchair. Wynne was on the sofa with Dudek; she would have preferred to be at the station. She didn't think Anderson was hiding anything, but you never knew, and she was of the opinion that people felt under more obligation to tell the truth when they were sitting at a table in a police interview room than when they were in an armchair in a family member's house.

'Thank you, Mr Anderson,' she said. He looked dreadful, his eyes red and his cheeks hollow. 'We'll make this as quick as we can.'

'Take all the time you want,' he said. 'If it helps find Annie then it's fine by me.'

'Where were you on Saturday evening?' Wynne said.

'I was here, from about nine thirty,' Mike said. 'Earlier on I was at the gym – near my home on the Wirral – and then I went for a drink with a friend.'

'Who was the friend?' Dudek said.

'Duncan. He goes to my gym.'

'His last name?'

'Telford.'

'We'd like to talk to him,' Dudek said. 'So if you could pass along his details, that would be appreciated.'

'Checking my alibi?' Mike said.

'It's standard practice, Mr Anderson,' Wynne said. 'Nothing more than that. After you had a drink with Mr Telford, what did you do?'

'I went home, which was when Matt called me to ask me to come here.'

Wynne folded her arms. 'How long have you known Mr Westbrook?'

'Since he met Annie. Maybe fifteen years?'

'And you and him have always got along well?' Dudek asked.

'Yeah. Matt's a great guy.'

'No fallings out?'

Mike shook his head. 'No. Nothing that stands out.'

'Did he ever mention anyone to you that he had fallen out with?' Wynne said.

'No. Matt's a pretty friendly guy. Everyone likes him. You've only seen him in these circumstances, but if you met him in the normal day-to-day, you'd know what I mean. He's funny, kind, relaxed.'

'What about in his professional life?' Dudek said.

'Same,' Mike said. 'It's possible he had a problem with someone, but he never mentioned it.'

'How about your sister,' Wynne said. 'Was there anyone who had a reason to dislike her?'

Mike held his hands up. 'No. I mean, she had friends who she was closer to, but no one with this kind of hatred towards her.'

'Can you think of anyone who she had a problem with, however minor?'

'She never mentioned anyone.'

'Any arguments with Matt, over the years?' Dudek said.

'Small ones. But no, nothing substantial.'

'His family?'

'His parents died a few years back, and Annabelle and Tessa are fine.'

Wynne paused. There was something out of place about what he had said.

'Fine?' she said. 'Or friends?'

'Friends,' Mike said, after a moment's hesitation. 'Now.'

'Not at the start?' Wynne said.

'They had a rocky patch,' Mike said. 'But that was years ago. And it wasn't really about Tessa at all. She was friends with Matt's ex-girlfriend. There was a bit of drama there, but it all blew over.'

'Who was the ex-girlfriend?' Dudek said.

'I don't remember her name now.'

'Do you remember what the drama was about?' Wynne said.

'I'm afraid I don't.' He pursed his lips. 'Although I do remember her showing up at Norman's christening. She was pretty wild, actually. But you'd have to ask Tessa for details.'

'We will,' Wynne said. 'Thank you, Mr Anderson.'

2

'Where could we contact Tessa?' Wynne asked.

'She's at the hospital now. She's a doctor.'

'Could we have her number?' Dudek said.

'Of course.' Mike dug his phone out of his jeans pocket. 'She works in A and E, so she doesn't always answer. I think she's busy today. There was an accident on the motorway so they're all hands on deck. That's why she's not here.'

'There was an accident?' Wynne said. 'I didn't hear about anything.'

Mike shrugged. 'That's what she said.'

'I'll check,' Wynne said. She glanced at Dudek. 'In the meantime, we'd like to speak to her. Urgently.'

'You don't think she has something to do with this?' Mike said. 'That's ridiculous.'

'I don't think anything, Mr Anderson. I just ask questions.'

'OK. I'll let her know.'

He held the phone to his ear.

'Voicemail,' he said.

He left a message telling her it was important and asking her to call him back as soon as possible.

Wynne turned to Dudek. 'Mr Westbrook may be able to tell us something about his ex-girlfriend,' she said. 'Would you ask him to come in?'

Matt

Matt sat in the armchair. It was still warm from Mike; he was in the kitchen with the kids.

'Mr Westbrook,' Wynne said. 'Your brother-in-law mentioned that Annabelle and your sister had a difficult start to their relationship. He indicated it was in part because of your ex-girlfriend.'

Matt put his hands on his knees. 'It was hardly anything,' he said. 'And it was a long time ago.'

'Would you mind giving us the details?' Wynne said.

'Lindsey – she was my girlfriend during the last year of high school – and Tessa became friends after we broke up. When I met Annabelle it was awkward, because Tessa was loyal to her friend. That was all it was. Loyalty.'

'And other than that, you would say they have a close relationship?'

He looked at DI Wynne. It was true that Tessa and Annabelle had not clicked when they met. Initially he had put it down to Tessa's friendship with Lindsey, but, although it had got better, they had never become best – or anything like best – friends.

'It's fine,' he said. 'They do OK.'

'But they're not close?' Dudek said.

'They're family. They like each other.'

'Do they socialize outside of family gatherings?' Wynne said.

'Not that much,' Matt said. 'But that's a long way from thinking Tessa would have anything to do with this.'

'We're not suggesting that,' Wynne said. 'Just trying to establish the facts. Mr Anderson also mentioned that your ex-girlfriend showed up at your son's christening and made threats?'

'Not really,' Matt said. 'I mean, yes, she showed up at the pub after we had Norman christened, but she was just drunk.'

'Did she threaten you?' Dudek said.

'You could say that,' Matt said. 'She said something like "You'll get what's coming", but it was the drink talking, that's all.'

'How long after the break-up was this?' Wynne said.

'I don't know. Nine, maybe ten years?' Matt said.

'That's a long time to hold a grudge,' Wynne said.

The door opened and Mike came in. He was holding his phone.

'It's Tessa,' he said. He passed it to Wynne. 'She's free now.'

Wynne

1

'Ms Westbrook,' Wynne said. 'Thank you for coming. How was the accident on the M6? Was it bad?'

'No,' Tessa said. 'It was only one injury I didn't have to go into the hospital after all.'

'That's not what Mr Anderson told us.'

'I know. I was thinking it would be worse when I spoke to him.'

'So where were you when he called?'

'I went for a run. To clear my mind.'

DI Wynne nodded. 'I see. We'll want to get your version of events in detail. But for now we'd like to focus on Lindsey Daley.'

'What about her?'

'It seems she had something against your brother and his wife?'

'A long time ago, yes.'

'Not now?' Wynne asked.

'No.'

'What was the nature of her complaint against them?' Wynne said.

'It was all teenage stuff,' Tessa said. 'Matt went to university and met Annabelle. Lindsey thought he'd been stolen away from her. She took it badly, but that's all it was.'

'In what way did she take it badly?'

Tessa stared at her. 'Is this about the baby?' she said. 'Did Matt tell you about the baby?'

Wynne glanced at Dudek. He raised an eyebrow. 'The baby? They had a baby?'

'No,' Tessa said. 'That's the point. Lindsey pretended to be pregnant so that Matt would stay with her.' She held up her hands. 'I know, it sounds bad. But she was a seventeen-year-old girl who thought she was in love.'

'What happened?' Dudek said.

'The truth came out and Matt broke up with her. Then he met Annabelle – well, they'd already met, which just made Lindsey think he'd been cheating on her, which he said he hadn't – and it was over with Lindsey.'

'But she didn't get over it?' Wynne said.

'She did, eventually.'

'And yet she came to Norman's christening? How did she know about it?'

'Oh, God,' Tessa said. 'I'd forgotten about that. It wasn't as though she was stalking them, though. It was sort of my fault. I mentioned it to her, and she showed up. I think Annabelle blamed me.'

'Were you still friends?'

'On and off. I saw her in town. She'd had a very hard time – mental health and substance abuse problems. But she's much better now.'

'She's better now?' Wynne said. 'Are you still in touch with her?'

There was a long pause.

'Yes, I am,' Tessa said.

2

They drove away from the Westbrooks' house. Tessa had given them an address for Lindsey Daley – now Meyer – and they had left her to explain to her brother why she had not mentioned they were still friends.

Lindsey lived a few miles away in a neat semi-detached house in Grappenhall. They parked outside and rang the doorbell.

A woman in her early thirties opened the door. She had shoulder-length brown hair and dark-framed glasses. She gave them a puzzled smile.

'Lindsey Meyer?' Wynne said.

'Yes. That's me.'

'I'm Detective Inspector Jane Wynne. This is Detective Sergeant Dudek. We were hoping you could help us with our enquiries.'

'About what?'

'Annabelle Westbrook.'

A weary look crossed her face.

'Come in,' she said.

Lindsey showed them into the living room. 'What happened to Annabelle?' she said.

'She's missing,' Wynne said. 'We're seeking any help we can get in locating her.'

'I don't know anything,' Lindsey said. 'I haven't seen her in years.'

Wynne studied her face. If she was lying, she was doing it well. There was no sign of nervousness.

The door opened and a boy – maybe six or seven years old – came in. He was pale, and looked like he'd just woken up.

'Mum,' he said. 'I'm hungry.'

Lindsey held out her arms and he settled onto her knee.

'He's got a bug,' she said. 'That's why he's off school. I had to take a sick day.'

'Where do you work?' Dudek said.

'I'm a nurse. His dad works away, so he can't be here.'

'Who are you?' the boy said.

'Wynne. My name is Jane Wynne.'

'She's a detective,' Lindsey said. 'This is the first detective you've met, Josh.'

'You're a detective?' Josh said.

'I am.'

'Who are you detecting?' he said.

'That's a long story. I'm sorry you don't feel well. But if you're hungry, that's a good sign.' Wynne smiled at Lindsey. 'Why don't you get him something to eat. We won't be too long, I hope.'

While Lindsey was in the kitchen, Wynne took the opportunity to take a look around the room. There were a number of photos of Lindsey, a tall, wiry man with curly dark hair, and Josh. There was also one of her and the man on their wedding day.

It didn't look like the home of someone bent on revenge for a decade-old slight, but then appearances, as Wynne had learned many times, meant nothing.

Lindsey came back and sat down.

'He's happy now,' she said. 'So how can I help?'

'We're trying to establish if anyone had a motive for hurting Annabelle Westbrook,' Wynne said. 'And we wanted to discuss your relationship with her.'

'We don't have a relationship,' Lindsey said.

'But you do know each other,' Wynne said.

'And you did attend the christening of her first son,' Dudek added.

Lindsey rubbed her temples.

'God, I can't believe that's coming back to haunt me,' she said. 'I was hoping it was in the past.'

'Can you tell us what happened?' Wynne said.

'I don't know what happened,' she said. 'It's so embarrassing. I was in a rough patch and somehow I thought it was a good idea to go there.'

'You thought it was a good idea to crash a party after the christening of your ex's first son?' Dudek said.

'Would you believe me if I said that I was intending to wish them all the best? Even though I was having a really hard time back then, I still knew I owed Matt an apology. And I was thinking that I'd show up and apologize and say all the best and let's let bygones be bygones. But that's not what happened.'

'What did happen?' Wynne said.

'I got there and saw them and realized that they didn't want my apologies. I was nothing to them. They hadn't given me a thought. And I just lost it. I'd been drinking, too, which didn't help.'

'Why were you having a hard time?' Wynne said.

'It's a long story,' Lindsey said. 'And I can tell you, if you want. But it's over now.'

'Maybe we'll come back to it,' Wynne said. 'Perhaps we can move to more recent events.'

'Of course.'

'You said your husband is away?'

'North Sea. He works in the oil industry.'

'When did he leave?'

'Last Wednesday.'

Wynne glanced at Dudek. He raised an eyebrow. He was thinking the same as she was. A husband conveniently absent. A husband who might have something against the man his wife had once loved.

'Who is your husband's employer?' Wynne asked.

Lindsey Meyer gave her a name. She noted it down. It would be easy enough to check his alibi.

'Could you tell us where you were on Saturday evening?' Wynne said.

'I could. I was working. I did the nightshift,' Lindsey said.

'Where was your son?' Dudek asked.

'You think I left him here alone? He was with my mum, Detective Sergeant. You can ask her. And you can ask the hospital – it's Warrington General – whether I'm telling the truth.'

'We'll check,' she said. 'That's all for now. We'll be in touch if we have more questions.'

'Look,' Lindsey said. 'I can see how you might think I have something against Annabelle Westbrook, and I can't tell you that we're ever going to be friends. But that was all a long time ago. I'm married, I have a job and a family. I'm happy, which has not always been the case for me. And I wouldn't do anything to risk that. I had nothing to do with this. Nothing at all.'

Annabelle

1

The door opened.

The kidnapper – still in dark jeans and a hoodie – came in and stood six inches inside the room. The door clicked shut.

There was no response.

'Are you just going to stand there?' she said. 'Or do something?'

Again, there was no response.

'At least show me your face,' she said. 'You'll have to, eventually.'

The figure shrugged, then lifted the hood slowly.

She did not understand what she was seeing. It made no sense. More than that – it was impossible.

'It's you?' she said. 'Guy? But—' she knew this was not the most profound question, but it was what she thought of – 'you were in Brighton, weren't you?'

'I made that up,' he said. 'I take it you weren't expecting me?'

He sounded genuinely interested, as though he'd thought she might be, but he was the last person she had expected to see. She had assumed it was a crazy fan or someone from her distant past. But Guy? The thought had never crossed her mind.

And, in the back of her mind, she wondered if maybe this made it better? It was Guy, after all, and not some monster.

'No,' she said. 'I wasn't expecting you.'

'Oh,' he said. He frowned, his brow creased in what looked like disappointment. 'You didn't guess? I thought you would have.'

'How the hell would I have guessed?' she said. 'You told me you were in Brighton.'

His frown deepened. 'I thought you might have worked it out,' he said. 'I was rather hoping you were looking forward to it?' He pointed to the champagne. 'I thought we might celebrate.'

'Looking *forward* to it?' she said. 'Celebrate? What would we celebrate?'

'Isn't it obvious?' Despite his words, there was a note of doubt in his voice.

'No,' she said. 'Why on earth have you done this? Why have you brought me here?'

'I think you know,' he said. 'Deep down.'

'No, I don't,' Annabelle replied. 'Trust me. I have no fucking idea. And I want to leave, now.'

'I'm afraid that won't be possible,' he said. 'This is your home now.'

'Guy,' Annabelle said. 'You know that's not true. You know I have a family. You know my home is with them. Whatever has happened, whatever made you do this – if you've had a problem – it's fine. Just take me home and we'll forget this ever happened. OK?'

He looked at her for a long time. She had the sense he

was like an eagle, sizing up its prey. There was a watchful, almost wild look in his eyes.

'Problem?' he said. 'You think I have a problem?'

'I don't see any other explanation. I'm confused, Guy.'

'I must say that I'm a little confused too. This is not what I anticipated.' He tilted his head to one side, his eyes, flat and expressionless, fixed on hers. 'And disappointed.'

'Disappointed?' Annabelle said. '*You're* disappointed?'

'Yes. I am. And I can get quite upset when I'm disappointed.'

'Well, I'm sorry to be such a disappointment,' Annabelle said. 'But you did kidnap me and half-rip my arm from its socket.'

'Yes,' he said. 'I'm sorry about that. It wasn't part of the plan. And neither was you attacking me.' His voice was reproachful. 'That was completely unnecessary.'

'Well, let me apologize,' she said, her voice heavy with sarcasm. 'I should have had better manners, but I don't know how you were expecting me to react after you kidnapped my kids.'

'You don't?' he said, and the last vestiges of his smile fell away, to reveal a face that looked less than human. 'I thought you'd be *glad*.'

2

Glad? He thought she'd be glad?

Of all the crazy things that had happened, this was almost the craziest.

She looked out of the window. At least she knew where she was now. She knew where she'd seen this view. It was in a photo Guy had sent her. He had bought a cottage by a lake, somewhere between Brighton and London, a few years back.

She couldn't remember the name, but it was pretty remote, she remembered him telling her that. They had met in London for lunch around that time, when one of her books was coming out, and he had explained how restful it was to have a bolthole to escape to when the pressures of the job and the city got on top of him.

What pressures? she had wanted to say. *You try having kids and a family and bills to pay and trying to write novels.*

She hadn't. She didn't want to be accused of complaining, so she had murmured *how lovely*. Now she wished she had told him what she actually thought.

'Guy,' she said. 'Why would I be glad?'

He smiled that uncertain smile.

'You know,' he said. 'You know why I'm doing this, and if you know that, then you know why you should be glad.'

'I don't,' she said. 'I have no idea. But whatever it is, it's over. I'm going home to my family.'

In an odd way it was almost a relief it was Guy. It might be scary and weird, but it was *Guy*. She'd known him since she was fourteen. He was – at least he had been – a known quantity. There was nothing for her to be afraid of. If it had been a crazed psychopath, that would have been different. But it was Guy. A friend. He had screwed up somehow, but she could handle him. She could *reach* him.

And she knew he would not hurt her, not *really* hurt her. He didn't have it in him. He couldn't, or she would have seen it over the years. You couldn't hide something that big for that long. No one could.

So she was going to leave. She was going to walk past him and leave this room and this house and this nightmare. And he would not stop her.

She walked towards him. He held up his hands and his lips twitched. 'Annabelle,' he began, 'I don't th—'

She tried to push past him and he grabbed her by the elbow and twisted. The pain bloomed through her shoulder and she screamed.

He increased the pressure.

'Guy!' she gasped. 'No. That hurts.'

'Annabelle. I don't think you understand.' Still holding her elbow, he pushed her back into the middle of the room. 'You can't leave.'

He levered her down until she was sitting on the end of the bed.

'And you don't *want* to leave,' he said.

'I do,' she said. 'I do.'

'No, you don't. More to the point, Annabelle, you *wanted*

310

this. It's your idea, Annabelle. You don't need to pretend any more.'

'Pretend what, Guy?'

'That you don't know what this is about.'

'I don't.'

The frantic look in his eyes grew wilder. He licked his lips. 'Annabelle—'

'I don't know what this is about, Guy. How could I? How could I know anything about this? It's fucking insane!'

'No, it isn't,' he said, his tone insistent. 'And you *do* know about it. It *was* your idea. You *made* me do it.' He frowned. 'I don't know why you're denying it. It's not helpful, Annabelle. It doesn't help us to move on with our plans.'

Our plans? She felt lost, bewildered by what he was saying. They had no shared plans. She had no idea what he was talking about.

'I have to say, I'm a little disappointed,' he said. 'I mean, I've gone to all this effort and we're finally here, together, like *you*' – he pointed at her, his arm fully outstretched, and his voice rose – 'wanted, and now you pretend you don't know what's happening? I mean, are you trying to ruin this deliberately? Because that's how it seems.'

She sat and looked at him. She had no idea what to say next.

He took a deep breath. 'Shall we start again?'

Even though she felt like she was lost in a thick fog with no sense of which way safety lay, starting again sounded like a good idea, because the terror was back, and the relief that it was Guy had vanished. This was not the Guy she knew. That Guy was gone, replaced by someone she did not recognize at all.

'OK. Let's start again.'

'Good.' He smiled. 'That's the right answer, Annabelle. Well done.'

Wynne

DI Wynne walked into DSI Marie Ryan's office and closed the door. Ryan looked up from the file she was reading. 'Take a seat.'

'No thanks,' Wynne said. 'I'll stand. I've been at my desk for the last hour or two,' she said. 'Good to get the blood flowing.'

'So, what do you have?'

Wynne looked at the window, then back at DSI Ryan. 'Nothing,' she said. 'We have absolutely nothing. Unless you count questions. We have plenty of those.'

'Take me through them.'

'Why, first of all. Not why does someone want Annabelle Westbrook – that could be revenge or obsession or another reason, although that leads us to who, and we have no suspects – but why kidnap the kids, and then exchange them for the wife?'

Ryan nodded. 'All that does is complicate matters. If it's revenge or obsession, why not just kidnap her and be done?'

'Right. There must be a reason to involve the kids.'

'Indeed, but it may be so specific we won't be able to guess it.'

'Which makes investigating it a challenge.'

'What if the kidnapper wanted to tie her in psychologically? Make her complicit.'

'We thought about that. But how does this make her part of it? She had no choice.'

Ryan shrugged. 'That's how we think about it. But we're rational people, DI Wynne. This person is not. Still, let's move on to question two. Who?'

'There's no one obvious. No disgruntled friend or colleague. We considered obsessive fans – one name came up, but we've ruled him out – and then there was an ex-girlfriend of the husband. She was pretty intense: lied about being pregnant to try and hang on to him, showed up at the christening of the first child threatening revenge.'

'Sounds promising.'

'We talked to her. We considered her husband, but his alibi checks out. Hers too. She's in the clear.'

'What about Annabelle's husband? He's a lawyer, right? Any enemies?'

'Not that he can think of. But we'll check. We'll interview his colleagues.'

Ryan bit her lip. 'Did the wife have a lover?'

'We can't ask her, obviously,' Wynne said. 'But she didn't mention anything to her husband before the handover.'

'She wouldn't.'

'You think? With the kids at stake? I think she would have confessed.'

'It's possible she didn't.'

'Possible,' Wynne conceded.

'And if it is that, find the lover and you find her,' Ryan said. 'What else have you got?'

'Nothing. We're looking for the van he put her in. We have it on CCTV leaving the car park at the truck stop, but there's been no trace since.'

'Vans don't just disappear, DI Wynne.'

'I know they don't. So the fact we can't find any sign of it suggests he hid it and switched to another vehicle.'

'In which case we would have no idea what we're looking for,' said Ryan. 'You have to find that van.'

'That's what we're working on,' Wynne said. 'It hasn't shown up on any of the ANPR cameras in the area, so we're assuming it was hidden quite close to the truck stop. Say within fifteen miles. But there's a lot of places to hide a van within fifteen miles of that truck stop.'

'Keep looking for it,' Ryan said. 'This isn't a random kidnap, DI Wynne. There's a reason for this, and if we can find out what that is, we'll find Annabelle Westbrook. Interview everyone you can think of, everyone who knows Matt and Annabelle. Friends, family, colleagues, ex-boyfriends and girlfriends. Find anything you can that might be a motive.'

'We will,' Wynne said, and she hoped for the sake of Matt, Annabelle and their kids that something came up, because as things stood she was completely in the dark.

Annabelle

1

'So,' he said, a thin smile on his lips. 'Aren't you glad we're finally here?'

She studied him. It was clear that something was wrong. This was not the Guy she knew; he was urbane, intelligent, kind. This person was unhinged. It was possible he had experienced a trauma she didn't know about which had left him like this, or he had suffered a breakdown of huge proportions.

Whatever it was, she couldn't think of him as harmless old Guy. Not now. Not until he was better.

Until then she had to treat him like he was dangerous. Which, the pain in her shoulder constantly reminded her, meant going along with him.

'Yes,' she said. 'I'm glad.'

'Glad?' he said. 'Only, I thought you'd be more than that. *Ecstatic*. After what you've been through.'

'I am,' she said. 'I said glad, but I meant delighted.'

He sat next to her on the bed and put his arm around her shoulder. He rested a hand on her thigh and she flinched away. 'I'm so happy to be near you.'

She shifted so their hips weren't touching. 'Me too,' she said.

His eyes narrowed, and he moved closer to her. 'Good,' he said.

She felt an intense discomfort at the touch of his hip. It was far too intimate. She didn't want to antagonize him, but she had to break the contact, or she was worried she might be sick.

She shuffled away. 'Sorry,' she said. 'It's – I need some space.'

He nodded. 'I understand. It's too soon. That's understandable. And we have all the time in the world.' He smiled, reassuringly. '*All* the time. He'll never find you here. I made sure of that. You're safe now. You've got everything you ever wanted.'

Her head spun. Safe? From what? From *Matt*? She tried to piece it all together. He had said it was her idea, that she had made him do this, that these were shared plans.

That she *wanted* to be here, was safe here, as though she was running from something.

But she had no idea what he was talking about. There was nothing in her life she wanted to flee; quite the opposite. And as for the fact that she'd made him do it – that was simply ridiculous. She had never told Guy that she needed him to kidnap her kids and then exchange them for her. Why would she?

But he believed it, and she needed to know what he thought and why or she would never get out of this mess.

Which meant swallowing her fear and playing along, for now.

'Guy,' she said. 'How did you know what I'd been through? I mean, we never talked about it.'

316

He raised his eyebrows in an exaggerated, theatrical gesture that said, *Are you crazy?*

'We didn't *talk* about it, but you told me everything. More than you could have by talking. I mean, come on, Annabelle. I can't even believe you're asking.'

'*I* know what I did,' she said. 'I want to make sure *you* do. So? How did you know?'

He turned to the shelves and held his hand up to her books.

'You wrote it all in these,' he said. 'In your books. As you well know. You wrote it all in your books, so I would know every detail. I suspected it as soon as I read the first one.'

'Suspected what, exactly?' Her mouth was dry, and the words came out softly.

'How unhappy you were.' He leaned forward, his eyes wide. 'But more than that, I understood the true message of the book.' He inhaled, his nostrils flared, as though he was about to taste a fine, vintage wine. 'And then you did not change your name. You remember that conversation with your publisher? We discussed publishing as Annabelle Westbrook, given you were engaged, but you chose to *stay* Annabelle Anderson. That was you telling me that what was in them was the true you. It was a relief, Annabelle. More than that. A *vindication*. I had suspected it all along, but it was a wonderful day when it was confirmed.'

She could see that what he was saying had an internal logic. If you took all the evidence he had amassed and looked at it the way he was looking at it, his conclusion made sense. He had built the entire edifice piece by piece.

The problem was that the foundations were entirely rotten.

'When what was confirmed?' she murmured.

'I'm glad you're testing me,' he said. 'It's proof that you are as serious about this as I am. I can tell you I was glad to finally find out that you loved me. That you had always

317

loved me, but hadn't realized it.' He smiled. 'And that you needed my help.'

She couldn't think of any response, so she just watched him.

He stepped towards the desk and picked up the champagne bottle. 'This can wait. I have to go now. Trust me – I know you'll understand – I want nothing more than to spend the day with you, but duty calls. I'm going into the office. They'll notice if I don't show up, and I can't risk calling any attention to myself by doing anything out of the ordinary. Not now. Not when they're looking. They'll stop soon enough, and then we can do whatever we want, but until then I'm afraid I have to be careful!'

She watched him leave the room and heard the click of the lock, then closed her eyes.

This – and she would not have thought such a thing was possible a few minutes earlier – was worse than she had thought.

2

Annabelle looked at the door, then the lake, and then the plastic champagne flutes.

She was starting to see what was happening, and it filled her with a sense of dread. There was something deep and longstanding and powerful and immensely troubling behind all this, and, although she didn't fully understand it, she could tell it was out of control.

Guy was in love with her, and it seemed like it had been that way for a long time. That alone was flabbergasting, but on top of that he thought she loved him. And the reason was her books.

He was mentally ill, she realized, and in the way that some people heard voices or saw secret codes all around them, he saw in her books a secret message, and his belief it was the truth was so profound that he was prepared to do all this as a result.

She tried to think through what he was seeing in her books. *Still Waters*, in which a woman marries a man she doesn't want to because he knows something secret about her and she has to resort to desperate measures – involving another man – to escape him. *Deep Cover*, a love story in which a

319

young couple fail to recognize they are meant to be together and marry other people, only to find each other when they are much older. *The Knot,* in which a wife, suddenly ill, discovers that her husband is not who he said he was, a discovery which changed everything for her and put her in danger. Danger she is rescued from when an old friend helps her out.

And then *This Is Not the End,* her most recent book, about a new mother suffering from post-natal depression, and, in the deepest stretch of her depression, questioning whether she even wants her child.

But deciding she does.

Evidently, Guy thought they were about her. He thought they were autobiographical. But there was more than that.

He thought they were a message from her to him. A woman forced into marriage, a wife in danger, a mother who questioned her motherhood. A coded plea. A cry for help.

A call to arms.

And he had responded by rescuing her.

But that left a question. Why kidnap the kids? Why not just abduct her?

She didn't know; she was sure he would tell her in time. For now she needed to be calm and figure out how to get away.

Annabelle looked out of the window at the lake. It was visible through a stand of tall trees. Pines maybe, but certainly evergreens. All the other trees around were deciduous.

She wondered if the pines had been planted to provide a year-round screen, shielding the house from the lake. Surely Guy had not gone to that much trouble?

She pictured a boat slowing to a stop by the shingle beach and rocking gently as two people got out for a picnic, then looking up at the window and seeing her frantically waving.

Except they wouldn't see her. She could see down to the

water, but the view up would be blocked by the trees. If someone really looked hard they might, at a stretch, see the window, but would they see her? And see that she was gesturing for help?

And no one would stop there, anyway. It was private land, and she was certain that Guy had thought all this through. He would have made sure there were signs telling people to stay away, and, even if they disobeyed them, it wouldn't help. There was no way he would have given her a window if there was any possibility that she would be visible to anyone. There might be boats out on the water – he couldn't control that – but all they would see was a peaceful lake house.

So she was going to have to get out of here herself.

She put her hand on the window. It was clear from looking at it that it was much thicker than normal glass. She pushed it; there was no movement at all. She looked at the frame, where the edge of the glass was visible.

It was perhaps three-quarters of an inch thick.

Unbreakable.

She turned the door handle. Locked, obviously. She tried to rattle it, but it was fixed, fast. It was made of a thick metal. She banged on the wall. Stone, she thought. Either the whole house was made that way – which was not impossible for an older house – or he had built this room specially.

However it had come about – and the architectural history of the room was of no interest to her – she was not going to smash her way out of her prison.

She would have to find another way.

She looked around for a weapon. There was nothing, especially since he had taken the champagne bottle.

Maybe she could persuade him to let her out for a bit of fresh air and run away. Or fake an illness.

He would not fall for that. He was too smart. He always had been.

She had known him since they were fourteen, when he had moved to the house down the street from her and started at her school. She had a boyfriend – Connor – and Guy had started going out with Heather Stanford, who was generally considered to be unattainable by every other boy in the school.

She had, for a few months, had a crush on him. One day, walking to school, she had tried to let him know.

What would you tell a friend to do if they were secretly interested in someone, but that person was just a friend? Should they tell them?

She had hoped he would guess that the friend she was talking about was her, and give her a sly look, then take her hand in his and stop walking and turn to look at her, and then they would kiss.

Sometimes it's better to say nothing, he said. *It'll pass.*

She had assumed he had guessed, and had given her the message he wasn't interested as kindly as he could.

After all, he was going out with Heather Stanford, who was five foot ten tall and looked like a model.

So she had moved on, and the crush had dissipated, and they had become friends. She liked having him as a friend – he was smart and handsome and charismatic and had something mysterious about him.

And now it turned out he'd been in love with her all along.

She could barely believe it. How had she missed it?

How had he *hidden* it? How had he managed to conceal something so powerful it had led him to this?

No – she was missing something. When he came back she would talk to him, calmly and rationally. She would ask him to explain and she would tell him the truth and he would see the mistake he was making.

And he would let her go.

She sat on the edge of the bed, her legs suddenly too weak

to support her. He had to let her go. She couldn't allow herself to think otherwise.

Because the alternative was too awful to contemplate.

1

She is where she has always belonged. Obviously she is a little bit fragile, for the moment. She's been through an emotional time, even if it is what she has been wanting.

She is also upset at how I did it. I can understand that. Perhaps I should have revealed myself immediately, then she would not have been hurt. I think this has turned her against me, for now at least. But she will come around. What's that trite saying people like so much? Love conquers all? Perhaps it is true.

And then we can get on with our lives.

It will be hard, of course. She will have to stay hidden, isolated in the lake house for quite some time. We can hardly go swanning around London together!

But, eventually, I will tell my friends I've met someone. I'll describe dates at the theatre and meals at smart restaurants. I'll show them photos of us together.

And one day they'll meet her. I know her name already – Angelica.

Angelica. Meaning: angel, or angelic.

She has always been my angel. And I have always been hers. I've wanted to tell her for years, but the time was never right. When we first met I lacked the confidence – ironic, given how everyone saw me, but that was all a front – and couldn't face the fear that she would reject me.

Because I loved her from the moment I saw her. I don't know why; I knew that she was the piece that would complete me, and that I had to wait for the right moment to make her mine.

She'll be surprised when I tell her how I waited. She thinks – like everyone – that I'm confident and sure of myself. Arrogant, even. I am, now – I've made myself that way – but back then I wasn't.

I was weak and nervous. I didn't let it show, but I was.

Hardly surprising, given what had been done to me by my bitch of a mother.

She drove my father away with her constant nagging, and then married Richie.

Richie. Just remembering his name makes me furious. I could kill all the world. Burn it down.

He had what they called a 'thing' for young boys.

Me included.

After the first time – I was twelve – he explained what he would do to me if I told anyone. It involved pain, and humiliation.

But I did tell someone, a year later, after fifty-two weeks of Richie coming to my room once or twice or three times a week.

I told my mother. I had to escape, so I told her.

And she did nothing. She called me a liar. Said I had never liked Richie and was making it up to split them apart.

So I had no alternative. Richie had to go. He was the first person I killed, and I did it from necessity.

The strange thing was that I found I enjoyed it. We went sailing on the River Dee and he fell overboard when I capsized the boat with a well-timed gybe.

He was not a swimmer, especially when encouraged to slip under the surface by the blade of an oar. The autopsy uncovered the bruises, but they were easily explained. He had banged his head in the chaos.

Killing him made me happy, because he was gone. It also made me calm, for the first time in my life.

Every time I've needed that calm I have been able to find it that way. I am not a serial killer – I am not tawdry like that, I do not need a fix – but I have a right to peace of mind, don't I? And all – well, most – of the people I have killed have deserved it.

My mother deserved it more than most. It was fitting that she died in the same way as Richie. A boating accident, which her young son survived.

A 'cruel irony' the local press called it. Poetic justice was the phrase I preferred. I made sure she understood that, before I pushed her head under the water.

They sent me to live with my uncle. I hated it, but then, a year later I met Annabelle. She was perfect.

She was my salvation.

I should have told her, but I was too weak. I let her slip away, and then she met that fool.

I never understood why she married him, but then she told me. He made her do it. I always knew he must have. Coercion and blackmail.

That was the message from the first book.

In the second she asked me to rescue her. The third; well, that could hardly have been any more obvious. And the latest? That was the final piece of the puzzle.

That one said, 'it's fine to do this. Put aside your doubts, and do it now.'

And I have her. We have each other.

Of course, there will be a problem with her meeting people if she looks like she does now. Someone will recognize her.

It's inevitable, in the modern world. Stuff gets all over social media. The only way to stop it would be to hide her away forever, and neither of us want that.

We might be exceptional people, but we want to live a normal life together. We want the world to witness our love.

So she will have to change her appearance. I have a plan for that, though. It will be hard and painful, but she will accept it.

Great love requires great sacrifice.

She knows that.

She may protest, but that is just proof of how great the sacrifice is.

Of how great our love is.

She will see it, in the end.

2

Now, to deal with her fool of a husband. I call him.

'Matt? It's Guy. Any news?'

'No.' *He sounds depressed, as he should. I'm looking forward to hearing it get worse.* 'The police lost the van. They think the kidnapper switched to a different vehicle.'

My plan worked. Useful information, and not the first useful information he has given me. The text messages immediately after the handover were vital – I had not anticipated a drone. If this idiot hadn't told me about it, I would have stuck to the A roads to get to the van.

And they would have followed me and seen what I had done.

As it was, I took the motorway. Thanks, Matt, you useless clown.

'Jesus. I'm sorry,' I say. 'What next?'

'I don't know. I really don't.'

'Can I help?'

'I don't think so.' *A pause, heavy with emotion.* 'Not at this point.'

'OK. Well, I'm in the office. Don't hesitate to let me know.'

'I won't.'

'And the kids? How are they?'

'Holding up, just. But it's going to be a tough road. They miss their mum.'

'I'll bet.'

She won't be missing them, though. That was the message of the fourth book, This Is Not the End. *She told me how to do this.*

A mother who didn't want her offspring. No surprise, given they came from the man who had forced her into marriage. Yes, in the book she changes her mind, but that was for public consumption. It was not part of the message. The message was that there was no reason to leave her there, trapped in her life with this fool. She didn't want the children. I was free to act.

And the title: how much clearer could it be?

There's a knock on my office door.

'I'll call later,' I said. 'And good luck, Matt.' *I put the phone down.* 'Come in.'

The door opens. It's Jenn. She joined a few months back, working in foreign rights.

She fucking annoyed me back then. She was nondescript. Brown, curly hair, a plain face. Nothing special about her at all.

And the bitch turned me down, a week after she started here. I was bored. I am often bored. I decided to use her to alleviate the mood, so I suggested a drink after work.

I have a boyfriend, *she said.*

Imagine: her *turning* me *down.*

It fucking pissed me off.

It's only a drink, *I said.* To say welcome.

The damage was done, though. I had asked her out and she had said no. I was enraged. It was humiliating. She should have been grateful; instead I was feeling like a fool.

And who was she to make me feel like that?

I taught her a lesson, though, not that she knows it was me.

'Hi, Jenn,' I say. 'Good weekend? Any news?'

Her face is narrow and her eyes sunken. She's lost quite a bit of weight in the last three weeks. That's what worry does to you.

'No,' she says.

'Still no word from him?'

It feels so good to twist the knife. A knife I had put there, with great pleasure.

'No.' She shakes her head. 'He's disappeared.'

'People don't just disappear,' I say. 'Something must have happened.'

'Or he got fed up of me. But he could have said something.'

'Jenn,' I say, 'there's no way he got fed up with you. You're amazing.'

She gives the ghost of a smile. 'Thanks. But I'm not sure that's true.'

Lovely. A bit of insecurity, accentuated by the fear that he simply left her because she is worthless.

He didn't, though. He is in the boot of his car, his neck snapped in two, in the corner of a scrapyard. Of course, I told him why he was going to die before I did it.

Because your stupid girlfriend didn't give me what I want, I said. And I am a man who gets what he wants.

And I do. I always do.

Matt

Matt put the phone down.

'Who was that?' DI Wynne said. She and DS Dudek had arrived at his house a few minutes earlier.

'Guy Sanderson,' Matt said. 'He's Annie's agent.'

Dudek made a note in his notebook. 'Might he know if there'd been a problem with a fan?'

'Maybe,' Matt said. 'But he would have mentioned it by now.'

'You never know,' Dudek said.

'We'll interview him,' Wynne said. 'Do you have his contact details?'

'I'll write them down. He lives in London. That's where his office is.'

'We can call him,' Wynne said. 'If he knows anything, we can go to see him.'

'He'd come here,' Matt said. 'He'd probably want to see me and the kids anyway.'

'Is he a friend? As well as an agent?' Wynne said.

Matt nodded. 'We go back a long way.' He pointed to a photo of Norman's christening. 'That's him.'

Wynne looked at it. 'I see,' she said. 'Give us his details.'

'In the meantime,' Dudek said, 'we need to make a list of people we should be talking to. Your colleagues, friends, family. We have to follow every possible avenue.'

'I understand,' Matt said. 'Where do you want to start?'

'How about your colleagues?' Wynne said. 'Could you give us their details?'

Wynne

1

DI Wynne and DS Dudek sat at a table in a conference room, a china cup of coffee on the table in front of each of them. There was a plate of biscuits; Dudek picked up a pink wafer and dipped it in his coffee.

'That's disgusting,' Wynne said.

'It's not,' Dudek said. 'It's the only way to eat biscuits. Keeps them moist.'

'When you finish there'll be bits of biscuit in the bottom of the cup.'

'That's a price I'm prepared to pay.'

Wynne sighed. 'They'll think we're savages.'

The door to the conference room opened and a tall woman in her fifties walked in. She was wearing a red skirt and red wedge shoes. She sat opposite them.

'I'm Valerie Cobb,' she said 'We're very concerned to hear about Annabelle. Do you have any updates?'

'Not at the moment,' Wynne said. 'Thank you for meeting us.'

'Of course. Whatever we can do.'

'We'd like to meet with Mr Westbrook's colleagues,' Dudek said.

'What exactly would you be looking for from us?'

Dudek sipped his coffee. 'We're looking for any information that might lead us to a motive. A reason someone would do this.'

'Someone who had something against Matt?' she said. She smiled. 'I think you might be barking up the wrong tree, to coin a phrase. I can't think of anyone who doesn't like Matt.'

'A client?' Wynne said.

'Matt does mainly small-to-medium-sized commercial transactions,' Valerie Cobb said. 'He has a group of clients he's been working with for years. I think they're all happy with his counsel.'

'Maybe he got something wrong,' Dudek said. 'And a client suffered a loss because of it.'

'I would have heard,' Cobb said. 'At least, I think I would. I suppose it *is* possible.' She smiled again. 'But very unlikely.'

She steepled her fingers.

'We – I included – will do whatever we can to help. Matt is a deeply valued colleague and an even more deeply valued friend. But I have to say that I don't expect you'll find what you are looking for in his professional life. I can't imagine how he would have hidden something of this magnitude.'

'You'd be surprised what people can hide,' Wynne said. 'For years. Decades. It used to surprise me. But not any more.'

'I suppose you have more experience in this arena than I do,' Cobb said. 'But please. Ask whatever you want, of whomever you want. We are at your disposal.'

'Thank you,' Wynne said. 'We appreciate it.'

2

Valerie Cobb was right. Wynne and Dudek talked to a procession of Matt Westbrook's colleagues and they all told the same story. He was kind and honest and well-liked, and none of them had any idea who would have anything serious against him, let alone something that could provide a motive for anyone to kidnap his wife.

They left in Dudek's Astra. He sucked his top lip.

'Nothing there,' he said.

'Nothing anywhere,' Wynne said. 'I'm going to call Sanderson. The agent.'

She dialled the number Matt had given her.

'Hello. Guy Sanderson.'

'Hello, Mr Sanderson. My name is Detective Inspector Jane Wynne. I'm working on the Annabelle Westbrook case. Would you be available to answer questions?'

'Of course. I was thinking you'd call. Matt mentioned you wanted to talk to me. That's why I answered, actually. Normally I don't pick up if it's a number I don't recognize. And you can ask me whatever you like.'

Wynne winced. She wished Matt Westbrook hadn't said anything. Even when the person she was talking to was not a suspect she didn't like them to have time to prepare.

'Thank you. I understand you are Mrs Westbrook's agent? But you have known her since you were at university?'

'Longer. I met Matt at university – Birmingham, in 2004 – but I'd known Annabelle since I moved to Richmond – the one in Yorkshire – when I was fourteen. We were at school together.'

'Were you friends?'

'Yes. Not super close. We became better friends at Birmingham.'

'Why was that?' Wynne said.

'I don't know. I think just because when we arrived we knew each other. We did quite different things, though.'

'Like what?'

'I was involved in theatre. She spent a lot of time with Matt.'

'How would you characterize your relationship with Mr Westbrook?' Wynne said.

'We're good friends. Very good friends. He's one of the people I'm closest to.'

Wynne looked out of the window. It was starting to go dark. It was how she felt about the investigation.

'I know this may be an awkward question . . .' she said.

'Go ahead,' he said. 'Ask me anything.'

'Did you and Annabelle Westbrook ever have a romantic relationship?'

'Before she met Matt?' he said. 'No. We didn't.'

'And after she met him?'

He laughed. 'No, Ms Wynne. We did not. I am very fond of Annabelle, but we have never been interested in each other in that way.'

Wynne pursed her lips. In her experience, it was near impossible for a boy and a girl and then a man and a woman to be friends for the length of time Guy Sanderson and

Annabelle Westbrook had been friends, and for there to be no romantic spark between them.

But she would have to take his word for it.

'Were you aware of any fan who may have behaved . . . unusually towards Mrs Westbrook?' Wynne said.

He made a noise as though he was blowing out his cheeks. 'I've been thinking about that,' he said. 'It's an obvious place to look. But there's nothing that comes to mind. Really nothing.'

He paused.

'Could I call you back?' he said. 'You're breaking up. I'll use my desk phone?'

'Yes,' Wynne said. 'Please do.'

Bumbling plod will see my number and know I'm in London. That's what I want – establish distance between me and the events that she's supposed to be investigating.

Although she has no clue what's going on. I was worried the police might be able to figure it out but they are just as useless as I expected.

Which is great. Everything is going perfectly. It's almost too easy.

Tap out the number. Let it ring. Here she is.

'Wynne.'

'Hi. Thanks for that.' *Pleasant, slightly submissive tone of voice. Make them think you're harmless. Like I said, too easy.*

'Not a problem. Could you tell me where you were over the weekend, Mr Sanderson?'

She's looking to see if I have an alibi.

As if I would not have an alibi. What kind of idiot would not have an alibi? I mean, no wonder the police never get anything done. Does she seriously think that someone who could plan and execute this would neglect to give themselves an alibi?

It's almost insulting.

'Let me see, I was in the office on Friday, left around four p.m. and went to my lake house.'

'Your lake house?'

'Yes. I have place by a lake. Between London and Brighton. I go there often, but this weekend I was there because I had a meeting in Brighton on Saturday morning.'

All true. All verifiable.

I left the office at four. Got to the house at six.

Then I drove the van up to a truck stop. Four long, boring hours.

But necessary. You see, I had decided that this was the weekend I was doing it. I'd been watching them for a while – since the most recent book, when I realized the children weren't an issue – and the time had come.

There will be travel restrictions soon, like in other countries. They will be here before long, and who knows how long they will last? I had to act, now.

The plan was to take one kid. Pick him or her up from the garden, or as they were walking to the corner shop.

It was just luck that had presented all three.

Another four hours back to the lake house, on the motor-bike I'd taken up in the back of the van. Small, but does the job.

I towed it back up North on Saturday afternoon, on a trailer hooked up to the Audi. It was how I got around while I was up there. No one recognizes you under a helmet. It's very useful. You can get very close to people, and they have no idea you're there. The bike's at the truck stop now. They might find it, one day, and trace it back to one Andrew Stephenson, of Skegness. Which won't help them.

'What was the meeting in Brighton?' the detective asks.

'It was to plan a literary festival. I was offering to do a talk on how to get an agent.'

'What time did that end?'

'About midday.'

'And then?'

'Back to the lake house.'

'Did anyone see you there?'

'I'm afraid not.' I put a regretful tone into my voice. 'It's quite remote.'

'There might be someone,' Wynne said. 'We'll ask around.'

Wynne

DI Wynne cut the connection. Dudek glanced at her.

'Anything?' he said.

She looked at the screen of her phone. It was dark, and her face looked back at her. There were no answers there.

'No. He's known her for years. Since they were teenagers. They're good friends.'

'Ever more than that?'

'He said not.'

'Believe him?' Dudek said.

'I think so. Even if there was something, it was a long time ago.'

'He could have been secretly in love with her, all along,' Dudek said, then shrugged. 'I know. Clutching at straws.'

'And he has an alibi,' Wynne said. 'He was in Brighton on Saturday at a literary thing. Until midday, at least. I'll check it, but I don't think it's him.'

Dudek's phone rang. He picked it up. 'Forensics,' he said. 'They might have something on the cars.'

Wynne held her hand out. 'I'll take it,' she said. 'No talking while driving.'

Matt

The kids were asleep. At different points during the night all three of them had been awake. Molly was first; around one in the morning she came into his room. He was awake anyway; he held out his arms and she climbed into bed with him.

Where's Mummy?

She's still gone.

I thought you were going to find her?

She was too young to understand that finding Mum might not be as easy as finding a lost teddy bear or book. For Molly, Mum being gone was a temporary thing. Confusing, yes, but soon to be over.

He wished he could be as confident.

Once she was asleep, he managed to nod off. He was woken by Norman. He was standing by the bed, shivering.

Hey, Matt said. *Come in the bed. Are you cold?*

Norman shook his head. *I'm scared.*

He held his son tight against him until his shaking stopped. He had not held him like that for a long time and he was shocked by how big he was. He was starting to become aware of the world in a way that younger kids weren't. These were key years, and it was possible he would be without his mum for them. Matt turned his face away. He didn't want his tears to run off his face and onto Norman's.

Last to come was Keith. He opened the door noisily; that was always how he had tried to get attention. He wouldn't come and tell you he wanted to talk, or burst into tears. He would stomp around a room, or kick something or open a door with a bang, so you'd ask how he was. Then he'd say *fine*, and you'd say *are you sure?* And he'd say, *yes, but* and whatever it was would come out.

Only because you asked, though. Not because he wanted to tell you.

Are you OK? Matt said.

Fine.

Come here and give me a hug.

I'm fine.

I want a hug anyway.

He came over. Matt moved to make space for him. *Everything OK?*

Yes. Then a pause. *Is Mum coming back?*

He kissed his forehead. *Yes.*

How do you know?

I believe it, Keith. I just believe it.

Norman would not have accepted that as an answer; he would have asked for proof and facts. Keith was a different type of person. He nodded.

I believe it too, he said.

Now – in the late afternoon – all three were asleep in the living room. Tiredness had caught up with them; they were too young to fight it.

He wasn't. He was exhausted but sleep seemed a distant possibility. He could fall asleep, but almost immediately he would jerk awake, his heart racing. The few minutes of rest were enough to – barely – keep him going. He'd read once about sailors who went solo around the world. They were

343

unable to sleep for more than a few minutes at a time in case something went wrong, and so that was what they did. Every hour they napped for ten minutes, which added up to four hours a day.

Hardly high-quality sleep hygiene, but clearly enough. Maybe that was his future.

He opened the drawer where they kept the tea and took out a teabag. Next to the Tetley's was a box of jasmine green tea.

It was what Annabelle drank. They had an ongoing debate about whether it was proper tea or not. She claimed it was; he said it wasn't. She was right, of course, and in truth he quite liked it, but it had become part of the furniture of their relationship.

Drinking that muck again?

You should try it, Matt.

He had various stock responses:

I did. Thought I'd picked up some warm drain cleaner by accident.

Or:

I have been using it, actually. It's good for cleaning your feet.

Or:

Someone came over the other day who I really don't like, so I made them a cup.

She would roll her eyes, and laugh, and he would say, *Go on then, I'll have a cup*, and they would sit on the couch and drink jasmine green tea together and enjoy the quiet and be happily in love, married now and forever.

He dropped the teabag and sank to his haunches, a huge sob heaving his chest painfully.

Was that all gone? Was their relationship – the bedrock of his entire adult life – over? Because of an unknown individual with an unknown reason?

It felt that way, and it felt like an unbearable fate. If that was what the world had in store for him, he wanted no part of it. He wanted oblivion.

But that was not an option. Norman and Keith and Molly needed him.

He wasn't sure he could do it.

The door opened. He wiped his eyes and got to his feet. Norman was looking at him, his eyes swollen and puffy.

'Daddy,' he said. 'I want Mum. Can you get her? Please?'

Annabelle

It was dark outside. She had watched the day pass by, the shadows of the trees growing longer. From the position of the sun she could tell that the house was facing south to the lake, not that the knowledge was much use to her.

She looked out across the water. There were no lights visible, no houses that she could see. Occasionally car headlights moved on the far side of the lake. There must be a road there, although it was very lightly used. The cars were very infrequent.

She tapped the glass again. It was much thicker than ordinary glass; her dad had taken her and Mike to Brittany one summer and it reminded her of the windows on the ferry. They were scratched and salt-caked, but they felt similarly robust and unbreakable.

She thought about the builder who had put the window in. Had they not wondered why Guy wanted a room like this? Or had Guy told them some story? It was hard to think what it could be. Either way, even if the builder had been suspicious, it didn't help her now.

She left the window. There was a door in the corner of the room which led to a small bathroom. There was a plastic cup next to the sink – anything heavier might be a weapon, she supposed – which she filled with water. Guy had left no food, although there was a small packet of ibuprofen. She had already taken six of them – her shoulder was throbbing – and there were only two left.

She popped them out of the foil and put them in her mouth, then washed them down with the water. It was cold, and delicious. Perhaps it came from the lake, or a well, but it tasted much better than what came from the tap at home.

That was something.

She tilted her neck to one side to stretch it. It pulled on her shoulder muscles and she grunted in pain. She would have to ask him for stronger painkillers. The ibuprofen just wasn't cutting it.

She was also starting to feel hungry. She had hardly eaten since the kids were taken, so she might try to eat when Guy came back.

There was a chance she would throw it all up, though. She had a constant, low-level nausea.

When would he be back? He had gone to the office, intending to keep up appearances. That was in London, so what? An hour away? If he left at five, he'd be here soon. She had no watch, but it began to get dark in the late afternoon at this time of year, so he should be here soon.

And then what? Food, more painkillers, but what else? Beg him to let her go? That didn't seem likely to work.

Which left one option. She could explain to him, calmly and rationally, that she did not love him, that the books were not secret messages, and that he was mistaken about the whole thing. If he knew that then surely he would see that this was pointless.

Let me leave, she'd say, *and I'll find my own way home. I'll say I have no memory of what happened to me. Everything can go back to normal.*

347

She turned back to the window. A car was passing on the far side of the lake.

She heard a noise behind her and jumped, startled.

There was a click, and the door unlocked.

She will be glad to see me, obviously. She was tentative earlier, which is to be expected. After all, she has been waiting for this for most of her adult life, ever since she realized – early on – what an error her marriage was and began to plan for how to get out of it.

She could have just asked me, but I understand it wasn't that easy for her. Maybe she didn't even fully understand her desperation herself. A kind of protection mechanism, maybe, to stop herself from losing her mind.

She was starting to see it, though, earlier. She wanted to test me, which I can accept. She needs to be sure.

Like I am. I am sure this is right, and that helps with everything. It provides clarity. Who could do what I have done if they had doubts? Even if she tells me she does not want this, I know she does. I see more clearly than her. It's my job to guide her to the light.

I have food for her. She will be hungry. Smoked trout. Greek salad. Feta, cucumbers, tomato. Fresh bread from my favourite bakery. The bottle of Piper Heidsieck I removed earlier: 2008, a vintage year. Very good with seafood.

Not the kind of crap she is used to. Last time I was at her house I was appalled at the swill her fool of a husband was letting her pollute herself with.

I think it was Australian. I could hardly bear to look. She deserves so much better. And this is the start of her getting what she deserves. It will take time for her to realize what she has been missing. In a way it is like deprogramming someone from a cult, but I have time. Time does not worry me. I am above time. Beyond it.

I unlock the door. I am looking forward to seeing her. This has been in the making for years but now I know she is there it is hard to be away.

She is standing by the window. Her face is pale. She looks tired.

It must be the pain. The package of ibuprofen is empty.

My poor darling.

'Here,' I say. 'Have a little food.'

Annabelle

1

The door opened. He was wearing a pair of dark grey trousers and a white, tailored shirt.

In his hands he held a tray with a plate of salad on it, and a bottle of champagne. Probably the one from earlier.

'Here,' he said. 'Have a little food.'

What hunger she had been feeling drained away.

'Maybe later,' she said.

'You're not hungry?'

'A little. I might try it in a bit.'

He put the tray on the table and gestured at the bottle.

'Drink? It's a good bottle. Vintage.'

She shrugged. 'I wouldn't know the difference.'

'I know,' he said. 'But you will. Should I open it?'

She didn't know what to say. Champagne was for moments of celebration: a wedding, or the birth of a child, or seeing a good friend after a long absence. It was not for *this*. It was a sign of how far apart they were: he was hoping to drink champagne; it was the last thing she wanted.

'Not for me,' she said. 'If you want to, go ahead.'

He frowned. 'I got it for you!'

'I'm not in the mood.'

He inhaled through his nostrils then blew out his cheeks as though dealing with an unreasonable child. 'Fine,' he said. 'I'll leave it. I don't want to drink alone. So. How was your day?'

He held her gaze, smiling a smile that did not reach his eyes. She had the sense that he was fighting to control a strong emotion.

The fear came back. He was not stable at all, and that terrified her.

'Great,' she said. 'It was . . . unusual.'

'Good, though?'

'Yes. Good.'

The smile stayed exactly as it was. 'Mine too. Nobody suspects anything. The police called me. They have no idea.' The smiled widened. 'Which is fantastic, isn't it?'

'Yes,' she said.

'You don't sound very convinced!' he said, his voice rising to a higher pitch. 'I mean, the least you could fucking do is try to sound fucking convinced!'

'Look,' she said. 'I'm sorry. It's just – you know – I miss my children.' It was not a good time to mention Matt. 'I'm worried about them.'

'You didn't even want them!' he shouted. 'You wrote a book about it. About the regret! About how you were depressed because of them!'

That was fiction, you moron, she wanted to say. *Are you that deluded?*

'Yes,' she said. 'I know. But I grew close to them.'

He sighed. 'Is that it?' he said. 'After all I've done, all you

352

can say is that you're worried about those brats? Those *irrelevant* brats?' He massaged his temples with his forefingers. His hands were shaking. 'OK,' he said. 'Let's start again.'

He rearranged his features into the smile that did not reach his eyes.

'So. How was your day?' he said.

2

She had a strong impression that if she antagonized him further he might snap, and she did not want to see what would happen then.

She took a deep breath. She could say whatever she needed to to get through this. It was just words.

'My day,' she said, 'was great.'

'Did you miss me?'

She nodded. 'Of course.'

'How much?'

How much? How much was enough for him?

'A lot. I missed you a lot.'

'More than you missed your children?'

No sane person would ask that of a mother, but then he was no sane person.

'Yes,' she said. 'More than them.'

'How much more?' he said. 'How many times more? Let's say you missed them a five. What did you miss me? A ten? A *fifty*?'

'A fifty,' she said.

He smiled. 'Wow. I never expected that. You *did* miss me!'

This was going nowhere. He was totally delusional. He

thought she was in love with him and had been secretly wanting him to rescue her from her husband and children, and nothing would change his mind.

That was the most frightening part. Nothing would change his mind.

At least she knew that now, but there was still one thing she did not understand.

'Guy,' she said. 'Why did you take the kids? Why did you arrange the ransom?'

He had been looking at the champagne; she had the idea he was about to suggest drinking it again, but he whipped around to look at her.

His eyes were narrow, his lips thin and white, pressed together in what looked like fury.

'What?' he said. 'What did you say?'

She had no idea why he was reacting like this, what it was that had tipped him into this fury.

'Never mind,' she said. 'It was nothing.'

'Did you ask why I arranged the ransom?' he said. 'Is that what you asked?'

His face was white, his eyes bulging in their sockets.

'Forget it,' she said. 'It doesn't matter.'

'Doesn't matter?' He clenched and unclenched his fists. 'You are such a *bitch*, Annabelle,' he said. 'Such a *bitch*. Well, I'm going to train you, you bitch. Like the dog you are. I should have done this years ago.'

He jumped across the room and grabbed her damaged arm.

'No,' she said. 'Please. Don't.' Then she screamed as he lifted her elbow and twisted it. She felt the bones in her shoulder grind together and it was agony, eye-watering agony, and then he stopped and her arm flopped by her side.

'The whole thing was about the ransom,' he muttered, deflated. 'And you pretend not to know why. How else could

355

you have done it? You could never have left him for me. I tried, before the wedding. I offered you an out, but he had you trapped—'

'That was you?' she said. 'You sent those emails?'

'Yes. And it taught me that you were stuck, which only got worse when he made you have children. So you had to leave them as well, which you made clear to me in your last book was what you wanted to do.'

'Why not just kidnap *me*?' she said.

'Because that would have been against your will! I had to give you the choice. You could have said no. You could have left the kids with me.' He held up his hand. 'It was perfect, right? It looked like you had no choice, because what mother would abandon her children like that? But I knew you didn't care about abandoning them, so for you it *was* a choice. And you made it. You chose me. That was the final proof I needed.'

There was so much wrong with this, she didn't know where to start. She hadn't known it was Guy, so she couldn't have chosen him. She had not been asking for his help. And she had never had any choice, because she did love her children, more than anything. She was not the mum he thought she was. She was the mum who would not have abandoned her children under any circumstances.

And that was the reason she was here. No other.

But she could not say that. She could not risk that anger again.

'Well,' he said. 'Here we are, again. Champagne?'

Tuesday, 10 March 2020, 7 a.m.

Wynne

1

They did not find his DNA in either vehicle.

Or hers. Wynne was still not sure this was a man. Pretty sure, but not certain. The kids thought it was, but they had described that high voice. It could have been a man with a high voice, of course, or a man disguising a low voice, or a woman.

The fact she couldn't even be sure of which one summed up this entire case: she had no idea what was going on.

And the question of why bother kidnapping the kids only to return them was still unanswered.

She thought about Matt Westbrook. For her this was an annoyance – an extreme annoyance, yes, but no more than that. For him it was a total disaster, a collapse of his and his kids' world. And he had no idea who or why, or whether he would ever see his wife again.

Wynne was beginning to think he wouldn't, and the forensic results from the Golf and the Land Rover were not giving her much hope that her opinion would be changing any time soon.

'So, yeah,' Dudek said. 'There was nothing. We found the kids' DNA, Matt and Annabelle's, but no one else's.'

'How's that possible?' she said. 'How does someone drive a car for that long and not leave a trace?'

'By being very careful,' Dudek said. 'And you know as well as I do. It's not television. The forensics people aren't miracle workers. You wear gloves and clean clothes, keep your hood up, maybe wear a face mask – you won't leave much behind.'

'Not much,' Wynne said. 'But nothing? That must have taken a lot of effort, which is telling in itself. They would only have taken such careful precautions if they felt that us getting their DNA presented a risk to them.'

'Because we already have it?'

'Right. Or because they think we could easily get it.'

Dudek nodded slowly. 'Which suggests it's someone she knows. They would assume that if we had DNA we would test everyone we could think of and find them.' He raised his hands in a gesture of helplessness. 'But we knew it might be someone she knows already. The question is who?'

'Or it's someone we have on file,' Wynne said. 'Which is new information.'

'OK,' Dudek said. 'I'll run a check for anyone with this kind of thing on their record, suspect or witness or interviewee.'

There was a knock on the office door. It opened and a uniformed officer came in. She gave a nod to Dudek then looked at Wynne.

'Good news,' she said. 'We found the van.'

'Where?' Wynne said.

'Near Sandbach. It was hidden away on a piece of wasteland. It's well off the beaten track.' The officer smiled. 'It was a stroke of luck. A guy with a construction business was there – looking for a place to do a bit of fly-tipping, we think, but we'll forgive him that – and he saw the van. Apparently it's pretty bashed up, so he thought he could get parts from it. Turned out it started right up.'

'The keys were in it?' Dudek said.

'I don't think so. He seems the type who wouldn't worry too much about keys. Anyway, he'd seen the news last night and remembered we were looking for a van that fit this description, so he called it in.'

Wynne stood up. 'Let's go. I want to see it. Then we can bring it in for forensics.' She glanced at Dudek. 'He may have been less careful with the van, or just in it for a longer period of time and so likely to have left more DNA. This could be it,' she said. 'This could be the break we needed.'

2

It was the van she had driven past. The windscreen smashed, the mirrors ripped off, the bonnet up, the metal creased and twisted: but the same van.

Wynne felt a chill in her back. She had been that close to Annabelle Westbrook. Mere feet away.

And now they had the van, maybe she'd be that close again, except this time she would not miss the opportunity.

It was clear now what the kidnapper had done. He had left the Golf at the pub, then walked to the truck stop and switched to the van, knowing that the police would figure out what they had done. So they had brought it to this deserted place and moved into another vehicle, well out of the sight of any cameras or prying eyes.

And then they had smashed it up so that it looked like another old van, abandoned so that the owner didn't have to deal with disposing of it.

It was a good hiding place. The kidnapper would know that the police would have alerted junkyards to look out for the van, and this was the next best thing. Perhaps they planned to come and move it at some point in the future, but for now this was a near-perfect solution.

But not perfect.

Someone *had* seen it, and wondered what it was, and now here she and Dudek were.

'Bring it in,' she said. 'I'll call forensics and make it a top priority. I want to know what's in that van as soon as possible.'

Annabelle

Annabelle lay on the bed, her shoulder throbbing. It was early; the dawn freshly broken, but she had been awake for a few hours, turning over what Guy had said.

She had a good idea of what he was thinking, and it terrified her. It was so outlandish and far from the truth that, if he believed this, he could believe – and do – anything. She had no idea how he had reached the conclusions he had, but that could wait. She had to deal in facts, and the fact was he thought she was secretly in love with him – so secretly she didn't fully realize it – and had been communicating with him through her books.

So he had constructed this monstrous plan to kidnap her children and then exchange them for her. For him, if she accepted the exchange it was proof he was right: she was choosing him over her family, all while being able to pretend to the world that she had no choice because she had to rescue her children. But since he thought she didn't really care about her kids – it was in the most recent book – that meant she was choosing him.

And everything else flowed from there. Every other fantasy he had constructed was proved right.

There was no point in trying to challenge the edifice he had built up. The whole point of the last book was that she *did* love her kids, but he was clearly beyond reason. She wondered how long his madness had been going on. Had he always been like this? It went at least as far back as the wedding – the emails proved that – but was it even deeper than that?

It hardly mattered, and she could hardly ask him. It would only provoke another painful attack on her damaged shoulder. Or worse. Maybe he would try to hurt her children, or do something awful to Matt.

So she had to tread carefully, try to find out his plans in a way that did not upset him.

She could make it sound like she was interested, that she merely wanted to know, for the good of them both.

Could she do that? She wasn't sure. But she was about to find out. There was a click as the door unlocked.

It opened, and there he was.

I'm going to have to get her better clothes. She looks scruffy. Bedraggled, almost. I want her to look her best. Sexy. I'll get her some lingerie, too. She'll want it. She's going to want me to think she's still a prize.

And right now she's slipping. There's no excuse, really – it's a lack of respect for herself – and for me – and I won't be able to accept that for long, but I can allow it this time.

This time.

She is in bed. She looks tired. She's going to need to sleep more. That's something else for her to work on.

'So,' I say. 'What are you?'

'I'm sorry,' she says. 'What do you mean?'

'A medium?' I look her up and down. Slim, but quite tall. She probably has problems getting things to fit, particularly coats, sweaters and shirts. It's those long arms. 'A twelve?'

'Twelve what?' She looked confused.

'Size twelve. In clothes.'

'Oh,' she says. 'Yes. More or less.'

'Long arms? That can be problematic. Most clothes are made for standard measurements – if you differ it can be a problem.' I give her a wide reassuring smile. Her reply – I am starting to lose my patience now – is a grimace. 'That's why I get my clothes bespoke. You will be too, soon enough.'

'We're going to a tailor?' she says. She sounds impressed.

'Of course. Life is going to get much better, for both of us.'

'Guy,' she says. 'What are you planning to do? You can't keep me here forever.'

I laugh. 'I know! I mean, we both want the same thing, right? To be together?'

She looks at me and there's fear in there – I'm not surprised, this is a brave new future for us – but also something else. Intrigue maybe.

'Yes,' she says. 'We both want the same thing. But this is no way to live.'

'I agree.' This is great. Fantastic. She's coming round sooner than I hoped. More proof – if more was needed – that I was right.

'So what are you planning?'

I smile again. I've been waiting for this moment. For the moment when it is no longer just me, but us, working out our future together.

And I've been looking forward to telling her the plan, because it is a *fucking* genius plan, and she will love me for it.

'Well,' I say. 'We want to live a normal life – as normal as two people like us can live, two extraordinary people—'

She interrupts me. Another opportunity for improvement. Interrupting is rude. 'I'm not extraordinary, Guy. You might be, but not me. I'm just a normal person.'

'Hardly!' I laugh, and this time I mean it. 'You are far from normal! Far above, that is. Anyway, we want to be able to go out and eat and have friends and go on holiday. Right?'

She nods again, still intrigued.

'And the problem is that people will see you and recognize you. Even if we avoid old friends, who knows what will pop up on Facebook or Instagram?' I raise a finger. 'But I have a solution.'

'Which is?' she says.

'It's obvious when you think about it,' I say, and I take

an envelope from my jacket pocket. I hand it to her. 'Take it out. Have a look.'

She reads it, and I see she is confused.

'I don't get it,' she says.

Annabelle

1

Guy was smiling, but not in his eyes. His eyes gave him away. It was a smile she recognized: wide, open, easy, charming. He had been doing it all his life, but now she realized it was all a sham. It was a mask. Had it always been? And why was he going on about clothes sizes?

He handed her an envelope. 'Take a look.' She unfolded a piece of A4 paper.

It was a birth certificate for someone called Angelica Rina Schmidt, born in Munich in 1984.

She caught his eye. 'I don't get it.'

He smiled. Again it did not reach his eyes. It was not like a smile at all; more like a deliberate rearrangement of his features.

'It's brilliant,' he said, his voice almost reverent. '*Genius.*'

'What is?' she said. 'Who is Angelica Schmidt?'

'She's you,' he said. 'This is a birth certificate I . . . procured. And with it I can get you a passport, everything you need for identification. You'll be Angelica. Angie. Guy and Angie. Got a ring to it, no?'

She was amazed he had not seen the flaw.

'But, Guy,' she said, 'people will still recognize me.'

'No they won't,' he said. 'Not if you change your appearance. Short hair, different colour.'

He was wrong. People would see through that, eventually. But that was fine by her. She'd get recognized and this would be over.

'OK,' she said.

'You're thinking that's not enough,' he said. 'And you're right. *That's* the plan. We are going to *fundamentally* change the way you look.' He leaned down, his face close to hers, his lizard smile fixed. 'Plastic surgery,' he said. 'Quite extensive.'

She stared at him.

'Great idea, no?' he said. 'I've spoken to a plastic surgeon already – an American, who can be relied on to keep quiet. He can't work any more, officially at least. He found his female patients a bit too appealing, shall we say. You'll be safe, though. I'll be there for your surgery, so he won't get up to any of his mischief with you. Anyway, he said that to make someone unrecognizable you need to do quite a lot of work. Nose shape, cheeks, jawline. None of it impossible, though. He'll be here this Friday. No point wasting time!'

He backed towards the door.

'I'll be the only person in the world who knows who you actually are,' he said. 'Think about that! You'll be all mine. I hope I still love you when you look different.'

She blinked. She had no idea what to say.

'Just joking,' he said. 'I'll *always* love you. Anyway, I have to go. I can't be out of the office. We don't want to mess this up when we're this close, do we?'

He held index finger and thumb a half-inch apart.
'This close,' he said. 'Right?'
She nodded. 'Right.'

2

So he was going to keep her here until his pet cosmetic surgeon had turned her into someone else.

Angelica Rina Schmidt.

Then Guy and Angie would sally forth into the world and dazzle it with their love for each other.

Her chest tightened. Every time she thought he couldn't get any crazier, he found a new level. It was like looking into an abyss, and she felt dizzy and unmoored.

She tried to breathe deeply. His plan was utterly grotesque, but at least she was clear now that they were beyond any possibility of reason. He could not be convinced to change his mind, and not only was it pointless – it was dangerous. If she succeeded in convincing him she did not love him, and had not been sending secret messages in her books, who knew what he would do?

It was perfectly possible – likely – that he would badly hurt her. Or kill her. She was trapped, but not in the way he thought.

Which might be an advantage. If she went along with the pretence and he started to believe her, his guard might slip. She might find an opportunity to get out of here.

Because that too was clear. She had to find a way to escape, and soon. If the surgeon was here Friday, it had to be before then.

She could not let Guy change her appearance. She would leave here the same person – but better, stronger – that had arrived.

She tapped the window. It thudded, reminding her of the thickness of the glass.

And reminding her how hard it was going to be to get out of here.

Matt

There was nothing to do but wait. It felt like a dream; he wandered from room to room, unable to sit still, and everything around him looked the same, but it was all different. It wasn't that the house lacked colour, or life, or looked flat: it just didn't seem real.

He kept thinking he was going to wake up and all this would be over.

But he also knew that wasn't going to happen. Not now, not ever.

He picked up his phone and unlocked it, then checked email and Facebook and his text messages. He didn't expect there to be anything. It was a few minutes past 2 p.m. and he had probably checked his phone fifty times already since midday, hoping there would be something.

Maybe a message from Annabelle, telling him where she was.

Nothing.

And then his phone rang. He recognized DI Wynne's number.

'Hello,' he said.

'Mr Westbrook? This is DI Wynne.'

'Do you have news?'

'Not of Mrs Westbrook. Not yet. But we have made significant progress.'

He stood straighter. 'What happened?'

'We found the van the kidnapper kept your children in. The assumption is it's the same one he used to transport Mrs Westbrook from the truck stop to the next vehicle. It was on a piece of wasteland in Sandbach.'

'And? Did you find out who owns it?'

'Not that. It was unregistered. But we did find DNA in it.'

'Do you know whose it is?'

She paused. 'No. We have no match.'

'Then I don't see how this helps.'

'I know it seems that way, but this is a big step. It means we can eliminate people, at the very least. I'd like to start with you, if I could. We'd like a sample of your DNA.' Before he could argue she carried on. 'It's standard practice,' she said. 'That's all. We'll be taking it from everyone who knows your wife.'

'Of course,' he said. 'How do you want to do it?'

'We'll send an officer,' she said. 'Hang tight, Mr Westbrook. We're making progress. *Real* progress.'

Tuesday, 10 March 2020, 6 p.m.

Finn

Finn Daniels veered between being shocked how unfair it was and shocked how upset he was. He was in love with Suneela, in the most profound way possible, and now it was over. He had always thought they might face their challenges, one day. Her parents – her mum, especially – didn't approve of him, and he had imagined them – her, mainly – trying to break him and Suneela up many times, finding an almost delicious enjoyment in the ways they found to circumvent her parents' – her mum's, that was – attempts to end their relationship.

In his imaginings, the attempts never succeeded. Their love was too strong. Who cared if Suneela was Hindu and he was Christian, more or less. Her mum had asked him once if he was a Catholic.

Maybe, he said. *We go to church sometimes. Weddings and things.*

You'd know if you were a Catholic, she said. *You must be Church of England.*

Yeah, he replied. *That rings a bell.*

She gave a sad shake of the head.

But who cared? Love conquered all, right?

Wrong.

He had accepted that her parents – her mum, primarily – might win out. Even that had been kind of OK. Their love was thwarted by forces beyond their control: it was almost heroic, and when they were older they would just find each other and be reunited in a glorious explosion of romantic joy.

At least in that – the worst case he could imagine – she loved him.

But it turned out it could be worse.

Because it wasn't her parents that were breaking them up. It was *her*.

She didn't want to marry him. He had asked, and she said, *Well, let me think about it* and he said, *What is there to think about?* and she said, *We're only sixteen* and he said, *So? We don't have to do it today, we can just promise* and she said *I've been meaning to talk to you about that* and he said, *What? Getting married?* and she said, *No, us.*

It turned out there was no 'us'. She didn't want to marry him; she didn't even want to go out with him any more.

It's me, she said. *Not you. You're too good for me.*

I've fucking heard that one before, he replied, then started crying. *I love you, Suneela, I really do. I can't live without you.*

I think you can, she said. *That's kind of what this is about. I feel a bit . . . crushed by you. At school you never leave me alone and then you call me as soon as you get home.*

This was *so* unfair. *You're my girlfriend! I love you! I miss you. Don't you miss me?*

I don't want to be mean, she said. *But I don't know if I miss you. You never give me the chance to find out.*

Well, he would. He'd give her the chance and she'd find out she *did* miss him. So he left. And now he was in his dad's old dinghy, rowing around on this stupid fucking lake wishing he'd stayed with her.

Because he'd said that four hours ago and hadn't heard from her since.

He rowed along, soothed by the sound of the oars dipping in and out of the water. God, life was unfair. What was the point, without Suneela? He could slip over the side and sink to the bottom of the lake, letting the water fill his lungs.

Except he wouldn't. He'd swim about like a crazy dolphin and end up going home wet and cold. He couldn't even kill himself properly.

And now, he realized, it was dark.

Well, at least he hadn't fucked that up. He'd anticipated the darkness and brought a headlamp. He switched it on. His dad had bought it for him last Christmas, and now it was coming in handy.

The beam of light illuminated the surface of the water.

He wasn't totally useless, after all.

Annabelle

There was someone on the lake, not far from the house. There was a light – a torch, or something like that – reflecting off the water.

She turned off the lamp so she could see it better. It was cloudy, but the torch gave off enough light for her to see the outline of a small rowing boat, with a single figure sitting in the middle.

And if she could see them, they could see her. She had to get their attention, somehow.

She picked up the lamp and held it up to the window. What was the Morse Code for SOS? Three dashes, three dots, three dashes? Or was it dots, dashes, dots?

Shit. She couldn't remember. She needed Google. But had no phone or computer.

Although she did *have* Google, or at least an earlier version of it. She ran her finger over the spines of the encyclopedias until she came to the volume L to N, then pulled it off the shelf.

There it was. Morse Code. She looked over the schematic showing the alphabet.

Three dots, three dashes, three dots.

S-O-S.

She held the lamp up to the window and flicked it on and off, three times, quickly.

Then three dashes, then three dots.

She counted ten seconds then repeated it.

And then again, and again, and again.

She watched, looking for a sign that the person on the lake had seen her.

And then the torch went out, then on, then out.

They knew she was there.

Finn

At first he didn't realize what it was. He saw the flashing light and thought that whatever kid was switching the lights on and off was going to get in trouble, but then he saw that it was in a pattern.

Three short flashes, three long, three short.

It rang a bell. That meant something, didn't it? It was a kind of universal signal asking for help. He typed it into Google.

Holy *shit*.

It meant SOS. Save our souls.

Someone was asking for help. Or maybe they were just messing around. That was more likely. It was a teenager who'd seen his headlamp and was trying to fool him.

Still, it might not be. He looked at the window.

It happened again, then there was a gap – maybe ten seconds – and there it was.

SOS.

It stopped. Maybe he should reply, but he had no idea what to say.

He looked on his phone. 'H' was four dots, 'I' was two.

He clicked his headlamp on and off quickly, four times, then paused and did it twice more.

379

Hi.

It was a bit lame, but what else was he supposed to say? He waited for a few seconds, and the reply came.

Annabelle

'A' was dot, dash.

'N' was dash, dot.

She started to spell out her name. Presumably the police were looking for her, so if someone showed up saying they'd seen an SOS signal followed by the name 'Annabelle Westbrook' the police would know immediately what was going on.

There may also have been a public information announcement so whoever was in the boat might recognize the name themselves.

Either way, this was her chance. And they didn't even need to know Morse Code. They just needed access to a phone so they could google it.

Dash, dot: 'N'.

Dot, dash: 'A'.

Dash, dot, dot, dot: 'B'.

Dot: 'E'.

Dot, dash, dot –

She heard the key in the door, and jumped. Her heart started to pound in her chest. She could not let Guy find her signalling to someone on the lake. There was no telling what he would do.

She finished the L, then put the lamp down, and lay on the bed. She clenched her fists to stop her hands shaking with the adrenaline that was flooding her system.

So near. So fucking near.

She'd got as far as ANNABEL. It would have to do. Now she needed the person in the boat to go to the police and tell them what had happened.

An SOS, and part of her name. It was enough. Surely, it was enough.

The door opened and Guy came in. He looked around the room, his lips pressed together. His gaze settled on her.

'Hello,' he said. 'Good day?'

'Yes,' she said. There was a tremor in her voice. She fought to control it.

His eyes narrowed. 'What's going on?'

'Nothing. I – I feel a bit ill.'

'Don't bother,' he said. 'I'm not getting a doctor.'

'I wasn't asking for one. I have a cold, or something.'

'Of course you do.' He shook his head. 'I suppose you're not hungry, either?'

'A bit.'

'Oh,' he said. 'Would you like me to bring food?'

I can hardly get it myself, she thought. 'Please.'

'Fine,' he said. 'I'll be back soon.'

Finn

ANAEL?

What the fuck did 'anael' mean? He had struggled to decipher the dots and dashes. The problem was he had to remember the sequence and then look at his phone to get the letters, by which time a new letter had started.

He'd missed a few, he was sure of that, but he'd hoped to be able to fill in the blanks. 'Aneal', though – that meant nothing to him. Was it a name? A Neal?

He had no idea.

Maybe he'd got a letter wrong. Maybe it was a real, but a real what? Or a near, but again, a near what?

He sat in the boat, patting the oars on the water and looking at the house. It was pretty big, and remote. You could easily hide someone in it.

He waited to see if the light would come again, but there was nothing.

His phone buzzed and he looked at the screen. It was Suneela.

Hey. You OK? Wanted to check in.

Ha. This was it. She had seen the error of her ways.

Fine, he replied. *Just out on the lake. Heading back. Will call when on dry land.*

He wanted to call right then and there, but that was a bit desperate. It could wait until he was out of the boat.

Which wouldn't be that long, especially if he rowed fast.

He grabbed the oars and set off.

Wynne

DI Wynne put the phone down. It had rung out to voicemail but she didn't want to leave a message. She preferred to hear people's reactions. She doubted there was anything to learn in this case – the Westbrooks' friend, Guy, was not a suspect – but you never knew.

She waited a few minutes then rang again. It was possible that he had seen the call but chosen not to answer it because he didn't recognize the number. She'd give him another chance to pick up.

He answered on the second ring.

'Guy Sanderson.'

'Mr Sanderson, this is Detective Inspector Jane Wynne. We spoke yesterday.'

'I remember. How can I help?'

'This is part of our routine enquiries, Mr Sanderson, but we'd like a sample of your DNA.'

'My DNA?'

Was that a slight hesitation before he answered? And a note of concern in his voice? It was hard to say, but she sat a bit more upright.

'Yes,' she said. 'That's right.'

'Why my DNA, if I may ask?' If there had been hesitation or concern, it was gone. 'I'm happy to help, of course, but why would you want mine?'

'Routine,' Wynne said. 'We take a sample from as many people as we can in cases like this, just in case anything turns up.'

'Has something turned up?' he asked.

'I'm not at liberty to discuss details of the case, Mr—'

'I'm a close friend of the family,' Guy said.

'I'm aware of that. But I'm afraid it doesn't change anything.'

'Very good.' His tone was brisk. 'How do I get you this sample? Send a few strands of my hair?'

'No. We'll make it as convenient as we can for you,' Wynne said. 'An officer will come and see you tomorrow. Will you be at your office?'

'Yes,' he said. 'And I'll make myself available.'

'Thank you, Mr Sanderson,' Wynne said. 'We appreciate your cooperation.'

1

What the fuck is this? They don't take everyone's DNA on a whim. No, they do it if they have something to match.

Which is impossible. The cars are clean. I made sure of that. The van was harder. I spent more time in it, so it is conceivable there is DNA in that, which is why it is well hidden. They have not found it. It is not possible. They are too stupid.

Still, I will get the van tomorrow – as soon as they have my DNA – and make sure it is never found. A quarry, maybe, or the ocean. The bike is at the truck stop, so I will have to get up there another way, but I will figure it out.

It'll be another long day.

And maybe unnecessary. Yes, they have something, but it is almost certainly not from me, so I can safely provide my DNA.

At least I think I can. I do have a way of finding out, though.

He – fool that he is – answers right away. He sounds terrible. Poor petal.

'Guy,' *he says.* 'How are you?'

'How are you, more like?' *I say.*

'Been better,' he says. 'Although there was some news today.'
Here it comes.

'News?' I make myself sound eager. 'What happened?'

'They found the van,' he says.

It is like I have been hit with a sledgehammer.

'And it has DNA in it. The kidnapper's. At least they think so.'

Another blow. My mind spins. I am dizzy.

'What?' I say. My shock – I cannot hide it – is in my voice. 'What?'

'I know,' he says. Thankfully he is too idiotic to interpret my tone correctly. 'It's amazing news. They're testing everybody's DNA. If it's someone we know, they'll find them, Guy. This could be over!'

'That's the best news we could have had,' I say. 'Apart from actually finding Annabelle.'

'I'm not getting my hopes up,' he says. 'Not yet. I can't face the disappointment.'

'Wise,' I say, knowing full well that disappointment is exactly what he faces. 'But this is wonderful, Matt. It truly is. Thanks for telling me. I'm very glad I know.'

For once I am telling him the truth.

2

I am struggling to think. My chest feels tight, and my heart is beating quickly. This is, I think, panic.

And I do not like it.

I take a deep breath and start to lay out the facts.

They have found my van and in it, DNA which may be mine.

It may not, of course, but I have to assume that it is. I have to proceed on that basis. So they have my DNA and it is linked to the van Annabelle and her children were kept in.

Once they test me, they will know who took Annabelle. This is incontrovertible evidence. I will not be able to argue my way out of this.

So I cannot let them test me. I have to avoid it, at all costs.

Which is impossible. Maybe tomorrow I can say I am ill, but that will merely delay it, and it may not even do that. It may make them suspicious.

So I have to let them test me, but find a way to stop them getting a good test.

Maybe I can give them someone else's DNA. I picture the scene. A police officer – maybe two – in my office, a test kit in his hand. He swabs the inside of my cheek. They have rules and protocols and evidence integrity shit that they do.

The idea I can fake the test is ludicrous.

So I have to avoid it.

Which means we will have to disappear. That is not impossible. I will have to think through the details, but it can be done.

Two weeks somewhere very remote. Scottish Highlands, in my camper van. I have used it in the past for this sort of thing. It is wonderful: an untraceable source of transport and accommodation.

I will use that time to figure out how best to solve this. I already have the bones of an idea. I can use the identity I have set up for Annabelle, so all I really need is an identity for myself.

By no means impossible.

So I will have to change the plan. But no matter.

I need to buy some time, though. I cannot have them showing up at my office in the morning to find I am not there. I need to delay them until the afternoon.

Then tomorrow morning we disappear, for good.

Wynne

Guy Sanderson was calling.

'Wynne.'

'DI Wynne? This Guy Sanderson.'

'Mr Sanderson. How can I help you?'

'Nothing urgent,' he said. 'I just wanted to ask if we could change the location of the test tomorrow. I checked my schedule and I have a couple of meetings in the morning. I'll be leaving London early in the afternoon, so could we do the test at my lake house? Maybe around three or four? If it's not convenient, I could make another arrangement.'

'I think that can work,' Wynne said. 'What's the address?'

When the call was over, she googled the address and looked at the house. A lawn ran down to a stand of trees by the lakeside. It was very isolated.

And there was something odd about Guy Sanderson. She couldn't put her finger on it, but she was looking forward to getting his DNA test and then sitting down to talk to him again.

Wednesday, 11 March 2020, 8 a.m.

Annabelle

She had spent most of the night awake, waiting for the sound of sirens, or a knock on the door and the voice of authority shouting, *Are you in there?* then someone kicking down the door and leading her from the room, past a handcuffed Guy.

Because her plan *had* to have worked.

In her wilder fantasies, Matt, Norman, Keith and Molly were there too, waiting for her to scoop them up in her arms and smother them with love and kisses.

Now, though, it was morning and nobody had come. She tried to think through what that meant; surely if the person in the boat had understood the message they would have contacted the police and the police would be here.

So they either hadn't understood, or they didn't think it was real.

Or maybe there was some other delay. That could be it: the police might not have it as a top priority, but rather something to look into when they got the chance. There could have been another event that was consuming their resources – a terrorist attack, or a shooting, or an outbreak of riots. She would have no idea; she was totally isolated from the outside world.

All she could do was hope her message had got through and they were on their way.

She was hungry, too. Guy had not come that morning – she thought it was around 8 a.m., so perhaps he had already gone into work.

Nothing to eat until tonight, then. She'd be fine. She didn't care.

She looked at the lake. It was still, and empty. Perhaps the person she had signalled would come back for another look. She would keep her eye on the lake, just in case.

There was a click as the lock turned. So Guy *was* here after all.

He walked into the room. He was in dark jeans, trainers and a black T-shirt. It didn't look like he was going to work at all. Was it the weekend? Had she missed some days?

'Morning,' he said. He looked tired, his expression serious. 'Big day, today.'

'You're not going to the office?'

'No.'

'Is it Saturday?'

'No. Wednesday. But I've had a rethink. Something came up.'

'What happened?' she said.

'The police called me. They're coming here, this afternoon.'

It was the SOS signal. It had worked. It had got out into the world, and its effects were rippling out, and now the police were coming here.

'Why?'

'It's a long story, but it means we have to leave. Now.'

'Where are we going?'

'I'll tell you on the way. But we have to go. Get yourself ready. I'll be back in five minutes.'

The doorbell rang. He started, and then a look of fury crossed his face.

'Fuck,' he said. 'Wait there.'

He slammed the door shut.

Annabelle smiled. This was it. This was the end.

Finn

1

Suneela had not wanted to get back together. She had not even really wanted to talk. She had only wanted to make sure he was all right.

I care about you, she said. *We can be friends.*

They could *not* be friends. Not now, not ever. If he couldn't be her boyfriend he wanted nothing to do with her. He didn't even want to think about her, not that he could stop himself.

What he wanted was to never have met her in the first place. It was too painful.

So he'd gone to see Eric, and play his PS4. As he was leaving, he'd remembered the SOS signal and mentioned it.

Eric raised an eyebrow. *You should tell someone.*

I will, he said. *Tomorrow.*

2

He was just past the Co-op on the way to school, when he saw two cops and remembered what Eric had said. He braked his bike to a stop next to them.

'Excuse me,' he said. The two cops turned to face him. One was a man; the other was a woman. He felt guilty talking to them, even though he knew he had done nothing.

'Yes?' the woman said.

'I wanted— something happened last night.'

'Keep going,' she said.

'It's a bit weird,' he said.

'We do weird,' the male officer said. He glanced at his colleague. 'We're all ears.'

'I was on the lake. You know, up past River Road.'

'I know it,' she said.

'I was on my dad's boat. It was dark and I was about to come back when I saw a light in a house.'

'A light in a house,' the man said. 'Keep going.'

'It was flashing on and off. I think it was SOS. You know, that signal.'

'Morse Code,' the female officer said. 'You think you saw an SOS distress signal from a house by the lake? Are you sure?'

'Yes. Pretty sure. I googled it.'

'There's no way it was just someone turning their light on and off? Or changing a bulb?' she said.

'They did it three times, at least,' Finn said. 'Then I flashed my headlamp back at them and they started on a message.'

'Which was?' the man said.

'Aneal. A, N, E, A, L.' Finn shrugged. 'No idea what it means.'

The female officer looked at him with a penetrating gaze. 'Are you having us on, young man? Because if you are, you're going to be in a *lot* of trouble.'

'No,' Finn said. 'I'm not.'

'OK,' she replied. 'We'll check it out. Which house was it?'

No one ever comes here. I don't have deliveries and if there are letters they are put in the letter box at the end of the drive.

It is my sanctuary.

And it is being violated.

I look out of the window at the top of the stairs. It affords a view of the front door.

There are two police officers there, a man and a woman. For a moment I consider killing them. I have acid in the basement and I picture myself running down and grabbing it and then throwing it in their faces when I open the door.

Then I drag them into the basement and torture them to death.

It is a delicious thought but I have to put it to one side. It will only invite more trouble.

What I have to do is get rid of them.

I descend the stairs step by step, making sure I am not breathing heavily and my expression is composed. I feel the ice in my veins. This is almost fun.

I open the door and raise my eyebrows to show I am surprised to see police officers at my door. Then I smile to show I am not worried by their presence.

'Hello,' I say. 'How can I help?'

The woman speaks. 'I'm PC Berry. This is PC Gibb. We had a report of an SOS signal from this location yesterday,' she says.

I make a baffled face. It is easy, as that is how I am feeling. 'SOS?' I say. 'I don't understand.'

Now the man speaks. I want to smash his face into the wall. 'There was someone on the lake last night. They saw a light from this house, flashing an SOS distress signal.'

Annabelle. She betrayed me. I feel my world start to collapse. There is something very wrong with her. I want to go to her immediately.

But first, these two.

'I'm afraid that's ludicrous,' I say. 'I'm here alone.'

'They were quite adamant that they saw the signal,' he says.

'I don't doubt it. But is it possible they were mistaken? I was watching television last night. Perhaps it was the light from that they saw?'

I see from the look that passes between them that it is possible this person was mistaken. Their witness is unreliable.

'Who saw it?' I say. 'If you don't mind me asking?'

'It was a teenager. He was out fishing.'

'Oh,' I say. 'I see. A teenage boy. Well, I'm sure he is sincere, but . . .' I let my voice tail away. The implication is obvious. This teenager is an idiot.

'Look,' I say. 'You're welcome to come in and look around. Take your time. I'm working in my office, but you can have the run of the place.'

I can offer this. The door to Annabelle's room is hidden. It is sunk into the wall, and, unless you know it's there, it looks like the wallpaper.

They would have to be looking very carefully to find it, and they won't. I can tell they already feel like they are wasting my – and their – time.

'That's OK,' the woman says. 'We'll be on our way.'

'If you have any further questions, please let me know,' I say, and then close the door behind them.

I sink to the floor. It has taken all my strength to hold myself together. What has she done? She is trying to escape.

Which means she does not want to be here, and that means – what? What else is she hiding from me?

I need to talk to her, now.

Annabelle

Annabelle waited for the door to open and the police – or anyone – to come in and put this to an end. She kicked and banged the door with her good arm in case anyone was passing by – she thought it was a safe assumption that Guy had somehow concealed the door from the outside.

No one came.

She looked out of the window, hoping to see people patrolling the grounds.

No one. Just the still waters of the lake and the trees standing sentinel over the garden.

And then the door opened.

It was not the police, or Matt, or a concerned neighbour.

It was Guy, and he looked *awful*.

Whatever had happened, had left him drained of colour, his cheeks sallow. He looked as though he was near to tears.

For a moment the friendship they had shared rose up and she almost felt sorry for him, then she remembered where she was and any sympathy vanished.

'What happened?' she said. 'Who was it?'

He did not reply. 'How could you?' he said. He blinked rapidly, then brushed his mouth with his fingers. He looked on the verge of losing whatever control he had. 'How could you do that?'

She felt suddenly uncertain. The way he was looking at her was different; the false cheerfulness and optimism was gone, replaced with suspicion and a hardness that made her very uncomfortable. The landscape had changed in a way she didn't understand.

'Do what?' she said.

'That was the police,' he said. 'They said someone signalled an SOS last night. It was seen by a teenager.'

It was the police? Then where the fuck were they? Why had they left?

'I got rid of them,' he said. 'I'm good at that.' His lips started to quiver and he steadied himself against the wall. 'But it was *hard*, because I couldn't believe you had done that.'

She bit her bottom lip. 'I – I want to see my family,' she said.

He clutched his head in his hands as though he was in severe pain. 'You made me do all this for nothing. For *nothing*.'

'I didn't make you do anything,' she said quietly. There was no longer any point in playing along with his delusions. 'This was all in your head, Guy.'

His head snapped up and he stared at her. 'No,' he said. 'No! It was not! This is my life! I did all this for *you*. All of it. We made a mistake, Annabelle, when we were younger. We didn't see we were meant to be together until it was too late. But we fixed it! Together, we fixed it!'

'No,' she said. 'You're mistaken.'

'Don't say that!' he shouted. 'I won't let you say that! Don't lie to me, Annabelle. You're treating me like I'm a fool. Like I made all this up. I *won't* have it. Maybe you changed your mind. I didn't change mine.'

'I didn't change my mind,' she said. She pointed at him, her finger jabbing. 'You think I wrote my novels as a secret message to you? That I'd think it was a clever idea for you to kidnap my children so I would have an excuse to leave my family?' She shook her head, her anger getting out of control. 'That's fucking insane, Guy. *You're* fucking insane. That's the problem here. You're crazy. You're utterly deluded. And in the end everyone will know it, because there'll be no Angelica and Guy. As soon as you turn your back, I'll be gone. So all you can do is keep me here forever, but that will mean you accept you got this wrong, and I'm not sure you want that.' She took a deep breath. 'So accept it, Guy. There's only one option left. Let me go, and I promise you'll never hear from me again. This is over, Guy. You must see that.'

There was a long pause. He seemed to be having an internal struggle. Then he looked at her, and the fury on his face was gone. He smiled his fake smile.

'I do,' he said. 'It's over, all right. But not in the way you think. We're leaving.'

'Where to, Guy? Wherever it is, you'll have to live with the knowledge that I detest you. I *loathe* you.'

'Detest? Loathe?' he said. 'No. You won't be detesting or loathing anybody. This *is* over, Annabelle.' He smiled. 'But I can't do it here. The police will be back – they're coming to take my DNA – and we have to be gone by then. So we're leaving.'

She felt suddenly deflated. In that moment he had changed, and not for the better. The mask was back; the anger had drained out of him. She got the distinct impression from the way he looked at her that she had almost ceased to exist, at least for him.

She did not know what had just happened, but she didn't like it at all.

Wynne

Wynne listened as the phone rang. The police station was in a small village so it was perfectly possible there was no one there. It was irritating; she'd have to try later, by which time it may be too late in the day to get Guy Sanderson's DNA test done. Maybe there was a large station in a nearby town she could use.

She was about to hang up when someone answered the phone.

'PC Rainford,' a male voice said.

She put the phone on speaker and beckoned to Dudek to join her.

'Hello,' Wynne said. 'I'm glad you're there. I'm Detective Inspector Jane Wynne. I'm with a colleague, DS Dudek. We're working on a missing person case.'

'How can I help?' Rainford said.

'We have a person of interest living nearby,' Wynne said. 'And we need him DNA tested.'

'OK,' Rainford said. 'How urgent is it?'

'Urgent. I need it today.'

'Oh.' His voice perked up; this was probably the most

interesting thing that had happened in a month. 'I could go myself. Who's the person.'

'Guy Sanderson. Do you know him?'

There was a pause. 'The name rings a bell,' Rainford said. 'But I don't think he's a local. Could be someone who has a second home here.'

'He is,' Wynne said. 'He has a house on the lake.'

'On the lake?' his voice rose another notch. 'Which house?'

Dudek gave him the address.

'Are you sure?' he said.

'I'm sure,' Dudek replied. 'What's going on?'

'That's the second time that address has come up today.'

Wynne glanced at Dudek. 'What was the first?'

'Two officers went out there earlier. A teenager told them he'd seen an SOS signal coming from the house last night. He was out on the lake.'

'They went out there?' Wynne said. 'What did they find?'

'Nothing.'

'Shit.' Wynne banged the table. 'It's him,' she said. 'It's Guy Sanderson. She's in his house.'

'We have to get down there,' Dudek said.

'We can't wait for that. If the police have been there, he knows we're coming. PC Rainford,' she said. 'What time did they leave the house?'

'About twenty minutes ago.'

'Then get them back there, right now. You as well. No one leaves that house, OK? Especially not Sanderson. He's keeping a woman prisoner in there. Take down my number and call me as soon as you get there. Got it?'

'Got it,' Rainford said. 'We're on our way.'

Wynne gave him her number and hung up. 'That's the second time,' she said. 'The second time we've been this close to him.'

'I know,' Dudek said. 'Let's make sure there's not a third.'

PC Gibb

1

PC George Gibb sat in the passenger seat. Next to him, PC Julie Berry switched on the siren and pulled out of the lay-by they had been waiting in, looking for people breaking the speed limit.

Get there as fast as you can, Ted Rainford had said. *And don't let anyone leave the house. There's a woman being held prisoner in there.*

She accelerated hard, the siren blaring. Cars moved out of the way to let them pass. When they were about a mile from the house, he reached up and turned the sirens off.

'Don't want him to know we're coming,' he said.

'When we arrive,' Julie said. 'I'll park across the drive. You go around the back of the house. If you see anything, shout. If not, meet me at the front. We can force our way in. Ted should be there shortly too.'

He watched from the window as the hedges and trees went past. He felt alert with adrenaline; it wasn't often he and

Julie did something like this, and a number of unfamiliar thoughts ran through his mind: what if he's armed? What if he's killed her? What kind of trouble are we going to be in for not going in and looking around earlier?

Because he realized now that was what they should have done. He could picture the conversation he'd be having with his boss later.

The fucking teenager told you he'd seen an SOS call, and you didn't go in?

The home owner was so convincing. And it was a teenager.

Shit. They'd probably both be fired.

He felt the car brake to a stop.

'Right,' Julie said. 'We're here.'

2

PC Gibb ran around the back of the house. There was a vast bay window and he peered inside. It was a dining room, with a long table. There was a candle in the middle of it; other than that, it was empty.

He continued onto a terrace. There was a gas barbecue next to a set of French doors. He tried them; they were locked, but he could see into a modern kitchen. It, too, was more or less empty.

He stepped back and looked up. There were four sets of windows, two with the curtains closed, one with the curtains drawn and the other with a set of blinds. He looked over his shoulder at the lake. This was the window she had signalled from. He was sure of it.

He ran back to the front of the house. PC Berry was standing by the front door, her finger on the bell.

'No answer,' she said.

He turned the handle and shook the door. 'We have to go in.'

'We have no warrant.'

'We have reason to believe someone is being held captive

in there.' He caught her eye. 'And we should have gone in earlier. I don't want to make that mistake again.'

'OK,' she said. 'Let's do it.'

He kicked the door with his heel, right where the lock was. It held, and he kicked it again. There was a sound of cracking wood, but the door remained shut.

'Let me try,' Julie said, and kicked the door.

It flew open.

'Don't worry,' she said. 'You loosened it.'

They walked into a large hall, a set of stairs directly in front of them.

'I'll go up,' PC Gibb said. 'You look down here.'

He ran up the stairs, two at a time. If she was here they needed to get to her as quickly as they could. Their presence here earlier would have alerted Sanderson to the fact they were close to him, and who knew how he might have reacted?

There was a landing running left and right from the top of the stairs. There were two doors to the left and one to the right.

But there were four windows upstairs. The one with the blinds was where the fourth door should be.

He walked along the landing, running his hands along the wall.

And then he felt a seam in the wallpaper. He pressed, the wall gave an inch, then sprang back, leaving a lip. He pulled and the door opened.

There was a small chamber, and then another door. This one was ajar. He pushed it open and walked into a small bedroom.

This was it. This was where she had been held.

But not any more. She was gone.

Wynne

Rainford had called. It was not good news. Wynne put the phone down and looked at Dudek.

'Godamnit,' she said. 'They're gone.'

'What happened?'

'The two PCs who were there earlier went back, but the house was empty.'

'Did they search the grounds? Basement, attic?'

'They're looking now,' Wynne said. 'But they're not hopeful. There was a hidden room and it was empty. They did have one piece of useful information, though.'

'What was that?'

'When they were there earlier there was a car parked outside, a silver Audi estate. They didn't take the registration – we can get that from the DVLA – but at least we know what he's driving this time.'

'Unless he did another swap.'

'Possible, but I think there's a good chance he didn't. He hasn't had time to plan this. He's fleeing.'

'OK,' Dudek said. 'I'll put out an alert. Anyone driving a

silver Audi estate could be in for a surprise. We'll stop every one we see.'

'Do it,' Wynne said. 'We're close. I can feel it.'

Annabelle

She sat in the back seat of his Audi. Her feet were bound at the ankles and her hands handcuffed in her lap. After strapping her in he had fully extended the seat belt then let it ratchet back, so it wouldn't give if she leaned forward.

It was a safety mechanism on seat belts. It had happened to her many times over the years and she often wondered why they were designed that way. She had never thought that it could be used to restrain someone.

Guy had, and she was stuck. The ball gag was back in her mouth so she couldn't even shout if they happened to stop beside someone. Not that they would be able to see her; the windows were tinted.

So all she could do right now was wait, and wonder what was coming.

Wonder where they were going.

They had been on a motorway, for a while. She had no idea which one, but they had left it and were now on a dual carriageway. She recognized some of the place names: Bexhill, Hastings.

They were heading south, then. Brighton, maybe. He had often mentioned Brighton. Perhaps he had another house

412

down there, on the beach, where he could hide her again, although now the police knew it was him, she thought – hoped – they would find him pretty quickly.

Or maybe it was something else entirely. She looked at him in the driver's seat. He was gripping the steering wheel tightly, his face brooding and serious. From time to time he muttered something and hit the dashboard. He seemed lost, almost totally deranged.

Inhuman, almost.

She felt the panic start to rise and closed her eyes. Whatever else, she had to think clearly. Eventually she would find out what he was planning to do, and she needed to be able to act.

It was her only chance.

So that fucking bitch ruined everything.

I can't stop thinking about what she has done, and all I want to do is turn round and put my hands around her throat and squeeze until she's gone.

That bitch.

She let me down. I gave her everything and she threw it back in my face.

So she will die. But I have to kill her in a special way. Otherwise everyone will know I did all this for nothing. They'll think I'm weak and foolish and I thought she loved me, but she never did. I will not allow her to humiliate me that way.

How did I get it so wrong? It's like my mother all over again. I trusted her, did everything for her, and she turned me away. Turned my world upside down.

That's what betrayal does.

And now Annabelle has done to me what my mother did, and so I will do to her what I did to my mother.

My mind clears. I feel myself smile. It's as though I am coming back into myself after a long journey away.

I'm me again.

And I didn't get it wrong. I was right all along. She sent me those messages. She loved me.

But something changed. She lost her nerve. In the final analysis, she was unable to go through with it. She is too weak.

Not me. Her.

So, she deserves the death I will deal to her. She led me to this and now she thinks she can just walk away? No.

And it will, as it always does, calm me. Which will be welcome.

But still, there is nothing left for me now. If I kill her, that will be the story. I'll escape – I have no doubt about that – but they'll think I was a fool who thought she loved me and had it all thrown back in my face.

And I cannot bear to live knowing they think that.

So I will set the record straight. The world will know the truth that I want it to.

And I know just how to make that happen.

Annabelle

She watched the road signs.

There was one town that had started appearing more and more often. Every time it did, they took that turn.

Eastbourne.

They were going to Eastbourne.

Guy glanced over his shoulder. He held her gaze for a moment, then smiled. All the angst and turmoil had gone. He looked as content as she had ever seen him.

He looked at peace. Like he had made up his mind and accepted his fate. And that worried her.

It more than worried her.

It *terrified* her.

He turned back to face the front and put on the left indicator. The car slowed as they pulled into a lay-by. When they had stopped, Guy put his arm around the passenger seat and turned to her.

'Well,' he said. 'I need you to do something for me.'

She shook her head. Whatever it was, she wasn't going to do it.

He rolled his eyes in mock exasperation. 'It's only a *little* thing, Annabelle.'

She shook her head again.

'Do we have to go through this? Really? I mean, *really*? Don't you want to know what it is I want?'

She ignored him, and looked out of the window.

'All I need is a signature,' he said. He opened the glove compartment and took out a pad of paper and a pen. 'Sign at the bottom,' he said, and put the pen into her right hand.

He held the pad up for her to sign. She scowled at him, and scribbled all over the paper.

He laughed. 'Next time you sign,' he said. 'Or I will rip your arm off your body.'

She shrugged. It was just pain. And she was not giving him what he wanted. Not now, not ever.

'I see,' he said. 'Well, how about this. After you're dead – and you will be, if you don't do what I'm asking – I will kill your children. I'll start with Molly. Keith is going to find it hard watching that, he's such a sensitive little soul. And as—'

She turned her head away. He would do it. She was sure he would. She gestured with the pen and he held up the pad.

As well as she could in the handcuffs, she signed her name.

'Thank you,' he said. 'I suppose you're wondering what I want it for?'

Wynne

It was out of her hands now.

Twice, Annabelle Westbrook had been in touching distance: when Wynne had passed the van, and when the two uniforms had gone to the house.

But that was not good enough to save her.

And Wynne thought that was what she needed now. Sanderson was aware they knew it was him, and if he knew that he also knew they would keep pursuing him until they found him.

And so he either had a plan for both of them to disappear for good – which was, if Annabelle wasn't totally committed to it, virtually impossible – or he was going to get rid of her and disappear himself, which was much more feasible.

And at this point, Guy Sanderson was in the realm of doing what was feasible.

She feared for Annabelle. She really did. Because whatever Sanderson had planned, she was on her own.

No one could help her now.

DI Wynne picked up her phone, her heart heavy. This was not going to be an easy phone call.

Matt

The phone rang. It was DI Wynne. Matt snatched it up.

'Hello,' he said. 'Did you find her?'

'We know where she was,' Wynne said. 'But she was gone when we got there. Still, it's progress.'

'Where is she now?'

'We're not sure, although we know who she's with.'

'Who?'

Wynne hesitated. 'She's with Guy Sanderson.'

Guy? What was Guy doing involved in this?

'Did he rescue her?' Matt said. 'I can call him.'

'He didn't rescue her,' Wynne said. 'He's the kidnapper.'

'Did you say Guy?' Matt said. 'Are you sure?'

What she was saying made no sense at all. Guy had been in Brighton. And he'd been calling them all the way through. Matt had been telling him what was going on.

And Guy was their friend. There was no way he had kidnapped anyone.

'I think you're getting this wrong somehow,' Matt said. 'Guy didn't do this.'

'We're quite certain,' Wynne said. 'There was a report of an SOS signal from the window of his lake house last night.

Two officers went to look into it this morning, but they found nothing.'

'So how can you be sure?'

'They didn't go into the house,' Wynne said. 'When I called the local station to ask if they could visit Mr Sanderson to perform his DNA test they mentioned the SOS signal, and I asked them to return immediately.'

'And?'

'The house was empty. The officers did find a hidden room that showed signs of recent occupancy. It seems very likely that your wife was being held there.'

'I can't believe Guy is involved,' Matt said. 'There must be a mistake.'

'I understand this is difficult to believe,' Wynne said. 'But there's no mistake.'

Matt felt a physical sensation, as though he'd been punched in the stomach. Guy? This was *Guy*? But why?

'They were gone?' he said.

'Yes. I'm afraid so.'

He felt a rising anger. 'You mean, you got an SOS from the house and didn't go in? And when you went back, he was gone? I mean, come on! You may as well have called ahead and warned him to run!'

'I'm aware that mistakes were made, Mr Westbrook, but—'

'Mistakes? I don't think that quite covers it. This is a total fuck-up!'

There was a long pause. 'I don't disagree,' Wynne said.

'So what's next?' Matt said.

'We have an alert out for his car. We think he's in his silver Audi.'

'And if that doesn't work?'

'We'll think of something else,' Wynne said. She did not sound convinced. 'I'm sorry, Mr Westbrook. I will call as soon as I hear anything.'

He put the phone down. He didn't know what was most unbelievable – that it was Guy or that the police had let him slip through their fingers.

No – he knew what was most unbelievable.

The fact it was Guy.

That *bastard* had been calling, offering support.

And getting information on what was happening. He'd told him about the drone, and then Guy had gone on the motorway, to escape. He'd told him *everything*.

Matt groaned and sank to his knees.

This was over. His wife was gone. And there was nothing he could do about it.

There it is. The final piece of the puzzle. Her name, in her own hand. I study it for a moment. Would she have thought quickly enough to sign differently to her normal signature?

I try to picture the contracts she has signed. I think it is her signature. But it is what I have, and I will go with it. I have no choice.

I begin to write.

TO WHOM IT MAY CONCERN:

   WE HAVE DECIDED THAT WE HAVE ONLY ONE COURSE OF ACTION AVAILABLE TO US.

   WE WANT TO BE TOGETHER, FOR ETERNITY, AND WE KNOW NOW THAT WILL BE IMPOSSIBLE, SO WE HAVE DECIDED TO TAKE MATTERS INTO OUR OWN HANDS.

   WHAT YOU MUST UNDERSTAND IS THAT WE LOVE EACH OTHER. WE ALWAYS HAVE. BUT ANNABELLE BECAME TRAPPED IN AN ABUSIVE MARRIAGE. WE WILL NOT SAY WHAT SHE SUFFERED, BUT SUFFICE IT TO SAY SHE WAS MISTREATED IN EVERY IMAGINABLE WAY BY HER SO-CALLED HUSBAND.

This may or may not be true, but I like the thought that the world will think it is. A final revenge on that fool.

WE HAVE DECIDED TO TAKE OUR LIVES TOGETHER. IT IS A FITTING END TO A GREAT LOVE STORY. DO NOT MOURN FOR US; WE ARE HAPPY. THIS IS WHAT WE WANT.

WITH LOVE,

I sign my name next to hers and read it again. It is perfect.

Annabelle

Annabelle watched him write on the paper she had signed. It was a letter, but she had no idea what.

He put the pad down on the passenger seat and started the engine. He turned to look at her, a complacent grin on his face.

She glared at him, and raised her fingers in a 'V'.

'Oh,' he said. 'You're feeling defiant. Better late than never, I suppose.' He held up the paper. 'You know what this is?'

She didn't respond.

'It's a suicide note.'

It was a suicide note. He was going to kill her and then claim she had committed suicide.

Oh God. That was why they were going to Eastbourne, but it wasn't Eastbourne that was their destination.

It was Beachy Head.

Some of the highest cliffs in the country and a popular – if that was the word – suicide spot.

And he was going to kill her there, then leave the suicide note on her body.

But there was a problem. Yes, he had her signature, but if he was writing the note it would be obvious what he had done. Matt – God, how her heart ached for Matt – would know immediately it wasn't her handwriting.

So there must be more to it. She felt exhausted. Every time she thought she had a handle on this, a new, unanticipated aspect of his plan appeared.

'So,' he said. 'Do you want to hear the rest of it? It's brilliant. I'm sure you'll agree. Absolutely brilliant.'

Even after all this I still hope she might be impressed by what I am doing, but then I push that aside. She is nothing to me now. Just another one of the ants swarming around my feet.

But I do have a problem.

The SOS. As soon as those two idiot police said there'd been an SOS from the house, I saw it. I'd thought she was at home, getting ready for the plastic surgery, getting ready for our new life, but in fact she was working on getting away from me.

And she had sent an SOS.

Here's the problem: whatever else happened, everybody would know she had tried to escape. It would be so embarrassing. The thought she could prefer that fool of a husband to me. Unbearable.

So yes, I can kill her, but I will still be humiliated. But this will change all that. At the very end, I will win. Yes, I may have lost battles, but the war will be mine.

They will think we chose to die together, lovers in each other's arms.

It does not matter what is true. I am creating an illusion. That is enough.

I will sacrifice her to avoid the shame and embarrassment this would cause me. She can hardly complain. She brought it on herself.

'So,' I say. 'Do you want to hear the rest of it? It's brilliant. I'm sure you'll agree. Absolutely brilliant.'

She shakes her head.

'It is,' I say. 'You may not like it, but you'll have to admit it is brilliant. Should I elaborate? Give you the details.'

She does not reply, so I start to read.

'To whom it may concern. We have decided that we have only one course of action available to us. We want to be together, for eternity, and we know now that will be impossible, so we have decided to take matters into our own hands.'

She closes her eyes and starts to hum. It is the equivalent of a child sticking its fingers in its ears and pretending it can't hear.

It's quite pitiful. I start to wonder what I ever saw in her. I thought she was like me, but maybe she is like the rest of them. A bug. An insect.

I continue reading.

'What you must understand is that we love each other. We always have. But Annabelle became trapped in an abusive marriage. We will not say what she suffered, but suffice it to say she was mistreated in every imaginable way by her so-called husband.'

Her humming grows louder. It sounds like an insect. She is pathetic.

'We have decided to take our lives together. It is a fitting end to a great love story. Do not mourn for us; we are happy. This is what we want. With love.'

I put the pad down.

'What do you think?' I say. 'Your idiot husband will believe it, I'm pretty confident. And even if he doesn't, he'll have his doubts. That's the great thing about it. Whether he thinks it's real or not, he'll never know for sure. And that will torture him.'

I smile at her.

'That's my final gift to you, Annabelle. You'll take to your grave the knowledge that your husband and children will never get over your betrayal of them.'

Annabelle

1

She just wanted to drown him out. Switch him off. Erase him from her life. Erase him from the universe.

There had been things about Guy – the supercilious manner, the arrogance, the aloofness – that had always annoyed her, but she had overlooked them. They were friends, and he had his good points: supportive, generous. And after all, no one was perfect, right?

Now she couldn't believe she had put up with him. She hated the sight of his smug face, and the sound of his whining voice.

And she didn't want to know what he was saying. She didn't want to hear him read his letter, didn't want to hear him crow about how Matt would be tortured by the doubts the letter would sow.

She couldn't help hearing it, though, and she had to face it. Not only would Matt – the man she loved more now than ever – have to deal with losing her, he would always wonder if she had been unfaithful to him.

He would think she hadn't, would suspect that the suicide note was faked, but he wouldn't know. That was Guy's final act of cruelty.

And it would extend to the children too. Had their mum abandoned them? Had she preferred to die with her lover than be there for their graduations and wedding and newborns?

The only silver lining was that Guy would die too. His master plan was a joint suicide. It didn't help her, but at least it stopped him doing this to other people.

She hummed louder.

'Quite pathetic,' Guy said. 'Infantile.' He frowned. 'You know,' he said. 'You're wasting your last minutes on earth like this? I don't know what I ever saw in you. It'll be a relief when I've killed you and I can get on with the rest of my life.'

She froze.

What was that? Get on with the rest of his life. She stared at him, eyes wide.

A smile spread across his face. It was thin and joyless and lizard-like, but this time it was real.

'Oh my,' he said. 'You thought I was actually planning a double suicide, didn't you? That was your solace.' He laughed. 'No, it's only you who's dying today, Annabelle. The suicide note will be for both of us – so they will assume I'm dead. They'll never find my body, though. They'll put it down to the tides.'

He tore off the paper and put it in his shirt pocket.

'Seriously, you think I'd kill myself for *you*? You're nothing. You're not *special*. You never deserved me in the first place. I thought you were like me, but I was wrong. I wouldn't do it for anyone, but wasting my life over *you*. I'm a lot more important than that. So I'm going to kill you. There's no need for me to die. Once you're gone, I can get on with my life. My new life. Because Guy Sanderson will have to disappear, obviously. But I'm glad about that. I'm sick of him. I can't wait. It's going to be fun.'

She didn't want to give him the satisfaction of knowing she was upset, but she could not stop herself from giving a low moan of desperation.

'Now you see,' he said. 'And what's more, I will come out of this even stronger. You will come out of it at the bottom of a cliff. I will throw you to your death – I'm quite looking forward to seeing you fall and watching what happens when you hit the ground. I've never seen anything like that. And then I will walk away.'

He turned and started the car. She closed her eyes as they pulled out of the lay-by.

2

Annabelle's stomach constricted and she was gripped by a sharp, debilitating panic.

She knew, in that moment, that she was going to die.

She was gagged and bound in the back of a car with a man – one of her oldest friends – who was intent on killing her and who seemed to have no concern whatsoever about getting caught. She had no idea what his plan was but he clearly thought he could disappear without trace, and he was probably right. She had no idea what he had set up, but it doubtless included a new identity, money and whatever else he needed.

And she was the last obstacle.

She wanted to say, *Leave me here, you don't need to kill me*, but even if she could have taken out the gag she knew there was no point. He was not going to change his mind. She had seen it in his eyes.

He was enjoying this. He was having *fun*.

As the car moved off, she closed her eyes and tried to curl up – the little she could – into the foetal position. A bolt of pain shot through her shoulder.

This was it. This was how her life ended.

Wynne

1

Her phone rang. She did not recognize the number.

'Wynne.'

'This is PC Jim Travis,' a male voice said. 'We think we may have seen your suspect.'

She sat up in the chair. She had been looking out of the window, turning over Annabelle Westbrook's case in her mind, looking for an angle that might give her an insight into her next step.

'Where?' she said.

'One of our cars passed a silver Audi parked in a lay-by outside Bexhill.'

She opened Google Maps on her computer and looked for Bexhill. It was on the south coast.

'Did they stop?' she said.

'No. They hadn't got the alert. When it came through they remembered the car and called it in.'

'They need to get back there, now,' Wynne said.

'They're on the way,' the PC said. 'Should be there in minutes.'

Wynne looked at the map. 'Which direction were they going in?'

'Eastbourne,' he said. 'They were heading that way.'

'Call me as soon as you hear anything,' Wynne said.

2

Wynne traced the road along the south coast with her finger until it reached Eastbourne. Was it them? A silver Audi in a lay-by? There must have been thousands of silver Audis in the country, some of them parked in lay-bys.

But not all of them were within striking distance of Guy Sanderson's house.

So it was possible Guy Sanderson was taking her to Eastbourne. But why? Probably not a day out at the seaside. Perhaps he had a boat there and was planning to flee to the continent.

Probably not that, either. It was too easy to trace, but she would make sure all the marinas and harbourmasters were alerted to look for a private boat leaving the Eastbourne area in the next few hours.

It might make sense to do that nationwide.

She googled Eastbourne and read the Wikipedia page. It was in the county of East Sussex, population 107,000 as of July 2019.

Nineteen miles east of Brighton.

And immediately east of Beachy Head.

There followed facts about Beachy Head. It was the highest chalk cliff in Great Britain, apparently.

It was also a famous suicide spot and, Wynne thought, the perfect spot for a murder.

She reached for her phone. As she did it rang. It was the same number.

'PC Travis?' she said.

'Yes. Our officers returned to the lay-by.'

'And?'

'The Audi was gone.'

'I think I know where they're headed,' Wynne said. 'We need people there, right away.'

'Where?'

'Beachy Head,' Wynne said. 'They're going to Beachy Head.'

Annabelle

He was *humming*.

He was about to end her life and he was humming.

She didn't know what she felt most: the fear of what was coming, or the terror she would never see Matt and Norman and Keith and Molly again or the hatred of Guy or the desire to survive, to get out of this at any cost.

No, she did know. It was the last of them.

It was the desire to survive.

At that moment she decided she would do whatever it took to stop this. There was no line she would not cross.

The car pulled to a stop. They were next to a hedge that bordered a field.

'Car parks are too busy,' he said. 'It's a short walk to the cliffs, but we'll be fine.' He looked out of the window at the grey skies. Drizzle spotted the windscreen. 'There won't be too many people out today. So we should be able to find a quiet place.'

He turned to look at her.

'Now,' he said. 'Let's you and me have us a little chat.' He was speaking in a faux-American accent, like a grotesque cowboy. 'You need to know a couple of things, buttercup.

Firstly' – now he was back to his normal voice – 'I'm going to untie your feet. Not your hands, of course, but you need to be able to walk. And I don't want you running away, or even trying to. I don't want you drawing attention to us. If you do' – he drew out the last word and, as he did, raised his right hand. He was holding a kitchen knife. Even in the dull light the blade glinted – 'I will slit your throat. It will take seconds. And I'll be gone.' He held her gaze. His eyes were flat and emotionless. 'And then I will do the same to your children. Remember that. You struggle, and you and they die. You don't, and it's just you.'

He opened the car door and got out, the knife tucked under his armpit, then opened her door.

'Put your feet out,' he said.

The seat belt made it difficult to move but she held them up enough for him to be able to reach down and untie her feet. He reached over and unclicked the seat belt.

'Get out. And no fuss.'

She stood up. The rain on her face was glorious. She looked around to see if anyone was nearby.

She would do whatever it took.

He grabbed her damaged elbow. She ignored the pain – it was hard, but she could not be put off by mere pain. Not now.

'Let's go,' he said.

I pull her towards a gap in the hedge. It's about two hundred yards to a path – where there might be people, so I will have to watch for that – and then from there about another fifty yards to a part of the cliff that can be descended to a small platform, which is hidden from view.

And it is from there she will fall to her death.

No one will see, no one will know, and I will be gone for good.

She resists, but not much. It feels like a token resistance. I wonder whether she has given up. I wouldn't be surprised. She is not like me. Maybe she will accept her fate.

Either way, it makes no difference. I will get my way.

And perhaps she knows that, which is why she has given up.

We cross the field. I slip the knife – part of me wants her to protest so I can follow through on my threat. I have never slit anyone's throat before, but there will be other opportunities – out from under my armpit and press it against her hip.

A little reminder of what awaits her, and her children, to keep her on the straight and narrow.

I can see the path ahead, and then the spot that goes down to the small platform. There is no one around, but I speed us up nonetheless. I don't want to rush this – it is too pleasurable – but I don't want to get caught. That would be a disaster.

My fun can wait until we are hidden from view.

She lets me hurry her along. I have to say I am a little disappointed that she does. I would enjoy a bit more fight, a bit more challenge.

This is all too easy.

Annabelle

She could smell the sea. It was a glorious smell; she wondered whether it would always remind her of this moment, whether it would be ruined by Guy.

That assumed, of course, she would ever smell it again.

She breathed in deeply and let it fill her lungs.

It gave her strength. She felt it fill her muscles.

Guy looked around, and then sped up. He must be worried about being seen. For a moment she considered fighting back in case someone was nearby, but then she felt the blade against her hip and decided not to.

Besides, it was no bad thing to let him think she had given up. It might make him complacent, and at this time, that was all she had.

She took another deep breath.

That salty tang of the sea air; it was too good to leave behind. She let him walk her along, let him think she was broken and submissive.

And she smiled.

Fine. If she wants to go this easily, I will let her. It simply confirms this is the right thing to do. Any lingering doubts that maybe she is worthy of me after all have gone.

She is worth nothing. It is a liberating feeling.

Like all the others. It is a burden, in some ways, being me. I realized I was different when I was about ten. I could see that other people were bothered if they said something and it upset someone. They cared what people thought.

I never even considered it.

I still don't. From a young age I thought other people didn't have minds. They were just hollow shells. It was only me that was truly real.

And so it was only me that mattered.

Then came Richie and I learned I could be hurt by them. I learned I had to fight, I had to do whatever I could to protect myself.

So killing him – and all the others – was a simple matter of survival. And every animal has the right to survive.

And if I happened to enjoy it? Well, that was simply the icing on the cake.

I know they have names for me: Narcissist, sociopath.

It is a sign of how different I am to all the others that they see those names as negative. They describe people like me as lacking something.

A conscience, empathy, a soul.

I see it as only positive. My life is simple: I want something, and I take it. Provided I don't get caught, there is no down-side.

No: what they think I lack is what makes them weak.

I am strong. I will prevail. People like me will prevail.

We are the next evolution of humans. A different species.

So killing her is like slaughtering a pig. Or a dog.

It is nothing.

We cross the path and approach the cliff. The wind whips the rain across my face. I can feel the salt air sting my cheeks.

It is a smell I have always hated. It is the smell of chaos, and I am a bringer of order.

Wynne

It was incredibly frustrating, but there was nothing she could do but wait. She was sure they were close and she would have given anything to be there, to get to Guy Sanderson before he was able to harm Annabelle Westbrook any more than he already had.

She stared at the phone, willing it to ring.

DS Dudek opened the office door. 'Any update?'

She shook her head.

'Well,' he said. 'It's in the lap of the gods now.'

'That's not where I want it,' Wynne said. 'I want it in *my* hands.'

Her phone buzzed. She looked at the number.

'It's him,' she said. 'PC Travis.'

'Looks like there might be some news after all,' Dudek said.

She shushed him and answered the phone. 'Hello?'

'We found the car,' Travis said. 'It's parked on a roadside near the cliffs. Two officers are at the scene.'

'Are you sure it's his car?'

'Yes. They ran the licence plates. It's him.'

'What are the officers doing?'

'They're looking for Sanderson and Annabelle. They haven't found them yet.'

'Tell them to look faster,' Wynne said. 'And get as many people as you can there, right now.'

'We are. I'll let you know as soon as I hear something.'

Wynne put the phone down and looked at Dudek.

'We've got him,' she said, but she did not feel any joy. 'I just hope that's good enough. Because this is a race against time, now. They have to get to him before he kills Annabelle Westbrook.'

Here we are.

The ledge is narrower and rougher than I remembered. It is chalky underfoot, of course, and slippery with rain. It is also hidden from view. I had a worry that it was not, but that worry was ill-founded.

I push her to the edge. It is a sheer drop to jagged rocks on which the sea is pounding.

'Fittingly dramatic,' I say. 'This would be a good place for someone in your books to commit suicide. Shame you won't be writing any more, though, isn't it?'

She tries to step back from the fall. I hold her in place. I want her to be able to contemplate what is going to happen to her, imagine herself falling, falling, to the hard ground below.

'Well,' I say. 'I must admit to a little disappointment, Annabelle. This is a lot easier than I imagined. It's such a shame it didn't work out for us. I mean, if only you had a little more imagination, you could have gone along with my plan. A bit of plastic surgery, a new look, and a life of pleasure. I would have got you whatever you wanted. You can see now that I am good at getting things.' I sigh. 'But, you chose this.'

She shakes her head and muffled sounds come out. She is trying to tell me she didn't choose this, or something equally banal. She thinks she didn't choose it because she doesn't

446

want it, but that's just another example of her lack of vision. She chose it implicitly when she rejected me.

'This is your doing,' I say. 'I want you to know that.'

I push her closer to the edge of the cliff. She resists. She pushes back, hard.

Good. There is some fight, after all. It won't help, but it might give me the pleasure of hearing her beg for mercy.

I reach behind her head and undo the ball gag. I cannot have them find it with her body.

I get a sudden déjà vu – it's positively Proustian – of all the other times I have used this gag. It's my favourite.

Then I let it drop to the ground. I will pick it up afterwards.

'So,' I say. 'Any last words?'

Annabelle

The gag dropped to the ground. It was a wonderful relief, although her tongue was swollen and her jaws were sore and were going to take ages to feel better.

Guy was smiling at her.

Fucking *smiling*.

'So,' he said. 'Any last words?'

She had nothing to say to him. Nothing at all, ever, just in case it made him happy. Although there was one thing that would let him know exactly how she felt.

She gathered a gob of saliva in her mouth and spat it into his face. It landed on his left eye and spread down his cheek.

His head jerked back, and his mouth twisted in disgust. Instinctively, he closed his eyes and wiped his hand across his face, flicking the phlegm from his face.

She hadn't done it for any reason other than to do the nastiest thing she could to him, but now, for a split second, his eyes were closed and his focus had switched from her to his disgust at being spat on. It was a hard-coded human reaction.

And it was her chance.

Not much of one.

But a chance.

And she had sworn she would grab whatever chance she got with both hands and not let go until there was no chance at all.

She slammed her forehead into the bridge of his nose as hard as she could. She felt a vicious pain – she was sure she must have fractured her skull – and then heard a crack as something broke.

It was his nose. He staggered back and she saw that it had moved across his face to somewhere beneath his left eye. Already, blood was streaming out of it, and his eyes were wide in shock.

She rammed her head into his ruined nose, then, when he tried to pull away, she clamped her teeth around his cheek and bit.

Hard.

She tasted the metallic taste of blood in her mouth and then there was a *lot* of blood, and she had to spit it out because it was threatening to choke her.

Guy screamed, and tried to pull away from her.

She felt, for the first time since this had started, as though she was in control.

She felt *powerful*.

And she was not going to waste the moment. She bit down again, as savagely as she could, and a chunk of his cheek tore off.

Which left him free. He stepped back from her, a ragged hole in his face. She let the piece of his cheek fall to the chalky ground.

'You bitch,' he said, his voice distorted. 'You'll pay for this.'

'No,' she said. 'This is the end, Guy.'

He was only a few feet from the edge of the cliff. He was focused on her, and she was not sure he knew how close he was.

She frowned, and glanced to her left, as though she'd heard something. When his gaze followed, she threw herself at him. When he saw her coming he held up his hands to hold her off, but he was too late, and she slammed into him, her shoulder in his chest.

He lurched backwards towards the cliff edge; she thought he was going to topple over it, but he managed to fall sideways, so that he was lying perpendicular to the edge.

It made no difference. He was at her mercy, now.

He looked up at her. There was no more than an inch of solid ground behind him.

She picked up a large rock between her cuffed hands and took a step in his direction.

'No,' he said. 'Annabelle, no. Please.'

She threw the rock at him. He fended it off with his forearm and she saw him wince in pain. She picked up another, larger, one.

'All I have to do to end this is kick you over,' she said. 'That's it. No one will ever know. You even have a suicide note in your pocket, if they ever find your body. I'll say I couldn't go through with it at the end, but you'd already jumped. No crime committed. And if they don't find your body? Who's going to care if it's true when I say you slipped and fell? They'll be glad to see the back of you. So there's nothing to stop me, Guy. Nothing at all.'

He stared at her, his eyes narrow.

'Or I walk away. And let the police deal with you. Maybe I'll do that. But this is the end, Guy. And I won.'

He closed his eyes. 'I know,' he said. 'You win, Annabelle.'

She thinks she has won.

She thinks she has me on the cliff edge, and all she has to do is push me over. Or leave and hand me to the authorities.

She is fool. *She does not know who she is dealing with. She thinks she is in control, but there is another option. There is* always *another option.*

I will take her with me. At the very least, I will take her with me. I will lunge at her and grab a foot. She can kick me and stamp on me, but I will not let go. I will drag her to this cliff edge and we will fall together to our deaths.

They will find the suicide note and – even though I will have died too – my plan will be complete.

Her husband will think she betrayed him.

Yes, they will wonder about the injuries, but my guess is they will put them down to our fall onto the jagged rocks below.

I will shout this into her ear as we fall, just so that it is her last thought.

'I know,' I say. 'You win, Annabelle.'

Then, before she can process my admission of failure, I spring at her. I see her eyes widen in shock, then hear her squeal as my hands grab her left ankle and yank it towards me.

She stumbles and slips to one knee, kicking out at me to shake me free.

She has no chance.

I begin to drag her to the cliff edge.

'Guy,' she says. 'No!'

I do not reply. I see the blow coming; the heel of her right foot, aimed at the side of my head. I take it; it makes me dizzy, but I am OK.

She does it again; I manage to twist my head out of the way.

And I still have her ankle. I drag again and we slide another few inches towards the cliff.

Then I feel it.

My feet are over the edge. Soon all I will have to do is fall, and gravity will do the rest. I inch further over the cliff.

'No,' she shouts. 'Stop it, Guy!'

She kicks at me again. She cannot use her hands, as reaching down would bring her closer to the cliff edge, and her kicks are nothing to me.

One more heave, and this is over.

PC Jessie Chalmers

1

PC Jessie Chalmers looked left and right along the path that bisected the field. The car was parked a couple of hundred yards away and she and Toby, her partner, had assumed that the man and woman they were looking for had gone through the gap in the hedge and headed for the cliff.

'I'll go left,' she said. 'You go right. If you see them, shout.'

'I'm not sure we should split up,' Toby said. 'He's supposed to be dangerous.'

Chalmers shrugged. She had met her husband in a boxing gym; he had come in to get fit and she had trained him. She had been close to the Olympic team in 2012, but a shoulder injury had put an end to that particular dream.

'I'll be OK,' she said.

'It's not you I'm worried about,' Toby said. 'But let's do it. We don't have a choice.'

She nodded, and set off to the left. She had not gone more than twenty yards when she froze.

'Holy shit,' she muttered. 'What is that?'

2

A woman's head had appeared above the cliff edge, as though she was climbing steps in the cliff itself. The head was followed by a torso.

Her hands were cuffed in front of her and she looked exhausted. She took a few steps towards her – she was limping horribly – then collapsed to the ground.

That wasn't what most stood out, however.

What most stood out was the blood smeared across her face.

She looked at PC Chalmers and sank to her knees. Chalmers ran over to her and knelt on the wet grass at her side.

'Are you Annabelle Westbrook?' she said, although she was pretty sure she already knew the answer to that question.

The woman nodded.

'It's OK,' she said. 'You're safe now.' She glanced up; Toby had seen what was happening and was running towards them.

'Thank you,' Annabelle Westbrook said. She was glassy-eyed and her breath was short. 'I can't believe it's over.'

'It is,' Chalmers said. 'It's all over. But I have to ask. Where is he?'

Annabelle pointed to the place on the cliff she had come from. 'He's over there,' she said.

3

Annabelle Westbrook was in shock; that much was obvious. PC Chalmers put her in the recovery position, and spoke into her radio.

'We have Ms Westbrook,' she said. 'She's safe. Request ambulance and back-up. Whereabouts of Guy Sanderson unknown.'

Toby arrived and knelt next to them. 'How is she?'

'Fine. She's in shock, but the blood doesn't seem to be hers – at least, I don't see any obvious injuries.' Chalmers put her hand on Annabelle's neck to feel her pulse. 'How are you?' she said. 'Are you hurt?'

'No,' Annabelle said. 'I'm tired. Do you have a phone?'

'Of course,' Chalmers said. 'Do you need to make a call?'

'I want to speak to my family.'

'What's the number?' Chalmers said.

Annabelle told her and she typed it into the keypad.

She put the phone on speaker and lay it on the grass next to Annabelle's head. Then she stood up.

'You hang back,' she said. 'Keep an eye on her. I'm going to find him.'

4

There had obviously been a fight. Blood streaked the chalky ground.

But there was no sign of Sanderson.

'Shit,' Chalmers muttered. She spoke into her radio. 'Need an alert on Sanderson. He's not here.'

She walked towards the edge of the cliff, studying the scene. There really was a *lot* of blood.

So much that no one could have gone anywhere without leaving an obvious trail.

But there was no trail.

Just the blood.

'Holy mother,' Chalmers said, and walked briskly to the edge of the cliff. She looked down and her head swam with vertigo.

It was a long way down.

A long way to fall. And someone had fallen.

She blinked the dizziness away and looked again, then spoke into her radio.

'I found him,' she said. 'I found Sanderson.'

Annabelle

She lay on the ground, the grass cool against her cheek. Her shoulder ached and her head throbbed where she had butted Guy, but she felt *wonderful*.

The tang of the sea air.

The noise of the gulls.

The phone ringing next to her.

'Hello?'

It was Matt. It was her husband, the love of her life, the father of her children.

It was a voice she had thought she would never hear again.

'Hello?' he said. 'Who is this? Is it Guy?'

'It's me,' she said. 'Matt, it's me.'

'Annabelle? Is it you? Where are you?'

'Beachy Head,' she said. 'I'm at Beachy Head.'

'Where's Guy?'

'He's gone.'

'Gone where? Are you OK, Annabelle?'

'He's gone forever. And I'm fine.'

'Where exactly are you? I'll call the police.'

'They're here.' She paused, and took a deep breath of the

salt air. 'And honestly, I'm fine. Can you believe it, Matt? This is *over*.'

'Oh my God,' he said. 'Annabelle, I was so *worried*.'

'Me too,' she said. 'But there's no need to worry now. I love you.'

'I love you too.' He started to cry. 'Wait,' he said. 'I'm going to get the kids.'

He called their names and then, moments later, she heard their shouts.

'Mum?' Norman said. 'Is that you?'

'It is,' she said. 'It's me.'

Wynne

DI Jane Wynne and DS Michael Dudek sat next to each other on a couch at the police station in Eastbourne. Annabelle Westbrook was opposite them. Her ankle was bandaged, but other than that she was unhurt.

On the outside, at least.

'Are they here?' she said.

'They're on their way,' Wynne said. 'They can't be far behind us. Maybe another ten minutes. You talked to them, earlier, I heard?'

'As soon as I could,' Annabelle said. 'I wanted to hear their voices. Now I want to see them.'

'I understand. That's our priority, too. And the minute they arrive we'll bring them here.' Wynne sipped her tea. 'While we wait, would you be OK to answer a few questions?'

'Yes,' Annabelle said. 'That's fine.'

'Thank you,' DS Dudek said. 'I think we have a reasonable idea of what happened up until you were on the cliff with Sanderson. We'll want to go through the details at some point, but that can wait.'

'Yes,' Wynne said. 'That can wait.'

'OK,' Annabelle said. 'Did you find Guy?'

'We did,' Wynne replied. 'PC Chalmers called the coast-guard, and they recovered his body.'

'So he's dead?'

'Yes,' Wynne said. 'He is. Would you be able to tell us what happened on the cliff top?'

'I think,' Annabelle said, 'that if I just said he fell that would be easier. But I'm sick of all the lies. So I'm going to tell the truth.'

'We appreciate that,' Wynne said. 'Go on.'

'He was going to push me off,' Annabelle said. 'And then leave a note saying it was a joint suicide. He was not going to kill himself, though. So when he came close to me, I attacked him. I bit his cheek and hit him and did whatever I could. I had no choice.'

'Self-defence,' Dudek said. 'That's fine.'

'And then he grabbed my ankle and started to drag me off the cliff edge. He was going to take us both over' – her voice faltered, but she collected herself – 'so I was kicking him, but it made no difference. I was trying to grab onto something, but my hands were cuffed, and then I felt the rock I'd hit him with. I picked it up and leaned down and smashed it onto his hands. I did it again, and again, so hard that I broke something in my ankle. I think I also broke his hands, because he let go.'

She looked away, tears in her eyes.

'I scrambled away from him, and when I looked back, he was gone. I didn't know if he'd fallen or if I'd kicked him over or if he'd escaped.'

'He didn't escape,' Dudek said. 'I can tell you that.'

'I didn't push him over,' Annabelle said. 'I was just trying to get him off me.'

Wynne folded her arms. 'I think' – she said – 'that in the interest of simplicity we can say he fell. You can leave it with us, Mrs Westbrook.'

461

There was a knock on the door, and an officer put her head around it.

'Hi,' she said. 'They're here.'

Matt

He had thought – really, totally, genuinely believed – that he would never see her again. He had pictured his life without her. Him, Norman, Keith and Molly struggling to find a way to live without her.

He could hardly believe she was back.

They walked along a corridor behind an officer – Farida, she'd said her name was – until they reached a door. Farida opened it, and said something, then turned to them.

'You can go in,' she said.

And there she was. He couldn't believe it was her. She was pale, with a big bruise on her forehead, and dark circles under her eyes, but she was smiling, and it was Annabelle, it was actually her, alive and in the flesh.

He had never loved anyone more than he did her, at that moment.

Norman, Keith and Molly froze for a second, and then they ran, arms outstretched across the room. Annabelle sank to her knees and they collapsed into her arms, kissing and hugging her and burying their faces in her neck and chest, as though they were trying to get as close to her as possible.

That's what he wanted to do, and then never let go.

She looked up at him, tears running down her face.

'Matt,' she said. 'It's actually you.'

He wiped the tears from his cheeks and knelt beside her. He wrapped his arms round them – as far as he could – and felt the warmth of their bodies.

They were together again. He had feared he had lost his family, feared this moment would never arrive, but now it was here.

'Annabelle,' he said. 'Let's go home.'

She leaned up and kissed him.

'Yes,' she said. 'Let's go home.'

Acknowledgements

Warmest thanks to:

Becky Ritchie, as always, for all your advice and support.

Kathryn Cheshire: your editorial guidance and input all through the process was vital and full of insight.

Anne O'Brien, for a thoughtful and detailed copy edit. I am in awe of your skills.

TMCG, O, F and A: for everything.

Read on for a sneak peek of Alex Lake's new novel, coming 2021 . . .

Early Summer, 2020

Chapter One

Carrie Lewis watched her fifteen-year-old daughter, Nancy, walk along the beach, waves lapping at her bare feet. It was an idyllic scene; the late afternoon sun glimmered on the surface of the water, families – suitably socially distanced, of course – talked or played ball or just soaked up the warmth, but she could not enjoy it.

She was too on edge, a pit lodged in her stomach.

Nancy had not wanted to come. Even though they had been housebound for weeks and the heat in town was muggy and sticky and oppressive, and the beaches were finally open, Nancy had shaken her head when Carrie suggested going out to the ocean.

But you love the beach, Carrie said.

Not today, Nancy replied. *Maybe tomorrow. Or next week.*

Come on, Rob, her husband, said. *It'll be fun. I'll buy you an ice cream.*

I'm not a kid, Dad, Nancy said. *You can't bribe me with ice cream.*

OK, Rob said. *Then I'll bribe you with something else. Cash? A new outfit? A pony?*

Nancy laughed. *A pony will do. You promise?*

Cross my heart.

Then Nancy shook her head again. *I think I'd still prefer not to go.*

Carrie – and Rob – didn't need to ask why. They had been dealing with why for months.

Look, Carrie said. *Let's try it. If you want to leave, we can. Any time you say. OK? We can't stay in the house forever.*

Nancy gave her a long look. *OK,* she said, finally. *But if I want to leave, we go. Agreed?*

It broke Carrie's heart that her daughter found it necessary to make sure she had that agreement in place. But they would sort it out. After this summer Nancy would never have to go through this again.

She glanced at Rob. He was reading a book about the 1918 Flu Pandemic. It was the last thing she would have read; they were living through their own version now, which was plenty for her. That was Rob, though. He watched documentaries and read history books and thought fiction was pointless because it was all made up.

It had been obvious when he bought her a book of Pulitzer Prize-winning photographs for their first Valentine's Day, so she couldn't complain. She'd had plenty of warning.

She took the lid from her cooler and reached in for a can of seltzer.

'You want one?' she said to Rob.

'Sure.'

She handed him a can. It hissed as he opened it.

'I feel so bad for her,' Carrie said. 'I could feel how tense she was when we arrived, wondering whether they were here.'

'Yeah,' Rob said. 'It'll take her a while to get over it. At least we have a plan for a fresh start after this summer. And they leave her alone now. One good thing to come from lockdown.'

'They' were Laura, Andi and Dana. Worst of all, Dana.

They had been friends since they were in kindergarten, but early in ninth grade something had changed. And it had changed for the worse.

There had always been something of an edge to Dana, a hint of cruelty, of taking pleasure in others' discomfort, but Carrie had dismissed it. She wished she hadn't – she wished she had never let them become friends at all – because, on the last day of school before the winter holiday, Nancy had come home and gone straight to her room.

Carrie went to talk to her.

Aren't you supposed to be going to the movies?

Nancy was sitting on her bed, staring out of the window.

I'm not going.

Why not?

I'm just not.

What happened? Tell me?

Nancy shook her head. She looked, in that moment, like the baby she had once been.

You can tell me. I'm your mom.

It's my friends. They don't – the sobs started, long racking sobs that Carrie would hear plenty of over the coming months – *they don't* like *me any more.*

Amidst the pain, there was a note of disbelief in her voice, as though she simply couldn't understand what was happening.

How long has this been going on?

I don't know. A few weeks. They've been doing things without me.

Carrie could hardly believe it herself. *But they're your friends! What have they been doing?*

Meeting up. Going out. Chatting online. Dana showed me all the threads I've not been on.

Dana. Fucking Dana. Why would she do that?

I don't know, Mom. But they don't like me any more. Dana tells them not to.

471

But why?

Because of George.

Carrie's head was spinning. *Who's George?*

The new guy at school. She likes him, but he's not inter-ested in her. Me and him are friends, and she said I turned him against her, which is crazy because I don't even like him, not in that way.

Then she needs to be a bit kinder, Carrie said. *She needs to stop being mean.*

Nancy gave a low laugh. *She likes being mean, Mom.*

At least it was the last day of the semester. Over the winter holiday Carrie had kept Nancy busy, hoping that when they got back to school it would blow over, but it had gotten worse.

Much worse.

Carrie had read about online bullying, but she had no idea how bad it could be. The things that were posted, the lies and rumours and insults, the sheer *cruelty* – she didn't even want to think about them.

It had reached a head when Nancy had refused to go to school at all. When Carrie pushed, she showed her a photo.

It was a naked woman in an obscene pose, with Nancy's head photoshopped onto the body. It looked very realistic, and, it turned out, many of her classmates thought it was her daughter – her then fourteen-year-old daughter. Nancy had received a barrage of messages from them, calling her a slut or a whore, others asking her for blowjobs or if she did threesomes, others simply taunting her with messages like *You'll always be porn girl* or *every town needs a bike for all the boys to ride.*

Nancy had begged her parents not to say anything to anyone – *You'll just make it worse*, she said, although Carrie didn't know how it could be worse – but they had insisted. The school and the police had done what they could, which, since the photo had come from an anonymous account, was nothing other than talk to the pupils to try and scare them into leaving Nancy alone.

Which they did. She was cold-shouldered and excluded and sniggered at in the corridor. Dana did all the things bullies did: she stared at her for long periods of time, whispered when she passed by, burst out laughing if she saw her.

So Carrie was glad the Coronavirus had come, glad when school closed early, glad to have her daughter back in the house where she could try to repair the damage.

Because Nancy was shattered. Pale, thin, drawn, unable to take pleasure in anything.

But gradually she started to eat and laugh and read and recover something of who she had been.

Carrie and Rob had looked for houses in another school district. They were going to make a new start, get their daughter out of the hell she had been in.

They were going to move on.

But first there was the summer to get through. And today was a good start. Sun, sea air, exercise.

Carrie sipped her seltzer. Nancy was about a hundred yards away, ambling along the beach by a low cliff. She started to climb it. It was not all that high – maybe thirty feet – but the far side was a sheer drop onto an outcrop of jagged rocks, against which the waves crashed and pounded.

When she reached the top she paused and looked out over the ocean, then took a deep breath.

Yes, Carrie thought, *breathe it in. Breathe in that strength and health and life.*

And then Nancy started, like a deer that has heard a rifle shot. She looked over her shoulder and froze.

Nancy followed her gaze. And there she was.

Standing behind her on the cliff.

Dana.